Ankara Fever: Journeys

Brian S. Vinson

ANKARA FEVER: JOURNEYS

Dedicated to Sheri

for believing when things are good

and being willing to suspend disbelief otherwise.

Special thanks to Linda for constantly requesting another page and to Bill for help with formatting. Further thanks to Mrs. Beeson: this book is part of my legacy and by extension, part of yours.

Prologue

Captain Martin Everett sniffed again, trying to keep the blood from leaking from his nostril. Lester, his copilot, was still relaxed and engrossed in the newspaper. The headline facing Martin was a taunt, an indictment.

CDC: Ankara Deaths Surpass Projections

Martin fished around beside his seat. He had already soaked through his handkerchief, and now he was approaching the end of the toilet paper roll he had taken from the crew latrine.

Thankfully they were about to enter the flight path to LAX. Once there, he could get to a hospital. He'd heard the hospitals were filling up, but he had good insurance. Surely there was something that could be done.

The first twitch went unnoticed. It was just a quick tightening of his right index finger. He had that hand on the yoke while the other was discarding the bloody wad of toilet paper.

Normally he wouldn't have a hand on the yoke. The plane flew itself for the most part. Right now, he was holding the yoke to keep his hands from shaking. Piloting a heavy aircraft with hundreds of people relying on you to do it safely could be a stressful job. Doing it cross country became routine, but that routine didn't completely alleviate the stress. Doing it while you knew a new pandemic virus was coursing through your veins took stress to a whole new level.

The second twitch was a little more forceful. His hand tightened on the yoke. Captain Everett lifted his right hand and shook it. *That was weird.*

He sniffed again, stopping a trickle that threatened to escape. The hand returned to the yoke as he reached for another wad of toilet paper.

The third contraction was massive.

His entire body seized. The hand gripped and arm pulled. His diaphragm contracted, forcing his breath out in a wet moan.

Too late, Lester looked up from the paper, "Oh, hell *no!*"

Martin was locked up, his entire torso contracted, his arms pulled tight to his chest. His legs were thrust forward, thrashing up and down. Martin's head was pressed back against the head rest, eyes stared at the roof of the cockpit, blood oozed from the corners of his mouth and ran from his nose.

Lester wasn't conscious of dropping the paper. He reached for the yoke, trying to push it forward. Martin had the controls locked. The plane nosed up, gaining altitude rapidly. Lester could feel the auto pilot trying to force the craft back to level flight, but it was failing. He had to get Martin to release.

The copilot thrust himself out of his seat and across the power controls. The electronic *wa-wa-wa* and flashing amber lights made sure he knew the plane was in trouble. It was more of an annoyance than a help at this point.

Martin had a white knuckle grip on the yoke, but blood leaked out around the base of his finger nails. Lester resisted revulsion and grabbed the bloody hand. He knew that the passengers had to be scared out of their minds. In pre-9/11 days, before the cockpit doors had been reinforced, he was sure he could have heard their screams. As it was, some disengaged portion of his mind wondered why Sabrina, the cabin crew lead, hadn't called in by now. He didn't let that thought distract him from his task.

Lester grabbed Martin's thumb, peeling it back from the yoke.

Overhead the amber lights switched to red. The angle of attack was too steep. The plane was approaching stall speed.

Martin's palm peeled up. Just the fingers remained.

Lester lifted the index finger, slipping it off the yoke.

Wa-wa-wa changed to *aun-aun-aun*.

The middle finger lifted.

Martin coughed, spraying Lester's face with a warm mist. The copilot didn't let his mind contemplate the content of that mist. He had to save the passengers.

Martin spasmed again. His foot stomped the right rudder pedal. The leg locked in place. Lester felt the plane slip starboard.

Over his head the *bong* of the cabin crew call button sounded. *Probably Sabrina.* Lester didn't take the time to answer. Within seconds her voice came over the cabin intercom. "Captain? Is there a problem?" She was the ultimate professional. From her tone you wouldn't have been able to tell whether the plane was in trouble or if she had run out of ice in the drink cart.

Lester pried the last finger off the yoke and the control slipped forward. He looked up at the intercom. "It's Martin. He's had a seizure."

The autopilot attempted to correct for the full rudder. Rudder controls turn the plane, the yoke uses the ailerons to bank the plane. It takes a coordinated effort to do it smoothly. There was nothing smooth happening at the moment.

Lester cast his eyes around the cockpit, looking for something he could use to pry Martin's leg off the rudder.

"What can we do? What's wrong," Sabrina asked, only the slightest sign of worry slipping into her voice.

"He's bleeding from his eyes, nose, fingers. Coughing blood." There was nothing in the cockpit he could use. Of course cockpits were deliberately kept free of debris that could injure the flight crew. The plane continued its hard turn, the ailerons trying to overcome the turn by banking in the other direction.

"Oh, shit," Sabrina's voice cracked, "That sounds like Ankara."

The plane heaved. The sound of a giant aluminum can being torn in half ripped through the plane. Lester was thrown against the ceiling, then rolled as the plane tumbled under him.

He was thrown against the windshield and managed to look back. Where the starboard side wing and engine should have been was just a torn stub.

The combined screeches of alarms reached a pitched level.

In slow motion Lester watched as the nose turned up. Another rending tore through the craft and he could see the top of the plane through his window. It passed by, the rudder flailing along behind.

Lester crossed himself and closed his eyes. The end would come soon enough. He didn't have to watch it.

1

Atlanta Hartsfield-Jackson Airport

The din of the concourse permeated his body. He hated air travel. Just not for the same reason most people hated it. Roger hated it because it took away everything that was important to him. His rational mind made him do it though. He knew it was safer than traveling by car and it allowed him to work across the country and still be home most weekends even if that didn't matter as much as it once had.

Roger found his gate and settled into one of the blue sling chairs that have been a part of Atlanta's Hartsfield-Jackson Airport Delta gates for as long as he could remember. A quick check of his watch told him it was almost 9:30AM, which meant he had almost two hours left on his layover. He adjusted his N95 respirator mask. Looking around the terminal he saw several others similarly covered, even more had the less effective surgical-style mask or even just a bandana. Of course they had to take them off for the TSA security check, but most people put their masks back on immediately thereafter.

His own mask received some furtive glances but most were either fear or envy. Still many walked through the crowd without a mask at all, and some of those looked at the masked with bemused pity.

A special news alert flashed on the flat screen television. The volume was turned down so as not to compete with the general din of the crowds in the terminal, but the closed captioning scrolled by as the co-anchors relayed some new details of Ankara Fever.

Ankara Fever, of course was the only reason Roger was in Atlanta. When the first signs of hemorrhagic fever surfaced in Ankara, Turkey it did not even hit the major networks in the United States. Even the 24 hour news cycles of cable failed to cover it for three days. When they did pick it up, Roger's email inbox had been flooded with requests. His clients needed him. Now!

That was ten days ago and Roger hadn't set foot in his house for nine of them. When words like *pandemic* surfaced, professionals such as Roger became incredibly busy. And that word, "pandemic" was exactly what had hit the news a week and a half ago. In less than four hours initial investigators in Ankara announced that the strain of hemorrhagic was not a direct match for any of the known forms. Lassa fever, Ebola and dengue fever were all relatives. They all had a commonality that made them relatively easy to fight, at least in developed countries. They were a generally short-lived phenomena. While tragic for those infected, as well as their loved ones, traditional hemorrhagic fevers generally infected their victims and caused extreme trauma. The patient was either killed or cured in a short period of time. This made containment of outbreaks fairly routine and very effective. Quarantine contained the viral spread and the patient was dead or significantly out of the woods within days.

Ankara was a different beast. It infected slowly, taking up to a week for symptoms to present. However, within two days of infection the victim became contagious. The first noted victim was a 67 year old British tourist who checked into a hospital in Ankara with complaints of flu-like symptoms and died two days later. Presentation of hemorrhagic symptoms preceded death by only several hours. Since then doctors had isolated the virus and given it an official designation, but everyone was still calling it Ankara Fever. Even Roger hadn't taken the time to devote the official designation to memory.

Last night another special report had filled in the information about victims being contagious for several days before presentation of symptoms, and that was why he was in an airport trying to make his way home. He had canceled his next two client visits, telling them he would conduct their review by video conference rather than face to face. Now he just had to hope that the overnight shipment of a webcam was delivered from Amazon, and that he could figure out how to hook it up. His son, Corey, said he'd walk him through the process if he couldn't get it working and if he could make time.

Roger snapped out of his revere, back to the situation at hand. A pair of nice shoes sat down across from his. Great shoes. Before she passed, Melissa had loved shoes and taught him, despite his attempts otherwise, quite a bit about them. He preferred a nice tactical boot or a good, solid Rockport shoe. His shoes said, 'working man'. What sat across the aisle said, 'good taste, lower upper income, willing to sacrifice comfort for style'. They also said, 'I am completely unfamiliar with Post-9/11 air travel.' The straps and buckles would make getting through security a challenge. The shoes lead up to a pair of great legs, a body concealed behind a professional skirt suit, elegant neck and some gorgeous eyes just above her own surgical mask.

She must have watched his eyes glide up because she waited for his eyes to firmly lock onto hers and then made a deliberate visual slide down then back up. What she saw was almost her polar opposite. Roger kept fit but he had on a light jacket over a short sleeved button-down that hadn't been pressed the last four or five times it had been washed. His blue jeans had been beaten and faded to the point that they were almost torn up enough to be considered *distressed* and put out on the shelf for Corey to purchase. They covered the tops of his beaten up and stained tactical boots similar to what SWAT team members or Special Forces troops would wear. Roger traveled by air often but he still wore his boots. He did make a concession and bought a pair with the industrial zipper so that it was a mere challenge to go through security rather than a completely futile event, but in his mind there was no excuse for getting caught out with bad foot gear.

When her eyes finally met his again they crinkled in what he thought was a mild smile. She pointed at her mask, "Quite the fashion statement, isn't it?"

His eyes crinkled back, "Oh, sure. If you want to say, 'Hi, I'm terrified of being in a public place, how are you'."

The crinkle faded from around her eyes, replaced momentarily by fear. He'd obviously struck too close to the truth. He simply wasn't any good at joking, and small talk wasn't natural for him either. It was at times like these that he really missed Melissa. She *got him* and he didn't have to feel like an idiot around her. "Sorry. Poor attempt at a joke."

Her head bobbed, seemingly forgiving his indiscretion but her hand came up and pressed the mask closer to her face.

A collective gasp from the terminal drew Roger's attention. The room dropped to silence and he was able to hear the television. Maybe his brain wasn't ready to comprehend what was being said so it marveled at how he thought the television had been muted when it had merely been drowned out by the noise in the terminal. It wasn't until everyone got quiet that he could hear the television. *Amazing, isn't it, how so many people talking at even a moderate level, could cover the sound of a television that was, by all logical standards, blaring now.*

That introspection lasted less than a minute, but it gave time for his brain to catch up and absorb the information. Others in the terminal were still staring at the screen or at one another in disbelief. Roger grabbed his carry-on duffel and started to make his way to the door. As he did so, all the televisions in his path seemed to be set at the same blaring level.

"To reiterate," said the female anchor in a very matter-of-fact voice that had just the edge of a very unprofessional quiver, "Flight 763 crashed near Golden, Colorado approximately five hours ago. One of the last transmissions is reported to be of someone – and we are assuming this to be either the pilot or copilot – saying, 'that looks like Ankara.'"

A male voice took over, "We have just received notification from the

FAA that all air traffic within the continental United States has been grounded for the immediate future."

As if to reinforce the point, Roger saw movement out of the corner of his eye. He glanced over to the departures board as all flight times changed to *delayed.*

The male voice continued, "...in conjunction with the Centers for Disease Control and the Department of Health, have declared all airports to be quarantined."

Roger increased the length of his stride and only then noticed the *clip-clip* of shoes behind him. He glanced over his shoulder to see Mrs. Fashion Statement following him.

"What are you doing?" He slung his duffel over his shoulders rather than carrying it in his hand.

"Following the only person who seems to have a plan." She had an attaché and a purse, and was struggling to keep up.

He slowed his steps, allowing her to close the distance. Roger turned the corner to the automated shuttle and pushed his way through the small gathered crowd. Taking in the scene, his heart dropped.

Blocking access to the shuttle were four armed National Guardsmen. Dressed in digital desert camouflage, they looked absurd standing in the middle of a concourse in the United States of America. *This doesn't happen here!* However, they had come equipped. Each had a standard issue M-4 slung at the shoulder, a chest rig full of spare magazines, hand grenades and miscellaneous other equipment. Some people gave the National Guard grief for being part-time warriors or weekend warriors, but many had been battle hardened in Iraq and/or Afghanistan. Even before that, they were well trained and dedicated soldiers. Roger never let the fact that they had civilian jobs take away from his appreciation of their service. Many Guardsmen, he couldn't make himself call them Guardspeople and Guardsmenandwomen just sounded weird in his head, had helped him out on several assignments.

"Well shit! Now what do we do?"

Roger looked at Mrs. Fashion Statement, "You kiss your mother with that mouth?"

"Like you haven't heard that before. Heard worse I'd bet!"

"Sure. I've heard worse, just never from someone wearing a pay check's worth of shoes. And my pay checks aren't all that small." He took a self-deprecating shrug, "Infrequent maybe, but not small!"

"Fine then, what next?"

"We get back to our terminal and see what happens. We're not getting through here any time soon."

The electronic sign above the shuttle doors changed from "Out of Service" to "Arriving in" with a ten second count down. The automated tram pulled up outside and the doors slid open, injecting a blast of warm humidity. Another camo-clad team stepped off the tram, wheeling a load of sandbags. Roger watched as they began building a wall of sand and plasticized canvas. After several minutes he shook his head.

Walking back down the concourse to their gate temporarily drew the attention of passengers, fixated by the television or arguing with the gate agents. He returned their questioning glances with downcast eyes or a slight shake of the head. They nodded or turned away, returned their attention to the television. This was the new America: watch TV long enough and someone will tell you what to do. He wondered what happened to the vibrant, self-guided, risk-taking individuals who'd made up the stories of his youth.

"By the way, I'm Jenny," Mrs. Fashion Statement said.

"Jenny? Aren't Jennys supposed to have braces and still be in pigtails or something?"

"Really? Is that how we're going to start? First you tell me I cuss too much and then you tell me my name is immature? Don't have many friends do you?" She stopped with a resounding *clop* on the concourse's tile.

"Nope. Don't have many friends and I'm not great with women."

"I bet most people would say you aren't great with *people*. I don't think being a woman is getting me special treatment, good or bad." Getting nothing but a shrug in response she placed her hands on her hips, leaning forward slightly. "So that's it? Not being good with people is a good enough excuse for being rude?"

"Well, my wife always took care of the people-thing. I didn't mean to offend. Sorry if you took it that way." Roger shrugged again, more pronounced this time in case she missed it the first time. People at the gates on either side of the concourse had started watching them now rather than the televisions.

"So it's my fault if I took it the wrong way? It couldn't be your fault for being rude?"

Roger shrugged again, making it very obvious that it was a shrug. This woman either didn't know what a shrug meant or was very unobservant.

"Sorry?" He made it a question because he wasn't sure what she wanted from him. If Melissa had been here, she'd have known what to do to smooth this over.

"Fine. Whatever. You have quite a bit to learn about politeness mister - ?"

"Oh, Westover. Roger Westover." He thrust his hand out. She looked at the extended hand for a moment, then shook it. Her grip was stronger than he had anticipated.

"Jenny, Jennifer. Jennifer Messeth." Roger nodded, still shaking her hand. She really did have beautiful eyes. He tried to make out the shape of her nose through the surgical mask. Her lips were a complete mystery because the mask, of course, hid her entire mouth. But if her nose and mouth were as nice as her eyes, she was probably very attractive. Now that she was standing and he could see how well the suit fit, she had a nice shape as well. All in all she was good looking, and she didn't have a wedding ring on. With that mask it was hard to tell, but she was probably in her late 30's, maybe early 40's. Right in line with an appropriate age group for him, maybe just a bit young.

He snapped back to the moment as she slipped her hand out of his.

"Quite a bit to learn," she said. *Whatever that meant.*

Roger forced a quick smile and resumed his walk back to his gate. Jennifer watched for a moment, shook her head, and followed after. Regardless of how little a people-person he was, he was still the only one in the whole freaking concourse who seemed to have a clue about what he was doing.

2

Denton, TX – Traditions Hall,
University of North Texas

Corey Westover slapped the bedside table three times before finally connecting with his alarm clock, sending it skidding to the floor. He cracked his eyes open and stared at the ceiling. It seemed brighter than it should be. But he had set his alarm so it couldn't be too late. Besides, he was only on the Xbox until 2:00, he could easily make his 8:15 Psych class, come back to the room and crash a bit longer before his 3:00 English Lit. Another quick crash and he'd be up by 7:00, ready for another night of stomping the mud out of Jacob and M-m-m-mitch.

Wusses.

He snagged his phone off the table to check his texts. *Damn! Sixteen missed messages. What the f-? 10:12? How can it be after 10:00? My stupid alarm! Whatever. Psych is overrated anyway. Besides, I've got almost a 2.3 in that class anyway. That's more than passing. Not like I have a scholarship to maintain. Those poor losers have to spend so much time studying!*

Corey cleared his missed texts. He'd get back with them later.

It looked like Dad called five times. Thank God for caller specific ringtones. Set Dad to silent, no vibrate and you never had to be bothered by a call you don't want. The old man left a message too. *He's the only one old enough to think that people still check voicemails.*

Two keystrokes, a pause, and three keystrokes later, voila, no messages. *Not like he won't call again and tell me what he said on the voicemail anyway. Learn to text ya weirdo!*

The low battery tone sounded. Corey turned the phone off. The charger was in the kitchen and he didn't feel like getting up to plug the thing in. He'd do it later. For now, *welcome back to Sleepland!*

Six minutes later the alarm squawked its electronic tone. Corey's hand slid out of the covers, snaked behind the nightstand, and switched the alarm from *auto* to *off.* No use letting a good day's sleep pass you by.

☣ ☣ ☣

Someone was pounding on his door. *Screw 'em.* Corey rolled over, pulling the pillow over his head. The pounding continued and was coupled with a voice. Ashley's voice. Ashley was the only thing he could think of that would get him out of bed. *With hopes of getting back in bed for an entirely different reason, of course.*

He threw the covers back and slipped on the shirt he'd worn yesterday. His boxers were good enough for the eight steps it took to get to the door of his dorm so he didn't worry about the pants.

Ashley pushed the door open as soon as he unlocked it. "Whoa! Wassup?" He was glad she'd come over, but still. Pushy!

"You haven't answered your phone all morning. Weren't you supposed to be in Psych this morning?"

"Yeah, but – "

"Doesn't matter. Have you seen the news? Didn't you say your dad was flying back to town today?"

For some reason Ashley actually *liked* his dad. They'd sit and talk for hours. Sure, they were at the University of North Texas, one of the best schools for emergency management, her major, in the country. And Dad is *the* Roger Westover, the Disaster Preparedness / Management master himself. He had consulted with the White House and Congress after a series of hurricanes tore up the Gulf Coast and Florida. That opened the door for him to be an adjunct professor at UNT even without a degree himself. That class is how Corey and Ashley met. Still, Corey didn't see why Ashley cared when his father was coming back to town. She could, and did, email him any time she wanted.

"So? No? What? I mean, no, I haven't seen the news. Who *watches* news anymore? Google it! And yeah, I think Dad is coming back today. Back to Fort Worth anyway, not here. Why?"

She crossed the room, picked up the remote and flicked on the television. She rolled her eyes when she saw it was set to the Xbox, and switched over to cable. Her eyes rolled again as Nickelodeon started blaring out. "Oh my god, Core, pretend like you're an adult just once in a while. Switch it to a news channel!"

Corey hit the Guide button and scrolled through the channels. He didn't even know where a news channel would be located. Hell, he didn't even know if he even got any news channels. After scrolling through several guide pages he found a target.

"Look!" Ashley pointed at the TV as if it was supposed to mean something to him. There was an image of a large airport. The caption said it was O'Hare, which was up north somewhere, he thought. It took a minute for the scene to register. All the planes had been pushed back from the gates and as the helicopter flew around it looked like nothing was moving on the ground. That seemed a bit strange.

The camera panned back then zoomed in on something that was definitely strange. All kinds of military vehicles were pulled up outside the airport, crowded between the massive parking structures and the terminal building itself. It looked like a parking lot of military vehicles ranging from HUMVEES to deuce-and-a-halfs and maybe a couple armored personnel carriers. Several white panel trucks were off to the side of the military vehicles and one big 18 wheeler and trailer was parked to the side as well. On top of the parking garages the military guys had built little walls of sandbags and had set up large guns of some sort. The road leading to the airport had been blocked off with military vehicles as well, causing a snarled mess of traffic for miles on the side roads and freeway.

"They're doing this at every airport!" Ashley started ticking off airport names on her fingers, "DFW, Atlanta, LAX, JFK. If your dad is flying home today then he is probably caught on a plane or in an airport!"

"Well, that'd suck for *him*, but I don't see what it has to do with *us* or why you're so freaked out." He picked his pants up from where he had discarded them last night. Obviously this wasn't going to be a *good* visit with Ashley.

"Core, don't you know what's been going on? There is a huge pandemic starting and your dad might be caught up in it! Hell, half the campus has already evacuated. Don't you keep up with anything?"

"Get off my ass, huh? I'm pulling a full load here and still trying to maintain some kind of life."

"Whatever," she said. "You're doing a 6 hour load and spend half your time playing video games. You don't study. You don't work. You barely show up to class! The least you could do is take some sort of interest in what's going on in the world around you!"

"I guess it's all coming out now, huh?" Corey brushed past Ashley, whipping the door open. "If I'm such a slacker in your eyes, maybe we just don't need to see each other right now."

"Maybe we don't!" Ashley stormed out, slamming the door.

Corey flung his hands in the air and threw himself on the foot of the bed. He picked up his Xbox controller and cussed under his breath that he had to get up to get the remote and change the television back over to the game box.

The picture on the screen showed military vehicles in a convoy driving across some suspension bridge. It looked like maybe a bridge in New York City or somewhere like that. Definitely wasn't anywhere close to Denton, Texas so Corey didn't see what Ashley was so upset about.

He flipped the TV over to the game console and restarted his game, locked and loaded, ready to take on an army of zombies.

☣ ☣ ☣

Ashley fumed out of the dorm. *Spoiled ass! How could I think he was worth my time? Maybe the apple doesn't fall far from the tree, but it can certainly roll a long way downhill.*

So close to lunch time the small courtyard, formed by two wings of Traditions Hall, normally had a couple of clusters of students talking, playing music, or just socializing. Every once in a while there was even a study group. Today as she stormed down the sidewalk to the guest parking in front of the Santa Fe Hall dorms, she saw only one other person and he was wearing a surgical mask, wide eyes staring out a bit fearfully, pausing a good distance away as Ashley crossed her path.

When did surgical masks become fashionable? This whole pandemic stuff is turning the world upside down. People afraid to go out of their house and be around others because they could catch the flu or something? This isn't China. Surely we have things under better control than they do. She caught herself and thought back to Professor Westover's, Roger's, class. *Oh my god, do we?*

She picked up her phone and scrolled through her contacts. Roger's cell phone was still listed as "Prof W". She pressed dial.

The phone switched immediately to voice mail. "Thank you for calling," just the familiarity of his voice was calming, "unfortunately I am unable to take your call at this time. Please do not leave a voice mail. Text or email instead as I am unsure of my recharging capabilities, I am conserving the battery on my phone. Thank you."

Ashley paused, leaned against her truck and disconnected the call. She immediately began her text message. "U OK? Fine here. Anything I can do?" She hit send.

The one person in the world she would trust in a situation like this was the very person caught in the situation. *Irony sucks!*

3

Atlanta Hartsfield-Jackson Airport

Roger turned on his phone: 3:47 PM. He filtered through the spam messages in his email and quickly wrote back to the two business inquiries, letting them know he was currently indisposed and that he would write back at more length when he could. The third email he read, nodded his head, and deleted. Four texts had come in, none from Corey, but Ashley's message was a welcome sight. He responded that he was OK but looking forward to finishing his trip; he'd be home in a week to ten days, maybe sooner. There wasn't anything else she could do for him.

Roger powered off his phone, slipping it back in to his pocket. His face must have betrayed some of his relief as Jennifer – Jenny nodded toward his pocket. "Your wife?"

"That'd be a miracle." Roger took the phone out of his pocket, making sure it was turned off.

"Oh, bad divorce?" Jenny had been through that herself. Not bad in that she got the shaft, but bad in that she thought it had been a great marriage until she found out just how bad he behaved while she wasn't around. For most women the greatest fear when their husbands were 'away on business' was that he might be cheating. That was her greatest fear for five years. Until he was arrested for murder out in Kansas of all places. *I mean, the person already lived in Kansas, how much worse could it get? Did he really need to kill someone who lived in Kansas?*

It turned out that Paul was a hit man for a certain group who preferred to remain unnamed in New York. She didn't know how he got mixed up with them but he must have made a killing, only a little pun intended, at it so he must have been pretty good. She didn't like to think about that part of it.

The strange part for her to come to grips with was that she was almost, *almost*, accepting of his profession. The thing that kept her up at night was that for seven years, five married and two before that, he had lied to her. Sitting back thinking about it logically she knew that if he had told her that he was 'off to whack someone' she would have left him. But since she didn't know what he was doing at the time, she was pissed that he hadn't told her what it was. Sometimes logic doesn't play into it.

On the upside, when your husband is convicted of multiple homicides across the country and awaiting trial in three foreign countries, the divorce proceedings are pretty smooth. With no kids and no *maintenance*, as Colorado calls alimony, things were pretty easy. Her lawyer proposed a one-half settlement of all assets and six months later it was all over. She just never would have thought how much one-half of their assets truly was! Plus Paul was good at investments and he still gave her investment advice from prison. He said he had plenty of time to do his research. All things considered he was a pretty stand-up guy for a mass murderer.

Roger shook his head. "No, not divorced. She died eight years ago."

"Oh! I'm sorry." Jenny sat back, not knowing what else to say.

"Why, you have something to do with it?"

Jenny's mind flicked to Paul for an instant, "Uh, no. Don't *think* so."

"Don't need to apologize for it then." Roger shrugged and tucked the phone into his pocket.

"I guess I just don't know what to say to that." Jenny quirked her head to the side, trying to figure this guy out. He had kind eyes, and people said the eyes were the window to the soul. But when you cover half your face with a mask there is so much that gets lost in translation.

"Sometimes when you don't know what to say, you just don't need to say anything."

"You're being rude again Roger." She held the 'u' sound in rude a little long and it came out as rooood. He found that a bit endearing.

"Am I? I thought I was being instructive." He shrugged. He'd have to think about that later.

Her eyes squinted over her mask. Since the sun was going down behind her the squint probably wasn't due to the sun so she must be trying to think something through.

"OK. We're setting that aside." She raised her eyebrows and tilted her head as if her statement was a question.

Roger shrugged with a slight nod, "OK." That seemed to satisfy her and she settled her shoulders as she continued on.

"So, what happened? How did she die?"

"Car accident. She was, as she termed it, my business manager. She basically sold my services, negotiated contracts; did all the people stuff. She traveled all over the country setting up my consulting business back when we were still trying to get off the ground. She was on one of those trips, returning her rental to the car lot and one of the staff was backing another car into the slot behind her. Something went wrong and when she bent over to pick up her bag, the kid backed into her. Freak accident. She was killed instantly. Better for her than lingering I guess, but I miss her. I thought I'd miss her, but I miss her more than I ever thought I would."

There was true emotion in his voice but Jenny was struck by the fact that if she were watching this conversation from across the room she would never have known Roger just told her such a tragic story. Even without the bottom half of the face showing most people would have had some emotional response in their eyes or body language. He just sat there and described it as if he were reading about someone else. She was beginning to feel he didn't process information the same way everyone else did.

"I'm sor-, I mean, that's terrible." She looked for an outlet to get away from that story. "What business were you in?"

"Oh, still am. Not as good as it was while Melissa was out there doing most of the work, but I'm still in it. I am a DP/DR/BC consultant. Disaster planning, disaster response and business continuity. I help people figure out what to plan for, how to respond to it, and how to keep the phones ringing and money flowing while they're trying to deal with it."

"Sounds like you're exactly the kind of person people need to be talking to right now!" Jenny's eyes lit up as she leaned toward him.

"Oh, I am. I was just in North Carolina helping a client get their business continuity plan rolling. I flew there from D.C. I was in a two day conference with a joint group of the CDC and Department of Health and Human Services. We saw this might be coming. Part of what's going on is right out of my plan. I didn't suggest an armed response at airports, but it makes sense. When you shut down the airports most people in the airports would probably want to get out so making sure they are contained is a wise move."

Jenny shook her head. This was just too disturbing. She just happened to meet probably the one and only guy in the country who knew all this was about to happen and then got caught up in it. Suddenly the idea struck, "You can get us out of here! Call your contacts and tell them where you are. They'll come get you!"

"Even if that were true, how would that get you out of here?"

"You could take me!" Maybe this guy was more challenged than she thought, "You could say we're friends, travelling companions, I'm your assistant, whatever."

"Um. OK. That might work. But it won't work. Against protocol." He shrugged as if that explained everything.

"Protocol? What's that?"

"Protocol. An established process to be followed in the event of a situation."

"A process? You mean a policy? You're not going to call your friends because it is against policy? Not everything can be anticipated, you have to have flexibility to respond to situations. All plans need a little give." She couldn't believe this guy.

"No, that's not why I'm not calling them. And they aren't friends." He settled in as if giving a lecture, "You're right. All plans need some flexibility. But that flexibility should be granted in order to deal with the unexpected. When you can anticipate an event, make a viable response for that event, which either strengthens the overall plan or at the very least does not serve to weaken the overall plan, the protocol should be followed. That is actually *part of the protocol*. This event, however, was not unanticipated and was, in fact, planned for.

"In the event," Roger's voice took on that far-away, as if reading tone, "a key member of the Response Team is compromised, the guidance, advice and continued participation of such member must also be considered compromised. For the security of the response, such a compromised member should therefore be excluded from consultation until the factor(s) of compromise are alleviated."

Jenny stared into Roger's eyes, waiting for them to give something away. "OK, so what does that mean?"

"That was my third email a minute ago. I was notified that the team was trying to track me down, found out I was here in the airport and that I was considered a compromised asset for the time being. You could say I've been voted off the island." The attempt at humor and crinkle around his eyes indicating he was smiling came close to sending Jenny into a rage.

She flung herself back in her seat, crossed her arms over her chest, and brooded. Overhead news reports continued about the closure of airports. Several groups had already formed in protest of the unlawful detention of American citizens in inhumane conditions. As the sun set in Atlanta, video of more westerly airports continued picture-in-picture with the news anchors, footage of protestors, a map showing known locations of Ankara Fever outbreaks both domestically and internationally.

Silence stretched for more than half an hour before Jenny looked at Roger again. He was leaning back in his chair, supporting his head on a pillar as he was apparently trying to sleep. "What's next?"

"Huh?" He sat up, blinking at her.

"What happens next in your protocol?"

"Well, they've already started with a combination first move. So some of my thoughts will be just educated speculation." Roger widened his eyes, leaning forward slightly as if awaiting for her response.

"OK. Educated speculation."

He nodded, "Right, educated speculation. They're going to have to start a feeding process. Some airports, and we listed them out, have restaurants that are accessible from all concourses so they are second tier concerns. We can get snacks here, but not an actual meal so we're a first tier concern. Pretty soon they'll start passing out MREs, meals-ready-to-eat, the stuff the military eats when in the field. Then they'll set up full food service kitchens.

"After that it is a hold-and-wait. If there are a lot of medical concerns then we'll be in prolonged quarantine. If there aren't we should be released soon."

"Define 'soon'."

"Initial indicators are that Ankara Fever has a three-day incubation, up to a seven-day dormant-yet-contagious period. I've forgotten the term for that, but there is a term for everything, you know?" He took the swishing motion of her hand to be acknowledgment, "And then we have a symptomatic period of hours up to three days before death. That gives us thirteen days. Give a fifty percent buffer and you arrive at approximately 20 days of quarantine."

"Twenty days! Three weeks!"

"Not quite, three weeks would be -"

"No, Roger. No. Not logic. Not specificity. Three weeks!" Several others in the concourse had started watching them again so Jenny lowered her voice until it came out as a string of hissing sounds. "You're telling me that we could be here for three weeks! I have things to do!"

"I'm sorry to have misled you." Roger realized this conversation wasn't going in the intended direction. "The twenty days is in case there are no signs of infection. If there is a considerable medical circumstance, it could go much longer."

"Shut up Roger." He opened his mouth but she cut him off. "No, seriously, shut up. If you say anything else right now, *you* are going to experience a *considerable medical circumstance*."

Roger shrugged and leaned back against his pillar. *I'm glad I met her. She is so much like Melissa.*

4

Atlanta Hartsfield-Jackson Airport

Jenny woke to an unexpected rattle. Her dreams had been of armed men in camouflage with pustules leaking blood from behind their face masks and around their gloves. They were wrapping people in chains and strapping on oversized padlocks despite the crying and wailing of the prisoners. She bolted up and an arm caught her across the shoulders, keeping her from falling out of her chair.

Her neck and shoulders immediately rebelled, complaining about not being properly supported as she dozed. When Roger was sure she wasn't going to fall out of the chair he lowered his arm. Jenny rubbed her eyes and tried to roll the kinks out of her shoulders. She slowly turned toward what woke her.

A small crowd gathered around an airplane catering cart where four of the National Guards, at least she thought they were National Guard based on what Roger said, were handing out large plastic pouches and plastic cups. She had watched enough news to know what an MRE looked like. Now it seemed she was going to get to find out what they taste like. She pushed herself to her feet but paused as one of the camo-clad people looked her way. The uniforms made them fairly androgynous but she was almost certain the person was male. The facemask was exactly like what she saw in her dream. She passed a glance around the seal of the mask as well as the wrists of the catering crew. Even though she didn't expect to see any blood leaking, she was still happy and somewhat relieved to be right.

Roger pushed himself up as well, looked at the Guardsmen and then back to Jennifer. "You OK? Want something to eat?"

"Yeah, sure." They walked over and stood in line.

The Guardsman handing out the MREs had his speech down. This must not have been his first concourse. "One meal per person. One cup per person. Water fountains are halfway down the concourse. Please save your cups. Heating instructions are contained in the packs. One meal per person. One cup per person..." Jenny and Roger took their packs then went to the line at the water fountains.

Jenny scanned the crowd. A full cross section of American society was represented and she estimated there were over five hundred people on this one concourse when you counted everyone who was waiting to get on a plane and everyone getting off. Add to that all the workers who were caught up when the airport was forced to shut down and then add all the people who were dropping off or picking up passengers and they were looking at some serious numbers. Maybe twenty-five to thirty thousand people just at this one airport. Atlanta is pretty busy so not all airports would have as many, but add in the top ten airports nationally and suddenly you're talking about 250,000 people. Conservatively double that to include every other airport and the United States of America had half a million of its own citizens and foreign travelers locked up.

"How many people do you think?"

Roger looked up from filling his plastic cup. "Huh? How many people what?"

Jennifer leaned in and whispered, "How many are trapped in an airport like us?"

"The plan called for covering up to 750,000 people for a period of up to six months."

She filled up her cup as well, refraining from talking until they were out of the crowd. "Six months? Are you guys f-ing nuts?"

"No. Of course we aren't going to keep everyone the entire time." He sat down in the corner of the terminal gate where no one else had taken up squatting rights. A quick dig through his duffle and he pulled out two bandanas. He handed one to Jenny. From the rattling sound she could tell there was quite a collection of items in the bag.

"We acknowledged some basic specs. In most instances it will take approximately one month to six weeks to develop a test for a known, yet previously untested, illness – in this case a virus. The test is pretty easy actually until you want to apply it to more than half a million people all at once. Then you have to package it and distribute it. All this is after you've made it and tested it."

Roger carefully tore open the MRE bag, a difficult feat considering how resilient the plastic packaging was, and laid out the contents on the floor between them. "Back in the 80s they had a ham and chicken loaf. That was my favorite. Haven't seen it in a while though.

"You gotta watch yourself with these things. They are made for people out in the field doing heavy manual labor and without a -. Hmm, um, without proper hygiene facilities." He raised his eyebrows, slightly leaning toward Jenny, a move she was learning meant he was asking if she needed clarification.

She nodded her understanding and he continued. "So there are a lot of calories packed into these things, about twelve to thirteen hundred calories each. That's more than enough calories in one of these bags for us to live on for the day at our current energy expenditure. But you have to have three a day to get all the vitamins recommended. We should be scheduled to get two per day until the food service unit start up.

"Now, like I said, they were designed for a different purpose than we're in. Two of those per day are still going to plug you up pretty good. Some people even say that MRE actually stands for Meals Requiring Enemas." He chuckled at that little slice of history stored away between his ears, then pointed to the small pack of toilet paper in the MRE contents. There wasn't much of it. "You're supposed to save those up. I'm going to take advantage of what we have in the facilities here until I have no other option. But the wet wipe there, that can be used for more delicate tasks than cleaning your fingers. Use the bandana as a napkin. We can always clean those." He tucked the wet wipes and toilet paper back into his empty bag.

Not enjoying the direction of the conversation, but appreciating his desire to make sure she had all the information she needed, she followed his lead and his advice, ripping open the bag and dropping her toilet paper and wet wipe into her bag as well.

"You're going to need plenty of water. You have some instant coffee there and those dehydrated pears will go down much better after soaking for a bit. You can still eat them dehydrated though," to illustrate his point, he ripped open the little pouch of peaches from his own kit. The chunks of peaches were held together by what Jenny assumed was the dehydrated juices. Roger removed his mask and took a bite. It sounded like biting a rice cake. He chewed it, swallowed and took a swig of water.

"Were you in the military? How'd you learn all this stuff?" Jenny poured some water into her pear pouch. She wasn't a huge fan of pears even when they were fresh. She didn't want to try her luck getting a pear-flavored sponge past her taste buds.

"No, I wasn't in the military. I like to go camping and when Melissa and I would go, back then even Corey went with us, we'd take MREs or dehydrated food with us on the trail. Melissa went a few times when I was practicing primitive survival but she didn't like that as much so I usually did that by myself or with some friends."

"How about the disaster planning stuff? Where'd you learn that good enough for the government to call you?" She started to peel open the pack of beef stew and Roger waved her off.

"Before you open it, do you want it hot?" She furrowed her eyebrows and he continued, "If you want it hot, leave it sealed up. Slide it into that paper sleeve there. It has a water activated heater. Pour in a little water, up to the line on the pack and slip the stew pouch in. Wait a little bit and it'll heat up, no flame. My chili and beans will go down fine without being heated so the heater joins the toilet paper." He slipped the flameless heater into the meal pouch he was saving. He also threw in the Tabasco sauce, sugar, creamer and instant coffee.

Jenny followed the instructions on the pack, poured in some water up to the fill line and then slid in her stew. A few seconds later the chemical pack started sizzling. She set the pack on the MRE pouch and watched. The white card-stock looking chemical pouch absorbed the water but nothing else really happened. When she held her hand close enough though, she could feel the heat radiating off.

"So," she asked, "How 'bout it? What's the story?"

"You know. Live and learn. I picked up stuff here and there, thought about it, put it together, thought about it some more. I had a friend who went to school for disaster planning and I read his books, helped him study for tests. That kind of thing. I kept up with the industry and found it fascinating." Roger ripped into his chili and macaroni, digging in with the spoon from the MRE pack. "He got a job at FEMA after a couple of years.

"Remember about 20 years ago there was that huge hurricane that took a bite out of Florida? Well, he and I started talking and I shared with him some ideas I had. He asked if I could come to D.C. and discuss those ideas. I'd just decided to propose to Melissa and thought that it was about time to settle down and get a real job – I'd been teaching some basic survival classes and if I didn't know how to forage for food, there would have been many meals I would have missed. This FEMA thing gave me an opportunity to maybe provide for Melissa and a family.

"I went to D.C. and didn't agree with anything any of what those guys said. They dismissed me pretty much out of hand. So I went back to Texas, ready to tell Melissa to move on and find someone who could provide for her. She surprised me by proposing herself. She said that if she'd waited for me, she would have been retiring before she got married.

"Anyway, she said that she made enough money and we could live frugally, that she didn't care if I was some, as she put it, caveman stuck in the twentieth century. We were supposed to get married eight months later but that summer we had a brutal wildfire season in the West and a brutal hurricane season in Texas. Turns out that the stuffed suits in D.C. remembered me and of all the miracles in the world, actually acknowledged that if they had taken my advice they could have saved quite a bit in logistic costs, saved time in deployments of personnel, and resources and been more effective in helping people be more proactive, reducing overall damages. They called me back and I've been consulting on various levels since. When others heard that I consulted for the government I got some credibility and Melissa went out there selling me across the country. It made for a pretty good life. She joined me most of the time and we always made sure to have weekends at home, together with Corey.

"I've picked up two honorary degrees and some people call me 'doctor' because one of the honoraries is a doctorate but I never went past high school. I'm still more accustomed to roaming around the backwoods than being in some office tower.

"Melissa and I lived in Fort Worth because it is close to a major airport but it isn't Dallas. We were going to retire to a cabin in Arkansas and we even bought the place and got it ready to meet our needs. Even had a bunch of friends buy adjoining property so we wouldn't be alone. The last time I saw her we were at the house in Fort Worth and I just haven't been able to unplug that last connection, so I still live there. I still go to the cabin and keep getting it ready for retirement, but it just feels a little empty now."

Jenny tried to redirect to a happier topic, "What about your son, Corey?"

"Yeah, that's a tricky one there. Things were good 'til Melissa died. Corey pretty much blames me because she was out on my behalf. His shrink said that was kinda normal," Jenny noticed that the more comfortable Roger became the more his accent slid toward Southern, "but that once Corey dealt with the loss, our relationship would normalize again. Trouble is that Corey never really dealt with the loss. He is twenty now and completely aimless. I thought getting him to go to school might give him some direction, even fixed him up with a nice girl. Nothin's workin'. Matter of fact, I couldn't even let him know that I wanted him to go to school. By the time he was eighteen he was just lookin' for a way to get away from me. I told him that his mom left a trust in his name. It would pay for college, which he had to pass, before it matured. Took me forever to get the lawyer to draw that up and make it look legit. So, at least he is going to college. His high school grades weren't great and no one really wanted to take him, but I pulled the few strings I had to pull and got him in where I teach sometimes.

"That's where I introduced him to Ashley. He doesn't know I fixed him up. Ashley is very cute, smart and funny, but he'd have turned away from her just to spite me if he knew. All he knows is she was in one of my classes and saw him with me one day then asked if I could introduce them. She's a couple of years older than him and I thought that might do him some good. Turns out I talk to Ashley more than him, and he hasn't really come out like I'd hoped.

"Wouldn't surprise me if she dropped him once she graduates or even if a brighter prospect comes along. She might have already. If she is as smart as I think she is, she'll recognize that he just might be a dead weight after all."

Roger gathered up the packages from his meal. Jenny had been so intent on listening she didn't even realize he had been eating the whole time or that her food, once hot, was now back on its way to getting cold.

She tried once again to change the subject. This time she knew that it wasn't to a happier topic. She'd had time to think about their predicament though and she'd rather be a bit depressed and educated on their situation than uneducated and uncertain. "What about us? You told me what will happen if there is no outbreak, but what happens if there is?"

"We're assuming that the outbreak doesn't happen to us?"

"Well, yah! I mean, come on. Do we even have to make that stipulation?"

"For proper planning, we have to consider -" she started waving her hand again, signaling him to move on. "Oh, rhetorical. OK."

Jenny unlooped her surgical mask from one ear, letting it hang down so she could start eating. Her nose was almost exactly as he'd imagined, very cute. Her mouth though. She had thinner lips than he thought she might, but they were still well shaped and somehow fit her face better than the fuller lips might have. Maybe she wasn't a Helen of Troy, but she'd draw more than her fair share of looks.

"OK. So we're not infected and don't die from the disease. Stipulated. If there is a considerable medical circumstance, then a multi-pronged decision tree is implemented. Since there are sick people and well people then either extreme of the tree is excluded from consideration." There goes that speed up motion from her hand again! *She really is impatient!* "OK. To summarize, there will likely be two responses. They'll either wait it out and we'll be contained here until no one shows further signs of infection or, option two, if the outbreak isn't overly large they will practice isolation and evacuation where they will keep the sick isolated from the healthy, test those who are asymptomatic to see if the virus is in its dormant phase, and then release those who are not infected.

"We'll need to be aware of two possible changes in condition. In option one there will be more healthy than sick so they will bring in a few tents in order to quarantine those who are sick and have the rest of the airport for testing and housing. Seeing tents go up would be a good sign.

"With option two, they know people won't be happy. People on the inside and people on the outside. No one wants to just put a bunch of people in a room and hope Darwinism isn't too harsh, so they want to take action – especially the people on the inside. In that instance, they'll reinforce the security presence. We'll see a transition from our National Guards friends to U.S. Army and or Marines."

"So, tents good, military bad?"

"That is far too simplistic, and our military isn't *bad*, they're trying to protect the greater population after all. But for our purposes, you are essentially correct. I'd just change the connotations, not the reasoning. Tents, favorable. Military, unfavorable."

"Great. I've always liked guys in uniform but I've never looked forward to seeing one any less than I do right now." Jenny stuck her spoon in the empty beef stew packet. She didn't remember eating it or the rehydrated pears, but she was full and right now that was the best she could wish for.

5

Atlanta Hartsfield-Jackson Airport

Roger awoke to a hand on his chest, shaking him. "Wake up!"

It took him a moment to recognize Jennifer's voice and remember where he was. The airport had long turned off the droning overhead announcements about suspicious luggage and he had spent enough uncomfortable nights sleeping in weird places that the catch in his lower back and neck wasn't much of a clue.

He opened his eyes and sat up, sliding his back against the wall. After a quick eye-cleansing rub he looked around. Jennifer was kneeling to his left but everyone else awake was staring, transfixed at the mounted televisions. "Wassup? Breakfast?"

"No, the news. Come on." Jennifer matched action to words, striding to the closest television. Roger stood, stretched, and joined her. He was digging through his duffle in search of his toothpaste and brush when the anchor's voice caught his attention. He looked up.

"So, Dr. Kreznyck, if I understand what you are saying correctly, you believe this to be an engineered virus. As an expert in infectious disease and in your more than thirty-five years experience you are saying that you have never encountered a virus with this infection rate – this communicability – and this mortality rate?"

Somehow the talking heads on cable news just seemed to fit the stereotypical look of their profession. Dr. Kreznyck was just on the graying side of middle aged with a full beard and mustache. Even Roger realized his tweed suit was out of style and Roger hadn't upgraded his wardrobe since Melissa's passing. This doctor looked like the guy you would cast for a movie if you were looking for a research scientist who must deliver bad news to a national audience. There were really only two things that kept Roger from thinking this guy might be a paid actor. First, Dr. Kreznyck was a colleague from the National Pandemic Planning and Response Group (NPPRG) and second, he looked *exhausted*.

"That is correct, Amber. From what we have been able to establish this early on, it appears the virus that is commonly being referred to as Ankara Fever – and I will refer to it as such for the benefit of your audience – is most likely a bioengineered agent. The infection rate of the H1N1 virus a few years ago is estimated to be below twenty percent. That is one component. The mortality rate, the rate at which the disease takes the life or leads to complications which take the life of the patient, for H1N1 was less than one percent except for very specific ethnic groups. The most deadly pandemic in modern times was termed the Spanish Flu and lasted from 1918 to 1920. The estimated mortality rate was approximately fifteen percent. The initial numbers we are seeing in relation to Ankara are significantly higher."

Just as Roger was wondering how the station had gotten Dr. Kreznyck to come on national television with such news, the doctor's cell phone began to ring. Roger only knew it because its ring tone was such a bizarre choice for such a staunch man of science. Transiberian Orchestra's *Christmas In Sarajevo* was the only ring tone the doctor ever had, winter, spring, summer or fall. Roger had actually wondered if someone had played a trick on the good doctor and changed the ring tone to that song and Kreznyck could not figure out how to change it to something else. The thought was never more than fleeting so he never asked, but with Dr. Kreznyck on the television and the Dum-da-da-dum Dum-da-da-dum going off in the background there was little doubt it was the doctor's phone.

"Doctor, according to the numbers you discussed with our producer just before coming on camera - . One moment." Amber pressed one finger to her ear, a questioningly look crossing her face. She gathered herself expertly and looked back to the camera. Off screen the doctor's phone stopped ringing. "It seems that question will have to wait until after this break."

The screen blanked but the normal cut scene the station used for commercial breaks did not appear. Amber's voice broke in, distant from a microphone but still clearly audible. "What the hell was that all about? I was just - ." The cut-scene rolled, drowning out the rest of what Amber had to say and leading to a commercial for an online trading company.

The crowd, Roger included, remained glued to the screen for more than ten minutes as commercial after commercial rolled. When live broadcasting was restored, the view was of the trading floor at the New York Stock Exchange with yet another perfectly coiffed announcer leading the audience through the expected day's trading. The market seemed to be set to continue its downward slide, but there was no mention of Ankara Fever. Melanie Brewer, the onscreen announcer, did pause at one point and had to visibly change what she was intending to say, "And as conditions surrounding the, um, uh, global environment continue to remain uncertain…," but that was as close as she came to directly addressing Ankara Fever.

Roger could see other groups around the terminals changing stations and his group started surfing for more news as well. No other news station was broadcasting information about Ankara and after it dominating the news for the majority of a week, not even a mention made it to the crawler at the bottom of the screen. Ankara had just become taboo.

"Whadaya gettin'?" One of Roger's terminal mates, a man in his early 30s probably, was looking to another who was on one of those tablet computers. His companion, close enough in age and looks to be brothers, just shook his head.

"I got a Facebook update and email about 1:30 this morning but nothing since. Looks like the WiFi is down and I can't connect."

A flurry of phone-grabbing rippled through the crowd. People stared at their screens, held them over their heads, and even a few slapped the phones as if that would change anything. The end result, mobile phone service was down. Roger slipped his arm through Jennifer's and stepped away from the crowd. He may not be as people-savvy as Melissa was but he knew that when most people were separated from their phones, the situation wasn't going to improve.

"What's going on?" Jennifer had the sense to lean close and whisper.

"Looks like an imposed communications blackout. I wasn't in on that part of the planning. No one but the highest levels knew the entire plan, but it makes sense."

"Makes sense? This is America! This is censorship, or at least a violation of the right to free speech!"

Roger nodded. "One time when Corey was about five we were kicking a ball around in the front yard. He kicked it as hard as his little legs would and it hit a tree. Bounced back over his head, and out into the street. He took off after it. I'd just caught him before he ran out between two cars on the street. Another car was coming. He looked up at me. That look told me he didn't appreciate being stopped. In his rush to go for the ball and then in his rush to pass judgment on me for stopping him, he completely missed that car coming down the road. I looked both ways and made sure no one was coming and let him go. He went out into the street, got the ball and walked back into the house without ever saying anything to me.

"To this day I'd rather him be upset with me for that little violation of his freedom than wonder what damage the car would have done to his little body."

"Good story. Noble." Jennifer looked around at the crowd. People were becoming frantic, trying to dial numbers even with no signal, pulling out laptops only to find the thirty-something was right and there was no WiFi coverage. "But I think whoever just did this has completely underestimated what the reaction is going to be. It is going to be more than a dirty look from a five year old."

"Jennifer, my new friend," Roger watched the others and saw the growing rage, "I think we've finally found a topic on which we can fully agree."

☣ ☣ ☣

Less than an hour later a rattling boom shook the terminal. The crowds surged from their gates, looking back toward the tram stop. Several Guardsmen were standing shoulder to shoulder, blocking the entire concourse, weapons held at the ready. Behind them a crew was standing up large mesh wire panels. Both sides were bolted to the walls, blocking off the entire width of the terminal.

Several in the crowd approached and demanded to know what was going on but the Guardsmen held their ground and did not respond. Roger shook his head. Behind those facemasks he knew that there were people, mostly ranging in age from 18 to 25, and they were likely as clueless about what was happening as the crowd here in the terminal. They knew they were following orders and they weren't hurting anyone. If they had a good leader, they were likely convinced they were helping to save the country. They were brave, but they were probably as scared as anyone else in the airport. The only difference was they had guns.

Finally someone in the back ranks turned on a bullhorn. "Please folks!" She waited for the din to die down a bit and tried again, "Please folks. We know you're frustrated and want to know what is going on. Right now we're trying to create a safe environment so we can tend to your needs. As soon as we get the 'all clear', we're going to open the doors. Believe me, please. You'll be no happier to get out of here than I will to open the door for you. Until that time, please let my soldiers do what they need to do."

Perhaps it was the compassion in the voice, perhaps that it was a woman's voice, maybe it was the mention of letting them go, but somehow that short speech calmed the crowd long enough for the soldiers to complete the mesh wall and gateway. A door was secured to one side. Structural reinforcements secured the panels in place and when it was tested, the Guardsmen fell back through to the other side.

When the crew emerged from the tram waiting area with the second set of mesh panels and started fixing them to the wall twenty feet back, no amount of quiet, calm compassion was enough to quell the uproar. The terminal had been sealed from the outside world and there was nothing that could be done about it. Roger watched as one of the gate agents snuck over to a door leading out to a boarding ramp. She quietly punched in several codes, checked the door handle, and returned to her chair at the podium. Her head went to her hands and her shoulder shook as she finally realized that she was just as trapped as everyone else.

6

Ashley's Apartment – Denton, TX

Ashley Sanderson sat transfixed, staring at her screen. Over the last two days she had stopped being able to process what was happening. Now the images and reports went straight from her eyes and ears, directly into her brain without pausing for interpretation. When she occasionally snapped out of the stupor, her brain refused to believe what she was seeing anyway. She wanted to go back to watching television where everything was safe and the world made sense, where complex social issues could be resolved in an hour if people just said and did the right thing. But she wasn't Corey. She couldn't just turn a blind eye to unfolding events.

She had left the television behind. Even cable news was focusing on old tired issues. The immigration debate was continuing. Unemployment was surging. The economy was lagging. Politicians were haranguing one another and the parties were ever more divided in their self-destructive attempts to see which party could be the furthest from the moderate center of the country's electorate.

Of course the riots were being covered by the news but the rationale for the riots was brushed by. Most often the riots were attributed to those disenfranchised with the government but no one was interviewed and no close-ups were shown. Not on national news at any rate. Yesterday morning Ashley received an email that directed her to StreamTheNews.com for *the real story* and except for a few brief hours once exhaustion completely overwhelmed her, she had been fixated by the site.

StreamTheNews had been up for less than a week but was receiving millions of views per day. It was for news what YouTube had been for entertainment, only unedited and uncut. Across the world independent people with cameras were capturing events as they unfolded, uploading them to STN. Channels were carved out by geographic region and metachannels linked stories from different regions, grouped by theme. The metachannel growing the fastest was labeled *Ankara Virus* and showed the spreading wave of fear and violence associated with the even more frightening wave of viral spread associated with the pandemic.

Within the last 36 hours reports and videos of the viral rampage flooded the StreamTheNews servers. Videos were being added faster than they could be viewed. When she first thought to look, Ashley had viewed 17 of 273 videos in the *Ankara Virus* metachannel. At the end of the next video she had viewed 18 of 337. The channel was growing exponentially. That was over 24 hours ago. More than 12,000 videos were now associated with the Ankara Virus with more coming in by the minute. Ashley applied the English language filter and still had over 7,000 unviewed.

Some videos were mere seconds long and most lacked the professionalism and polish of traditional reports but the simple reality displayed in the videos trumped all the polish in the world. Ashley scrolled through the list and clicked a report from close to home titled, "Parkland Hospital, Dallas". It had been uploaded over five hours ago.

A young male voice narrated. Ashley guessed he was about her age and his voice cracked with emotion as the camera took in the view, starting with a shaky close-up of a back-lit sign. A thin white strip with gray letters stated "Parkland" over a red square with the white letters "ER". A somewhat dated tan brick multistory building rose in the background. When the camera zoomed out, the image steadied and Ashley could see what was making her narrator's voice crack.

"I'm here at Parkland Memorial. The sun is about to come up and I don't wanna get caught so I have to make this quick." The camera scanned over rows of bed sheets tucked in around human forms, all with their heads covered. In the dim lighting dark smears stained the sheets especially around the groin and face region. From similar videos Ashley knew those stains would be a sickly red, fading to brown. "I took a quick count," the narrator stated, "and it looks like between seventy-five and eighty people have been laid-out here behind this make-shift barrier." The camera zoomed out even further to show where garbage bags had been hastily stapled to surveyor stakes.

The camera swung violently to another stretch of grass where even more rows of bodies were positioned on the grass, covered with sheets. The same dark stains were apparent but these bodies wriggled and moaned in pain as medical staff stepped between them. "I brought -," the voice broke for a moment. "I brought my little brother and mom here yesterday and there wasn't anyone in the grass but the Emergency Room was already full. "Mom and Chris died before a doctor could even see them. I just wanted to get this out to people."

The camera panned down to his pants where a red stain had begun to soak through. "I don't have much time left. I've got to get this uploaded, but anyone who sees this, stay away from the hospitals. They can't do anything for you but watch you die and pile you up with everyone else."

The camera turned to the narrator's face. A dark streak ran from his right eye, down his cheek. Another ran from his right ear, down to his jaw and puddled on his collar. "I think it is too late for me. Stay inside, stay away from other people and pray. This is probably my last video. It's starting to hurt too much now. Bye." The image shifted to black.

Ashley pushed back from her computer, the bloody kid's face burned into her mind's eye. His plea to stay away from everyone else struck a nerve. Her mind had simply been absorbing the images, recording data, filing it away like some information for a research paper. This anonymous kid from less than 100 miles away had done what more than a day's worth of viewing could not. He made her brain engage.

Professor Westover's class had focused on disaster response in a business context but he also alluded to disaster preparedness for individuals. In ongoing conversations he'd talked in-depth about how to assess your needs, how to assess your potential trigger events, and how to prepare yourself. Both mentally and with supplies.

Too bad Corey never listened to a single word his dad said. Ashley froze halfway through pushing herself out of her chair. *Oh shit! Corey!*

☣ ☣ ☣

Corey looked at the 7-11 like it was some kind of bad joke. He even remembered a bad joke about 7-11s. *Why does a store that stays open 24 hours a day, 7 days a week have locks on its doors? Ha, ha.* But it wasn't a joke. He'd finally run out of Mountain Dew and Totino's Pizza Rolls. Since his car was broken down again he'd borrowed a bike someone had left unlocked outside the dorm.

It had taken less than five minutes to ride to the store but it had been a creepy five minutes. No one was out. No one. He heard sirens in the distance and there were cars clogging up the streets everywhere. He probably couldn't have made it to the store in his car anyway. But now that he had arrived, he saw something he had never before witnessed. The 7-11 was closed *and locked*!

He rattled the door and looked inside to see if anyone was in there. No one was. Not only that, but almost all the sodas were gone. And the chips. Even the little sandwiches in the refrigerated section were gone. The store looked ransacked – in a very orderly manner. *Maybe this one closed. They really should have put up a sign or something.*

Corey looked around. The Jack in the Box was closed too. Lights off even. Same with the Chinese buffet. *That sucks! I loved that place.* And the pizza shop. *What the hell? Is this whole block being condemned or something? You'd think it was by the smell! The garbage people really need to make the rounds.*

For the first time Corey really looked around. It was weird that no one else was out, but now what had only crept around the edge of his brain was starting to settle in. The roads were full of cars but there were no people. Even I-35 was quiet. It was several blocks away but, with as silent as the rest of the city was, he should have been able to hear cars and trucks speeding by at freeway speeds. Instead he again heard a distant siren and the occasional dog bark. In a city of over 110,000 people, Corey was alone.

Now that his attention was captured, he began to notice more. The cars had stopped, not wrecked. Some had pulled over but most had simply stopped in the middle of the road. Doors were opened or closed, however the previous occupants had left them. Only one car half a block away still emitted the *ding-ding-ding* of the door being left ajar. The others had dead batteries or closed doors. These cars had been here a while.

He pedaled his bike back onto the road, looking down the row of cars. At the lead of the pack, one car seemed to have drifted to an intersection. What was in that intersection made Corey's heart skip a beat.

A Ford pickup had obviously rear-ended a Chevy of much the same size. In Texas, this would be cause for at least harsh words, if not an out-and-out fist fight. In this instance, it looked like even more. Laying just outside the driver's side door was the apparent Ford driver. She was in a white shirt tucked into the waist of tight jeans. What drew his attention was the blood.

Bent in the fetal position the lady – girl?, teen? – looked to have been tightly clutching her stomach when she died. Blood leaked from her eyes and ears and Corey supposed she had been stabbed in the stomach as she was laying mostly face down and mostly in a pool of dried blood. It seemed the smell might be coming from the cars rather than trash cans because this one was getting ripe.

Corey stopped beside the body, outside the ring of blood and dropped his kickstand. He walked a half circle around the body. She was definitely dead. Her face was bloated and it even looked like blood had dried *under the skin. Someone was really pissed! No reason to do this for a fender-bender!*

Not understanding why, Corey needed a better look at her face and at the wound that had killed her. He had killed hundreds, maybe thousands, of people in his video games but he'd never seen a dead body before. Even when his mom died he hadn't been able to see the body. The funeral had been closed-casket so he never really had a chance to say goodbye. Now here was this lady, maybe close to his mom's age and she'd been killed in the middle of the street. He had to see what death looked like.

He knelt at the edge of the blood smear, positioning himself to both see what he needed to see and to spring up and run if he needed to. Being this close, he could smell the putrefaction already working through the body. He reached out but pulled back, his hand clamping over his mouth to quell the bile rising in his throat. *Steady damn it! She can't hurt you!*

He reached out again, the bile receding through an effort of will. He started to push at her waist but it was too far away. He'd lose his balance and might fall into the blood. Even though it was dry, it was still disgusting and somehow wrong. He decided on her shoulder. It would give him leverage and it was close enough to not make him lose his balance.

His hand inched closer. A light breeze ruffled the thin cotton of her shirt. Closer still. He was almost there. He steeled himself for one last push forward, this time to touch the shoulder and push her over. His hand moved.

"Stop!"

Corey jerked back, his hand slapped against chest as he spilled over backward, bumping his head against the asphalt of the road.

"Did you touch her?!" The voice was familiar but Corey tossed his head, trying to shake off the pain. Ashley came in to focus as he opened his eyes. "Did you touch her?"

"No! It's not like that. I wasn't going to do anything to her!" Corey sat up, rubbing the back of his head.

"I didn't ask if you were doing anything. I asked if you touched her!"

Corey looked up. Ashley was always so calm, so composed. Now she looked scared. Frightened out of her skin really. Seeing her so frightened actually frightened Corey more than her yelling had. And she was backing away, her hands behind her, making sure she didn't bump into anything too hard. "No. I didn't touch her. She was like that when I found her."

"You idiot! This isn't about you. This is about *her*. About *all of them*."

"All of who?" Corey pushed himself to his feet, wiping his skinned hands against his jeans. His right elbow had also taken a whack and now it throbbed. Ashley was still backing away.

"Haven't you been watching the news or anything? There is a disease. People are dying all over the place. You sure you didn't touch her? None of the blood, nothing?"

"Positive. I -" His thought changed course. "What do you mean people are dying? Where?"

"Like I said. Everywhere." People in Dallas, in Austin. All over the state. All over the country. In every country!" Her shaking hands formed a tent over her nose and mouth. "People are dying everywhere, Corey. They thought it was bloodborne but there are too many people dying so now they think it must be airborne. But they are dying everywhere."

Ashley held up a finger to forestall him, whatever he was about to do. She retreated a couple of cars back and pulled her own bike out. She had what Corey always thought of as the DadPack strapped to the bike. He hated that DadPack. It was the emergency gear his dad recommended all of his students have on hand at all times. Ashley maintained hers like some kind of religious ritual. Every month she went through it, organized it and refreshed any contents like prepackaged food or sealed water that might have expired.

"Where'd you get the bike?" Corey started to walk toward her and she held up a finger again. He stopped.

"I guess the same place you got yours. No one was using it, and its easier than driving with all these cars everywhere. I borrowed it." Finding what she was looking for, she pulled out a yellow biohazard suit, goggles and a facemask. She bundled the goggles and mask into the suit and tossed it to him. She kept something else tucked behind her back and tucked into her waistband.

"What's this for?" He pushed the suit with the toe of his sneaker.

"Put it on. You may have been exposed. Since I can't be sure and since we need to get back somewhere safe, I need you to put that on."

Corey looked at the suit. He looked up at Ashley, then decisively and purposefully kicked the yellow tangle. The goggles went flying. The mask was caught by a gust of wind, skittering a little way down the road before getting tangled under a car tire. "No way. That's stupid. Let's just get out of here and find something to eat."

He stepped toward her. In a smooth motion she reached behind her back, and pulled out a handgun. Corey jerked back as if she had already fired, his hands flying in the air.

He was struck by the irony that just a few moments ago he had been frightened by her fear. The calm that she was exhibiting now trumped that fright a thousandfold. Only the smallest twitch of the gun barrel indicated that she was anything but absolutely calm and that twitch may have easily been caused by her bicycling the seven miles from her house.

"Ok, Corey." That calm was completely unnerving when someone was pointing a gun at you. He noticed that she wasn't pointing at his head. Headshots were hard. Video games had taught him that. Go for center mass and you were more likely to score a hit. If you score one hit that makes it easier to score another if you need to. *She is friggin' serious about this!*

"Here is the situation," she said, " I came here because I once cared for you and I still respect your dad enough that I didn't want him to have to come home and find a dead son because that son never listened to a damn thing his dad said."

Corey started to say something. His hands began to drift down. Ashley stomped her foot and her eyes lined up behind the sites of the gun. Corey didn't know what caliber it was, but the black void at the end of the barrel changed his plans. He shut his mouth and his hands rose back up to shoulder level.

"Good. I see we have an understanding." Ashley backed up another couple of steps. Reaching behind herself with her free hand she fumbled again in the DadPack. This time he saw what she pulled out. It was another magazine for the gun. She slipped it into her back pocket, easily accessible in case she needed it. "Like I said, I cared for you. I am *so* getting over that. Very quickly. But regardless of how utterly self-centered you are, I still don't want to see you dead.

"With the magazine I just put in my back pocket I now have thirty-four chances to hit you. Well, thirty-five if you count the one already in the chamber. Please don't make me see if I can do it." Corey stepped back, his hands drifting just a bit higher.

"Ok, Corey. Ok. Now there are a couple of ways to play this. Well, there are three ways but the third way ends up with you with a bunch of holes in you and neither of us want that. So let's focus on the other two. Do you feel focused? Do I have your undivided attention?"

Corey nodded emphatically. So far he had just barely been able to keep his bladder in check and the sudden urge was quieting. Somehow he still would have felt better if she seemed to even have the slightest amount of reluctance about shooting him. "You got it Ash. My full attention is totally on you."

"Good. Now your hands are going to get tired so you can put them down, but I want you to stick them in your back pockets."

"Back pockets?"

"Yup. Back pockets. That'll keep your arms from getting tired and so we can avoid potential miscommunication. But it'll keep you just enough off balance that you can't really run at me and if you try to take your hands out I'll have enough time to pull the trigger." She wasn't sure if that was true but she remembered from a Psych class that issuing orders led to compliance and one act of compliance led to another. When Corey slowly lowered his hands and slipped them in his back pockets she knew that they were well on the path of him following her next order. She just couldn't believe he couldn't see how nervous she was. Her palm was slick with sweat and her fingers were numb. She was surprised she'd held on to the gun a couple of times.

"Now: the two scenarios we'll let ourselves talk about." She retreated to her bike and propped her hand up on the handlebars so that her arms would stop feeling like rubber. "First, you walk about halfway down the block behind you then you wait until I get out of here. Then you're on your own. Second, you put on the HAZMAT suit, put on the goggles and mask and bike back to your house. I'll bring you food and if you don't turn up dead in a week or so then we can move to phase two. Since I don't really like being out and exposed like this, you get to choose right here, right now."

Corey thought for a moment and dropped his chin to his chest. Without a word he turned around. For a moment she thought he was going to walk away. When he stopped at the HAZMAT suit she didn't know if she was relieved or saddened. He just stood there, then looked quizzically over his shoulder at her. She realized that he was waiting on her for something and then it hit her.

"You can take your hands out of your pockets if you're going to put on the suit."

A few minutes later they were pedaling back down West Oak. Corey's HAZMAT suit made a strange *vip-vip* sound as it rubbed against itself and the bike. He was huffing and puffing from trying to draw breath through the filter mask. She almost felt sorry enough to let him take off the fogged goggles. But she had finally established dominance and wasn't about to give it up and possibly cost herself her life.

When she left him at the dorm she also left two day's rations from what Corey called the DadPack and she called the Go-Bag. She could replenish it when she got home. For the next week though, she was going to have to scrounge to make sure she didn't put herself at too much of a disadvantage for the days to come.

7

Atlanta Hartsfield-Jackson Airport

Roger woke to a scream.

The sound reverberated through the otherwise quiet and dark concourse, rebounding and magnifying as it rolled across the tiled floors and vinyl-covered walls. People went from deep slumber to sudden wakefulness. The second round of screaming enveloped the crowd. Roger checked his watch. The tritium impregnated hands and dial meant he didn't need light to read it: 11:05.

Down at the other end of the terminal, a group of travelers, mostly German from what Roger could tell, were scurrying away from another couple. Roger assumed it was a husband and wife. She was holding her husband's head in her lap, sobbing. Even from this distance Roger could see dark stains on the husband's cheeks.

They had an outbreak on the concourse.

Jennifer joined him in staring, her hand grasping his forearm. She had been doing that lately. He recognized this as a comfort-seeking device and at first it hadn't bother him, if that was what she needed. Now he looked forward to it a little bit. This was something about Jennifer that didn't remind him of Melissa, but that was OK too.

"What now?"

"Now I think tents are less likely and military is more likely." Roger didn't look at her while he spoke and she didn't look at him. They spoke quietly enough that no one else could hear.

Jennifer couldn't believe how calm she felt. She not only knew that someone she had been locked away with had an incredibly contagious disease, but she just received confirmation that she was probably going to be locked away even longer. Maybe exposed even more. These last few days had taught her more about herself than she thought she needed to learn.

"So now you'd classify our situation as 'unfavorable', huh?"

This time he did look at her. "You know that was a euphemism, right? No. I'd classify our situation as *bad*." Jennifer nodded. Their eyes locked for a moment and then they looked back toward the other end of the concourse.

"So, what now," she asked.

"Following pure logic, we sit here and wait it out. If we go out in public and we've been exposed then we could be responsible for hundreds, even thousands of deaths. Now that we know that we've been subject to exposure, even if not directly exposed, it would be irresponsible for us to leave."

She kept her voice very low but Roger knew her well enough now to know a little about her vocal inflections. Jennifer was scared and more than a little angry. "So you're saying that we just stay here and get stuffed into tents with other potentially sick people?"

"Hell no." Her head jerked, twisting to look at him. "I said pure logic would dictate that. But I'm not Mr. Spock from *Star Trek*. I say we get out of here before we're exposed to even more infected!"

"Finally," she leaned over and kissed him on the cheek through her mask. "After almost a week together we've found the second thing we both agree on. Now, how?"

"This is the trick in all our planning. These Guardsmen are great people and great soldiers. They'll follow orders. But, we have two situations. First, they now know that there is infection in this concourse. Second, they are about to receive orders telling them that they either have to step aside and let the military take action on American soil or they have to take action themselves and not just *secure* other Americans where they are, but actively *restrain* other Americans and impose on them a reduction in freedom.

"The first priority in any living being is self preservation. They're going to be conflicted about coming in here. Secondly, some of them have been talking to us through the gates and they've been feeding us. They feel like our caretakers. They're going to be conflicted about following the orders they are about to receive. By sun up I expect the military to have tents set up outside."

He glanced at his watch, then out the huge panel windows into the blackness of night. "It's 11:13. I'd estimate we have less than five hours to take advantage of our situation and get ourselves out of here."

"Well, let me know about thirty minutes before you're ready and I'll see if I can arrange a distraction."

She knew that squinting look from him. He was asking a question without asking. "Hey, you know this stuff. I know people. You let me know when and we'll have a distraction."

☣ ☣ ☣

Roger had hoped this day would never come but it would have gone against his nature and, indeed against his profession, not to prepare for it. The main issue with attempting to escape an airport is that it is an airport. In modern America that, by its nature, means it is a secure facility. The restrooms do not have convenient windows for escape. The air vents were barely big enough to slip in a boot much less a full sized body. Even if he could fit into the air vent he knew that the conduit would never support the weight of a human body. That only happened in movies. The restrooms were out as a means of escape. That left the concourse.

The obvious point of egress would be the huge panel windows. Over the last several days, Roger had spent hours studying these windows. They were double paned and thicker than the windows at home. Based on a quick sampling, they even appeared to be bulletproof or something close enough as to not matter. They were held in place by a rubberized strip and that was his first option of escape. Closer examination late at night showed that the windows sat well into the frames. The thickness would have retained the windows even if he somehow managed to remove the rubber gasket without being observed and stopped.

He had paced the entirety of the concourse multiple times each day of confinement. The walking itself was good exercise and it gave him an opportunity to thoroughly examine his environment. The doors were locked. As he had witnessed earlier, even the security codes had been blocked. The doors opened into the jet ways, meaning the hinges were on the outside and inaccessible. Almost immediately he ruled out the doors as escape points.

It was only after discounting every other option that Roger returned to the doors as a solution. Rather than viewing them as obstacles, he changed his perspective and began to view them as enablers. The jet way doors had an additional benefit in that they were mostly hidden behind gate agent booths and walls displaying departure boards.

From years of airport travel he knew the doors were thick, fireproof, and probably bulletproof. There was no battering down the door, at least not with anything Roger had in his bag of tricks. Even the small crowbar would do little but bend should he attempt to use it. The only avenue of escape would be through the window. However, like the air vent, they were too small to fit through. Again relying on years of experienced air travel and his experience with American safety laws, Roger was almost certain that these doors would need to be able to be opened from the jet way in order to allow escape if a plane had a major issue calling for evacuation. He peaked through one of the windows.

It was interlaced with a crisscross of wires to help prevent shattering. He knew that breaking the window out would be loud and would likely draw more attention than he preferred, regardless of the distraction

Jennifer had planned. Casting an eye further down the jet way he spied a round mirror mounted high on the wall at the bend in the corridor. Such mirrors were used to help prevent collisions at corners. As he stared he could just make out the emergency bar on the backside of the door. If he could get his hand through, he could press the bar and possibly effect escape. Seeing the emergency bar only furthered his frustration. There was still no way to get an arm through to make use of it.

Thankfully his mind did not stop working as he resumed his strolls around the concourse. Of the more than forty gates in the concourse, thirty -seven were identical. There was no way to penetrate the doors. On the other three, the workmen had gotten sloppy. The frames on each of these three by fourteen inch windows were reversed. On all the other doors the little screws which held the metal windowpanes in place were on the jet way side. On these, the panes were reversed and the little metal covers used to conceal the screws were on the inside. Taking a mental inventory of the tools in his bag of tricks Roger knew he had a screwdriver that would do what he needed.

Of course all that planning had been at a time when he was working the idea through purely for theoretical purposes. Now that it appeared he was going to need to implement it, he had his doubts. Those doubts, however, did not reduce his conviction that he needed to get clear of the building. If he ended up in a tent with another person who was infected by the Ankara virus he knew he'd probably never get out of that tent alive. According to protocol, he would likely end his days in that tent. All that would remain to be buried would be a pile of ashes intermixed with the others in the same tent, all presented to Corey – if he still lived – in a generic box delivered by nondescript people in dark suits and stern faces.

He found Jennifer and told her he was ready when she could create the distraction.

☣ ☣ ☣

As Jennifer told Roger, he may know everything about preparing and surviving, but he certainly wasn't good with people. Other than Jennifer, he hadn't even spoken with more than five people since being stuck here. On the other hand, Jennifer had spoken with hundreds and probably knew the names of over one hundred. She thrived in social situations. That was another reason her ex's deception had hurt her so much. She had been certain she would have known if he was lying. When she thought back about it though, he never lied. He just never told the truth. He told her he worked for an equity exchange group and that he helped them settle difficult transactions. Finance was always boring to her so she never looked beyond that.

When Roger told her it was time, she regretted what she was about to do, but not as much as she knew she would regret not doing it. It was going to be difficult once she got away from the airport. She didn't even know what she was going to do, but she couldn't stay and wait to die with stomach cramps, fever, seizures and blood leaking from every opening. Just thinking about it hardened her resolve.

She walked to the gate where the soldiers were stationed and looked across the space between the two fences. "Hey, excuse me," she called to the soldier on the other side. With their gas masks on she couldn't tell if the soldier was looking at her or not. The covered head nodded and the left hand came off the gun long enough to signal her to continue.

"Um, do you guys have a nurse?"

The solder took an unconscious step backward. "Why ma'am? What's wrong."

"Oh nothing, really. Just I've now run out of my feminine products and I was wondering if a nurse could bring some for me."

"Oh, um." He looked around and waved another soldier closer in. "This lady needs some feminine products she says."

"Yes. I do. But, I really need the nurse as well." Jennifer looked around. Several people were watching but she was trying to keep her voice pitched low enough to not be overheard. "See, the lack of feminine products has led to a feminine problem and I think…well, I think that I would prefer not to go in to detail with someone who isn't a medical professional."

The soldier held up a restraining hand. She was sure it was an unconscious gesture but he didn't want to hear any more himself. She could imagine him behind that mask, a late-teen or early twenties young man who hadn't had many experiences of women 'sharing' their personal, female, medical issues. She almost felt sorry for him.

"Yes ma'am. We'll see what we can do."

"Thank you," Jennifer said a little too loudly, smiled broadly and she turned away from the cage. She cast a self-conscious glance around at those watching her and quickly set her face to a more serious expression. She crossed the room and leaned against the wall next to a small group she knew from her socializing.

"What was that about?" Steve was one of the guys she remembered from the first day – one of the ones trying to get signal on his tablet.

"I'm not supposed to say." She looked over her shoulder, then looked back conspiratorially. Clark, Steve's friend from that first day, was in this group. So was a young lady who appeared to have gotten close to Clark but who spent most of her time with another group. "But if you guys promise not to tell, I want to make sure you know what to do."

"I just asked the people at the gate how long they were going to hold us, what with the guy dying and all." She cast a furtive glance over her shoulder again, quickly turning back to the group. "He said not to worry. About half of us were getting out. See they've come up with a vaccine."

Jennifer leaned in closer, making sure to look only at Steve and Clark, speaking quietly but loud enough for all seven in this group to hear. "The problem is that there are over a thousand of us stuck in this concourse and they only have about 700 vaccines so some people are going to have to wait until next week when the next shipment gets in." She pitched her voice low again, "So there is going to be a nurse or doctor show up. When they do, be sure to be close to the gate to make sure you're at the front of the line."

She placed a conspiratorial finger to her lips and slowly turned away. Before she was even ten feet away she heard the scuffling of shoes as the members of the group slipped up to notify their friends and family.

Jennifer joined Roger in one of the sling chairs further down the concourse. "Well," he asked.

"Just wait a few. I kind of hated to do it, but there is going to be a distraction. It'll probably be ten to fifteen minutes but it is going to be big."

Roger nodded his head. "Big is good."

☣ ☣ ☣

When the distraction came, it was not just big. It was huge. Jennifer never saw whether the person who came to the gate was a doctor or a nurse, or even a medical officer at all. The next time a soldier approached the gate the crowd surged. The heavy gage wire buckled under the onslaught as people pushed, shoved and stepped over one another to be the first to the gate. Even those who did not know what was going on rushed the gate, the mob mentality taking over.

Roger sprang into action. Jennifer followed him behind the wall to one of the jet way doors. He pulled a small multi-tool out of his pocket. Roger brandished it triumphantly. "No knife, no awl, no file. TSA has cleared it more times that I can count."

"Brag later. Work now." Jennifer waved at the door, not understanding what he hoped to accomplish with such a small tool.

Roger flipped out the flat blade screwdriver and quickly flipped the screw covers off the window frame. Another couple of twists of the tool and the Phillips tip was out. He skillfully applied it to the screws. As the crowd reached a fevered peak of yelling, Roger broke out in a sweat as he went to work.

Six of the eight screws pulled out cleanly. Two were stripped in place. No amount of pressure or leverage was going to work them out. Roger reverted to the flat blade and worked it under the frame edge. Slowly the edge pried away from the door until the gap was big enough to get a finger under. First one finger, then a second. Then a third. Roger pulled and bent the frame back.

Jennifer looked over her shoulder and around the divider wall again. It appeared the full concourse had congregated at the gate and a group of young men, apparently led by Steve and Clark, were pushing and pulling, trying to work the gate loose. A padded thud drew her attention back to the door.

Roger was shaking blood off the finger tips of one hand while reaching through the window with the other. The wire reinforced window was laying at his feet. When the door popped open it was all she could do to restrain a cheer.

Roger grabbed her wrist and together they sprinted down the jet way, their long strides echoing loudly. Roger turned the corner first and pulled up short.

They knew the planes had been pushed away from the gates but Roger had underestimated just how far the jet way was from the ground. He looked around for some way to lower themselves to the ground while avoiding injury. Nothing was at hand. He doubled back to what he thought of as the baggage door – where carry-on luggage that didn't fit was sent down to the tarmac. This time the door was no trouble. The lock was on the inside.

Hand-in-hand they burst through the door and down the metal grate steps. The planes had been pushed back but the vehicles needed for operations were still parked in their assigned locations, marked out by white lines on the ground. Concession trucks, luggage trolleys and septic work trucks had been left as if ready to go back to work. Even the pushback tractors used to move planes around were still connected to the front landing gear of the closest plane.

Roger sprinted to the closest vehicle, a luggage trolley. The controls appeared simple enough but there was no key and the exterior lights were not turned on, leaving the control panel in the dark. Without light and at almost 2:00AM, he was unable to identify anything that would start the tractor-looking contraption. Instead he cast a glance around and found something more familiar.

Together they ran under the jet ways for the next two gates. In the residual light from the concourse above, they had just caught the gleam of a large decal on the front of a golf cart. Reflective letters surrounding a badge emblem said "Security". At least he knew how to drive a golf cart.

Jennifer took the right side, Roger the left. The steering bar and accelerator were positioned in the middle. When Roger stomped the pedal nothing happened. Jennifer reached down and flipped the selector switch on the panel under the seat from "Off" to "Forward". The electric powered cart rolled forward and gained speed.

Roger had chosen the door they exited for two reasons. First, of the three potential doors, only two were on the opposite side of the concourse from where the soldiers were stationed. He wanted the building between him and any observing eyes. Second, the airport was hemmed in on three sides by interstates. Of the two remaining gates, he chose the one furthest toward the end so he would be as close to the interstate as possible. In his estimation, once he was to the freeway, he was in the clear.

It was only once he had moved away from the terminals and onto the actual runways itself that he realized there may be a flaw in his logic.

No traffic was moving on the freeway. As Roger attempted to navigate the taxiways and runways, he looked out across the city, then back over his shoulder, in an attempt to see a broader view. He was pressing on to the northeast where Interstate 85 came closest to the airport property. Rather than following the curve of the runway, Roger guided the golf cart off the tarmac and onto a patch of grass toward a service road that appeared to converge closer to the fence.

Just as the wheels hit the grass, the front plastic fender of the cart ripped off. That piece fell forward and slipped under the cart's wheels, causing it to lose traction and lurch forward. An instant later the fiberglass top of the cart shattered. Roger glanced up and saw a half-inch hole with a spider web of cracks forming around it.

"Get down!" He matched actions to words and ducked down into the floorboard of the cart, his knee now firmly pressing the accelerator to the floor.

Jennifer joined him yelling her question, "What? What's happening?"

"Someone is shooting at us!" Roger began steering erratically, shifting from side to side across the field while still heading for the service road he could just make out in the moonlight. Roger's seatback exploded in a shower of plastic and foam, the bullet whizzing by mere inches from his scalp. He heard a yelp and wasn't sure whether it was Jennifer or himself.

"But we're Americans! They can't do this!" Jennifer turned so she could look back over the seats but ducked back down as she almost lost her balance to Rogers's maniacal zigzags.

"Not right now." The ground dropped off toward the fence and Roger took the opportunity to make his escape, hoping the slope would somewhat conceal the golf cart. "Right now we're potential viral time bombs and they're trying to protect the uninfected. They'll kill us and that will probably result in some guilt in the shooter but - "

Roger was cut off as a round impacted on the back of the vehicle. The cart immediately began to slow. The batteries must have been penetrated.

He looked back and saw the cart was below the edge of the hill but in the distance he thought he could hear a high powered engine revving. He turned the cart directly at the fence, aiming just to the left of the closest pole.

"But, he'll get over that guilt because he followed orders and saved the country from a couple of runaway lunatics. Hold on!"

At the last instant Roger realized the bottom foot of the fence was reinforced with concrete. The crash flipped the cart into the fence. With their added weight and what momentum was left from the downhill, semi-powered roll, the aluminum support ties were ripped away from the fence's vertical pole. Roger and Jennifer were thrown over the remainder of the fender by the impact, briefly wedged between the wreckage of the cart and the security grade fencing. Neither took time to check their injuries, instead they threw themselves off the cart and squeezed through the gap under the fence created by the impact.

Roger slung his bag over one shoulder, grabbed Jennifer's hand to help her through the hole, and stumbled onto the access ramp for Interstate 85. The northbound lane was congested with cars. The two fugitives ducked around an older model Toyota Celica just as the back window exploded, showering them in glass. Staying even lower, they ducked around several other cars, always keeping their heads below window level.

They cleared the wide swath of grass between the access lane and the freeway itself and stayed in their bent crouch as they continued crossing through stopped traffic. When they came to the median wall Roger stopped.

"All right, we have to put this concrete wall between us and the bullets. It's going to be tricky though." He looked up and down the freeway, taking a moment to catch his breath.

"It looks pretty empty to the north. If we get out there we'll probably be out of range but we'll be exposed for any pursuit. Over there," he waved vaguely toward the south, "it looks like business and residential and we can hide a bit better."

The vehicle with the revving engine slid to a stop next to the fence and Roger could hear yelling but couldn't quite make out what was being said.

"If we go over together we present a bigger target. If we go over one at a time they'll know where to shoot for the second person. We have to spread out, at least a few car lengths and get to the other side of the divider. Stay low and run down to the overpass."

Jennifer just nodded. She wasn't a submissive person but she couldn't find a flaw in his plan so she accepted it. "I'll get on the other side of that pickup. You get down," she pointed a few cars down to the north, "behind that Mercedes. When we're set, count to three and I'll go for it."

Roger nodded and duck-ran toward the Mercedes. When he was in place he looked back, seeing Jennifer beside her truck. He nodded again, this time knowing that she probably couldn't see it in the dark. He yelled. "One!"

She yelled back. "Two!"

They yelled, "Three," together and sprinted for the wall.

Both executed a quick grab and roll to the other side. Roger was half surprised not to hear a bullet impact aimed at either of them. Jennifer didn't wait to make sure he made it over the wall. She began her bent run toward the overpass. Roger followed quickly behind. There weren't any cars in the southbound lanes so they stayed hunched close to the wall. They made good time over the 300 yards to the overpass.

Once the bridge blocked the view of the airport Roger knew it also obstructed the sniper's view of their position. Using the concrete support pilings as a shield from the soldiers by the fence, he stood up and stretched out his back. From what he could tell, the soldiers had not followed under the fence.

"Just guessing," Roger waved back toward the soldiers, "the airport is under lockdown but I think the soldiers are confused whether that applies to the rest of the city. We need to get out of here before they figure it out."

Jennifer reached up and turned Roger's face into the dim cast of moonlight filtering under the bridge. "I agree, but I think we can scratch the idea of blending in."

Roger furrowed his brows and she ran a finger down the side of his face. It came away with a dark stain. Then she did a two-hand model sweep down herself. The dark stain must have been blood and her clothes had been torn to shreds in their flight. Roger looked at himself and saw that he wasn't much better. Now that he took a moment to think about it, he felt the burn of sweat in a scratch that must go from his forehead to his jaw. Several burning sensations were scattered across his back. Those must have been from the wreck or crawling under the fence. Taken together, Roger thought they must look like they had just fled a warzone. When he considered the heavily armed troops firing at them and pursuit from some military vehicle, perhaps that wasn't too far from the truth.

"Well," he said, "there's nothing to it but to do it." Jennifer nodded and followed him up the concrete embankment under Airport Boulevard, and across the field. They crossed Lee St. Con, then Main Street and into one of the off-site parking lots for the airport. Thankfully Atlanta was an old city with plenty of large trees. It was relatively easy to stay under the tree canopy as they made their way westward. On a couple of occasions they heard a helicopter. Each time they took a risk and stepped up on porches or under carports to provide an extra layer of protection. By the time the sun cleared the horizon, they had made it to a shopping center where Loop 285 where Hwy 6 intersects.

It was the sights at this intersection that gave Roger the first true sign on just how bad things had gotten and just how much worse they may become.

8

Corey's Apartment – Denton, TX

Corey just stared at the television screen. He had his game controller in one hand and the television remote in the other. The screen had gone off, with every other electrical device in the apartment, plunging him into darkness. That was three hours ago but he still tried all the buttons every couple of minutes just to make sure. Earlier he had looked out the window and it looked like all the lights were off in town. At least they were everywhere he could see. He tried his front door before remembering that Ashley had installed a latch and pad lock on the outside. The door didn't even open far enough to get a breeze. Of course he could still get out through his window if he really wanted to but, he'd have to drop two floors down to the ground. There hadn't been any reason to do that as long as the TV and Xbox were working. He tossed the controllers on the couch, pushing himself to a standing position.

Thankfully, he thought, *I still have Plan B!* He crossed the room, kicking a table leg with a wayward toe and stumbled to his bedside table. He tried the lamp so he could get a better look at the toe and remembered the electricity had gone out. Pulling back the curtain let in enough moonlight so he could see the toe wasn't bleeding, but it didn't help the pain any. He wondered briefly if he still had any of the hydrocodone from his root canal a few months back but then remembered he'd traded the last of them for the latest *Grand Theft Auto*.

Oh well, he thought as he reached for his iPhone, *I'll just have to tough it out*. He pressed the Home button on the phone. Nothing happened. He pressed it again. Pressed the power button. Pressed the Home button. *Damn it!*

Corey grabbed the power plug and jammed it into the phone's charging port, staring at the screen. Again nothing happened.

Damn it! He threw the phone across the room, cracking the screen and making a divot in the wall. *Fucking power outage! Why do these things always happen to me?*

He thrust himself from the bed, onto the hurt toe, cried in pain and flung himself back in bed. His anger still in full bloom, Corey grabbed his lamp and flung it across the room. At least it would have flown across the room had it not been plugged in with the cord wedged behind his table. As it was, the lamp reached the end of the cord and recoiled. The bulb shattered on the table and glass fragments exploded across the room, showering his bed and the carpeted floor around the bed with tiny shards.

Not fair! I can't catch a break! He raked at the slivers of glass knocking some to the floor and embedding others in his hand. Throwing his hands in the air he finally let the anger subside.

☣ ☣ ☣

An hour and a half later, he was still sitting in sulking silence when he heard the lock being removed from his door and saw it crack open. Ashley, dressed in a smaller version of the HAZMAT suit she had made him wear earlier, shined a flashlight into the room. When it crossed over him, she paused. Her voice was muffled as she spoke.

"What happened?" Corey noticed that she didn't sound all that concerned. She just sounded like she knew she was supposed to ask.

Screw that, he thought. *If she really wants to know she'll have to ask it like she means it!*

As if reading his mind, Ashley just said, "Fine." The bulky suit made it difficult, but she turned around and lifted a big cardboard box. She set it just inside his door and pushed it in with her booted foot. Next she slid in two two-gallon jugs of water.

"I'll be back in a couple of days. If you are still here I'll give you more water. There are twenty-one MREs in that box and a first aid kit. Looks like you'll need that. The food should last you a week easy. Since you aren't really doing anything it should last even longer but I'm not expecting you to ration yourself so I'm doing it for you. I won't be bringing more food when I come back so don't eat it all. If you're still alive in a week then we'll get out of here."

She started closing the door.

Corey yelled at the shrinking sliver of light, "What the fuck makes you think I want to go anywhere with you, bitch!"

The door stopped. He saw the inflated head of the HAZMAT suit obstruct some of the moonlight as it moved to where she could see him again. "Corey. You have food, water, shelter and medical supplies. You can survive in your room for at least a couple of days until I get back. I will - "

"Don't bother! I don't even care if you come back."

Corey always hated that Ashley could stay calm no matter what he said and she did it again this time. "OK Corey. If that's how you feel. Maybe I won't."

The door closed and Corey threw himself off his bed to burst through the door. Immediately he felt the glass shards slash into his foot. He screamed in pain and fell back on the bed where glass embedded itself in his back. By the time his screaming was over Ashley had the lock back in place and Corey was alone again. In the dark.

☣ ☣ ☣

Ashley unzipped the HAZMAT suit, letting fresh air touch her skin again. She stripped out of it, folding it carefully and placing it in the bag on the back of her bike. It was safest to move about with the suit on but even on an early October evening in Texas it was too hot to do much without air flow around you. She just made sure to stay away from other people she saw. That wasn't much of a problem since she didn't see many people and they were interested in keeping their distance as well.

She leaned against the wall and ran her fingers through her auburn hair. The sweat had stuck it to her forehead and neck. The evening breeze felt cool, if only in contrast to being inside the suit. Though the breeze felt good, the underlying smell of rot and decay that it brought made her desperately want a shower. *Only a few days in and it already smells like this? It getting worse is just one more thing to add to the list of things I'm not looking forward to.*

Corey was infuriating. Their relationship had always been a bit strange. She started dating Corey because he was Roger's son. It had taken her a while to come to terms with that. Corey was basically a romantic surrogate of sorts. It wasn't that Ashley was sexually attracted to Roger. It wasn't even that she used Corey to try and get as close as she could. It was just that Roger was smart, and though he had his quirks, he was funny in the right situation. She enjoyed being around him, and he was somewhat of a surrogate father figure.

Thinking of her father made her wipe a tear from her eye and clear her throat. She had talked to her mother yesterday, and her father was getting a cough. Mom thought there might be some blood in what he spit up, but he was hiding it. When Ashley called this morning no one answered and with the electricity failing, she wasn't sure when she would hear from them again.

The thing with Corey was a mixture of idol worship for Roger and assigning unearned positive characteristics to his son. Her Pysch professor would have called that an erroneous attribution. Ashley called it a pain in the ass.

Thinking positively of Roger had led her to believe that Corey had that same good heart, innate intelligence and underlying humor. His haughty arrogance, she had thought, was just a cover. Over the five months of their relationship she discovered she was wrong. There wasn't an inner depth. He was just a self-indulgent spoiled brat of a man-child. He had the emotional maturity of a kindergartener and spent his time blaming others for his own character flaws and misdeeds. As far as Ashley could tell the only thing Corey shared with either of his parents is half a set of genes.

But she was stuck with him. It wasn't that she wanted to resume a relationship. That thought made her skin crawl more than the breeze across her sweat-slicked neck and its sickly sweet scent. But since she had taken some responsibility for him during their relationship she felt somewhat responsible to ensure he was taken care of until he could be returned to Roger. Reverting back to her Psych education, it was almost like she had undertaken the role of a protective – yet pissed – older sibling. Once Corey was safe and returned to Roger, her responsibility to him was done. If that meant he had to sit in his room and pout until she was sure he was not infected, she had no problem with that.

Ashley cast her gaze around, ensuring no one had gotten close. In fact no one was even within sight. She threw her leg over the bike and hooked her foot into the pedal cleat, pushing off.

Riding through a town that had been vibrant and full of energy from thousands of college-aged students just a week ago was somewhat eerie with the streetlights dark, cars clogging the roads with the only signs of human life being a week old, with trash blowing across the pavement. Even those signs were better than the occasional lumps scattered around town which Ashley desperately tried not to recognize. The only electric light she could see in the entire city came from the hospital.

Up to now she had diligently stayed away from the hospital. She figured it would be overwhelmed with people infected by the Ankara virus. Going to the hospital would only expose her to a higher potential of contamination. Now that it was a shining beacon in an otherwise dark city, she felt drawn to it. She cruised up West Oak and Thomas, squeezing the hand brake to stop a block from the building itself.

She carefully unpacked her HAZMAT suit, zipping herself back into its stiff, crinkly confines. Once everything was back in place with gloves and booties on and arms and legs sealed with duct tape, she climbed back on the bike and pushed off once more.

She cruised past the tan brick hulking structure of Vintage Retirement Community, behind Yorkshire Place apartments and across the parking lot in front of a physicians' office complex. The bicycle bearings clicked as Ashley glided toward the hospital door. Further to her left, the parking lot was beyond full. Cars and trucks were parked in every available spot with more along the grassy field beside the fountain pond decorating the entrance driveway. Cars continued up and down the service road to the freeway and even more were parked on the hard shoulder of the freeway a couple hundred yards away. Most of the cars were parked in orderly fashion, but some were butted right up against others and more than a few had collided, especially along the field.

With all the vehicles, the most disturbing part of the scene was the movement and sound. There wasn't any. No one was visible in the parking lot. With the crowd of cars Ashley expected to hear a din of voices as people yelled over one another to get help for themselves or a loved one. Even the crickets were silent. Ashley shivered within her PVC suit. The only sound was her breathing, the crunch of the suit and the bearings of the wheels as she skimmed along the sidewalk.

She knew the Emergency Room entrance was behind the hospital. She'd had a tour of the hospital and its Emergency Operations Plan in one of her classes. She cruised by the front door first, hopefully taking in the situation in small enough bits that her mind would accept it without becoming overwhelmed.

She was not prepared for what she saw inside the front door. Even here, half the building away from the ER, there were sheet-covered bodies lying on the floor. Red blotches turning brown, traced distorted Rorschach images. She didn't want to let her mind engage and try to figure out those abstract blotches. The bicycle had almost stopped and she had to push quickly on the pedal to regain her balance, thankful to have something to draw her attention away.

Someone had taken long strips of tape printed with the word "QUARANTINE, DO NOT CROSS" in a continuous scroll and taped it across the door. Of course, she had no idea who had done it but no one had violated the quarantine since it was put in place.

Ashley paused on the sidewalk between the parking lot and the front door. She waited, forcing herself to avoid looking at the covered bodies. A helpful clock inside and opposite the door clicked off the seconds and then the minutes. She waited for seventeen minutes without seeing movement and pushed off again, continuing the circuit of the hospital. The bike carried her around the side of the building. Off to her left was the crammed ER parking lot, a little further out sat the helipad, the helicopter missing, and to the right was the ER entrance.

Again, quarantine tape stretched across the door. *Did the person tape it up and then just leave? Did they carry the virus out with them?*

Beyond the tape she could see into the ER waiting room and down the hall. More bodies, some stacked atop one another, cluttered the room. Crimson and brown blotches leaked through white sheets. Propped against one wall sat a woman in blue scrubs, her N95 facemask still in place, completely blood soaked. In her hand she still held a syringe, obviously succumbing even as she attempted to provide potential life-saving duties.

Ashley found warm trails sliding down her cheeks, dripping down into the V of her shirt. Even if she could reach her face through the mask she wasn't sure she would even try to stop the tears. This was a tragedy of unimaginable scope. These people deserved to have someone mourn for them.

She turned away from the scene. It was obvious that no one was still alive in the Emergency Room, but she and Corey had a trek ahead of them and if she could get in there, she might be able to find medical supplies that would be helpful. Maybe even medications. Grabbing a small pry bar from the Go Bag strapped above the rear fender of her bike, she turned toward the ER door. As a final precaution, she checked the 9mm tucked in her waistband. She made a mental note that she needed to find a way to secure the weapon outside the HAZMAT suit in the near future. For now though, she'd make do. In all honesty she hoped she never had to use the thing.

Ten minutes and a fog-clouded face mask later Ashley slumped down, back pressed against the sliding glass doors that would not slide. The pry bar was too small for popping the doors open and did not have enough weight to break through the double paned, reinforced glass. She had only hit it once but it had made so much noise and had so little result that she hadn't tried again. The noise factor also ruled out using the 9mm to shoot the door.

As her breathing slowed and softened, the facemask slowly cleared and with it her mind. During the tour she remembered that some of the staff went out a back door around the corner from the cafeteria where there was a smoking area.

Weird that healthcare professionals seem inordinately susceptible to the lures of smoking. She slid the pry bar back into her pack, slung her leg over the bike and pushed off down the sidewalk again. When she pulled up next to the door, her brows knitted over questioning eyes.

A man, obviously several days dead now, lay half in and half out of the door. Rather than the now signature marks of the Ankara virus infection, this guy had three holes in his chest. The shooter had a nice grouping. You might not be able to cover the holes with a silver dollar but you could cover them with a dollar bill.

What the hell? Two weeks ago you'd be all freaked out just to see a dead person. Now you make mental commentary on shot groupings? She shook her head and pulled her spare flashlight from her pack. Again she noted that she needed access to things while in the HAZMAT suit. Maybe Batman's utility belt wasn't such a bad idea.

As she approached, Ashley painted the dead man with the flashlight. His right hand was held at an odd angle like it was holding something. It was long enough that rigor had already faded but nothing had come along to disturb the body. Beside the body was a ring of blood. Obviously this guy had bled-out here but it looked like something was sitting beside him while it happened. She assumed it was a bag that someone else had found.

Looking inside the doorway she found more evidence that someone else had come along. Another man lay sprawled on the floor about twenty feet inside. The flashlight showed his dark blue uniform top crumpled next to him, the shoulder patch verifying he was a member of Denton's finest. It appeared that the looter who had come along had even stolen the badge from the uniform along with the weapon, radio and big belt with all the gear. *Do they still call that a Sam Brown belt or is it just a duty belt now*, she asked herself absently.

It looked like the officer had taken a grazing shot to the neck. Despite being in a hospital, he had died from blood loss. Looking up the hallway Ashley saw several holes in the wall. The crook didn't have near the shot placement as the officer, but it only took one shot to get lucky.

Ashley moved gingerly against the door. She could see a bar of light leaking in under the door from the main hall. Waiting several minutes – having a watch outside the HAZMAT suit would be invaluable too – with her ear pressed against the suit and the suit pressed against the door, she heard nothing but the beating of her heart and her own slow, steady respiration. Her hand gently pressed down on the door handle. With the slightest shoulder pressure she leaned against the door. It wouldn't budge.

She lifted the handle and pushed again. Nothing. She lowered the handle again. Pushed. Nothing. The hospital was so close! If she could just get in she –

Ashley paused, stepped back and tried the handle again, this time pulling gently on the door. It was a big, heavy, fire resistant door but as she pulled it shifted toward her. *I'm coming from the outside. Fire code. Doors are supposed to get out of your way. Keep it together there missy!*

The door opened smoothly but before there was even enough room to fit the bubble head of the suit into the hallway Ashley was practically hyperventilating. Obviously someone had already been here to look for stuff. The dead officer and dead, presumably, crook were proof enough of that. But someone had also looted their bodies. Hopefully that was days ago and she wouldn't be meeting anyone in the halls. Equally, she hoped there was still something worth collecting.

9

Outside Atlanta

Roger and Jennifer trudged up the embankment from where they had crossed Loop 285. The stop light at 285 and 6 was out. A major pileup of cars streamed in all directions from the intersection, clogging this major artery as far as the eye could see. The tracks and scattered mud around the intersection showed where several vehicles had bypassed the pile ups.

Such scenes had become standard in their short trip across the city. What made Roger stop in his tracks was the scene behind the pileup. Just a week ago this would have been a busy retail center. The shopping area north of Highway 6 looked to be about three-quarters of a mile long and about a quarter mile wide, populated with stores large and small. Next to the road were major franchise restaurants as was usual all across the country. Except in this instance, the restaurants were *gone*.

Three of the burned out husks sat in one cluster on one side of the entrance to the shopping center. Four sat on the other side. Each had a nice stand of trees surrounding it, giving a bit of a visual block to the competition back in the good old days of last week. While the trees appeared singed from the heat of the fires, none of them were destroyed and none showed enough damage to indicate that the fire raged through the trees. Each fire had been individually set. Another smaller cluster of restaurants sat untouched by fire, but each had obviously been looted. The large windows had been broken and the Popeye's chicken place still had a 4x4 stuck through the front glass.

Back to the north, Roger cast a glance over the parking lot, looking for movement. Other than blowing plastic bags and the scattered decorative tree, the parking lot was lifeless. Cars were jumbled throughout the lot and in the aisles but there was no sign of their owners. Stores lined the parking lot with no signs of shoppers.

He had hoped that when they found a store they'd be able to pick up some items they'd need. Now he was just happy that no one was around.

Well, not exactly no one, Roger thought. He cast a wary eye to the buzzards that were just beginning to circle above. Though he could not see what they saw at this point, he was afraid he knew why they were gathering. His nose told him part of the story and even that was more than he really cared to know. One of the birds swooped down below car level and didn't immediately take flight again. The pressure of Jennifer's hand on his shoulder told him she understood what was happening as well.

"I don't want to go in there," she said.

"It isn't a matter of want, is it?" Roger looked at her but her eyes were still fixed on where the buzzard disappeared. "We have to go in. We need supplies. At the very least, we need to get you in a better pair of shoes."

Jennifer couldn't argue with that. The high heels had been impractical for someone on the run. At first she had simply carried them. When she realized they were just in the way she had thrown them in a yard. Now her feet were raw from running barefoot on concrete and asphalt. If she was going to be of any value she was going to have to get some shoes. The big marquee sign promised all kinds of potential, including a Shoe Carnival and Payless Shoes. She nodded silently and followed as he trudged up the last few steps.

They crossed the barren wastes created by the burned-out restaurants and ducked down behind some trees. Again Roger stopped to scan for movement but it was Jennifer who saw three buzzards take flight near the corner of a island of shops. Roger was looking right and the birds took flight on the left. She tapped his shoulder and pointed where the buzzards had been.

Together they stared at the corner. Jennifer began to doubt that the birds taking flight had meant anything when she caught a glimpse of movement from a windshield. Her hand tightened again on Roger's shoulder and his head jerked back instinctively to where she had pointed.

"I saw it this time," she whispered. "Not sure what it is, but I saw movement reflected on a car."

He nodded. "OK," he said, his voice low, "I'll keep an eye out but don't whisper. Just talk low. Whispers carry much further."

Jennifer started to respond when Roger put his finger to his lips. "But silence is even better."

Jennifer raised her eyebrows but nodded in agreement. Roger returned his attention to the parking lot, looking for movement. Just as he was beginning to think that Jennifer had been imaging things he caught movement as well. The barrel of a rifle slid from behind a car halfway across the parking lot. If he hadn't been looking specifically in that direction he would have missed it. Roger looked at her and used his first two fingers to point at his own eyes and then point at the rifle. It was pointing across the parking lot so he wasn't yet too concerned.

Jennifer squinted, shaking her head slightly. The barrel shifted a bit and caught her attention. She nodded her acquisition of the target. Roger kept scanning the area, looking for anything else out of the ordinary, returning his attention to the barrel on each scan.

Suddenly a flock of pigeons erupted over the parking lot. A boy, no older than his early teens, stood casually holding the weapon as he jogged across the parking lot. He bent over, retrieved a pigeon from the ground and hefted it in triumph. Judging by the size of the rifle and the lack of noise when it was fired Roger guessed it was a BB gun or pellet rifle.

Jennifer relaxed a bit, and released a breath neither of them knew she had been holding. She turned to look at Roger and started to say something when Roger's eyes bulged. She turned to look back at the parking lot, and her eyes popped as well.

The teen, dressed in a blue T-shirt jogged toward the island of shops. Toward the rest of the group. Two other young men stood at the corner of the shop, both with long guns. The one on the right had what looked to be a deer rifle with a scope and the other had a pump shotgun. They were joined by an older man, perhaps their father, who had an AR-style rifle on a sling at his chest.

The older man patted the back of the boy and tucked the bird into a pouch on the back of his own hunting vest. The group exchanged a short conversation and the hunting rifle man lifted it to his shoulder and used the scope to scan the area. Roger adverted his eyes and again spoke quietly to Jennifer, "Don't look at the scope. Look off to his side. Don't try to hide. He'll more likely see movement than see us behind this tree."

Jennifer gave a quick nod and Roger made a *tsk* noise, sucking his teeth. "Don't nod. Quick movements like that are easy to see, even at a distance."

"Gothcha." Jennifer held her head still and focused just off the man's left shoulder, trying not to stare. After a few moments the scope swept past their tree. She wasn't sure but the scope seemed to slow and pause as it passed by her position. Under its gaze, Jenny felt exposed, like a convict jumping the wall while in the glare of the spotlight.

The moment passed and after completing the scan, the young man dropped the rifle to a carry position. The group shared another brief conversation then turned and walked back out of sight.

Roger placed his hand on her shoulder. "I think they are gone but we need to wait a few to make sure. Watch the south side of that set of shops to make sure they don't sneak through between there and the Wendy's. Keep your eyes in the area but don't focus on any one thing. Keep your eyes moving. It will help spot more movement and keep you from getting tunnel vision."

She nodded and forestalled his reprimand. "Gotcha. And I'll stop nodding."

After about thirty minutes of no further movement Roger again patted her shoulder. "I think we're good." He stood and helped her to her feet. They both brushed loose grass and leaves from their clothes. Roger led her on a circuitous route between cars and toward the Payless Shoes.

The panel windows had been destroyed and the interior was in shambles. Roger waved her in, then knelt behind a table. Again he used the two-finger point at his eyes before pointing the fingers toward the parking lot. He then pointed at her with one-finger, did the two-finger thing at his eyes and then used the same two-finger point to scan across the store. Though Jennifer had never been given directions this way, it was fairly intuitive. "I'll watch the parking lot. You look around in back."

She started to nod, stopped herself and then just turned to go about her task. With the sun well up, there was plenty of light to explore the store. Unfortunately there wasn't much left to explore. It seems shoes were top-of-the-list items for the looting crews. Luckily she had fairly small feet so they weren't picked over as much, but then the selection probably hadn't been that great before the looters arrived. After a few minutes digging through the pile she finally emerged with a pair of cheap plastic sandals. Roger looked at the footwear and shrugged.

"We'll try another store but those sandals are at least one notch better than nothing."

"Two notches better than high heels." Jennifer smiled and did her best 'model pose' for the shoes.

"Confirmed." Roger returned his attention to the parking lot. "Looks like the Target over there got it too, but maybe there are still some shoes left. Plus we can look for other things."

They started to step forward and Jenny placed a hand on Roger's shoulder. "When you're using your hand signals, how do you say 'yes' or 'ok'?"

"Nod."

"But I didn't think I was supposed to nod!"

"Not when someone is looking." Roger's brows knitted as he examined her face, looking for signs of whether she was just attempting to be difficult. *It really isn't that hard to understand.*

They stepped out of the store and ducked between the cars. Weaving back and forth, they made it halfway across the lot. Roger held a hand up with the fingers together and thumb along side. If he had been pushing the hand forward it would have looked like a police officer directing traffic holding up a 'stop' hand. He matched his action to the hand signal and stopped behind a car. He scanned the area and when he was sure they were not under observation he looked at Jennifer. "That hand signal means to stop as soon as you can. If I hold up a fist, that means to stop immediately. Don't even finish your step. Pretend you're about to step on a tripwire. The best bet is to freeze. Then follow my lead. If I crouch down, you crouch down. If I settle into a position you can settle into a position."

"OK." Jenny smiled and asked jokingly, "but what if there really *is* a tripwire?"

"I'll point at it and you'll step over it." Roger scanned the parking lot again then used a flat hand over-arm wave – a signal most people would recognize as *let's get going*. They maneuvered through the remaining maze of vehicles toward the Target. Roger held up the flat-hand stop signal again and they both settled behind a car.

"All right. This is what the military would call a kill zone. We're going to be in the open and exposed long enough for someone to acquire a target and pull the trigger. Nothing we can do about that. What we can do is make their job harder."

He pointed at the store. "We're going over there. If we were a military unit and had weapons where we could cover one another, we'd move one at a time with you covering me. Then I would cover you. But we're just two unarmed people. The best defensive advantage we have is speed and mobility. So we go at the same time to confuse a potential shooter and we go in different doors. If they see us converging on a central point they can aim at that point. Doubles their chances of a hit. You go to the right broken door I'll go to the far left broken one."

Jenny scanned the parking lot, looking for the mystery sniper. "You really think there is someone waiting for us to make a break for it?"

"Always assume a gun is loaded until it is verified." He locked eyes with her and she didn't see even a hint of humor. "When entering a danger zone always assume you're exposed to the danger until proven otherwise. Ready?"

"Well, no. But we don't have a choice, do we?"

"That's the spirit!" It was amazing how much cheer his quiet voice could carry when talking about potentially being shot.

They both prepared for their sprint. Roger held one finger out and gave it a flick. The second finger. A flick. The third finger. They raised onto the balls of their feet. The flick.

His boots and her sandals slapped against the asphalt. He stretched his legs, taking long strides. His feet drove him forward. Five strides to go.

Four. He drove his arms, slinging himself forward.

Three. Drive and push.

Two. Stretch forward.

One.

He grabbed the doorframe and let it stall his forward momentum and sling him around, against the interior wall. As his back made contact, he whipped his head to the side, just as Jennifer cleared the doorframe. She tried to stop in those cheap sandals but ended up skidding across the floor mat just inside the door. One of the shoes caught on the mat and tripped her. She fell on her hip and slid across the tile, into an overturned basket. Jennifer bounded away from the basket and threw herself to the side, out of the spill of light coming in to the store.

Roger gave her a moment to collect herself then asked, "You OK?"

She patted herself down, checking a couple of specific spots. "A bit banged up but I'll get through it."

Roger ducked a head around the door frame, scanned the parking lot and adjacent rooftops, withdrew his head, knelt and scanned again. He changed the height of his head several more times and examined the area. "Looks like we're clear."

"Nice to know I'm going to have bruises for weeks. All for nothing." She stretched her left arm, working out a charley horse.

"Next time you can stroll across and draw fire while I take it seriously." Roger backed into the store, staying in the shadow while watching outside.

"Hey," she said, "I appreciate the offer but I'll take some bruises to keep from taking fire."

"Smart."

Once they were both fully shrouded by shadow and well away from the door they paused to take a look. By comparison the Payless was in better shape. People had just looted the shoe store. Here it looked like they actively sought out ways to destroy the store. Baskets were smashed together and even piled upon one another. Tile from the floor had been peeled up and thrown across the store. Clothing racks were overturned, and cash registers were thrown to the floor, smashed open.

Widely spaced skylights provided enough illumination to navigate the store and read labels. Since most Targets are similarly laid out, Jennifer easily found the shoes section and riffled through empty boxes and single shoes. After almost twenty minutes she gave up. Either her size had been stolen or hadn't been stocked in the first place. Roger had split his time between watching her sort through the litter and watching the rest of the store. When she looked up and shrugged he nodded and they moved through the rest of the store.

Spending about an hour rummaging through piles of former-goods-and -packages-made-trash and sorting through bent, broken and discarded products, they rounded up several items still of use. In the Sports and Outdoors department Roger rounded up three knives, two sturdy lock-blade folders and one fixed blade with a blade about three and a half inches long. Not exactly what his first choice would have been, but it was much better than he had. Jennifer turned up a Katadyn pump water filter and two spare filters along with a 5 gallon collapsible jug. They each found a backpack. Roger put his gear, including the duffle bag he already had into his backpack. Jennifer started loading hers with newly acquired gear including a couple of cheap first aid kits, a few canned goods and apples that had somehow been overlooked at the back of shelves in the groceries department.

Outside the Target the two ducked from store to store. Everything had been picked over. Nothing had been left untouched but that didn't mean that others had been looking for precisely what they were seeking. Going through a full roster of franchised megastores such as Lowe's, Marshall's and Barnes and Noble, along with more specialized stores such as GNC, Hibbett Sports and even PetSmart, rendered them much better prepared than they had been just hours earlier. Roger leaned against a stack of exercise pads as he finished strapping a yoga mat to his pack and watched Jennifer doing the same.

The LA Fitness location was huge and there were a lot of resources available, if you knew what you were looking for. Compared to the other locations they had gone through it was also remarkable untouched. Of course most items here were heavy and difficult to move but obviously there weren't a lot of creative thinkers. Though most of the snacks had been removed from the juice bar, there were still bottles of water and a few snacks in the store room. There were plenty of towels to provide additional padding for the shoulder straps on the backpacks. The packs were a good find but they were designed for kids to take books to school and would prove uncomfortable soon enough. The yoga mats would serve as a ground barrier and a little padding for sleeping on their trek. Several lockers had tennis shoes that fit Jennifer. Roger guided her to choose the ones that offered the best arch and ankle support. Cordage was incredibly important on the type of scenario they were about to engage in and the various nets, cables and elastic bands provide quite a variety of cordage.

Jennifer finished tying the yoga mat in place and blew out a sigh. She had been virtually silent since they entered Target earlier, just following along and doing what needed to be done. After the night they had, and the constant stress of the day, she was looking tired and worn. The sigh must not have gotten whatever she was thinking out of her head because she looked at him, her head still tilted down, eyes just visible through her hanging hair.

"I can't believe it. I can't believe what the looters have done to all those shops!" She shook her head again, her mind tracing back over the events of the day.

Roger smiled grimly, "Don't knock looters too much." When she looked up again, his smile lost some of its grimness. "We're looters too. Now."

"But we –"

"Don't try to justify it. Yes, we're in need. But that doesn't change it. That doesn't make it something other than what it is. I bet most of the people who have come through have felt they were in need of something. Definitely more than the greedy stores who closed their doors.

"But that's just part of it. We can't allow ourselves to justify it. We have to recognize that we're making a break with the traditional rules that held our society together. For now at least that society doesn't exist.

"Trying to hold on to yesterday too much may limit the number of tomorrows we have. So just accept that we looted. We looted because we were in need. This will be the first break from social convention that we're going to experience. Go ahead and get your head wrapped around it now so that the next step is that much easier to take."

Jennifer just stared at him, her hair-shrouded eyes locked on his. He just said it. He had basically just told her that they had broken the law and that they were likely to break even more laws in the days to come. By taking the first step he had let her know that her life had changed and she needed to get on board. And he just said it like it was the most normal thing possible.

"You know, you're kind of warped."

Roger nodded, the smiling losing the last grim vestige. "Yup. Lucky for us it appears the rest of the world has caught up with me."

The absurdity of the comment settled onto Jenny, and for the first time since leaving the airport she felt the urge to laugh. She tried to hold it back but that just increased the pressure. It exploded from her and rocked her body for several minutes. When she finished and wiped the tears from her eyes she saw Roger was chuckling as well, shaking his head with a shy smile.

"All right now," he said, still smiling, "let's get some rest. We've got a long way to go."

Using a roll of shower towels as a pillow and a beach towel from the swimming area as a sheet, he settled in to get comfortable.

"You think it is safe?" Jennifer cast a glance to the floor below where the front doors were still pushed open.

"Nope." Roger fluffed the towel pillow, trying to conform it to his head. "But safer than walking during the daylight with both of us too tired to keep watch. Get some sleep. You'll be better for it."

She laid down on her stack of mats, casting one more glance at the front door. "I don't know if I can sleep with guys walking around out there with guns."

Roger smiled, "You can. And as soon as I can be, I'm going to be one of the guys with a gun."

Jennifer's next breath was deep and even. She was asleep even before the smile faded from Roger's face.

10

The Hospital – Denton, TX

Ashley scanned the hall to her left, right and left again, a habit established in Driver's Ed. Left, right, left. Nothing. She hoped her safety didn't depend on hearing. The only thing she was able to hear was the beating of her heart and the crinkle of her plastic suit. Of course she could take off the suit but that would expose her to more of the virus. As Roger would say, the best solution has two components: first, it provides a protection that is a significant increase from your unprepared state; second, you can do it. No use pursuing an option you simply cannot enact and no reason to pursue an option – and spend resources pursing an option – that you will never be able to put in place. Spend time concentrating on what you can do and that which improves your situation. Right now she *could* stay in her suit and it *was* a substantial improvement in her protective state.

OK, she thought, *enough with the theoretical evaluations. Get to your objective and reduce your exposure to the hazard.*

She navigated the halls, approaching corners with caution, using the big mounted mirrors in the corners to check for movement when the mirrors were available and approached from across the hall to increase her field of view when the mirrors were unavailable. At the first non-mirrored corner she approached, she tried quick head bobs around the corner to check for movement but the suit crinkled so loudly she was practically deafened and she was sure anyone within 100 feet would have been able to hear in the otherwise silent building.

She was somewhat disappointed in herself and somewhat pleased with herself that she was so easily able to look past the bodies lining the walls in the tiled areas of the hospital. It seemed that human nature wouldn't allow the staff to move the dead and dying to the carpeted area. Maybe it wasn't human nature. It would be harder to disinfect carpets. Maybe there was an internal protocol about bodily fluids and carpeting. They didn't get that deep into operations during her class walk-through. Nevertheless, she only got turned around once on her way to the dispensary and avoided breaking down in misery from being surrounded by such death.

Perhaps unsurprisingly, the dispensary was trashed. The heavy, code-keyed door was propped open by shelving. Rolling chairs and rolling trays were pushed to the side. Paperwork was scattered about, practically carpeting the floor. Ashley shook her head as she looked across the room. A body dressed in scrubs and a lab coat lay crumpled on the floor, the coat soaked through with blood from three holes – two in the chest and one in the upper right arm. The blood was already dried to rust brown and flies had already begun buzzing. It was obvious this was not a recent shooting.

Ashley began to dismiss the room, but took the time for a serious second look. Bottles and loose pills were scattered across the floor, but she noticed some bottles still had their lids intact. As she sorted through the mess, she found that the easily recognizable items had been taken. Hydrocodone and Valium bottles were emptied, not just missing. Certainly there had been other bottles as well, and they were missing, but it slowly dawned on her that the person who ransacked the room was apparently looking more for recreational than medicinal drugs. There were many medications remaining, but she had no better idea what they were than the previous looters. She remembered that doctor's used something called a PDR or *Physician's Desk Reference* when prescribing medicines. It only took a few seconds to find the almost three-inch-thick book. It took far more time to find some way to carry her horde. There wasn't anything in the dispensary except trays, cups and rolling carts. She needed something that she could carry out.

Suddenly she remembered passing the laundry – she had gotten very turned around – and thought she could gather some towels to wrap the haul in. Now with a purpose, she crunched down the halls and back to the laundry. Turning back to the door with an armload of towels she spied another option. Stacks of scrubs were sorted by size into bins. Ashley dropped the towels and picked up several pairs of pants. As she jogged back to the dispensary she tied the pant legs into knots. It was clumsy work with her plastic gloves but she managed and had four sets of pants ready by the time she reentered the pharmacy.

She quickly stuffed the *PDR*s into one of the legs. The book was followed by bottles and boxes of every description. She would sort them later. For now she was going to carry out everything she could. Suture kits and tiny glass bottles with rubber tops followed bulk count white plastic bottles. The gauze had been picked over but a few sealed rolls had escaped the previous thief. In less than five minutes all eight pant legs were stuffed to capacity.

Ashley draped the pants over her shoulders and began crunching back down the halls toward the cafeteria and her door to the outside world. Just as she passed the cafeteria someone called out, "Hey!"

She didn't even pause. Her arms squeezed the stuffed pant legs to her chest and her feet jumped to running speed. There wasn't a second call. As her hands banged against the door, a boom sounded behind her.

Her back screamed in pain. The fireproof door barely budged, but it was enough for her to slip behind it. Two more shots rang out. They slapped the door. She didn't take the time to see if they had penetrated the door. She fled down the short hallway, hurdling the dead bodies. The thought of moving one of the bodies to block a door flashed through her mind but it would take too long. Instead, Ashley sprinted for her bike.

She slammed her foot into the cleat and pushed with the other foot. Her right foot pressed down. Her back screamed in protest. Ashley pushed it to the back of her mind. She didn't have time to think about it. Quick weaves took her across the sidewalk leading to the employee parking. Her head was down, body as parallel to the bike as possible. Two shots rang out. A hole opened in a car hood. A headlight shattered. Then she was shielded by the cars.

Despite the protest from her back, Ashley kept pedaling hard. She shot across the swatch of grass between the parking lot and the faculty building. The ride smoothed as she flashed across the faculty parking lot, then over another lawn. Another shot sounded, this time barely audible over her breathing and the crunching of the HAZMAT suit. With a building between Ashley and the shooter, she took a moment to think of how to leave.

A concrete lined ditch ran opposite the faculty building from the hospital. If she used it she would be below the line of sight for a good distance. Plus she'd be doubling back, moving in a direction the shooter may not anticipate. Decision made, she coasted into the ditch. It was wet but not impassable. The bike kicked up a rooster tail as she powered back toward West Oak. Using the side of the ditch as a ramp she blasted up and out, her back wheel made contact with a patch of grass. The front wheel came down on the northernmost driveway into Yorkshire Place apartments. A hard left and she was back on West Oak, hurdling away from the hospital. Once she was past St. Maximum, three blocks further on, she finally paid heed to her back. She slowed to a more casual pace and glided back to her apartment.

☣ ☣ ☣

At least she had preplanned what she was going to need to do once she got home. A garden hose was attached to an exterior faucet and she had soap and a long-handled brush staged behind some bushes. She hosed herself down, still in the HAZMAT suit, and proceeded to scrub every inch she could reach with the brush. The water that ran into the suit at the bullet hole worried her. That means she was exposed to potentially contaminated air in the hospital. Not only that, she got an open wound while in the hospital. Strangely, the wound didn't hurt as much as she expected, at least once the initial trauma had settled. There was little she could do at this point though, so she put it out of her mind for the moment and scrubbed down the bike.

After the thorough washing, she stripped off the plastic suit, leaving her gloves on. She wadded the suit up and discarded it in a Dumpster in the parking lot, along with the gloves. She had never thought about it until the walk-through at the hospital, but most people took gloves off wrong. They just grabbed and ripped. But that could sling infected materials across the room. At the very least, if you grabbed wrong you could touch contaminated areas. So she was careful. With her gloved left hand she firmly grabbed the right wrist and pulled down, uncovering half her right hand while turning the glove inside out. Using the still covered fingers of the right hand she pulled at the left wrist, peeling the glove all the way off. With her now exposed left hand she gripped what had been the interior of the right glove and finished pulling it off. The right glove turned inside out and completely encapsulated the left glove, considerably reducing the risk of contamination. It took a little more time to do properly but she now knew the state of medical treatment in the area. She really couldn't afford to get sick. Even a minor infection could be a death sentence until things settled down.

Ashley jogged up to her apartment, unlocked the door and swept the interior with her handgun, looking for anyone who shouldn't be there. It was a traditional one-room, economy apartment like so many of her fellow students had, so there weren't many places for someone to hide. Still, it paid to be cautious these days. The room was clear.

She picked up a Sharpie marker, a write-in-the-rain notebook, a pen and a couple of dish towels. Rubber dish gloves came out of a plastic bin marked MISC CLEANING. Three shallow tubs, bleach and some dishwashing liquid stacked together. She filled the top tub with water – *Thankfully the water hasn't lost all pressure yet* – and returned with her cleaning gear back to where she had dropped the scrub pants.

She divided the water up into the three tubs and settled in for a long piece of work. Her back was to the building so she could keep an eye out for anyone approaching. The 9mm was out of its holster and sitting beside her on its own towel on the sidewalk. No use in setting the weapon on the grass and letting moisture settle on it when she had the option to head off the problem.

Taking her headlamp from the bike bag she settled in for work. To the first tub she added dishwashing detergent. The second got a dose of bleach and the third remained clean. The gloves went on and she started her process. First she wrote the name of the medication and its strength on her notebook. She then dunked it in the dishwashing mixture, then the bleach solution and set it to the side to let the bleach mixture dry then went on to the next item, making sure to keep everything orderly. As she suspected, many of the labels did not survive the process. When the first bottles were dry she rinsed them with the water to get the bleach off and then dried them with the hand towel. Finally she used the Sharpie to assign a number to the bottle and wrote the corresponding number next to the description she had already entered.

It took forever. She estimated that she began around 10:00 in the evening and it was well past 1:00 in the morning when she finally dumped the water pans out, gathered her contraband and headed back upstairs. Her back screamed in pain, both from tense muscles and from the gunshot. But she did find something that explained why the pain wasn't as intense as she had thought it would be. It appeared the *PDR* had deflected the bullet. There was also a small glass bottle that was shattered. Ashley figured the book had taken the brunt of the shot and deflected the bullet into the bottle.

She didn't bother to clean that bottle, there wasn't anything worth salvaging in it. However when she looked up Rocephin, the former contents of the bottle, she discovered it was an injectable antibiotic. Of all the things to have splattered into her, many ranked worse than an antibiotic. Ashley used the bathroom mirror, a battery powered lantern and some hemostats that she had gathered, in their hermetically sealed package, to dig at the wound and remove a couple of tiny shards that had embedded themselves. She applied an adhesive bandage and made a note to check it at least twice a day until it healed to ensure there wasn't any infection.

One final trip downstairs to retrieve her bike and once again hide her scrub brush and soap in the bushes left her exhausted. When she crawled into bed she didn't even remember closing her eyes.

11

L.A. Fitness – Atlanta

Thunder slapped Jennifer across the face. She recoiled from the noise and flash of light, rolling off the exercise mats. Her brain raced as she started putting the pieces together and the events of the previous day came back to her. She peered over the stack of mats. In the flashes of lightning coming through the windows high on the wall she could see Roger, tucked in the half fetal position, arm wrapped around the roll of towel pillows. For all intents and purposes he could have been snuggled into some five star hotel suite.

On second thought, Roger probably would be less comfortable in a suite than he was right here. Jennifer, on the other hand, would be just fine right about now with a big bathtub where she could sink up to her chin in hot, scented bubbles. She had gotten accustomed to the good life during her marriage. Not that she had taken it for granted. She came from a poor family and she knew how the other half lived. While they weren't in the top 1% as the media had come to call the very wealthy, they definitely weren't in bottom 60% either.

As the rain and lightning continued, Jennifer leaned back against the stack of mats, thinking about their situation. While they had been at the airport the most important thing seemed to be *leaving the airport*. Now part of her wondered if it was the right decision. Sure, there was an outbreak on the concourse, but since leaving the airport she had seen more dead bodies than she cared to recall. She had no idea the situation had gone so wrong so quickly. In the America she remembered, people didn't just bust the windows out of stores. Kids didn't hunt with their families in the local Target parking lot! Traffic jams were cleared before the morning news got a good look at it and you certainly didn't stack up exercise mats in the back of a fitness center and spend the night hoping that the hunters didn't just wander in and take the stuff you just looted from an entire shopping center.

Jennifer brushed non-existent fluff from the black velour jogging suit she had found earlier. Lacking pajamas and unwilling to sleep in just a long shirt like she would at home, she had chosen what she thought would be most comfortable. Turned out that she probably could have slept in a suit of crushed glass. She had been so tired. Now that she was awake she had to take care of other bodily needs. She didn't want to leave Roger in case he woke up, but since they had 'hydrated' – to use his word for it – before going to bed, she really needed to *de*hydrate just a bit.

Roger was still sleeping deeply so Jenny decided to risk it. The bathrooms were still working yesterday and they had even taken a chance and had showers. That was probably what had helped the exhaustion to take over so fiercely last night. The shower hadn't been hot but it had been welcome and relaxing. She decided to risk it and walked down the stairs, crossing to the restrooms.

A few minutes later she had wrapped up her business and was heading for the stairs when a sound stopped her in her tracks. The first thing to flash through her mind was that the hunters had returned. Two voices were talking just inside the front door. Lightning flashed and illuminated the two figures. They definitely weren't the hunters. One was long haired and with a female body. The other was a bit taller and with shorter hair but still with a more feminine than masculine shape.

It struck Jennifer as interesting that Roger was right about whispering. Even standing this far away she could hear that they were whispering. Not precisely what they were saying but that someone was saying *something*. Even stranger was that she expected the rain would wash out the sound of the whispering, but there was a chaos to rain and there was a pattern to whispering. It was that speech rhythm that had stopped her.

Now what? Jenny looked up the stairs, hoping that Roger wouldn't stand up and call for her, hoping, that he did, just so that the situation would move forward. She took stealthy steps backward until her back was against the wall. The two in the doorway had a pile of belongings at their feet. It looked like they may have just ducked in to escape the weather. However, a quick check of her watch set in a bit of concern. It was 4:30 in the morning and she knew that the sun would be coming up. Within an hour and a half there wouldn't be anywhere to hide. Jenny had less than that to make up her mind and take action. Judging by the conditions going on outside, the weather wasn't going to do her any favors.

It only took moments for the women at the door to settle in. They moved their bundles well back from the doorway, inside the foyer. They seemed hesitant to enter the open, dark expanse of the fitness center, and for the moment that was to Jenny's benefit. The tall one hunched into a corner in the foyer while the shorter one stood by the entrance and watched the parking lot.

The interior doors to the foyer were shattered so there was no sound protection, but Jen knew she needed to get upstairs before Roger stirred and made a noise of his own. Quietly, she slinked out of the alcove to the restrooms, crossed the carpeted floor on silent feet and slowly backed up the stairs. Once she reached the top, she turned toward their sleeping area, slamming head first into a man's chest.

Roger wrapped one arm around Jennifer's shoulders, quickly putting a finger to her lips. Even as quick as she realized who he was, a squeak still slipped from between her lips. They both ducked, squatting together at the top of the stairs, arms wrapped around one another. Looking at the main door, the sentinel appeared oblivious to the events inside. The storm must have drowned out all sounds from within.

They sat that way for several moments, watching. Somehow Jennifer felt more secure huddled in Roger's arms with potential danger mere yards away than she had guarded by armed soldiers back at the airport. *He is a strange guy but there are worse things than strange mixed with kind, competent and confident.*

Subtly her weight settled against him, his arm wrapped across her chest with firm but steady pressure, supporting her without crushing her. It had to be a delicate balance of strength and consideration, and he seemed to manage it unconsciously. The relief from a burden she hadn't even known she was carrying was so great that she settled even more in to his embrace.

"Oh, sorry," he spoke quietly into her ear. "Didn't mean to squish you." He slowly duck-walked backward, guiding her away from the edge of the stairs, then stood well behind the angle where they could be seen.

Of course he didn't get it. It's Roger. "No harm, no foul," she said. She wasn't even sure he would understand if she tried to explain what she was thinking.

"This presents quite a pickle, doesn't it?" He stared her in the eyes. They were standing close enough that she could see the whites of his eyes even in storm-clouded night darkness. She could smell the soap he had used in the shower last night and she wasn't sure, but she thought she could feel the warmth radiating off of him.

"What does?" Maybe he did understand.

He stepped toward the top of the stairs, nodding toward the door. "Those two. It's a whole do-we-stay-or-do-we-go kinda thing."

Nope! No clue! Don't even know why I got my hopes up. She nodded, "Yup," doing her best Roger impersonation, "a real pickle." *Hang on. Did I really say 'get my hopes up'? Is that what I'm hoping for?*

"Yup. Quite a deal," he said. Or did he say "dill"? *Standing here in a life-threatening situation did he just make a joke?* He cast a quick look over his shoulder. Was that a smile? It was too dark and he was now too far away for her to be certain, but it seemed Mr. Westover may have a sense of humor hiding deep down inside after all. *Or I'm projecting favorable traits on this guy and* that's *all I need right now. At least he isn't in the mob though.*

He backed away again and led her behind the stacked exercise mats where they had stashed their gear. "Two ways I see this going. Several variants but two essential ways. First, they leave and we're clear. No hassle. Second, there's a hassle. They stick around, they come in, someone sees them so close to the door and comes to investigate. Hassle, hassle, hassle."

"What if they stay and are friendly?"

"And they want to walk with us back to Texas? Where do we find food to feed four people? Hassle. Taking care of the medical needs of two more people. Hassle."

"What about there's safety in numbers?"

"Only when those numbers aren't negative. We don't know who they are, what their situation is, or anything else that would make me inclined to risk an encounter." He rubbed his hand over his pack, feeling the various bulges like he was tactilely reinventorying his pack, looking for something to use in this situation.

"But you took me on before you knew anything about me. From that first day you were giving me tips to get through. We don't know. Maybe these people are like that."

"You were -," Roger paused. His eyes shifted from his pack to her and back to the pack quickly. "You're worth the tow. I could see it then and you've just proved it since."

"Worth the tow?"

"Yeah, you know. You see a broke down car in the junk yard and you see what you can make out of it? You decide, what the hell, I'll tow that back to the house and restore it."

"Worth the tow." This time it wasn't a question. It was a flat statement. He had just equated her to a junked car.

His eyes shot back up. "Hey. I know that tone. Melissa used it quite a bit. There wasn't an insult in there unless you want to find one." His accent was coming through thicker with each word. "I was just saying you're worth the effort. That's all. And I knew it even back then."

'You're worth the effort.' It seemed like such a simple, and on some level, even insulting sentiment. But from Roger, it was possibly even more romantic than the $10,000 getaway Paul scheduled for them when he proposed. She fought down the flutter in her stomach and shook her head, *Damn! I've got to get over this. That really wasn't a compliment to get all stirred up over!* Her thoughts paused for a moment. *Unless it comes from a guy who is so unfamiliar with compliments that he just doesn't know how to give them.*

Jennifer grabbed the shoulder strap for her pack and found the little plastic size-adjuster-slide-thing. She wrapped her hand around the hard square of plastic and squeezed. The corner digging into her palm was just enough pain for her mind to disengage from that line of thought. "OK. You meant it as a compliment. Fine. But we don't know maybe they are worth the tow as well."

"Maybe, but now I don't want to risk anything happenin' to ya."

Aww!

☣ ☣ ☣

Roger glanced at his watch. The tritium glow said they didn't have enough time to think this through much more. It was almost 5:00 and the sun would be lighting the sky soon, even if it was dimmed by the clouds. They might have a couple of hours, maybe even three until full sun up. The sky would start getting light much sooner than that. The storm seemed to be dying down a bit. That was good because it might encourage the others to leave. Bad because if they didn't leave, it might make them brave enough to come further into the gym.

That whole conversation with Jennifer had left Roger just a little uneasy. He was sure she was hearing something that was coming through in the *female frequency* which he had a real hard time hearing. Melissa had been very tuned into the frequency. The infuriating part was that Melissa was usually right. It's a shame most men couldn't hear that frequency. *Doesn't really matter right now though, we've got more pressing matters.*

Roger didn't want to hurt these people if he didn't have to. A gun would be a good deterrent, but he'd always lived by the adage of *never pull a gun if you aren't going to shoot it.* There were any number of things he could use to hurt someone in the gym. Weight plates and weight bars were the first items that came to mind. But he wasn't trained with those kinds of weapons, and if the others had guns then a hand-to-hand situation could be over before it even started.

"There's gotta be a back door."

"What," Jennifer quiet-asked.

"A back door. All these places have a back door. We could just sneak out." The sun had just set when they entered the gym so the details weren't crystal clear in his mind. But he knew there were some offices downstairs and there might be a way out through the back office.

"OK. Sneak out the back door. But we're going to have to talk about your trust issues when we're clear."

Roger squinted at her in the darkness. Why would she want to discuss trust issues? As Robert DeNiro said in those movies, she is in the 'circle of trust'. Why would she want to talk about that? From the tone she wasn't going to express gratitude.

They gathered their supplies, careful to be as silent as possible, Jennifer two steps behind Roger. With their packs on their shoulders, they treaded down the stairs, one step at a time, careful to stay close to the edge of each step where the tread has the most support and is least likely to squeak under strain. At the base of the stairs Roger turned right, keeping an eye on the two newcomers up front, but making his way toward the back of the building. He pointed at Jennifer, did the two-finger point to his eyes, then pointed toward the darkness in back.

His hand dropped to hers, clasping it gently. She paused for a moment then took the lead, navigating through the dark and threading her way past various exercise machines with arms and levers and other appendages protruding at odd angles. Somehow she made it to the offices without rattling the machines or tripping them both. Once the stairs blocked the view of the front door and thus the other's view of them, Roger turned and followed more closely but didn't drop her hand. He tried not to think about it too much but he just didn't *want* to let go.

As fate would have it, once they reached the doors they encountered the only intact windows and closed doors they had seen since entering the shopping area. Jennifer tried the door handle. Locked.

There were large panel windows allowing the workers to look onto the workout floor. Now Roger leaned in, cupping a hand around one side of his face to block what little light was filtering in from the windows above. His other hand was still interlocked with Jennifer's. It had moved from a simple clasp to interlocked fingers. He couldn't claim it was a comfortable grip considering the circumstances and the need to move around, but he still wasn't inclined to retrieve his hand. For the moment Jennifer didn't appear to be in a rush either.

"If we want to go out the back," she quiet-talked, "we're going to have to break some glass."

"Not necessarily." Roger unslung his bag and they finally let go of hands. Jennifer kept watch for movement at the front door as Roger dug through the pack. At last he stood with a small pouch in his hand. "Here we go."

The pouch was about three inches wide and four inches tall, almost flat. A fold-over flap was secured with a snap. Roger opened it with a flick of his thumbnail. Inside was an assortment of small, flat and oddly shaped metal pieces. He pulled out one shaped like and "L" and another that was straight but with a squiggly tip. He held them up to Jennifer and in the dimness he could just make out her questioning squint.

"Lock picks."

"Aren't those illegal?"

"In some places. If questioned you usually have to show a need for carrying them." He turned to the door, inserted the "L" shaped piece, the torsion wrench, and then the half-diamond pick.

"And how did you get away with it?"

Roger was concentrating on the door. "Most people who would ask only ask if they have reason to." He paused as he wiggled the tool in the lock, feeling for the tumblers and trying to move them into place. "And others are easily impressed by credentials. Funny how people just take for granted what you say."

That comment went without explanation as he continued to dig at the lock. He reset the lock by releasing tension and shrugged his shoulders to loosen them up before another attempt.

"Credentials? Take for granted?"

Roger looked up at Jennifer questioningly then his brain reengaged. "Oh, yeah. I'm a professor of Emergency Preparedness, here is my card. Credentials. I wrote this paper for the DHS, or testified in that hearing before Congress on emergency planning. I keep them to determine if they should be considered as part of a publicly identified readiness item. That kind of thing."

He returned to the lock, feeling around, applying tension and releasing it, lifting pins, searching for spacing that he could take advantage of.

"So you lie to keep your lock picks?"

"Well, that and other reasons. I'm not doing anything illegal with them. If I was, I'd be better practiced!" He pulled the picks out of the door and stood, giving the door a quick nod. "Perishable skill. Maybe I should have been practicing."

"But how long have you been lying just so you can keep carrying lock picks?"

From her tone Roger suspected that the question wasn't solely for curiosity's sake. It seemed she may have another motive for asking.

"Well, there are two answers to that question," he rolled his shoulders again, twisting his neck, loosening muscles. "First, it isn't a lie. I have done all those things and if someone asks I would let them know that I think they should not be included in a standard, publicly disseminated readiness items list.

"But that is just part of the answer. If I am understanding your intent, then that isn't the part you were interested in. So, how long have I been saying that so that I could carry them? Just long enough so that they'd be here in my pack when we need them."

She was standing with her back to the door and windows, blocking the very little light that was available. Heavy shadows draped her face, making it so that he couldn't see if she showed any expression. Since she didn't say anything, he assumed she accepted that answer and returned to his work. After several more attempts, he peeled back the cover to his watch again, the tritium showing 5:47.

"This is taking too long." He tucked the tools back into the pouch. "Perishable skill. I needed more practice."

"What's that mean?" Jennifer reached over and tried the handle on the door again as if, maybe, it would open simply because she wanted it to open.

"Well, the good news is that we're no worse off than if we didn't have lock picks." Roger shrugged trying the handle himself. "Bad news is we're no better off for having them."

"So what do we do now?"

A female voice came from the shadows beneath the stairs, "I suggest you put your hands up and keep 'em where I can see 'em!"

Jenny and Roger turned toward the voice. A boxy gun emerged from the shadow, followed by a finely boned hand with fingerless gloves. Logically Roger knew the barrel couldn't be as big as it looked but logic had nothing to do with it at the moment. Standing in front of the barrel he'd swear he could stick his head in the gaping hole.

12

Ashley's Apartment – Denton, TX

Ashley awoke with a twinge in her back. She slid from under her covers and stumbled to her bathroom. Glancing at the mirror on the way to the toilet she was impressed by what a late night, lack of shower, an hour or so in a plastic hood, and restless night of sleep could do to her hair. Just a couple of weeks earlier people would have paid good money and used quite a bit of hair product to achieve the same affect.

She combed her fingers through her hair while taking care of morning business. As she rationed her toilet paper usage she was glad she'd thought ahead to stock up. Even in a little apartment such as hers there was room to put aside appropriate supplies for short term self reliance. Unfortunately her plan had been for *short term* survival. FEMA recommended a three day supply. Ashley had planned for three weeks all-round and three months of essentials. She was already depleting a considerable bit of her stores, and throwing a week of food in for Corey didn't help her situation at all. *It would have helped if he had just taken a little of what his dad taught to heart. He would be lucky if his act of rebellion didn't cost him his life.*

Pressing the handle for the toilet produced her first disappointment for the day. The toilet flushed but the refill cycle started slow and ended in failure. Apparently the municipal water supply had finally petered out. With the mass death and wholesale exodus, it was a little surprising that the water ran out so soon. But every leaky toilet, dripping faucet and garden hose in use watering lawns served to drain the finite resource. Once the electricity failed it was just a matter of time before the water ran out.

She lifted the over-sized Maroon5 t-shirt which, along with a pair of jogging shorts, was what she used for sleepwear. Peeling off the adhesive bandage, she evaluated the wound in the light of day. Well, as close to the light of day as you could get in a bathroom with a tiny, pebbled glass window that even her small frame would find difficult to squeeze through. The wound was bruised but it had scabbed over, wasn't leaking and wasn't rimmed with a pink halo that would indicate infection setting in. She peeled and stuck another bandage and dropped her shirt back in place.

Crossing the apartment to her kitchenette she lit a can of Sterno and placed it in the foldable stove she had acquired just for this purpose. A standard metal canteen cup received water from a jug in her water stores and then sat on top of the Sterno stove. While it heated she scooped two heaping spoonfuls of coffee into a coffee press. She also had a manual coffee grinder for when the pre-ground stuff ran out, one of the many of the things she had for emergency situations. The coffee press, though purchased for a lights-out scenario, had become her chosen method of coffee prep even before the lights went out.

The water still hadn't reached a simmer so Ashley flicked on her radio scanner. It was just a citizen band scanner, but she had been able to pick up emergency radio traffic until two days ago. Now there was nothing but static. It would have been great to get some idea of what was going on. Being from a generation that was so accustomed to instant access to virtually any information, being uninformed was incredibly uncomfortable. She really missed the news. Not the media, but the news.

One of her goals had been to get an amateur broadcast license but between school, work, writing her thesis, other preps and simply attempting to have enough of a social life that she actually *wanted to survive* an emergency, there just wasn't enough time or money. Jeremy and Rosa were HAM operator friends, but she hadn't seen them since the day before the outbreak. She hadn't seen anyone from the group since that day. Hopefully they had gotten out of the city and she hadn't walked past their sheet-shrouded body in the hospital.

Pushing that thought from her mind she checked the water, saw the simmer, and poured it over the coffee grounds. Putting the cap back on the Sterno put out the flame and saved the remainder for next time.

She pulled out the medical supplies from last night and settled in for a task. One by one she read the number on the bottle, consulted her notebook and the *PDR* then wrote a label: name, strength and use – antibiotic, anti-inflammatory, blood pressure, antacids, anesthetic, analgesic, etc. The label was put in place by a piece of cellophane tape and the medicines sorted by type.

Corey was *fuming*! That bitch had locked him in his own apartment! There was no electricity. The water stopped for some reason, and his cell phone was shattered across the room. Glass was scattered across the floor and he had already cut himself twice trying to pick it up so he had just declared that half of the room off limits. He'd even had to fold out the couch last night and sleep with that damn bar pressing against his back. Now the sun was up and he couldn't even go outside. He looked out his window and waited for someone to walk by. He would try to get them to open the door. After waiting almost a full five minutes no one had come by.

The bitch!

He looked out the window again. He had already knocked the screen out, but that was more of an accident than a plan. His Nintendo handheld console was dead as well. A wayward throw had sent the small game system through the open window with enough force to rip half the screen out. Corey had rushed to the window as if he could still catch the device. When he saw the system shattered on the sidewalk below, his animated arm flailing had finished off the screen.

Glancing back and forth through the window, Corey would even welcome seeing that stuttering ass-hat Mitch coming. But no one was out there. No one at all. He knew that Ashley was all spun up about this virus – and he was going to press kidnapping charges or something when he got out of here – but surely everyone can't be as stupid as she is. He poked the remote again, cussed, and threw it back on the couch then returned to the window.

Usually he could hear cars or something, even see people. Surely the cops had cleared the streets of all those broken down cars by now. People should be coming back. The kids around here were so serious about school. Sure, they'd cut up and have a long Saturday night, but when it came down to class these people went. However, Corey hadn't heard anyone outside since the lights went out and he'd opened the window to get a breeze.

Maybe if I get my sheet I can make rope to get me down to the ground. He leaned out the window and was overcome by a brief moment of dizziness. Heights had never been his favorite thing and it was like a whole two floors down to the ground. *Maybe I should concentrate on getting through the door rather than out the window.*

He tried the knob again, like he had done a dozen times since waking up. It was still locked. The door opened inward so he couldn't bust it open. He'd kicked open a couple of doors in his life. You have to break the door frame at the latch to get it to open. On the outside of the door a support runs the entire length, keeping it from being kicked open. The hinges were on the inside so the door wouldn't swing inward anyway.

The hinges! Corey ducked into the kitchen and dug through the junk drawer. His dad had given him all kinds of stupid crap when he moved in. Who needed a hammer or nails in a friggin' dorm? You had a problem, you called someone. But he could take that stupid crap and make something good out of it. *Hah! Dad thinks he is the King of the Readiness. Now see what I can do! Who needs all that other stuff?*

Corey crossed back to the door with his hammer and a long nail. He put the nail on the base of the hinge and tapped. Nothing. He tapped harder. Nothing. Harder. The pin moved. It was just a little pop, but it moved. He tried again. It moved more. A few more taps and a return to the kitchen for pliers left the door still sitting on the hinges but all the pins out, laying where they fell.

He used the claw on the hammer to pry the bottom hinge apart. A sudden pop shifted the door. It fell off the hinges, resting against the latch Ashley had installed outside. With just a little maneuvering, Corey had the door open and could see into the hallway, into freedom.

☣ ☣ ☣

Out on the street Corey was confused. The cars were still parked in the middle of the streets. If anything, there were even more windows busted out and the smell had gotten even worse. Everything looked deserted. Nothing manmade moved on Prairie or Avenue E. The old convenience store right there on the corner had looked pretty trashed at the best of times. Now it was completely abandoned, its front windows destroyed and contents emptied. From this intersection he could have walked to the freeway in less than five minutes, at a casual stroll, and yet he heard no traffic on I35. Way off in the distance there was the sound of an engine revving followed by a rapid succession of semi-auto fire.

At least that was one thing his dad had done that Corey liked. Back when Corey was in high school, he and his dad had gone to the range a couple of times a month. Though it was begrudging respect, he did have to give it to the old man. *Dad could shoot the wings off a fly at 50 yards – with a handgun.* Corey was better than his father with a rifle but not so much as would make a difference.

Corey wandered the streets, past the UNT Bookstore on the left and the Rec Center on the right. He looked down Sycamore. About a block down two cars had collided in the middle of the street. Apparently a sedan had tried to pull around where other vehicles were blocking the road. The oncoming SUV t-boned the sedan. The driver's side sedan door was open. Airbags had deployed but it looked like they hadn't done much good. The driver was dead, tangled in the seatbelt and laying half out the door with head and shoulders on the ground. Blood had leaked from her eyes and mouth and soaked into her UNT Mean Green sweatshirt, drying to a deep rust brown.

He walked up to the intersection and remembered the last time he was out. He looked around for Ashley but didn't see her. He didn't see anyone. No one alive at least.

There were a bunch of cars on the road and if Corey knew anything about his fellow Texans, he knew that they loved their guns. If someone was shooting within hearing range and if Ashley had a gun, he wanted one too. His dad had bought him a Glock 17 back when they were going to the range. The old man thought that the gun was locked up somewhere safe because it wasn't allowed on campus or in the dorms. In reality that gun helped finance the Xbox. If his Dad had wanted him to keep the gun he should have bought the Xbox when Corey asked for it. *The old man just didn't get how the world worked.*

Corey started to walk toward the cars to begin a search, but remembered how adamant Ashley had been that he not touch anything that had been touched by one of the dead people. *Hell, she might be the last piece of ass left in town, better not piss her off too much.*

He walked over to the Rec Center. He had visited a couple of times when he was trying to get into the pants of another coed, and she had invited him to come watch a soccer match she was in. He ended up leaving with another chick each time so she stopped inviting him. Anyway, he still remembered the basic layout of the building. There was even a janitor's closet he remembered.

At one point he planned on breaking in with Jeremy and Mitch to steal some ammonia and bleach and shut the school down one day. But as they were making their plans they got too stoned and by the time they woke up the next morning they decided to just skip class instead. Plus they all had classes in different buildings and that would be a lot of trouble to shut it all down at once. Skipping was a lot less work.

The Rec Center was one of the few buildings in town that still had its glass intact. *Guess when people start getting a case of bloody crotch they don't just naturally want to go workout.*

He pushed the door open and walked in. The entry was open with light coming in from the front windows. However, the internal hall was much darker. When he found the janitor's closet he was in virtual blackness and the door was locked. He went around and opened doors. Thankfully, people liked seeing the great outdoors when they fled the brutal Texas summers and exercised indoors.

With all the interior doors open and the windows letting in light onto the basketball courts and the weight room, enough light got reflected around that he could see what he was doing. He found a fire extinguisher on a wall and took it over to the janitor's closet. Two whacks with the base of the red cylinder and the door knob shattered, clattering to the floor. Corey ducked into an admin office, picking up a pair of scissors. He jammed them in the latch of the door, pushed out the other side of the knob, then twisted the internal mechanism, pulling the latch out of the way. Just like that, the door swung open.

After a bit of rummaging, he came out with what he was looking for. He slipped on a pair of rubber gloves that stretched up to his elbows. Corey stuck another three packs of gloves in an empty five gallon bucket along with an assortment of tools and a whole pack of those white face masks with the stretchy bands that wrapped around your head. For good measure he added a box of blue paper-cloth towels and a pair of goggles. *No way that bitch-cow can tell me I'm not being safe this time!*

He took his bucket and went back outside. All the cars around here were for students and faculty so the likelihood that these vehicles had guns in them was minimal. There wasn't much town out west of I35 and there was still a lot of the college to the east. It only took a second to decide on heading south. He cut across the grounds next to the Physical Education Building, past the Coliseum and a few more buildings associated with the school, and then the freeway. The frontage road was clear of vehicles. It looked like a couple of people had gotten into a bit of a fender bender. Several more cars piled up behind them and blocked the freeway. This was where anyone coming from the south would exit for the hospital, which probably explained why so many people had tried to exit here.

Since the freeway ran between two low hills and a concrete wall divided the main lanes, there wasn't anywhere to go. A few more cars had gotten caught up in the wreckage. Corey guessed any cars that were still mobile had driven up the on ramp or driven the wrong way back down the freeway to get out of the area. Nothing that could move under its own power was left down here. Still, he had seventeen vehicles to scrounge through. As he got closer he marked more of them off his list. It looked like eight of the vehicles had been purposefully evacuated, doors opened and everything of value removed.

That left nine; three pickups, four SUVs, a compact and a Jeep. He hit the pickups first. Back when he was a kid, people had driven around with rifles or shotguns in racks in their back windows. Now that there were so many restrictions on where you could take guns you didn't see that as much. He searched the center consoles, behind the back seats, under the seats and in the doors. No guns, but he picked up two small first aid kits and a large Maglite flashlight that held six D-cell batteries. It was a good, resilient flashlight and it could be used as a club. He shoved it into his belt and kept scrounging.

Out of the beds he picked up several lengths of rope, about twelve wire clothes hangers and some tie-down straps. He also found half a six-pack of Bud in a back floorboard. With a 'don't mind if I do', Corey popped a top and took a swig of the warm beer. It went down a bit rough – cold beer was much better. But, being free, it was his favorite kind of beer.

In the second SUV he hit pay dirt. The steering wheel airbag had gone off and there was quite a bit of blood in the seat and floorboard, so Corey suspected that the driver had been hurt pretty bad. The front of the SUV was buried into the concrete dividing wall – maybe they had tried to dodge around the pile-up. Shattered safety glass was scattered all over the cab, except the driver's seat. Probably no passengers. Strapped in a holster mounted under the steering column Corey found what he was looking for. The Smith and Wesson .357 revolver had a 2 inch barrel, so it was for very short range. Stainless steel and hammerless, it was a great concealed carry weapon. The stainless would allow it to resist the moisture from being next to the body and the lack of hammer would reduce snags when being drawn. On the downside, it had only a five-round cylinder which reduced its capacity, but it also reduced its size, so score another point for concealability.

The cylinder was loaded with five rounds of .38 special. The console of the vehicle had two speed loaders, one with more .38 specials and the other filled with .357 magnums. All of them were hollow points. The console also held a magazine that Corey was very familiar with. It was a 17-round magazine for the Glock 17. He checked the seat and on the right side, just on the outer edge of the seat, he found a worn spot where the seat had been rubbed repeatedly over the years. Obviously the driver had a concealed carry permit and carried the 17. That would make the driver a big guy. It took a large frame to be able to effectively conceal a full sized weapon such as the Glock 17. The revolver under the steering column was probably a back-up. He put the speed loaders into his front left pocket and slipped the magazine in his left hip pocket.

The final piece of gear retrieved from the console rounded things out quite nicely. A pancake holster was essentially two pieces of leather sewn together with a gap in the middle where the weapon fits. A slit on each side of the middle gap allowed a belt to be fed through. The difference with this one was that instead of those two long belt holes, this one had metal hoops. These allowed the holster to hook over the belt while being situated *inside* the waistband of your pants. Appropriately named an 'inside the waistband', or IWB holster, it was yet another indicator that the owner was a concealed carry permit holder. Corey loosened his belt and slid the holster in place then slid the weapon into the holster. *Well, that's a bit better.*

Corey sorted through the remaining vehicles picking up a few more tools. The sedan had a blanket, an umbrella and a pair of galoshes in the trunk, along with the traditional scissor jack. The final item was an old tire iron. Not the new chrome-plated 4-way tire irons which had become popular recently, but the old school black powder coat type with the lug wrench on one side and a narrow tapered end on the other. After a cursory inspection he slipped it inside his belt, opposite the .357. That would signal to anyone else who might see him that he was armed and not to be taken lightly but without being as confrontational as wearing the gun for all to see.

Just as he was beginning to feel more comfortable with this situation, an explosion tore through the air washing Corey in a wave of heat, throwing him to the ground.

13

L.A. Fitness – Atlanta, GA

"Keep 'em up," the young lady repeated. Roger and Jennifer stood there with their hands at ear level. The fingers shifted their grip on the weapon's handle. The one finger that really concerned Roger was worthy of that concern. Her index finger was inside the trigger guard and constantly shifting on the trigger. If the woman had any decent training she would have either kept her finger out of the trigger well or provided steady pressure on the trigger. The fact that she was violating two basic rules of firearms handling meant she either had poor training or no training. It was far more favorable to be held at gunpoint by someone you could trust not to shoot you by accident.

Another shadow crept out of the shadow. The tall one. That made the shadow with the gun the shorter of the two.

"OK, they're up." Jenny twitched her hands as if to confirm they were in the air.

The gun twitched in her direction, "Good, now shut up."

"Naomi," the short shadow said, "it's good. Keep calm." She stepped out of the shadow, into the light from the windows above.

The one called Naomi twitched the gun at Jennifer, "First you. Turn around slowly." Jennifer turned, leaving her hands in the air. "No good. Take off the top. I wanna see if you've got a gun."

"I don't," Jennifer said. She moved her hands down and grabbed the front of the velour top. "I don't have anything on under it either." She nodded at Roger, "And I'm a bit shy."

"Bitch, I don't care if you-" Naomi flicked the weapon again. "If I tell you to strip down and I have the gun, you're going to strip down."

"Hang on. Hang on." The taller one stepped up to her compatriot. "We're not doing it this way."

"Look," Jennifer said, "you can frisk me if you want-"

"Are you fucking kidding me?" The gun bobbed around as Naomi appeared to have a tendency to speak with her hands. "You know what's going on out there? People's dyin' in the streets out there. There's some kind of bug goin' round killin' people. You think we wanna touch your ass? Unzip the top and lift it up!"

"Ok. Ok." Jennifer took a half step back, behind Roger's line of sight. She ran the zipper down and grabbed the hem, opening the top and lifting it higher. She exposed herself and slowly turned, verifying her lack of weapons. At a nod from Naomi she dropped the flaps, her hands still at shoulder level.

"Good. Now zip it up." When Jennifer complied the gun shifted toward Roger. "Now you. Shirt off. Turn around."

Roger shrugged, slowly lowered his hands and slipped the shirt over his head. He turned around slowly, showing a body that had once been an athletic teen but had slid only somewhat gracefully into middle age. When no weapon was revealed, Naomi relaxed a bit and lowered her own. Roger noticed that her finger never left the trigger, even now that she was effectively pointing the weapon at her own foot.

"If I could make a suggestion?" He pulled the shirt back over his head.

"Prolly not but whacha got?" Naomi flicked the weapon with the question.

"Your trigger finger." Roger waved vaguely in the direction of her hand. "It's good practice not to put your finger on the trigger until you're ready to pull it."

"Oh, don't you worry 'bout that." Naomi gesticulated with the weapon again, "I'm ready to pull it any time I need."

"I'm sure." Roger pointed at the gun again, obviously this girl needed to be stepped through the thought process. "What I mean is you could accidentally shoot someone if your finger is on the trigger."

"Roger?" Jennifer said, "Maybe this is not the correct time."

"No, it's good." He made calming motions at Jennifer then turned back to Naomi. "See, you're pointing the gun at your foot. You could shoot yourself. When you talk with your hands you could shoot your friend."

Naomi looked at the gun, almost as if really seeing it for the first time. She wrapped her index finger around the hand grip, crowding the other fingers down and throwing off the balance of the weapon.

"Ok, safer, but not better." Roger made a fist of his right hand then pointed his index finger. He turned so that she could see how the hand was positioned. "Like this, but place your finger along the frame of the weapon until you're ready to shoot. That way you have just a short distance to move and you don't have to move your other fingers."

She positioned her hand as shown, gripped the handle and relaxed her hand. "Yeah, that's good. Much better."

She lifted it again, horizontally so the ejection port was pointing up. "That's real good. Just a flick and I can pop a cap in your ass."

Roger shook his head. "Didn't anyone teach you anything about gun handling? Don't hold it like that. Turn your hand so it is up and down, not on the side."

"What are you some kind of professor? If I want - "

"Oh. Sorry, yes. I can see the confusion."

"Yes what?" Naomi dropped the hand so the gun pointed at the ground again. This time Roger was somewhat proud that her finger rode the frame rather than riding the trigger.

"Yes, I'm a professor. Well, adjunct faculty to be more precise."

"Roger!" Everyone looked at Jennifer. "It was rhetorical. And is this really the best time to be giving shooting lessons? To our captors?"

"Oh, I see your point." Roger looked back at Naomi, "Sorry. You'll have to figure out the rest on your own."

"You some kind a - " Naomi was cut short by her companion.

"That's enough Naomi. I think these two are safe enough." She turned to the captives when Naomi shrugged. "What were you doing in here?"

"We just ducked in earlier to get some rest." Jennifer adjusted the waist of her jogging suit now that it looked like the immediate danger had passed.

"When we woke up we saw you and tried to sneak out the back." Roger tossed a thumb over his shoulder toward the offices. "Seems I needed more practice picking locks and then you know the rest."

Naomi twitched the gun but it mostly still remained pointing downward. "Why didn't you just say sumthin'?"

Roger used a corresponding twitch to signal her weapon. "Kinda don't like having guns pointed at us. Didn't want to get in a situation where that might happen."

"Oh. Um." Almost appearing embarrassed, Naomi slipped the gun into the waistband of her pants.

The taller woman spoke up, "I'm Sheila. We've been running since this thing started. Guess we forgot how to be polite."

"Probably for the best." Roger tucked his shirt back into the waistband of his pants. "If you don't have personal protective equipment it's best not to interact with others more than necessary."

Naomi seemed unable to say anything without using her hands. "What we thought. If I knew you was tryin' to leave I never woulda stopped you." They were all still maintaining twenty or more feet of spacing between the groups.

"So we can go?" Jennifer slowly lowered her hands and shrugged some relaxation back into her shoulders.

"Can, but I wouldn't." Sheila backed away a few steps, making sure the path out of the fitness center was unobstructed or, more likely, that Roger and Jennifer didn't get close enough to cough or sneeze on her if they chose to make a break for it.

"Why not?" Jennifer bent down to pick up her pack. Naomi's hand jumped to the handle of her pistol.

Sheila swatted Naomi's hand before replying, "Because the sun's almost up." Jennifer's eyebrows crinkled a question so Sheila continued, "People are out there who'll shoot you just to see if you have anything they want. Best to wait until after dark if you want to move about. Some of 'em have night vision so that's no guarantee but it's sumthin."

"But we really need to get home." Roger retrieved his pack and slung it over his shoulder. "Long way to go."

"Didn't think you was from here." Naomi stepped back beside Sheila, making sure there was plenty of room for Roger and Jennifer if they decided to leave.

"Nope." Roger shrugged the pack straps on his shoulders. "It'll be great if we can find a car or something, but we've got to get some distance behind us."

"Where you goin?" Sheila made it a question of curiosity, but she had been so quiet to this point even Roger figured there was some hidden reason behind the question.

Jennifer responded before Roger had a chance, "Why, you got a car we can use?"

"Naw. Just wonderin. We from here. Really ain't got nowhere else to go. Just wonderin what's better than here." Jennifer didn't think that was the complete answer but suspected that she wouldn't get a complete answer, so she let it drop.

"Wouldn't stay around too long." Roger nodded toward the door and Jennifer nodded back.

"Why not? Ain't you worried about people shootin at 'cha?" Naomi stepped further back, keeping away from the professor and the woman.

"Very worried. That's why I wouldn't stay around here much longer. When people start coming back to the city it won't be a fun place to be. That's when the shooting will start in earnest."

☣ ☣ ☣

Jennifer stuck close to Roger as they made their way out of the LA Fitness and across the car-strewn parking lot. They crossed the highway, then ducked into the woods on the other side. The entire time she was expecting a yell or a gun shot from behind. Once the view was blocked from the shopping center she let out a tense sigh. "So," she asked, "did you mean that? Or were you just trying to scare them?"

"Mean what?"

"About the city and people coming back." She sped up her steps so she'd be even with him and not just talking to his back.

"Oh, of course. It will be much more dangerous very soon. I'm surprised it hasn't started already. The timeline seems to be off by a few days." Roger shrugged as if it was of no consequence.

"I need more than that Roger."

"What?" He paused in his hike. "Oh! Right. For future reference, if I ask if you meant something *I* only meant to ask if you *meant* something. It is a point of clarification, not necessarily a request for elaboration."

"Good to know." Jennifer looked at him. Some days he seemed so normal. Others he was so *Roger*. "For future reference, there are more people who mean it the way I do than the way you do."

"I'll take that under advisement." He nodded as if he were, seriously, filing it away for future contemplation. "Back to your original question, yes, I expect things are about to get much worse. This is a massive event.

"Humans are creatures of habit. Traditionally we do the same things in a routine manner, in a routine place. Left to our own we tend to stay with what is comfortable and familiar. Like addiction, familiarity is one of the reasons that people continue to do things which are unhealthy even if they know it is unhealthy. It is familiar and they take comfort in the familiarity." When he paused it was almost for dramatic effect. For the first time Jennifer got the impression of what Roger may have been like as an instructor. "When the stimulus that inspired a departure from the norm is removed, or sufficiently reduced, we tend to return to our habitual behaviors.

"In this instance people were dying all around and as a society we are unfamiliar with death. We do virtually everything we can do to remain unfamiliar with it. We don't even acknowledge that people die anymore. They 'pass on', 'cross over', or 'join their maker'. The word death is becoming taboo. You see-"

"Are you still on track to answer my question?"

"Oh, right. So we had this major event that made people break their habits. Fear is a primary motivator for humans." Jennifer marveled that he said the word 'humans' as if they were some test subject he had studied rather than a species to which he belonged. "It is enough of a motivator to cause a deviation from normal behavior. However, once the fear stimulus is removed entirely or replaced to a sufficient capacity by another stimulus, the subjects may return to pre-fear activities.

"The hypothesis is that fear of the unknown, coupled with starvation once readily available food sources are depleted, will force those who are fearful to return to previous activities in familiar environments. So I am operating under the supposition that people are going to quickly run out of food. Once they have developed a high enough degree of hunger, they will return *en masse* to the city and try to scrounge whatever they can find. If what we have encountered is any indication, they will not find much and will begin turning against others who are attempting to scavenge resources. When parents see starving children, or spouses see their starving spouses, there will be very little they will not do to get food. Certainly some will try to live by yesterday's rules, but they will be the first victims of those who have accepted the change."

"Not a lot of happy thoughts in there Roger." Jennifer shrugged to settle her pack on her back, but she wasn't sure if the shrug was for the physical or psychological discomfort she was feeling.

"Not a lot of happy thoughts flying around these days. Best to understand what we're dealing with so we're not caught by surprise. We haven't seen many yet, but they're here. And there's about to be more of them."

"And you think they are going to be trouble makers?"

"No. Survivors." In a moment of clarity Jennifer rarely witnessed with Roger, he turned to her, his face completely serious. "The rules have changed. We can't judge by old standards. There is still good and evil. We used to have an easier time determining which is which though. Now it won't be about the specific actions, it will be about the motives."

"You're kind of scaring me Roger." Jennifer shrugged the backpack again, watching her feet as they trudged through the woods.

"Well, I'm not trying to." His clear-eyed gaze pierced her again, "But I'm not trying not to either. We're in a world of trouble here and got a long way to go."

"So, Texas, huh? You're walking all the way to Texas?"

"I hope to drive part of the way. If we can find a vehicle it would certainly improve our chances of making it. And the goal is Arkansas, assuming everything is still turned upside down by then. Just Arkansas by way of Texas."

"But isn't Arkansas closer? Why not just straight there?"

They crouched in the woods as they came to a road cutting across their path. Roger gave his hand signals. After a few moments of waiting and listening he signaled for her to go. Once she made it safely across he low-ran over to join her. Again they crouched and waited. When it appeared they had made the crossing unobserved, Roger signaled for them to move out. Jennifer had just begun to wonder if he had forgotten that she had asked a question when he finally answered.

"I gotta find the kids. My boy is in Denton. North of Fort Worth. So is Ashley. Probably his ex by now but she'll always be a daughter to me." The serious look from earlier was replaced by a wistful look now. "I heard from her just as the airport was closing down. Nothing since. Nothing at all from Corey. I just hope nothin's happened to 'em."

14

On I-35 – Denton, TX

Corey picked himself up and brushed the dirt from his pants. Less than a half mile away, right where Avenue D crossed over the freeway, a pillar of smoke was blossoming into a dense black flower. The stem was trailing down to a gas station across from the entrance to the university. He couldn't see it from where he was, but he had passed it often enough to know what was there.

Over the ringing in his ears he could make out someone yelling. Bending at the waist he ran to the edge of the freeway, staying low to the grassy embankment. The yelling continued as he made his way closer to the smoke. He crouched as he walked up the onramp, keeping low, hoping he would see what was going on before anyone saw him. As luck would have it, the people were preoccupied at the gas station and Corey was able to make it all the way up the onramp and across the frontage road to the lawn in front of the performing arts building. About two hundred yards away, the entrance to UNT was signified by a large sign on a small hill. He positioned himself where the sign blocked his view of the gas station, and thus the station's view of him, then jogged up to the sign. Now about a football field away from the station he could more easily hear the yelling but still could not make out what was being said.

Taking quick peeks around the sign, he scoped out the situation. Three men were arguing toward the south side of the gas station building. The building itself was on fire with a car embedded in the north side. The ports to the underground fuel tanks were geysers of flame. Fire shot up fifty feet, and the heavy black smoke continued to boil out. The awning over the gas pumps was rolled back, the paint seared off. Further north several cars set in an old IHOP parking lot, their windows a spider web of cracks where any glass remained. It appeared to be a war zone where a huge bomb had gone off.

The gas station building provided some shelter to the three men who argued in its shadow. Corey knew that he would be in the open too long to avoid being seen if he tried to sneak up. The roar of the fire would be too loud for him to hear anything even if he made it to the building unnoticed. The choice came down to leaving these guys alone or approaching in the open. As these were the first people he'd seen – other than the bitch – in over a week, he was finding it difficult to just walk away.

Finally, he set down his five gallon bucket with his scavenged supplies behind the sign. A quick check to make sure the tire iron was still wedged in his belt. The .357 was still tucked in the holster, hidden under his shirt. It gave him the extra slice of confidence he needed. Placing his back against the University of North Texas sign one more time and taking a deep, cleansing breath allowed him to clear his mind. He turned and headed across the street without further hesitation.

It seemed the roar from the flames was getting louder with each step. The distance from the sign to the gas station was close to 100 yards. He was surprised that he made the first sixty to seventy yards without drawing their attention. Once he was spotted though, their argument ended and they formed up in a V. The front man kept his eyes on Corey. The two in the rear scanned the area, looking for anyone else who might be sneaking up on them. Corey held his hands up at chest level, not really an indication of surrender but high enough that they could see he wasn't holding any weapons.

The guys were dressed similarly enough that they probably shopped at the same stores. Each had on black biker boots and faded blue jeans with greasy dirt stains. A wide black leather belt made the transition to the faded black T-shirt the lead man wore. On the left of the belt he had a hunting knife strapped in a leather holster. On the right was another leather holster. This one held a handgun but Corey couldn't identify it at this distance. A ragged beard outlined an even more ragged face. Without running water it was difficult to keep up proper hygiene, but Corey suspected this guy's greasy long hair was probably in the same style and condition it had been last month, last year, or even last decade. The other two had on filthy old blue jean jackets with the sleeves cut out. Similar hunting knives and sidearms rounded out the ensembles with the guy in the back right adding a hunting rifle across his back.

The hunting rifle slid off the man's shoulder to be held causally across his chest. He had red splotches on his neck and face that pretty much matched the size of the lead-man's fist. The rifleman's left eye was already beginning to swell shut. From long experience with rough and tumble nights, Corey knew the thing would be completely swollen and three shades of purple by this time tomorrow.

Together the guys must have had a good bit of confidence. Corey walked up to the curb to the gas station, less than 20 yards from the group before the leader held up his hand for Corey to stop. "Whatcha got there, Chief?"

Corey shook his head, keeping his hands up at chest level, "Nothing. Just heard the explosion and the yelling. First people I've seen in a week. Thought I'd come check it out."

"Well, now you've done that. You can be on your way." The leader hooked his thumbs in his belt, the right hand laying on the handgun holster.

All his life Corey had been dismissed by people who thought they were cooler, better looking, smarter or just plain tougher. The world had changed and it was time he changed with it. *Nothing tough guys appreciate more than toughness.*

"Naw," he said, "I ain't done looking." He took a step off the curb, into the parking lot for the station. This prompted the leader and the other hand gunner in the back to shift their weapons. They still hadn't drawn them, but they were attempting to show they were willing.

"See, Chief, I think you didn't understand. I'm letting you go. You stick around and I might not be so nice." The leader wrapped his hand around the handle of the weapon, fingers curled, index finger laying along the length of the slide. At this distance Corey could tell it was an auto-loader and not a revolver.

"I'll go in a minute." Corey didn't risk the next step forward but thought he was setting himself up to be shot in the back if he turned back now. He dropped his hands to a more relaxed position though he was anything but relaxed. *No use letting these guys think they're intimidating me.* "What happened here?"

The rifleman had obviously had enough, he raised the rifle in a show of force but didn't settle it to his shoulder. "Hell of a lotta none-your-fuckin-business!"

Corey smiled at the guy, trying out his best, go-screw-yourself grin. His guts were turning flips as he tried to cover his fear. "You know, you might want to shut your fucking pie hole, asswipe."

"Yeah, or what?" The rifle finally seated itself against the guy's shoulder.

"Or your friend here," Corey nodded to the leader, "might just decide he needs to beat the shit out of you a little more."

The leader chuckled, apparently honestly amused by the display of bravado. He raised his hand and signaled the rifleman to lower the weapon. The rifle dropped and was slung over the man's shoulder. "I gotta say, Chief, you got some *cajoles*. Whatcha wanna know?"

It looked like the stand-off had come to its end. For now Corey's bowels relaxed. The urge to soil himself receded.

"So, what happened?" He nodded toward the geysers of flame and black smoke.

"Sammy-boy." The leader dropped his hand off his weapon and the three crossed the parking lot so they could see the inferno. "One of our guys. He was using the fuel pump from the car" he jabbed his thumb toward the vehicle protruding from the building, "and there must have been a spark or something. Pretty heavy fumes though. Sammy wasn't the smartest. Maybe he stopped to light up a smoke."

They crossed the parking lot and stood next to Corey to watch the flames. He didn't realize until too late that they had positioned themselves on three sides. At some unspoken prompt they jumped him.

The first hit was a straight jab from the second hand gunner. It caught Corey on the left jaw and was just enough to stun him. The rifleman hit him from behind, making him stumble forward into the leader, who quickly grabbed him by the back of the head and forced Corey's head downward as his own knee came up. The combined impact was so jarring Corey had no idea how he ended up on the ground or how long it had been. All he knew was that he woke up with something warm splattering his face.

Corey shrugged out of the stream to look up. The leader was relieving himself and using Corey's face as a target. The second handgunner had a firm grasp on Corey's tire iron and the pain from his left knee told him it had already been used at least once.

Rolling on his side, trying to dodge the stream of urine, he still had enough presence of mind to roll to his right. That allowed his hand to slip under his shirt and grasp the revolver. The move was hidden from the trio who were more intent on talking about their next move than watching him.

The leader laughed at the sight of Corey writhing on the ground. "He wants to play with the big boys? He wants to show us he has balls? Let's see 'em. Rolling 'im over and get those pants down."

Handgunner and Rifleman grabbed Corey by his feet and rolled him. He resisted rolling on his back so they twisted the other direction. He allowed them to roll him to the left. He swung the revolver into position and pulled the trigger.

The boom immediately cut the trio's laughter short. Rifleman took the shot to his gut. Corey had tried to shoot him in the head but he had never shot from this angle and everything was off. The second was rushed, and caught Handgunner in the left thigh. The leader, was scrambling for his handgun, ducking away from the screaming Rifleman. That position just brought his head within easy range and Corey fired point blank, just above the guy's ear. He crumpled, dead before hitting the pavement.

Rifleman was backing up, his hands trying to keep the spill of blood from leaving his stomach. With staggering steps he turned and began to walk away. Corey lined up another shot and realized the blood-soaked spot on the back of the man's shirt must be the exit wound. It was already the size of a large man's fist and getting larger.

Handgunner had fallen over his shattered left leg. He captured Corey's attention by grunting when he tried to pull his weapon from its holster. The force of the fall had carried the man down and now the gun was trapped under him. Corey snapped off another shot, catching the man above the left breast pocket of the denim vest, and another in the man's neck.

He turned his attention back to the rifleman, carefully lined up the shot and pulled the trigger. The hammer fell on a dead chamber. Corey was out of bullets. He forced himself to his feet and dug for the speed loader in his pocket. He wasn't sure if they were .38s or if they were .357s, but he shoved them in the cylinder as soon as the empty shells were ejected. With shaking hands this took much longer than he anticipated.

By the time he was loaded and ready again, he was out of targets. Whether through shock or death, all three of his assailants lay in motionless heaps on the ground. Corey retrieved his tire iron and approached each man. The leader was absolutely dead, N*o way to survive that much of your head missing.*

Handgunner appeared to have expired as well. Corey wasn't sure if any of the bullets had inflicted a fatal wound or if it was shock that did the trick. Whatever it was, the guy was dead and not just faking. Finally, Corey crossed to the Rifleman.

This guy wasn't moving but he was still breathing. Corey raised the revolver, his finger tightened. *Hang on*, he thought. *No use wasting bullets!*

He hefted the tire iron and as his vision clouded red, he pounded downward. Several blood-soaked minutes later he sat back, out of breath. His hand was somehow slick and sticky at the same time. Somewhere along the way he had lost the tire iron. It lay a few feet away and his hand hurt as if he had been punching the ground. *Maybe I was.*

He stood and started to wipe his hands on his shirt but thought better of it. He crossed back to the leader and ripped off a large panel of his T-shirt. Using that to wipe his hands, he threw the rag to the ground and stepped back. Surveying the scene, he took it all in. The columns of flame and smoke, the burned out, blown up car and gas station, three dead bodies leaking on the old faded asphalt parking lot. *Somehow I thought I'd feel worse about killing someone. Maybe I* was *born for this world after all.*

☣ ☣ ☣

Ashley was sitting at her table still processing the medicines when she heard the explosion that rattled her window and door. Stepping to the window she couldn't see anything. Opening the front door earned her a view to the south where a roiling black cloud was still inflating like a greasy black balloon. Birds were scattering in all directions, scattered from their perches by the sudden noise.

This was the first sign of human activity she had seen for days - if it was human activity. She returned to the table and continued researching her inventory. The last thing she needed to do was get entangled with the situation going on out there. After sundown was early enough to investigate, and she needed to get this inventory done during daylight while she didn't have to use fuel for light and possibly give away her location. When gun shots rang out from the direction of the explosion she stood, crossed to the door and closed it, ensuring the deadbolt was set.

Maybe I'll wait until tomorrow to see what that was.

15

Outskirts of Atlanta

Just after Highway 6 crossed Old Fairburn Road it took a northward turn. At the end of that bend in the road a utility corridor cut through the woods, providing a cross-country route that was off any major roadway. Except for a few close encounters with dogs where the corridor butted up against neighborhoods, the way was clear and mostly uneventful. It was good travelling until they reached the Chattahoochee River and there was a 200 foot wet gap in their throughway. It had only been about six miles of walking but trying to stay concealed in the edge of the woods and not attract any attention had slowed them considerably. Consulting his McNally Road Atlas, something he had kept in his carry-on bag for years, Roger could see that Highway 92 crossed the river about a mile and a half to the south.

Highway 154 to the north with more neighborhood-like roads shown on the map, an indicator of greater habitation to Roger's mind. The closer, less populated crossing made the most sense. Besides, if Roger was guessing the lay of the land correctly, he might be able to pick up the utility lane again after the south crossing. He wished such things were shown on the map. At least he had appropriate maps for his homestead back home. But getting there almost seemed to be a dream at this point. That dream gave him something to fight for.

Roger looked up at the sun. "It's going to be dark in about two hours. I don't wanna try that bridge until after that." They were settled about fifteen feet into the tree line, watching the bridge. He dug out a couple of power bars and a water bottle, passing one of the bars to Jennifer. "Try to get some rest. I'll keep an eye on the bridge. Once we get across and somewhere safe on the other side, we'll bed down and I'll get some rest."

Jennifer was exhausted. Back when she was married to Paul she had been the workout queen in her social circle. Five miles on the treadmill was just a good start to her day. She would usually do that at home *before* going to the gym. Sure, since the arrest and the divorce she had slacked off with the workouts a bit, but she still jogged at least five miles three times a week either on the treadmill or out on the streets of her neighborhood. She had the cardio of a race horse. At least that is what she thought before hiking six miles next to Roger.

Somehow this middle aged not-quite-dumpy guy had out paced her over the course of the day. He had scouted forward, cleared areas and come back to her time and again, probably covering at least eight or nine miles while she covered six. Now that they were stopped he looked like he'd had a bad day at the office. She felt like an office building had fallen on her.

"How do you do it?" She cracked open the bottle of water. It was warm but the taste was better than any ice cold water she ever remembered. "How do you keep up that pace like that? You don't look like the gym type to me."

Roger nodded, taking a swig of his water as well. She noticed that he actually drizzled a little water into his mouth, swished it around and then drank it down. He did it every time they stopped. "I don't go to the gym. You're right I'm not that type."

She tried the drizzle, swish, swallow routine. Strange, with the cold water she was accustomed to, you got the water in you and went on with your day. The warm water wasn't as refreshing. However, when she swished first, it covered her entire mouth and seemed to alleviate the thirst better. She'd have to try it next time before taking the first big gulp. "So, how then? I thought I was in pretty good shape before today."

He nodded again, "From everything I can tell, you're in excellent shape." He cast an eye up and down. She remembered a similar look back on the first day they'd met. At that time it seemed rude and inappropriate. Now she felt he was simply confirming his opinion, like a vet verifying a horse's leg was still intact. She gave him the 'come-on' rolling hand gesture and he continued. "From what I can tell, you're probably one of those gym people. For being a gym person you're in good shape.

"I like the outdoors. I like hiking and camping. I like to camp where no one is around. I don't like spending money so I don't go for all the new ultra light-weight gadgets they are coming out with for the rich preppy hikers. So I use heavy gear and walk in the woods or into the hills or up the mountain, and I take whatever I need with me. The military has a saying, paraphrased: 'you fight the way you train'.

"You go to the gym in the air conditioning with light weight tennis shoes or soft soled running shoes on level ground, your Spandex pants and a tank top with a towel over your shoulder in case you start to sweat. That is better than nothing, but it isn't training for this type of movement. Where I go, the terrain is much worse than this. The pack is usually heavier and the air thinner. But don't kick yourself, you're doing well enough."

"Well enough?" She laughed but what he said made sense. Somehow the energy bar he had given her had magically disappeared down her throat along with the last of her water. She packed her trash away, *leave only footprints*, but there was one lingering question, "So why don't you have the bod of some Greek god then? If you're in such good shape?"

He quirked his head and his eyebrows knitted together. Not like he was confused, but like he expected she would have been able to figure that out for herself. "Because I like food and don't give in to the aesthetics of others. Instead of doing crunches to have six-pack abs, I'd rather get where I'm going and sit back with a six pack. Much more enjoyable."

She started to ask another question but he held up a finger. "You're tired," he said, "and your brain is fighting it because you're not used to traveling like this. Lay down and go to sleep. I'll wake you when we're ready."

As if his command had some mystic quality, Jenny found she truly was sleepy. She laid down, only intending to rest her eye. For the second night in a row she couldn't remember her eyelids fully closing.

☣ ☣ ☣

Roger gathered the empty water bottles and slipped down to the river. He found an area where he was somewhat sheltered from sight by a stand of trees which ran right up to the water. Taking a bandana from his pack, he folded it into a tight square of at least eight layers and held this to the mouth of the bottle. Using that as an improvised large-particle filter, he strained the river water into four bottles. Returning to the sleeping Jennifer, he dug in his pack again and pulled out a small brown bottle with several tiny tablets in it. The iodine would kill enough of the microorganisms in the water that it should be safe enough to drink. He wished he knew more about the Chattahoochee because no amount of iodine tablets and bandana filtering would keep out toxins. It was an unfortunate truth that gas, oil and fertilizers were toxic and found in pretty good concentrations in most of the country's free flowing waterways. *Well, trying it might kill you, not trying it definitely will. Survival is all about playing the averages. No use worrying Jennifer with this particular calculation though.*

If he had the time, and an area where he wouldn't easily be witnessed, he would have built a small fire and boiled the water in the canteen cup he carried just for that purpose. Boiling was better because it didn't require the use of a nonsustainable resource, the iodine tablets, and because the water tasted better after boiling than after iodine treatment. *I'm sure there will be plenty of time to boil water on this trip.*

☣ ☣ ☣

Roger watched a few people cross the bridge. Three went from the east to the west and one traveled from the west to the east. None of them appeared to be walking too carefully or obviously avoiding any particular spot on the bridge. When night fell a few people crossed using flashlights. They didn't pause, just walked across and there appeared to be no one guarding the bridge or conducting a check point. If Roger had lived in the area he would definitely have encouraged guards and checkpoints. For now, this served his purpose better.

Using a common military tactic, he settled in and waited. Now that people had become accustomed to a lack of openly available electricity, their sleep schedules would be changing to accommodate a new light schedule. It was a biological drive to sleep during the dark. Without artificial lights to keep them stimulated, people would start going to sleep when the sun went down. Of course this wouldn't happen immediately, and he wasn't sure when the light had actually gone out this far away from the city, but he knew the new rhythm would be taking over. He had to fight to stay awake himself.

Originally he had intended to make the crossing around 2:00 AM. This was traditionally thought to be the time when people were the least aware. Sleepers would be in deep slumber and people on night watch would be in that twilight stage between just being woken up and the giddiness that comes with extended sleep deprivation. As preferable as that would have been, he was simply having too much difficulty staying awake. It was midnight and if he waited two more hours it was likely he'd just wake up with the sunrise.

He gently rocked Jennifer's shoulder. In groggy stages she slipped the bonds of sleep, and after a few minutes she was sitting up, rubbing her eyes. Roger poured a pack of instant coffee saved from an airport MRE into one of the treated water bottles and shook it until he was pretty sure it was mixed.

"It isn't hot. There will be a chemical aftertaste, but we'll get a bit of caffeine in our system. Cream or sugar?"

Jennifer took the proffered bottle and unscrewed the cap. She took a swig, swished it around in her mouth and swallowed it down. The taste hit her like a kick in the teeth. She tried to hold it back, but the brown sludge made its way back up and she barely had time to turn away from Roger before emptying the coffee and a good bit of bile on the ground.

"Gotcha," he said, "cream *and* sugar." Roger retrieved the bottle and dumped in three packs of non-dairy creamer and three packs of sugar. After another vigorous shake he returned it to her. This time she took a smaller drink and simply swallowed. The cream and sugar helped but it was the second most vile thing she had ever put in her mouth. Second only to the same stuff before the cream and sugar.

She marveled at Roger. He sat there drinking the stuff like he was in a diner back home. "What about you? Don't you have any taste buds?"

"Taste buds?" He thought about it. "Yup, plenty of taste buds. Just lower expectations." If she hadn't known better she would have thought Roger smiled after saying that, as if at a joke.

Crazy man!

☣ ☣ ☣

All that preparation, observation and worry was for nothing. Roger and Jennifer crept along the bank of the river until they were practically under the bridge. They climbed the bank, hopped over the wood-post-and-corrugated-metal guardrail and jogged across the football field length bridge. On the other side a green sign informed them they were entering Douglas County. Another 100 yards and the road made a tangle of itself by splitting into three forks. The couple continued through the intersection and reentered the woods just beyond. Less than twenty feet into the woods and it cleared again for the utility corridor. Since there weren't any high voltage lines visible, Roger assumed it was probably a pipeline.

They sprinted across the flat, open field that served as a runway for a little airport and took a few minutes to find their way into the gap between the trees on the other side. Staying near the edge of the trees, but moving quickly carried them across a two lane highway, up an embankment, across another small road and once again along the utility clearing. The sound of generators told where a few houses were nestled in the woods. Roger kept the pace until they were well clear of those noises. Just as the eastern sky started to lighten he led Jennifer into the woods. He threw out a couple of large beach-type towels from the fitness center to serve as bedding, gave his good-night and dropped immediately to sleep.

☣ ☣ ☣

He rolled over and the sun was directly overhead. A root was burrowing into his back and the beach towel he'd laid down as a sheet was crumpled in a ball. The other one was wrapped around his upper torso, shoulder and head. At first he thought someone had bound him in his own bedding. He jolted up, throwing off the make-shift blanket.

A finger immediately pressed to his lips. Squinting against the sun, it took a moment to make out Jennifer's face. Even after a trek like they'd had the last few days, sleeping when and where they could, no shower and no make-up, she was still a beautiful woman. Roger shook the cobwebs from his mind and opened his mouth to say something. She pushed her finger more firmly to his lips, then did the same to her own.

Using a nod of the chin Jennifer indicated the direction of the path then cupped a hand to her ear. Roger froze in place and listened.

It sounded like several people were walking down the utility corridor, moving back toward Atlanta. They were speaking quietly but they were still loud enough that Roger was able to make out at least five distinct voices. The sound of the voices, however, was second only to the sounds of their trudging along the path. It almost sounded like they were deliberately making noise. Branches snapped and there were the various metal-on-metal or plastic-on-plastic sounds of poorly secured backpacks and hiking gear.

Jennifer quiet-spoke, "Someone else came through about fifteen minutes ago. I almost didn't hear that one. Then these came through and I think they woke you up." She passed him a water bottle and a power bar, saying, "Last one."

Roger nodded and took a swig of the water. It was more of the treated water and with the chemical taste he would have almost preferred to remain thirsty. No time for taste right now though, it was about hydration and survival. He broke the bar in half, and passed a portion back to Jennifer. He'd thought that she might protest and he'd have to force her to take it. She didn't. She ate her portion without protest and with more a look of gratitude than disapproval.

The sounds were fading off in the distance as the group continued on its way. "Did you get a look at them" he asked.

Jennifer shook her head, "Didn't want to draw any attention. Stayed here and tried to keep you from snoring." A shy smile curled her lips. "Must only happen when you're really tired. You snored a bit back at the fitness center but none at the airport. This time, wow. I thought some lumberjacks were going to come over and tell you to keep it down!"

"Oh, sorry about that." Melissa had told him that he snored when he went to bed unusually tired but that had been so long ago he had forgotten. Other than disturbing his wife, snoring wasn't a major issue previously. Now it really could get you killed. He vowed to try to control it but the best way he could think to do that was simply to get more sleep! *A Catch-22.*

"All right," he said aloud, "there was someone fifteen minutes ahead of that group, let's wait fifteen to thirty once we can't hear them any more and move out. A group that size would draw the attention of anyone with ill will and enough strength to do something about it. So we should be clear for a couple of hours. Let's see if we can make some headway."

No one else came through during the next half hour.

They moved out, through areas where generators were running in the distance. This gave some clue as to where homes were hidden in the canopy. Now, they had been in the quiet of nature for a while. Animals still scampered through the woods, birds sang and crickets chirped, but there had been no sound of other people. What made them pause was the smell.

They had become far too familiar with the smell of putrefaction on their journey out of the city and coming across it here so far removed from that horror somehow made the smell even worse. Roger glanced around as they slowly moved up the cleared route through the woods. Finally he saw another area deeper in the woods where there was a gap in the tree canopy. Focusing his attention lower toward the ground, he was able to make out the side of a house. With the next breeze he understood this was the origin of the smell. Someone had died in that house and they were still there.

16

Corey's Apartment – Denton, TX

Ashley unlatched the padlock and opened Corey's door. Since the explosion and gun fire she had been worried about him. He was stuck here without any idea of what was going on in the world. *Surely there is some part of him interested about what's going on now.*

She no longer had her HAZMAT suit. Once it was penetrated she lost trust in its integrity and had trashed it in the dumpster. That left her with a lower grade of protection. Rather than the bulky plasticized yellow suit, she now wore two layers of white painter's jumpsuits, complete with booties, a respirator and rubber gloves. Corey had shown no sign of the virus yet, and she doubted he had it, but protocols were established for a reason. She needed to wait the full week before she lowered her guard.

When the door swung open Ashley was a bit surprised by what she saw. There hadn't been a solid image of what she was expecting but the reality was disappointing. Nothing had changed. His dirty clothes were still piled in the floor. The shattered light bulb glass was pushed to the side rather than swept up. Opened food packages were strewn about the room and Corey was laying in his bed with the sheets pulled up, completely covering his head.

"Hey, sleepy," she tried to force levity into her voice but the room had taken some wind out of her sails. *I thought he'd clean up with nothing else to do. Maybe he'd be taking this situation seriously. Guess not.* "Hey, it's me."

"Who else could it be? You're my prison guard, right? What do you want?" His voice was groggy and he didn't move to lower the sheet.

"Um, I had a spare radio and thought you might want it." She held up the small hand-held, crank-powered radio. When he didn't look she let out an exasperated sigh. "Look. I'm sorry that I've had to lock you up like this. It really is for the best though."

"Sorry enough to let me out?" The form under the sheet moved as if he was turning toward her.

"No." She hung her head. *Protocols are protocols.* "Just a few more days. It's as much for your protection as mine. I might be sick and you don't want to be exposed to me either."

He didn't respond. "Look," she said again, still trying to hold on to a little empathy for him, "I know it sucks-"

"Do you? Really? You get to run around all day and do whatever you want and I'm stuck here! Do you really know how much that sucks?"

"No. OK? I'll give you that." She hung her head and took another cleansing breath. *It really had to suck, but he had to bored. He doesn't read, doesn't do anything away from his damn games. This must be killing him. But protocols are protocols and they are in place for a reason.* "That doesn't change what we have to do. It won't be much longer.

"I was thinking," she tried to change the subject, "that we should try to press on once we know we're both healthy. Your Dad's cabin. I know he had several people who were planning to go there if something happened. And something *has happened,* so I bet there are quite a few people who have bugged out up there. I was thinking we might try to make our way to the cabin. It's gotta be safer there with more people than it is here, trying to live off a city with a bunch of dead people everywhere."

"So you're not here to let me out?" He sounded hurt, like she had disappointed him. The sheet over his head didn't allow her to see his face, but she had known him long enough to know his tone of voice.

"No. I just came to check on you. And talk about planning to go to-"

"You know, you can just plan on going to Hell for all I'm concerned! If you aren't here to let me out, just fuck off why doncha?" The sheets spasmed as Corey rolled away from her.

"But I-"

"You don't get it. Fuck the *fuck* off! When you're ready to let me out I'll talk but I won't talk to someone keeping me in prison!"

Ashley hung her head again. She placed the radio just inside the doorway and closed the door. She clasped the padlock again and carefully laid it against the door before making her way outside, back to her bike.

☣ ☣ ☣

Corey waited until he heard the padlock close and lowered the covers. He'd almost screamed out when he rolled over. He wasn't sure if his ribs were broken or if they were just bruised from the beating he'd taken yesterday. He did know that he had one heck of a black eye and some scrapes to his face that would be hard to explain. *Hopefully I pissed her off enough that she won't come back until I've healed a little.*

He crossed to the radio and turned it on. He tried to tune in to the two stations he listened to, but they were static. Since he used his iPhone for most of his listening he didn't even know what other stations to try. As it was, only two stations came in. One weak, the other weaker. Both were playing the same recording, "This is a public service announcement. Please stay tuned for an emergency message. New information will be given at the top of the hour when available." It was stuck on an endless loop. Corey shut the radio off and tossed it to the side. *Worthless.*

The idea Ash had about going to Dad's place isn't terrible. I should have thought about that, actually. I could go today. He ran his fingers through his hair and flinched at the pain in his side. *But she has more supplies than I do...and I bet we could rekindle that old fire if I could get her alone for a bit. Hell, I might even be the last man on earth!*

The prospect of getting back into Ashley pants cheered him up more than he thought it would. But first things first. If she knew he had snuck out she'd be even more pissed. Maybe even try to keep him locked up longer. If she secured the other side of the door he'd have to climb out the window and it was a long way down. Best if she never found out.

That doesn't mean I have to stay in though! Overnight he had heard sounds from outside. There were a few cars driving by, a few windows breaking and a few screams and yells in the distance. If people were coming back, they must be looking for something and if they were looking for something, there must be things of value out there. He wasn't about to let people come in and steal stuff from his city without getting his fair share!

Taking the pins out of the hinges was much easier this time. He set the pins to the side and checked to make sure the coast was clear.

The first thing he needed was a pharmacy so he could get some tape or a bandage to support his ribs. Those assholes really knew how to kick just where it would hurt. Not that they were planning on Corey living long enough to hurt. *But still, they had fantastic aim for scumbags.*

He looked across the hall to the stairwell. Traditions Hall was designed like a huge letter H. At the end of each leg was a stairwell leading to the bottom floor. His room was situated at the end of one leg, these being the choicest rooms because they were larger and didn't have to share a bathroom with their neighbors. Roger paid a little more for the room and Corey felt it was well worth the expense. Looking down the hallway, the floor looked like a hotel. Doors lined the hallway with no windows to break the monotony of the view except on each end.

Corey walked each floor, starting at his room, crossing the connecting bar on the middle of the H, and then across the hall catty-cornered to his. When he reached the end, he used the stairs to go to the second level, crossed again and then used the stairs to move to the first floor. There were almost 400 rooms in the building. Several of those rooms were double occupancy. All told, there might have been 450 people living here when the outbreak started. Sure, most of them were freshmen, but some fish had good stuff. He looked around with a gleam in his eye. *As they say, charity begins at home.*

Now that he was certain no one else remained in the building, he developed a plan. He had noticed some of the doors were still ajar. He also noticed that there was a distinct absence of dead-stink. So first thing to do was to go through the rooms that were open or unlocked. This would leave the least trace that he had been out and about and it would be the quickest route to scoring some loot.

Each leg of the H had about twenty rooms with the remainder in the center section. The center section on the first floor was also occupied by a common area with a TV room, a computer room and the main desk. For this trip, that area was pretty much worthless. Until the electricity came back on no one would be needing computers or TVs. When they did, he'd know where to go.

He started in the southeast corner, testing the doors and rummaging through anything that wasn't locked tight. Not knowing exactly what he was looking for ended up being quite a benefit. Since everything was potential loot, he looked at all the items of the previous residents' through a new light. Even before leaving the first floor, he found he was going to need a backpack. It just so happened that backpacks were very easy to acquire in a college dorm rooms. He dumped out textbooks and papers and filled three packs before getting back to his room. At just past 2:00 in the afternoon the search had taken far more time than he had expected. It wasn't until safely behind his door once again, with the hinge pins back in place, that he really stopped to examine what he'd acquired.

It was quite a haul; even more than he had expected. The small, orange, plastic bottles with the white child-proof lids were his favorite finds. Immediately he decided that these were 'not for sale'. These bottles contained a variety of medications. Of course he recognized the hydrocodone, oxycontin, oxycodone, Ritalin and Valium as well as others, but there were several that he had no idea about. Some of the labels were very vague and simply said to take them 'as needed'. Corey decided he needed a couple of those and popped them into his mouth as he continued sorting through the rest of the loot. He went ahead and slugged down two of the hydrocodone as well, to take the edge off the pain from the ribs.

Corey didn't remember passing out but woke up still sitting in the floor. He was bent at the waist with his forehead against his right knee, drool soaking his pant leg. Both of his hands were trapped under his torso and were numb from lack of circulation. When he tried to sit up, the spasm in his back and side caused him to cry out and slump to the side. His legs didn't want to cooperate, and it took far more concentration than usual to straighten them out. Once this was accomplished, he lay on the floor and waited for the pain to subside. After a few minutes he snaked a hand over to the hydrocodone bottle, fished out two more pills, and washed them down with the last of his water. About twenty minutes later the pain had subsided enough for him to go on with the sorting and inventory.

In addition to the prescription medication, Corey had found a remarkable amount of recreational drugs. The quantity was only remarkable because these rooms had obviously been abandoned and had been left unlocked. Most of it was so easily found that a simple search was all that was needed. The prescription medicines were harder to find. It was interesting that ten bottles, all found in different rooms, were prescribed to just two people. *They must have needed a little extra 'book money'.* He rolled a joint from a baggie and sat back to enjoy the relaxation. He had a few more baggies for future use but those would be for very special occasions.

He'd found two hunting knives, several pocket knives and one very naughty coed had a .380 automatic handgun tucked into her underwear drawer along with a half box of ammunition. Of course he snagged the gun, and he also tucked away a half dozen of her panties and several of those slick tops he had always thought of as a camisole but Ash referred to as a 'shell'. He thought he'd pamper his weapons – this one as well as the ones retrieved from his trip outside yesterday – by giving them a nice cleaning with the silk underthings from a young college girl. From the pictures plastering her walls, she would have made a nice replacement for Ashley if he had only known she lived in the building. *Oh well, she's probably dead in the street somewhere now...still though, a nice piece of ass.*

He rounded up the candies, snacks and power bars, bottles of water, more radios – though none of them were cranks like the one Ashley gave him – and flashlights. A couple of kids must have been real outdoor-types because they left behind sleeping bags as well as some camping items like folding stoves, whistles, tarps and ropes. Strange that they didn't take their stuff with them. Maybe they didn't have a choice when they left, and they were just never able to make it back to get the stuff. *Either way, too late now. Finders keepers.*

Once the joint was down far enough that it burned his fingers, he flicked the cherry off and tossed the roach into an old Coke can that had dried out. No use wasting your limited supplies!

He spied the tire iron and began plotting of how to get into the locked rooms. If possible he'd prefer to make little visible damage and the tire iron gave him an idea. He stuffed his newly-gained stash under his bed and in his small closet in case Ashley came by before he woke up, then settled in bed with ideas of plunder tugging up the corners of his mouth.

17

Western Georgia

"Tell me again, why are we doing this?" Jennifer looked at the house with its faded green paint and once-white trim that had yellowed in the sun. There was a detached garage with the same color scheme, one of those old single panel garage doors that lifted up and out rather than the traditional roll-up modern garage doors. There weren't any windows in the garage door and the windows on the sides had so much stuff packed against them that she couldn't see in. One thing was sure though, someone had died in the garage and no one had removed them. The stench was overwhelming and in this little clearing in the trees where the humidity was over 80% and the wind was virtually non-existent, you just couldn't get away from the smell. Not that the garage was the worst of it. The house absolutely reeked as well.

Roger had retrieved a long sleeved shirt from his bag, slipped on another of the N-95 masks, tied a bandana over the mask to keep it even closer to his face than the elastic band allowed. He pulled on a pair of rubber gloves and a set of goggles. Truth be told, he looked like an extra from some really bad, really low budget sci-fi flick. Unfortunately, this was all too real.

"This is the best chance we have of stocking up. I think they may have some canned food in there. It will still be good. Maybe even keys to these cars." He jabbed a gloved thumb over his shoulder to indicate the two sedans and pickup that were parked in the grass beside the gravel driveway. A Bobcat multi-purpose vehicle sat behind the garage, probably used in moving timber and other heavy yard usage.

"It just doesn't feel right stealing from the dead. You know what I mean?" Jennifer looked down and absently kicked a dirt clod. When

Roger woke up this morning and gave her the second half of his power bar she had been thankful. She had never been this hungry in her entire life, and that half of the bar just ratcheted up the hunger a notch rather than taking it down a notch. If it wasn't for the feeling of her stomach trying to eat itself and the weakness that was now going hand-in-hand with the hunger, she probably wouldn't even consider standing here while Roger went in the death house. With the hunger, she was considering going in herself but there was still a strand of guilt that went with the thought.

"Yes, I do know what you mean. It doesn't feel right." Roger looked at her and with his face completely covered with the goggles and bandana she couldn't make out any expression. His voice, however, conveyed an extraordinary amount of emotion for someone who always seemed so stoic. "This is not something I want to do. What I want to do less is leave this behind and have one, or both, of us fall dead from starvation while food rots here."

It wasn't that Jennifer had not thought about it. She had. It was just that she did not want to accept the fact that they could wander around until they died. Now that it was said though, going in seemed to be the most logical choice. She gave a nod, and Roger walked up to the house.

This was rural Georgia. Roger turned the knob on the front door and it opened without protest. This door didn't even have a deadbolt on it, Roger wondered if the knob lock had ever even been used. Just inside the door he got half the answer to the thought. A plaque hung just above the light switch for the living room. Three sets of keys hung from the hooks on the plaques. Each set had a key for four vehicles. One of the key rings also had a house key. *If this house had ever been locked it wasn't very often.*

Inside the house the stench was even more oppressive. It hung so heavily in the air that it almost felt like a physical weight. He tried to keep his breathing shallow and through his mouth, but even that helped only a little. This was a terrible task and he just had to force the stench out of his mind so he could do what he had come to do.

He worked his way through the living room and the adjacent dining room. In the back was a small kitchen with a pantry. He opened the pantry and was surprised to see such an expansive selection of canned food. The real surprise was that most was home canned in glass jars rather than store bought in metal cans. He used his flashlight to read the labels. Almost everything had been processed within the last few months, some even while he and Jennifer were stuck in the airport. He made a mental note not to take any of those. Almost certainly the canning process had killed any potential pathogens but *almost certainly* and *certainly* were different enough to make him want to exercise an extreme abundance of caution. Besides, there was more food in the pantry than he'd be able to fit safely in any of the vehicles, including the pickup.

On the floor sat several gallon bottles of water. These people were in a hurricane zone and knew how to prepare. At the back of the pantry was an emergency kit with tarps, batteries, two radios, five flashlights of various intensity but all using C cell batteries. They had matches and cigarette lighters along with some lighter fluid, all packed away in a large pot which, he supposed, was meant to be used to boil water. Roger grabbed the pot and the well-stocked first aid kit next to it, then opened the back door, exiting to the screened in back porch. He walked out into the yard and set the pot down beside the pickup. Jennifer looked at him and raised an eyebrow while flicking her head toward the house. Roger somberly shook his head and walked back to the house without comment.

After rummaging around on the bottom floor for a few more minutes he found a duffle bag in the front hall closet and used it to shuttle food out to Jennifer. On his second trip he snagged a set of keys and she started the pickup, made sure it was in working order, and began filling the bed with supplies. Roger brought out dish towels to pack around the jars. Jennifer discarded them due to the smell. Instead she pulled up handfuls of tall grass and leaves to provide padding.

Roger found an old breach-load double barrel shotgun atop the hutch in the dining room, with shells in each barrel. Next to it was a twenty-shell box with only five rounds left. It was rabbit shot but that was a lot better than what he had, plus it was more versatile than buckshot or a slug. Next to that box was another, this one with over one hundred rounds of .22 ammunition. Since he hadn't seen a .22 downstairs he figured it must be upstairs.

He had delayed going upstairs as long as he could. The trip past generations of old pictures showed him the gradual evolution of the family. The house was old enough that the stairs weren't carpeted. They were covered with a runner down the center of the steps, held in place with a brass bar at the base of each tread. Each bar was polished and the interior of the house, except for the stench of death, was in immaculate condition. Obviously the family had taken pride in their home. No doubt the lady of the house would be scandalized if she had known the smell would be the first and most dominant impression a stranger would have of her domain.

The top floor was just as orderly as the bottom and, if anything, the stench was even greater. The stairs came up to a small landing. There were two bedrooms in the back, two more in the front. A single bathroom was positioned in the middle of the wall opposite the stairs. Next to the bath was what Roger guessed to be a closet. All the doors were closed but windows at each end of the hall let a breeze through and let the smell out into the woods.

He made sure his mask was firmly in place. It was more for a sense of security than for actual protection, but he still felt better for it. He found what he expected behind the first door. Based on what he could tell, a young man was covered head to toe with his bed sheet. The now familiar dried rust stains in the predictable places. Trying not to disturb the body,

Roger searched the room. In the bottom of the closet Roger found a slingshot with a mesh bag of marbles for ammunition. On the dresser he found two nice quality hunting knives and a sharpening kit. Otherwise he left the kid's memorabilia intact and untouched. He did grab three sets of socks from the chest of drawers.

The second room was a mirror-image of the first. A bed, chest of drawers, bed side table and closet. Another dead young man covered with stained sheets. This time Roger came out with a .22 rifle to go with the ammo from downstairs. Under different circumstances this would be a find worth celebrating.

The third room was an identical setup. This time with a young woman lying under the sheets. He had no idea what she looked like but for some reason seeing her lying there, completely concealed, Roger overlayed an image of Ashley. Strangely, neither of the men had forced the same flash of imagery for Corey.

He searched the room quickly and had to force himself not to look at the stained shape again. There were a couple pairs of boots that Roger thought might fit Jennifer and he added those to his haul, then dumped in all the socks he could find. If the boots were a bit large, Jennifer could add another pair of socks or two so they wouldn't rub her feet.

The final room was the master bedroom. The double bed had only one occupant. Based on the pictures on the wall, he knew exactly what she'd looked like while she was alive. This had to be the happy smiling mother whose life was traced from her preschool years to probably just months ago. She had been a handsome woman rather than beautiful. You could tell she'd had a life full of a happiness that she just could not hold in. To see her covered form and know that someone so apparently good had come to the same end as hundreds of thousands of regular people, or even some truly evil people, made Roger wonder if there really was justice in the world.

This sad room was a bonanza. In the one closet was another .22 rifle, this one with a low power scope. There was a 12 gauge pump shotgun with an assortment of shells Roger didn't bother to inventory. Several 'bricks' of .22 ammunition followed the shotgun shells into the bag. Each brick was 500 rounds. Even those small bullets added up to a good bit of weight. After realizing that all the clothing was for a man, he checked the sizes on the shoes and discovered they were a size too small. No use carrying them out.

Roger closed the door, walked down the stairs, out of the house. He placed his load in the bed of the truck. Taking off the bandana and mask allowed a little fresh air to brush across his sweat-soaked face. The first thing that had alerted them to the house was the smell but after leaving it and standing here in the yard, all Roger could smell was clean, fresh air. He looked at Jennifer but still didn't have anything he could say. The look in her eyes told him she understood just fine. It took a few minutes of silence before he felt better. When he looked up again Jennifer let him know what she had been up to.

"The truck runs fine. None of the dash lights are on and all the gauges seem to be in the middle so I don't think there are any immediate issues with them. The biggest problem is gas. There's only half a tank. Maybe two hundred miles?" She sat in the driver's seat with the door open, letting the information sink in.

"We'll siphon it from the others. Maybe get it to top off."

"Tried that." Jennifer nodded toward a piece of garden hose lying on the ground next to one of the sedans, the flap for the gas tank still open.

Roger nodded. "Late model. Most cars have anti-siphon devices, some kind of screen in there. We're going to have to do it the hard way then. Poke a hole and let it drain out into a pan or something."

Jennifer nodded. "Thought of that too." At his look of incredulity she shrugged, "Hey, I was married to a mobster. I didn't *know* I was married to a mobster, but maybe some of that underworld stuff just soaked in by osmosis. Anyway, there aren't any tools out there." Her grin was welcome enough that he let it go without pressing her for more information.

"Well," he said, "only one thing to do." Roger strapped the mask on again and tied the bandana back in place. "I'll open the garage and see what we can find. You might want to stand back. I think the man of the house is in there. Everyone else is dead and covered – they couldn't have done that for themselves. His clothes are still in the closet."

Jennifer nodded grimly and took a step back. She wasn't in the way of anything but it was more of a subconscious impulse than anything else. Roger tried the 'house key' on the keychain and found that it fit the garage's T-lock perfectly. He twisted the key and unlocked the handle. Rotating the T pulled the latches back inside the garage. Roger stepped back and heaved the door up, stepping further back to allow it to open completely. Once again the smell of decomposition washed over him. Back by the truck he immediately heard the sounds of retching.

The scene inside made it pretty evident what had happened. A final car was parked in the garage. A rubber hose was stuffed over the exhaust pipe with a garden hose taped in place. The hose was then routed into the back window of the car. The driver's seat was occupied by an older-middle-aged man. His arm was sitting on the edge of his window, poised as if he was going for a casual drive. In his lap was a pack of cigarettes appearing as if only two had been removed. One butt was in an otherwise clean ashtray. The other had fallen into the passenger seat where it had burned a hole in the cloth seat cover and melted into the foam cushion. The man had the thinnest thread of dried blood trailing from his right eye and left nostril.

Roger knew many religions thought that suicide was the ultimate betrayal, the unforgivable sin. If so, he hoped this man's action had been seen simply as speeding up a forgone condition. Anyone who had watched as his family died and taken such good care of them, surely had the right to choose the timing and method of his own death when the end was obviously at hand.

He turned away from the car to check on Jennifer. She had stopped her retching and was rinsing her mouth out. When she saw Roger looking, she gave him a halfhearted wave that told him she was OK and he should continue.

Checking the car one last time, Roger saw the key was still in the 'on' position. The fuel gauge pointed to empty and the dash lights were dead. Obviously it had run until out of gas and remained on until the battery had died. Casting a longer glance over the vehicle he saw nothing else of immediate use. He turned to take in the rest of the garage.

There was the normal assortment of toolboxes. More tools hung from a pegboard mounted on the wall. Shovels, rakes, posthole diggers and other yard tools were sorted and stored. Two lawn mowers and three weed trimmers were in their assigned places. On a shelf above the tools was one thing Roger was seeking. Four plastic tubs were stacked inside one another and safely secured. Over by the lawn mowers was an even more promising find. Four five gallon gas cans were situated on a shelf with a half empty bottle of Sta-bil, the fuel stabilizer, sitting next to them. On the next shelf down was a smaller gas can with several small bottles of two cycle engine oil waiting to be mixed for the weed trimmer.

Roger made quick work of moving tools to the truck before turning to the task of draining the fuel from the other vehicles. First he drained the five gallon cans into the pickup. Jennifer had been correct that there was only half a tank left, but that was only one of the tanks. The truck had another tank that needed to be manually switched. That tank was full. It seemed that these guys took seriously the local habit of staying prepared for hard times. Whatever drove them to it, Roger was grateful for their forethought. One of the cans was completely full. Another was just over half full. The other five gallon cans were empty. He went ahead and drained the two gallon can as well, that low ratio of two cycle oil would have virtually no effect on the truck. If anything, it might blow a little extra smoke out the tail pipe but when a few ounces of oil were mixed into over thirty gallons of gas, even that was doubtful.

The remaining fuel was dirty work. He used a shop towel to wipe clean a fist-sized area on the bottom of the first sedan's gas tank at its lowest point. Using a Philips screwdriver and hammer he punched a hole in the thin sheet metal and began draining the gas into one of the tubs. As one filled he moved another in place and handed the first to Jennifer who used a funnel to refill the gas cans. By the time they had completed both sedans, the pickup was full and they had about fifteen extra gallons stored in the pickup bed.

"Well," he said as he brushed off his knees, "we have what we need to move on." He walked around the pickup, surveying their hoard. Jennifer nodded at the bed and helped him secure a tarp in place. It might help protect against the elements but more importantly, it might protect against prying eyes.

"There is one more thing though." Roger fastened the last corner of the tarp in place with a bungee cord. "I don't feel right taking all this stuff and leaving them so undignified."

Jennifer nodded but had nothing to offer.

"There's that Bobcat behind the garage. There were a few attachments for it too. I think I might be able to figure it out enough to get some holes dug."

Jennifer nodded again.

"The problem is," Roger continued, "I don't know if I can get them all downstairs and in the holes on my own."

Jennifer's eyes grew big as she understood what he was asking. She hadn't said anything since he opened the garage. Now she stared at the tarp strapped to the back of the pickup they were about to steal from a family who had died and left them everything they would need to survive. "I can do it. I can help."

"You sure?"

"It's the least I can do for them."

☣ ☣ ☣

As night fell they were miles away, following the back roads. Both rode in silence except for Jennifer calling out directions and Roger acknowledging them. Their headlights were off so they were going slowly, relying on moonlight and more than a little luck. They were on the road and they were already making better time than on their feet. Neither Roger nor Jennifer wanted to admit that they weren't sure if they would ever get the smell out of their noses. They both felt better for the grisly work they had accomplished. Jennifer even steadied herself long enough to find identification for everyone so each had a grave marker to record their passing.

One thing was sure: even if they shed the smell, those memories would remain forever.

18

Sack & Save - Denton, TX

Ashley had been cautious cruising down Avenue C toward the freeway. The explosion yesterday sounded like it came from this direction. There were still thin streamers of smoke drifting up from something a block over, closer to the freeway. Once she cleared the side of the big grocery store she could tell that the explosion had most likely come from the gas station on the corner. Most of the building was blocked from sight by a McDonald's but it looked like the whole place had burned down.

More importantly, there was traffic on the freeway. It wasn't full rush hour type traffic, not that rush hour was that bad in Denton, but there were a few cars coming and going. There had even been a couple of cars cruising slowly down the streets in town. She had stayed clear of them, but it looked like people were starting to come back and that had her a little on edge.

The Sack & Save was right on the service road to the freeway. She figured that if any place was going to get hit by looters it would be a grocery store. *Best to get what I can before others come get it.* She was now kicking herself for not coming immediately when she realized they were in a real *situation,* as Professor Westover would call it. She knew she was prepared for a reasonable amount of time. The problem was that she wasn't prepared to support Corey as well, and the amount of time had become distinctly *un*reasonable. If she had time, she was going to try the hardware stores as well. Based on the amount of movement she was seeing and hearing, time was running out quickly. Already today there were at least three gunshots in the distance and one instance where it sounded like a prolonged gunfight.

For now she needed to focus on the task at hand. The sliding glass doors appeared to have been ripped off their tracks and were discarded in the parking lot in front of the store. This served her purpose because she could ride her bike into the store and not worry about it alerting someone she was in the store. She coasted in and leaned the bike against the first checkout stand she came to. It was an old-style store with no skylights and no windows. The only light getting into the store was from the front. She quickly made sure the bike was steady and ducked inside. If someone was in the store Ashley didn't want to remain silhouetted against the windows.

She calmed herself, sitting hunched next to the cigarette case which had been completely emptied, and took a moment to let her eyes adjust to the gloom of the store. From what she could see, the store was absolutely trashed. On the plus side, there were still a few boxes and packages scattered around, but she couldn't tell what they were or even if they still had their contents intact. *Give it a few minutes. Let your eyes adjust. Keep listening for movement.*

That was just what she had intended until she heard tires crunch to a slow stop in the parking lot. Her eyes were just adjusted enough that she could see a jumble of grocery baskets clogging the front of the store. There was a path between them, but she had to move slowly to ensure she didn't bump them and make too much noise. Perhaps whoever it was would just keep going.

"Hey girlie!" It was a male voice from just outside. "How 'bout we have a bit of fun?"

So much for them just passing by. Obviously someone had watched her enter the store.

"Nice bike you got here." Ashley crouched down and saw the man enter the store. "I'll make sure we take real good care of it for you."

Another man walked in. Either of them could have walked directly off the campus on any given day. She expected for them to be dirty biker types or some Backwoods Bubba. Instead her stereotypes were blown out of the water. The first guy had on nice western boots and blue jeans that may have been starched when this whole thing started. Now they had been worn too long for the crease to still be sharp. He had on a pull-over golf shirt and a baseball cap with some logo on it. The second guy was similar except with a button-down shirt and a wind breaker. He seemed a little shy though. He just rolled the bike out the front door, his head down, not saying a word.

Moving slowly and quietly, Ashley continued further into the store. It seemed this guy didn't worry so much about being silhouetted by the light. He just squinted and gazed into the store. "Hey, sweetie, just come on out and it'll be a lot nicer for you. We got boys at all the exits. You can't go nowhere. You come out nicely and we might even try and make it enjoyable for ya."

Well, ain't you the romantic? Jerk. Ashley slipped into the cashier's stall behind the last cash register in the line. She slipped her handgun from its holster in her waistband. *It was time to break out the outside-the-waistband holster too. Easier to draw, easier to reholster. Let's hope I have a chance to do that.*

The distance to the man was just over fifty feet. She was fairly certain she could put a hole in him from this range. She'd done it with paper targets. But this wasn't paper. Paper didn't make you nervous. When you were just a long range hole punch you had all the time in the world, you didn't have to worry about the consequences of your actions and the paper didn't return fire. Add all that up and drawing a gun on a real live person was a totally different thing than shooting paper.

The second man returned, his head still hung in apparent resignation. Where the first guy seemed to be excited, almost bouncing on the balls of his feet, the second guy just seemed to be along for the ride. For convenience sake she started thinking of them as *Pullover* and *Button-up*.

Pullover flicked a hand and Button-up started to the right, toward Ashley. "Come on out, sweetie. You're just about to make me mad and no one's gunna like it when I'm mad." He walked down the row of check stands, pushing baskets out of his way, making room and making a lot of noise in the process.

Button-up kept moving as well. He was moving the baskets out of his way, but in a more orderly, less violent fashion. Ashley trained her weapon on him as he got ever closer and kept track of Pullover more by sound than sight. When Button-up was two stands over, he paused and their eyes locked. Ashley leveled the gun at his chest and he slowly elevated his hands to waist level, in a low-level *hands-up* kind of posture. He slowly glanced over his shoulder to where Pullover was ranting. Equally slowly he raised one finger to his lips in a shushing motion. Still moving slowly, he continued past her to where a chrome rail blocked his progress, then turned and walked back.

She watched for any sudden moves or change in posture that would indicate he was about to do something. He just went back to gazing into the store. Pullover was in a rage now. She spared a look at him just in time to see him lift a shopping cart and throw it. It didn't go far, but crashed into a cash register. Both the register and cart slammed to the floor with a sound loud enough to be a gun shot. She checked her sight picture and saw the barrel was still pointing squarely at Button-up's chest. She shifted the point of aim so that she was pointing at the ceiling and made sure her finger was again on the frame. So far this guy was decent. She didn't want to shoot him accidentally.

Pullover yelled at Button-up, "Well? You find the bitch?"

How quickly I turned from sweetie and honey to bitch. Why do guys always call girls bitches, even when the guy is obviously in the wrong?

Button-up just shook his head, held his hands up and backed away a step. Pullover continued to rage. He pulled baskets and pushed baskets, flinging them around with contempt. "Come on out, ya whore! I wasn't gunna hurt you but, now I just won't hurt you as bad if you come out. Don't make it worse for yourself!"

Ashley changed the point of aim from the ceiling to his chest as he started in her direction. His arms were flailing and he was still yelling but now the rapid fire of her heartbeat in her ears was drowning out all other sound. He was four check stands away, slapping away the chrome stands for plastic bags.

Three check stands, raging at the back of the store.

Two check stands, flailing and looking back at Button-up.

One stand away, yelling at the top of his lungs.

Her stand.

He glanced down.

Their eyes locked.

The yelling stopped.

He looked at her, a smile split his lips.

He reached for her.

The 9mm barked twice.

Pullover spun, his right hand flying up to cover his left shoulder. His feet slipped out from under him. He fell to the floor, making first contact with his right shoulder. A scream, then a mad scramble. He started running while still on his knees, making his way to his feet and out the door. Button-up had already disappeared.

Ashley pursued just far enough to make sure they were loading into the car and not preparing for a bigger fight. As Pullover threw himself in the passenger seat, Ashley could see where the two bullets had made their exit: one just below the ball joint of his left shoulder, the other just above the narrow of his waist.

She lowered the weapon as the car sped away. *Not bad shot placement. Not great, but they both got him. Shoulda aimed for his balls.*

❈ ❈ ❈

Corey was covered in fine white powder. He was standing in the middle of the room, bent over coughing. Sweat made thin rivulets through the powder and dripped as white spots onto the carpet.

This was the third room he had *burrowed* into. It was messy work. Starting at one of the unlocked rooms on the first floor, he stripped away enough drywall to fit himself between the wall studs. The goal was the administrative office, where he was sure they would have spare keys for all the rooms. If he remembered right, the resident assistants had a master key for each floor. He hadn't found them in the one unlocked RA room where he had looked so he assumed the RAs had probably taken their keys with them. *Still sucks no one came by to tell me they were leaving. Bunch of assholes.* But it was almost a certainty that there would be a master set. The trouble was getting there.

Still trying to stay somewhat anonymous and keep the signs of looting to a minimum, he decided not to just try and break into the office through the door. Instead he'd thought of going through the walls. Drywall was easy to get through, especially with his tire iron. Just knock a couple of holes with the wrench end and dig it out with the bladed end. But with no air conditioning and five walls to get through, it was taking longer than he had expected.

Once enough of the drywall was cleared out he could squeeze through the framing easily enough. The problem was getting rid of the drywall. It kicked dirt into the air, making it difficult to breath. It coated his skin making it hotter, and caused him to sweat more. It just got into places where he would prefer not to have some dry powder thickening into a sweat-mixed paste. Finally he'd cut a piece of top sheet from the bed and used it as a rag to wipe off his face, then cut another piece to use as a bandana mask.

He swung the tire iron again, popping a hole in the next wall.

☣ ☣ ☣

An hour later Corey was in the admin office. Gypsum was caked from head to toe and stuck to the sweat on his shirt and jeans. He had pulled up a chair and tried to relax a bit. It wasn't that any part of the plan had been difficult to do. It was just that there was so much of it. *Shit, a few less hours of Xbox, a few more of jogging or weights would have made that go much easier. I didn't realize how out of shape I was!*

Corey had always prided himself on his looks. He had the hair, the bone structure, the slimness that was so desired these days. While he didn't worry much about how he dressed, he kept himself clean and reasonably well groomed, especially when going out in public. He never would have thought that someone who was as thin as he was could be so unfit. The heavy breathing, gallons of sweat and ache in his back gave him the truth of the situation.

Once behind the locked door, the administrative section of the building was an open area with a couple of desks and one other door. He opened that door and found a lockbox mounted on the wall of the small supply closet. Inside he found what he was looking for: the master keys. There were four keys on three rings. Each set had keys marked '1', '2', '3' and 'M'. Two more sets of keys hung from the last hook in the box and were unmarked. Corey took them all, just to make sure.

Now that he was filthy and exhausted, he decided to head up to his room. A change of clothes and a good rinse were in order. *Maybe a nice nap as well.*

He exited the office and crossed the foyer to the double glass doors leading out to the courtyard. Checking the keys he found that the unmarked sets opened the exterior doors. He walked to the end of the northeast hallway and tried those same keys on the outside doors and they worked there as well. The ones marked 1 through 3 operated the room locks on the respective floors.

Things were looking up. He had keys so he didn't have to worry about burrowing through the walls. His face and ribs were healing. Soon he'd be back to full strength. He had the run of the building, plenty of water for now, and quite a stock of food from the various dorm rooms. In this new world, he was a king.

He walked up to his door. It was still propped open, hanging by the padlocked latch. Moving it out of the way, he looked in to his room. Everything had changed.

His water was laid out on the bed alongside the snack packs, potato chips, power bars and beef jerky acquired from the other rooms. Even the guns were on the bed, except for the revolver that he still had in the holster inside his waistband. He started to open his mouth to yell when Ashley stepped into view.

Immediately his face wilted and his mouth started to form words but nothing would come out. He pointed at the supplies on the bed but still couldn't say anything. He stopped pointing and could only stutter something that sounded like a croak. Ashley crossed her arms as she watched him try to work up an excuse or some rationale behind his stash.

Corey stepped into the room, still unable to make a coherent sound.

Ashley uncrossed her arms and slipped past him, out the door. She crossed to the stairs, flung the door open, and said over her shoulder, "Well, at least you don't need any more of my food or water. I'll be back when I'm ready to go to Arkansas."

Finally Corey's mouth started functioning again, "When?"

She turned to face him, "As soon as I'm damn good and ready."

The door closed, shutting off further discussion.

19

Eastern Alabama

Roger had followed the roads only far enough to get back to the pipe-line clearing in the trees. Using these corridors as their personal highway, they crossed the remainder of Georgia then paralleled Interstate 20 until they reached Talladega National Forest. On the north shore of a small body of water marked as "Bonner Lake" on his road atlas, Roger finally felt they were in deep enough woods to not be noticed. He parked the truck.

Roger unloaded a tarp from the back of the truck. They had several now, so he picked one that was medium sized, about eight feet by ten feet. He ran a length of cord between two trees, feeding the cord in and out of the grommet holes along one side of the tarp. A few small sticks served as tent spikes. He showed Jennifer how to carve them to shape. One end pointed, the other end with a slight hook to catch a grommet hole. She finished the work, whittling the sticks and stretching the tarp between the waist-high line and the ground. After that was done, she scooped a huge pile of pine needles and leaves under the tarp and laid down another tarp to serve as a moisture barrier. It might not be a bed, but it would be the most comfortable night they'd spent in a while if she had anything to say about it.

While Jennifer was preparing the shelter, Roger worked on the fire. He helped clear a spot of leaves and needles then used the shovel to dig a shallow hole. He dug short trenches about three feet in length, in an X pattern with the hole at the center of the X. These trenches started at the same depth as the hole in the middle, tapering off to ground level at the end. It would allow air flow into the fire while allowing the fire to be somewhat recessed in the ground, thus more hidden from accidental onlookers. Setting the fire too low would be fine for cooking but wouldn't provide much heat. The last few nights had been chilly and the extra warmth would be appreciated.

Jennifer completed her shelter building. Once he had the fire pit prepared he checked over the tarp lean-to and nodded at the work. She was a novice but she was smart, learned fast and cared about her task. If anything she was over-exacting with her work. As long as it didn't take too long though, he wasn't going to complain. Better to have something done right than have it done again.

"All right. Good work." Roger gave her a pat on the shoulder and was a bit confused by the glare she gave him. *Examine the work. Check. Praise the work. Check. Provide positive physical reinforcement. Check. Maybe she isn't familiar with the proper procedure for showing approval. Poor thing. Must not have gotten a lot of positive feedback when she was a kid.* He made a mental note to try and give her more kudos.

☣ ☣ ☣

Condescending prick! I don't need to be petted like a dog. You said it was a good job, so – but then again, he is Roger and Roger probably doesn't know any better. Jennifer was proud of the shelter. She'd never done anything like it before, hadn't even watched anyone do anything like it. Until leaving the airport, her idea of 'roughing it' was a four-star hotel after the restaurant had closed. A five-star with room service was just about the right speed for her. Somehow though, she was actually enjoying parts of the trip. Obviously not the death or the part with guns being pointed at her, but she liked being in nature and didn't even mind that her manicure had been destroyed.

"Fire's next." Roger used his hands to illustrate dimensions, "We need to fill up a space this big with deadfall branches. About six feet long, three wide and up to your hip high. If you can find dead stuff that is still in the tree it'll be drier, so that'll be best."

Six by three feet? "Really, we need that much?"

"At this temp? Yup. If it was cold we'd need more. We might not use it all, but it's better to have too much and get through the night than too little and have it go out and sprain your knee tromping around the woods looking for it at night. Gonna be dark in a bit and I don't want either of us gettin' hurt."

Considering the number of trees surrounding them, it didn't take long to gather the wood. It seemed the rain from Atlanta didn't make it this far and everything was very dry. Roger stripped the limbs and sorted the wood.

"OK. We have three things here. The big stuff, larger than a finger, up to the size of your wrist. That's as big as you need in a survival situation. That's fuel. Save wood splitting for when you want a nice cozy fire in your living room. Fuel wood is the last thing you put on the fire for longer burns. The next size down, the size of a pencil to the size of your thumb. That's kindling. It's the second thing to go on. It provides enough heat to catch the fuel but isn't so big that the tinder can't get it going. Tinder is the first stuff. Even pencil size can be too big here. Save that for kindling."

He picked up a handful of pine needles and started twisting them together in a bunch. "Pine needles are hard to catch when they are laid together. At some point we might have to start a fire with a spark. When a spark hits a branch, all the heat can be absorbed without catching fire. Some people say you have to increase the surface area so that your spark can catch. What you really need to do is get things that are so thin that they absorb the heat without displacing it. That absorption of heat is what catches the stuff on fire. Not the amount of surface area."

He unwound the bunch, then wadded it up and ground it between his hands. "See that powder? It'll take a spark. Then it'll share its heat with its neighbor and so on until you get a fire. Of course that's if there's enough air and everything is really dry. We'll try that some day but we're losing light. Today I'll just use this." He pulled a lighter from his pocket and flicked a flame. It easily caught the pine needle dust.

"So here we go. That was just the first part." He indicated the tiny flame flicking across from one needle to the next. "That's just a flame. It's not a fire. You don't have a fire until you've got something you can't just blow out."

He laid a few more pine needles on the pile. The flame grew and consumed them. "Once you have a flame, add more kindling until you have a sustained flame. Then you add tinder. You gotta watch close though. You can put it out if you throw on too much. Remember, everything you throw on will absorb heat until it gets hot enough to burn. Throw on too much and all your heat gets absorbed. Or you smother it. The trenches should allow for good airflow so our worst enemy is impatience right now. It's alive. Let it breathe and let it grow."

Roger matched action, or inaction, to words. He waited while the pine needles caught and the flame spread. Once the flame grew again, he began with the match stick sized pieces. "Place it on deliberately. Don't just dump a handful. Piece by piece."

The flame grew for a moment then settled down. "Wait for the flame to get higher than the fuel you've given it." The match stick sized kindling caught and the flame shot up to twice the height of the pile. "OK. Now add a bit more."

Little by little Roger repeated the process. He added progressively larger pieces, forming them in a loose 'teepee'. The flame retreated with each new volume of fuel, then slowly grew again. Roger worked his way through the small kindling then up to the larger bits. Once they were consumed, he started with the smaller pieces of true fuel. In short order the flame had transformed to a fire and it was blazing.

To Jennifer, the process was a mixture of simplicity and fascination. As someone who had never started a fire – even her fireplace fires were started by Paul and he used those long matches with firestarting logs wrapped in paper – she had no idea of how delicate the techniques needed to be. There was nothing difficult, but it was exacting. In some inner corner of her mind she was anxious to try it herself. For now though, there were other things to be done.

She looked over at the lake. "You know," she said, catching Roger's eyes, "now that we have a fire and can get warm, that lake is right over there and I'd love to get clean."

"Hygiene is important. Probably not a bad idea. Once we're clean though, we need to replace the water we drank today." He stood up and brushed his knees, looking back at the fire with an almost fond look in his eyes. Grabbing a pot he said, "Let's see what we can see at the lake."

They walked together to the shore. The lake was obviously man-made. Its shore was made up of angles which had been weathered but were obviously originally straight lines. Across the narrow expanse of water, the dying sun was being caught on the window of a house hidden in the woods. It was a good ways off, but in such a quiet environment they would have to be cautious of noise in order to not alert any potential residents. Roger looked back toward their camp to make sure their fire was not visible. It wasn't, but that would be another point of caution.

He crouched beside the water and invited Jennifer to do the same with a wave of his hand. When she squatted as well he let her know what was on his mind. "So we need to replace water. What I want to do is make sure this water is moving and determine the direction of movement."

He picked up a leaf and tossed it in water. It settled for a moment then started a lazy drift left to right along the bank. The water was definitely moving. Roger pointed at the leaf, a smile on his face. "Now we know the direction of flow. That's important. We want to take water for processing from upstream and take our baths downstream. There is an order to things.

"Starting from the top, the first spot upstream, you get your water for drinking and food preparation. Next is water for cleaning. Food first then clothing, then bathing. After that is waste disposal, if we were using this water for that purpose. Since this leg of the lake dead ends and flows back out, I suggest we keep burying our waste and not pollute the water."

"There really is something to consider every step of the way, isn't there?" Jennifer shook her head as she looked up at Roger. *This guy has so much crap stuffed in that head! It all makes sense, but there is just so much to consider.*

Roger walked back to the truck and retrieved an empty two liter bottle and pot. Back at the shore he wrapped the bandana around the mouth and filled the bottle. Bottle by bottle he filled the pot halfway. "If you wanna get your bath, I'll take this back to the camp and start it boiling."

She walked back to camp with Roger and gathered a set of sweats, a towel, and some toiletries from her pack. She moved downstream and felt a bit self conscious as she prepared to go skinny dipping for the first time since her teens. The sun was fully down now, and she couldn't see Roger, so she was pretty sure he couldn't see her either. Across the lake there was still no light coming from the house. It was just barely visible even when the sun was up so it was unlikely that anyone over there could see her either.

She finally decided there was nothing else to do and just stripped out of her shirt. Kicking off her shoes, she took a deep breath and stripped off pants and underwear in one swift move. Reaching around, her fingers found the clasp for the bra. It came off with a flick and a shrug. Dropping the last of her clothing into a pile, she moved from apprehensive to liberated. Somehow it felt natural to be out in the middle of nowhere standing naked beside a lake. She breathed in the cool night air, feeling it wrap itself around her. It was a cool caress that brought up goose bumps. As she rubbed her hands over her skin, smoothing down the pebbled flesh, she felt more free than she had in years.

The water was cool as she stepped in. Taking slow, graceful strokes she propelled herself out, away from the shore and then back to her supplies. She retrieved the soap and shampoo. There wasn't a wash cloth available, so she simply rubbed herself down with the soap and rinsed in the slow moving water. As she did, her mind retraced the last couple of weeks.

As strange as it sounded, Roger was one of the most bizarre people Jennifer had ever met, but in this short period he had established himself as completely trustworthy. It was probably because he wasn't trying to establish trust that he had earned it. After the divorce from Paul, Jennifer wasn't sure if she'd ever completely trust again. Roger didn't seem to have any inclination that there might even be times when it was appropriate to be less than completely honest.

There was just something about him. Well, it wasn't just *something*, there were many things about him that were attractive. He wasn't bad looking. Perhaps he could lose a few pounds and maybe tighten up a bit. Paul had been in great shape. The perfect physical specimen. She was pretty sure that Roger could literally walk circles around Paul if it came down to backpacks and rough terrain. Roger would never think of showing off like that, and Paul would be so ticked off that he'd have found an excuse why he wasn't able to 'perform at peak'. He'd never admit he was simply outdone by a guy a few years older and several inches further around.

Jennifer smiled at the thought of Roger showing Paul up. As she stood there rinsing the last of the shampoo from her hair she started coming to terms with how she felt. Certainly it wasn't love. She didn't know Roger *that* well. But there were other feelings that weren't as strong as love that were just as respectable. Wrapping up that train of thought, she snapped to a quick decision.

She climbed out of the lake and quickly swabbed herself off with the towel. She drew on her sweat shirt and combed her hair back, tying it back with an elastic band. There wasn't any makeup to be had, but she knew she was still a nice looking woman even without it. Besides, all she had on was a long sweatshirt and a smile. What else did she need?

Jenny bundled her clothes and toiletries and walked back to the camp area. When she reached the truck she laid everything on the hood and stepped around the front. Roger squatted next to the fire, studying the atlas.

"Hey there." Jennifer stood there, her bare legs poking out from under the sweatshirt, the arms pushed up to her elbows.

"Hey." He traced his finger across some roads.

"Wha'cha doing?" *Will you please look up?*

"Trying to find out where we're going tomorrow. How best to get across Alabama." He shifted to get better light on the map.

"Yeah? What do you think?" She stepped closer. *Maybe getting in his personal space will draw him into my personal space.*

"Not sure. Addison is just up the road and there is a major Army base there. Not sure if we should try to go through or if we should go around."

"Gotta do that tonight?" She used that low, raspy voice that always made Paul respond. "It's kind of cool out tonight. Shouldn't we do something to maybe warm up?"

"Oh!" Roger closed the map and looked up at Jennifer. When he faced her, his nose was at the level of the hem of the sweatshirt, which was a bit long but still just barely long enough to provide any modesty. "You're right! It is cool."

He stood up. They were face to face, inches apart. He hadn't had his bath yet but somehow the smell was just the smell of *man*, not *filthy man*. It was intoxicating. His eyes met hers and a shy smile crept up his lips.

She looked up, her smile mimicking his for a moment, then hooking her lower lip with a tooth, giving him a bit of a pout. "So, what can we do about it?"

His hands slipped up to her shoulders. Quicker than Jennifer knew what was happening, Roger acted. He scrubbed her upper arms, patted her back and turned to the wood pile. "I'll get the fire going. That'll help."

He broke a limb in two and tossed it on the fire. "And, you know, I don't mean to criticize, but you might put on some pants! That'll help warm ya up." He gave her a light punch to the shoulder. "Crazy lady! I'm gunna catch my bath now. Be back in a few."

By the time he returned Jennifer had on a pair of pants, covered with the sweatpants, and a T-shirt under a sweatshirt. She was lying on the needle-tarp mattress, her back to the fire. He announced "I'm back," but she had nothing to say to him.

20

Traditions Hall – Denton, TX

Corey looked around. Someone was yelling. Ashley was standing in his doorway, shaking a fist and yelling at the top of her lungs. "Dude, no! Wake up, man. Come on Jerry, come on! Don't give in man!"

What the hell was she talking about? Who is Jerry? Hang on. That doesn't sound like Ash.

He shook his head and looked around. He was laying in his bed, the door closed, hinge pins in place. Ashley wasn't even in the room. Corey sat up in his bed, rubbed his eyes and ran fingers through his hair.

"Come on, man!" It was a man's voice, coming through the window. "Oh, thank God!" There was a pause. "Yeah, man. Sure. I'll be right back!"

Corey hung his head out the window and saw a man next to a car in the parking lot of the convenience store. He was walking into the store. Corey couldn't see the other person, Jerry, but assumed he was in the car.

"Dude," the small guy in a baseball cap and button-up shirt said, "It's empty man! Nothing here at all."

He looked around and saw Corey looking out the window. "Hey! Man! Dude, my friend has been shot. He really needs water. You got any water, man?"

Corey thought about it a minute. These guys might have something to trade. Maybe they had information or something else.

"Yeah, man." Corey ducked into the room, grabbed a gallon of water and held it out the window. "I got some water. I'll be right down." He slipped back into his room again and made sure the revolver was stowed in the holster inside his pants. Just in case, he also tucked one of the auto-loaders from the gas station between the belt and his back.

He emerged from the building at the northeast stairwell door. Now that he had keys, he could come and go from any door he chose. The store was just across the street but he waited for a moment and scoped out the situation. The guy had returned to his car. Now that Corey was on the same level he could see the second man. It looked like he also had on a baseball cap. Through the open driver's side door Corey could see the guy had on a pullover shirt that was soaked through with blood. The cloth seat had soaked up quite a bit of blood and the cloth cover was saturated.

He raised the water. "Here it is, man."

The smaller guy started toward Corey. "I really appreciate it! Man, you're a life-saver."

"No prob, dude." Corey lowered the jug and turned his side to the guy. "But nothin's free these days."

That made the man stop, almost mid-step. "Shit man, Jerry's about to die. He just needs some water."

"I know. You can have it. We just need to come to an understanding." Corey gave the young man a shrewd look. "This was what, a buck fifty before the lights went out? I've been around man, ain't much left."

"I know. He was shot this morning and I've been trying to find water ever since. Hell, we were looking for water when he was shot!"

"Not a problem, man." Corey smiled, he knew he had this guy now. "A buck fifty in the old days. Call it twenty bucks now and you got yourself some water."

"What?" The guy was stunned. Corey knew he had the guy on the ropes. He must have been stunned because he didn't realize how good Corey was going to be at bargaining. "Twenty bucks? Like twenty dollars?"

"That's the price man. Take it or leave it."

"Dude! I'll take it!" He dug into his pocket and pulled out a wad of paper and started to sort through it. The first bill he came across was a

$50. He tossed it at Corey. "Keep the change man!" He grabbed the jug of water as Corey bent over to pick up the bill.

He followed the guy to his car. The passenger was in bad shape. He was all pale and his left arm was just hanging there. "Man, what happened? Who shot him?"

"Some girl, man. She -. He -. We were going into that grocery store over by the freeway. She was in there and shot him."

"Wha, where did you find that?" The bleeding guy swallowed two huge mouths-full of water. It seemed to revive him. "Where'd you get the water?"

"This guy sold it to us Jer." The first guy hooked a thumb over his shoulder at Corey.

"S, s, sold? Wha'd you give 'im?"

"Twenty bucks. Well, a fifty, that's what I had. Don't worry about it, we got the water now." He helped Jerry take another swallow from the jug.

Jerry gulped the water down, "Stupid shit."

"Hey there, *Jerry*." Corey couldn't believe this guy. His friend was probably saving his life, and he had the nerve to sit there and catch attitude while he bled out. "You don't have to talk to him like that. He-"

"Not him, asswipe." Jerry turned his head, locking eyes with Corey. "You're stupid if you traded water for money."

"Jerry," the other guy started, "it's all right man. He did us a solid, man. Don't be such an ass."

"Money ain't worth shit man." Jerry smiled and a trickle of blood dribbled from the corner of his mouth. "Where you been hiding?" He started to cough and blood flew in flecks from his lips. "So stupid man."

The coughing continued. More blood sprayed the car interior, his wounds opened again. A laughing cough turned into a prolonged wheeze, then faded to silence. It took less than two minutes for the laugh to transform to death. The smaller guy sat there the whole time, getting sprayed by blood, holding a hand on his friend's shoulder, trying to keep him calm. When the last breath leaked out, he relaxed back in the driver's seat, staring at the roof lining of the car. It was splattered in blood.

It took a few minutes but he finally spoke. "Thanks man. I know it doesn't look like it helped, but at least he didn't die thirsty."

"Don't thank me." Corey used his thumb to cock the hammer of the revolver. "You bought the water with money your friend said is worthless." It could have been a question but Corey made it into a statement.

"Dude," the small guy said, his hands creeping slowly to the steering wheel. "I wasn't screwing with you. I thought you were screwing with me."

"You told me to keep the change. You knew it was worthless." There was no tone, no inflection in his voice. Just a simple statement.

"Yeah, man, but I thought you knew!" He gripped the wheel tighter, his knuckles turning white.

"Why the *fuck* would I give you water for something worthless?"

"I don't know, man! Like I said, I thought you were screwing with me!"

"Well listen up. I'm not screwing with you this time. Things are going to happen pretty fast so you might not be able to keep up."

"Ok. I'm listening. What's up?" He relaxed his grip on the wheel, blood flowing back into his fingers and knuckles.

Corey pressed the barrel of the revolver into the guy's ear canal. "Here's what's going to happen."

"Yeah, man. Yeah. I'm listening."

"Good." He released the pressure a bit, unclogging the guy's ear. "I only need to exert about three pounds of pressure and the bullet will rip its way right through your head."

"Got it man! No funny stuff, I'm listening." The day was cool for North Texas in mid October but the guy was sweating profusely.

"Good. Listen real good. You screwed me man. You screwed me and you knew it." The man started to protest but Corey poked the barrel into his ear again and the protest quieted immediately. "So. You screwed me.

"You gave me a fifty for a gallon of water. You told me to keep the change. But that puts me in your debt and I don't like being in debt to people. So I tell you what. I'll sell you something else. How 'bout I sell you a bullet? Not just any bullet, a thirty-eight special, hollow point. Not just any thirty-eight special hollow point, but the thirty-eight special hollow point in the next chamber of this very gun. How's that sound?"

"Man! That sounds good! I'll by all the bullets in that gun if you want me to!" His hands flexed on the steering wheel, knuckles going from white to red then back to white.

"I'm just selling one. The very next one. I'll sell it for thirty bucks. That'll make us even, right? Well, not even because you screwed me, but we'll make this deal and then I won't be in your debt. Then we can work on settling that score, whacha think?"

The man broke out into a giddy laugh. "That sounds great man! I'll take it. Thirty bucks! Sounds like a deal to me!"

"Glad to hear it." Corey relieved the pressure on the man's ear. "Now that's settled. You did screw me though. So I think I should get to set the terms of delivery. Wouldn't you agree?"

"Dude! Yeah man, absolutely. Give it to me now, later, whatever man! You choose."

"Good. I agree." Corey smiled as he looked down at the man. "Here ya go." Corey didn't anticipate the guy turning toward him. When the gun went off the bullet thundered in just above the guy's left eye and blew the back of his head over Jerry in the passenger seat.

Corey reached into the car and pulled the driver's shirt up, using it to wipe the splatter off the stainless steel of the revolver. "Glad we were able to come to a mutually acceptable agreement."

He released the shirt and poked the button that unlatched the trunk. "Now that you guys won't be needing anything anymore, let's see what you've been up to."

☣ ☣ ☣

Ashley was lying across her bed. The iPod cranked away in her ears with Lady Gaga repeating, "Show Me Your Teeth." There were any number of interpretations for the song, but right now Ashley just wanted the drive of the music to purge everything else from her mind. The problem was that she had the volume turned up so loud it almost hurt and she still couldn't get her thoughts to quiet.

How on Earth could Corey be Roger's son? He is just such an ass!

When she'd left the Sack & Save, she had been shaken. Taking the time to scavenge what she could, after literally having to fight for it, just made sense and she was happy to have gotten a few more supplies but pretty much anything of use had already been taken. What she had needed was a friend. Someone to talk to. She had just shot a man. Maybe killed him. She purged that thought almost as quickly as it came. She didn't know that, so she wouldn't carry that burden if she didn't have to carry it.

Getting up to his room and seeing the door propped open from inside was a slap in the face. She had seen the stock of a rifle sticking out from under the bed and she knew that he didn't have a rifle in his room. Obviously that meant he had been out. When she looked under the bed and confirmed what she was seeing, all the scavenged goods, all the weapons and then all the food in the cabinet, she just flashed to everything she had done for him.

It wasn't just about these last few days. When she wanted to go to dinner, could he pay? Nope. But if he needed a video game it somehow just materialized on the first day of release. Could they go to a movie? Sure, if she paid and if it was something he wanted to see. Go visit her parents? She went by herself and he didn't even answer when she tried to call. For all of Christmas break last year she'd had a very one-sided relationship with his voicemail. When she returned, he just bragged about how good he had gotten at some stupid game.

Now she had a true issue and was in dire need of a friend. She realized the person she thought of as the only friend left alive in the world, never had been her friend. She needed to talk about what had happened, but there was no one to talk to. So instead of talking, she was drowning herself in music. Her small solar charger was more than enough to keep the iPod powered but she felt just a little guilty using electricity so frivolously.

The only thing to do was seriously get ready and get to Roger's place in Arkansas. She knew there were a bunch of people who were going to gather there, but she still thought of it as Roger's place. The only other people she had met from the group were Eric and Stephanie. They actually lived at the ranch and made sure it stayed active. Hopefully they would remember her and would accept her being there. *Geeze, hopefully they are still* alive *and still there.*

If she could simply go without Corey, she would. Unfortunately, she didn't know how to get there. The one time she went was with him driving, and she was still more interested in trying to get him to return her attempts at affection. Of course he had always been ready for sex, when it got to that point - but in a truck with his dad, that wasn't an option. Since sex wasn't involved, he'd driven or played with his handheld game system. She should have known it wouldn't work out and paid more attention. In the end, all she knew was that it was somewhere outside Dierks, Arkansas and there was a lot of land outside Dierks.

For now, Roger's last text message had said he would be here in seven to ten days. She just hoped that he would get here sooner, but the time was almost up. *He has two days to get here. If he doesn't make it, hopefully he'll make it to the ranch.*

She fast forwarded to the next song. *Why the hell is Justin Bieber on my iPod anyway?* Beyonce' was calling out to all the single ladies. *That'll do.* Ashley settled in, trying to come to terms with the events of the day.

21

Outside Anniston, AL

Roger broke out of the woods where the utility corridor opened up into a farmer's field just south of Highway 4. He stopped and consulted the map again. It had taken less than an hour to get to this location but that had been the last leg of certainty he'd had for today's travels.

Anniston itself was attached to a sizable military base. From his own knowledge of working within the government, he knew there was also a Department of Homeland Security contingent on the base as well. It was a training facility for DHS and a major repair facility for the Army's tracked vehicles. At this point in time Roger wasn't exactly relishing the thought of seeing employees of either department. He had a long way to go and just didn't want the hassle. As it was, he was surprised that he had been able to get this close to the base without encountering a roadblock. *Maybe I would have if I'd taken the roads. I might be inside the perimeter without permission. That can't be good.*

He turned to Jennifer who had been remarkably quiet this morning. Of all the possible responses she had to choose from with any of the questions or comments he had asked or said this morning, she seemed to be able to find the one with the fewest syllables. Usually just 'yes' or 'no'. *Poor thing must not have slept well.*

Still, this was a sticky situation and he needed her buy-in if he was going to put her life in danger. "Here we are," he pointed to the map in the best approximation of where he thought they were. "Right ahead of us is Route 4. If we keep going, we'll run right into Anniston where that base is. If we try to go north on 9, we hit a couple of small communities and then cross I-59. There are several hills and a few water crossings between here and there.

"Go south, we hit Talladega. That's a pretty small size population center but it is kind of iconic, so there might be some kind of presence there." Roger looked over at Jennifer but she still remained silent. "So," he said, "what do you want to do?"

"Obviously what I want to do doesn't matter." She crossed her arms, her eyebrows narrowing.

Roger quirked his head. *When Melissa looked like that she was being defiant. What does Jennifer have to be defiant about?* "Yes, what you want matters. We could be in a serious situation. I need to know your opinion."

"So it's about your needs? Figures." She turned to looked out the window. "Whatever you want."

"Hey, did I miss something?" Roger dropped the map in the seat and reached a hand out.

Somehow she knew what he was doing, "You touch me with that thing and you'll be pulling back a stump." His hand stopped in mid motion and slowly retreated. She paused for a moment then looked over her shoulder. "Yes, Roger. You missed something. You missed quite a bit. You'll never even know what you missed. Now make a decision and just do what you're going to do."

Well, Roger thought, *at least that is an answer.* He picked up the map, studied it a few more minutes and made his decision. Route 4 split about half a mile north, with Highway 78 going back toward the east for a bit. It would mean some backtracking, but he could catch Route 281 and take that south, through the Talladega National Forest. If all went well, he would come out at the Coosa River about halfway between Birmingham and Montgomery. If he could keep a good speed, that would be about 100 miles and he could get that done in less than three hours.

Roger kept a careful eye on the odometer as he set off.

His plan stayed intact for exactly six miles.

☣ ☣ ☣

Damn it! Jennifer was easily as mad at herself as she was at Roger. Somehow she just couldn't make herself snap out of it. She had never been the type to just throw herself into bed with any strange guy, but Roger wasn't a stranger anymore. They'd been through a good bit in a short time, and he really was *that guy* most women say they want, but would never give a chance. His biggest failing was that he just didn't get *people*, doubly handicapped when it came to *women people*. She had known that before she'd thrown herself at him last night.

On the other side, when she did decide to make a pass at a guy, she certainly wasn't accustomed to being turned away. That was the troubling part. Roger hadn't turned her away. He had been completely *oblivious* as to what was happening. If he had turned her away, she'd be perfectly fine with being mad at him. Other than stripping down completely and giving him an instruction book, there wasn't much more she could have done last night. She already felt kind of trashy for as far as she had taken it. Any further and her ego just might not have been able to recover.

She just- *Oh, shit, what is that?*

☣ ☣ ☣

They passed by the utility lane they had used when leaving camp this morning. Roger recognized the deadfall tree he'd had to negotiate around earlier. *So, here we are almost three hours into the day just to get back within half a mile of where we started.*

The intersection with I-20 was going to be a big challenge. Of course the military couldn't afford to guard every intersection of every road in the entire state. If they were truly inside an established perimeter then there would be even fewer guard stations. However, if the perimeter was to the east at Heflin, as he suspected, this intersection would be three to five miles in, a reasonable distance for a checkpoint.

The road had enough twists to make a snake proud. Unfortunately, it was cut into miles of trees, and visibility was practically zero except directly ahead and directly behind. When Roger came out of the curve leading up to the intersection, there was no chance to deviate from his course.

The I-20 bridge was an old concrete two-lane. Below it were four lanes divided by enough of a grassy median to double the size of the interstate. All in all, the bridge was less than a quarter mile long and it was less than a quarter mile away. It might as well have been on the other side of the moon.

As sturdy as the bridge appeared, it likely would not have supported either of the M1 Abrams main battle tanks posted on either end. The turrets were pointed along the east and west lanes. For north and south Route 281, two Stryker armored fighting vehicles had their main turrets poised to keep watch. On these turrets were mounted M2 .50 caliber machine guns. All four vehicles looked quite out of place. Here in the green woodlands of Alabama the vehicles still had their desert camouflage paint jobs. The packs of supplies stuffed in bags and duffles and cans, strapped to the tops and sides of the vehicles gave more of an indicator of the deteriorated situation the country had fallen to. The supply lines must be collapsing if a unit less than 20 miles from a base, on friendly territory, had to keep several days worth of supplies. Within an established perimeter Roger was surprised that troops were stationed anywhere for such a long period. But, then again, Roger wasn't a military strategist.

Between Roger and the armored vehicles were concrete barriers. The same barriers that lined the lanes of highways in construction areas to keep lanes separated were being used here to block off the road. There were five of them laid out in a zigzag fashion. People coming down the road would have no option but to slow down or crash into the walls. Between the walls was just enough room to comfortably maneuver a sedan. Roger was going to have to pull through, backup, turn, pull through and repeat several times to get the truck through. There would be no way to do it quickly and if you had malicious intent, there would be no way to do it without taking fire from at least two .50 machine guns. There were also about twenty soldiers behind the barricade, alert, but not standing at attention. Another twenty were on the other side.

Two soldiers were standing, each on one side of the road just in front of the barriers. The one on the driver's side held up a hand, indicating Roger should stop before proceeding into the slalom. He pulled up and rolled down the window.

"Morning sir," the young soldier said. Like his compatriot, he was dressed in desert camouflage which made him stand out rather than be concealed in this stretch of heavily wooded road. The name strip above his right breast pocket said 'Jerriton' and the small metal insignia fastened to the front of his gear was a single chevron. Private Jerriton stepped up to the truck. "Could I ask you to exit the vehicle, please?"

The other soldier, 'Schopp' by name, and with a three-chevron rank insignia stepped up to the passenger side.

"Sure, if you can tell me why?" Roger had been a resident of the United States all his life. He knew his rights and knew that he could not be searched or have his vehicle searched without probable cause or his giving consent.

For some reason the question seemed to flip a switch with Jerriton. "Because I fucking told you to get out." The young soldier stepped back and didn't quite raise his rifle but left little doubt as to his intent if Roger did not comply.

Roger held up his hands and out of the corner of his eye, saw Jennifer do so as well. He slowly reached out of the vehicle toward the door handle and this seemed to calm the soldier a bit. "Private Jerriton, it is Private, isn't it? I am willing to do as you say but I know my rights in this country you signed on to defend. You took an oath to protect the very document I am now relying on." He unlatched the door. The solder stepped back as it opened.

"With all due respect, sir," Jerriton started, "you must have been hiding in one deep shit hole. The president declared martial law. All that constitution shit is out the window until I'm told otherwise."

"Private!" It was the first word from the other soldier. It had enough authority that even Roger snapped to attention in his seat. "The word 'constitution' and the word 'shit' will not be stated in the same sentence in this Army or in my presence, is that understood?"

"Yes, Sergeant," the private muttered. He shrugged his shoulders and resettled the weapon across his chest.

"Private, you aren't going to make me create a demonstration of military discipline right here, on the side of the road, in front of these good people, are you?"

"No, Sergeant." It was said a bit louder, still lacking all enthusiasm.

The older soldier moved so he could lay eyes on the private across the tarp-covered bed of the truck. "Are we understood then?"

"Yes, Sergeant." A bit louder.

"Un-der-stood?"

"Yes, Sergeant!" The private yelled the response.

Sergeant Schoop stepped around in front of the truck. "Please exit the vehicle, folks. In accordance with orders, we have established martial law to reestablish and maintain order. The constitution has been temporarily suspended in this time of national tragedy."

"Seems to me," Roger said, climbing out of the truck, "suspending the constitution is the greatest tragedy our nation could face."

The sergeant simply stared at Roger for a moment before returning to his duties. "Private, search the vehicle."

Jerriton unhooked the bungee straps holding the tarp in place. When he threw the tarp back, he let out a low whistle. "Ho-o-oly shit, sarge, lookit this."

Still staying in front of the vehicle, Schoop moved further to the side where he could crane his neck to look into the bed of the truck. He nodded and returned his gaze to Roger, sparing only a quick glance for the silent Jennifer. "That's quite a supply of food and tools you have there. Do you have some ID?"

"I do, but I-" Roger stepped back, as if creating some space between himself and the sergeant would change the situation.

"Sir, I am attempting to be as polite as possible, considering the circumstances." The sergeant released his grip on his rifle, but the rifle stayed in place, suspended by an over-the-shoulder sling rig holding it to his chest. "I can continue to ask you questions and you can continue to rely on a set of rights and circumstances that will, hopefully be restored soon. However, in the meantime, those rights are not currently in effect. I can, and if necessary will, detain you for any reason, or none.

"I can, and may, remove any property that I believe, at my sole discretion, will assist in establishing or maintaining order.

"I can, and may, forcibly enlist your service in an activity that I believe, at my sole discretion, assists in establishing or maintaining order."

The sergeant flexed his back as if the weight of gear was bearing down just a little too heavy. "Those are the things I can and may do. Please note that none of them had the word 'law' in it anywhere. I truly hope to avoid exercising my sole discretion in any of those matters.

"So I ask you once again, do you have some ID?"

Roger dug his wallet out of his pocket, Private Jerriton covering the action from behind. Roger handed the ID to the sergeant. Schoop turned to Jennifer. "Ma'am?"

She reached into the truck, again with Jerriton carefully watching her actions, and dug her pocket book out of the bottom of the pack. She riffled through the various credit and debit cards and produced her driver's license.

"Texas and Colorado." Schoop looked up at Roger. "Where you coming from?"

"Atlanta." The word was out before Roger even thought. This guy might know someone broke out of the airport. They might even have their names on some watch list. "Charlotte before that." *Maybe that'll throw him off the trail.*

"You've come a long way. Where you going?"

"Texas."

"Big state."

"Yup."

"Anywhere specific?"

"Yup."

"You going to tell me where that is?"

"Only if you make me."

Obviously the sergeant had had enough. "That's fine Mr. Westover. I am able to practice my sole discretion and allow you to pass through."

Roger retrieved his license and slid it back into his wallet with a sigh of relief. Jennifer smiled as he handed her license back to her with a nod.

"However," Roger felt his heart sink as the sergeant uttered that one word, "I am first charged with establishing and maintaining order in my jurisdiction." The sergeant turned to the troops back behind the barricade.

"To that end, I wish to express the thanks of a grateful nation in exchange for your donation to the cause of order. These soldiers will ensure the food goes to feed the citizens who have come under our protection in Anniston.

"I am authorized by my command to extend the safety and protection of our facilities to all citizens who seek sanctuary. If you would like to seek sanctuary I can call for an escort."

Roger smirked as he watched the soldiers carry away armloads of food. Sergeant Schoop watched the smirk and nodded, "I can see that won't be necessary. With that being the case, I expect that it will take you two days to get to Texas. As such I'll leave you with enough food to make that journey.

"However," Roger's stomach sunk again. He'd hate that word the rest of his life. "Being as my primary duty is the safety and security of this jurisdiction, I will be confiscating the firearms I can see in the vehicle."

Roger opened his mouth to protest and Schoop held up a finger, forestalling the comment. "I will be confiscating the firearms I can see in the vehicle," in a lower tone and with a serious eye, "Do not tempt me to search the vehicle to determine if there is anything else I need to remove for the establishment and maintenance of order within my jurisdiction."

Roger stepped back. Sergeant Schoop nodded toward the cab of the truck. "Private Jerriton. Retrieve the firearms I can see."

The private stepped up to the truck and withdrew one of the .22 rifles. His next reach retrieved the pump shotgun. He leaned them against the side of the vehicle and reached in again. "What are you doing, Private?" Jerriton looked to his sergeant, "I can't see what you're reaching for."

"It's a-"

"Private. I did not instruct you to retrieve what you could describe. I told you to retrieve what I could see."

The private glanced around, then looked back at the sergeant, "Can you see several boxes of ammunition on the floorboard, sarge."

"Not a chance, son."

"Looks like that's it then, sergeant." The private stepped away from the vehicle, taking the weapons with him. He stacked them atop the jars one of the other soldiers was carrying to the bridge.

Sergeant Schoop nodded and returned his glance to Roger. "Last chance, Mr. Westover. There is food and medical care available in Anniston and any citizen is welcomed to it. We cannot guarantee your safety outside the confines of our aid camps."

"Can you guarantee it within the camps?"

"Well, uh-"

"How many new cases of the virus are showing up in the camps, sergeant?"

"Fewer each day." The sergeant, for the first time, appeared to lose some of his confidence.

"But still, new cases every day." Roger shook his head.

"I should let you know," Sergeant Schoop changed the subject, "looting is a criminal offense and is punishable. Up to execution. Just thought I should let you know."

Roger nodded, "Appreciate the warning. That's only within your jurisdiction, right."

"That's all we can take care of right now."

"I think I understand what you're saying."

"I hope you do Mr. Westover. I hope you also understand that every NCO in the military has been given orders very similar to the orders I have received. However, communications and command infrastructure are not as intact as we may like them to be. Ankara has hit the military as hard as anyone else.

"All I'm saying is that we've all gotten the same information but there will be those who interpret those orders differently than I do."

"Thank you, Sergeant. I believe I understand you perfectly."

As Roger started the truck and began making his way through the barriers Sergeant Schoop thought to himself, *I hope you do Mr. Westover, I truly hope you do.*

22

Central Alabama

Jenny was still a bit shaken three hours later when they'd made it to the Coosa River. After several days being isolated from the rest of society, it had almost been a welcomed sight to see the military. It was a sign of civilization to her mind. Of course having large caliber weapons trained on United States roadways was unnervingly odd, but she had been raised that the military, like police officers, put their lives on the line in order to protect civilians. Now that philosophy had been challenged.

Jenny sat with the .22 rifle in her lap, the barrel pointed toward the door so as not to be a danger to herself or Roger. Sergeant Schoop had been polite. He had probably even let them have more weapons than he strictly needed to. But that was part of the problem.

She flexed her grip on the rifle. When Roger had mentioned that he wanted to be one of *those guys with guns* it had made her a bit nervous. She had been around guns a time or two but she had never really been exposed to them. Paul had shown her a handgun that he'd owned, she shivered unconsciously at the thought of what he may have used it for, and the thing that struck her most was that it was so heavy for its size.

She wasn't the type to go shooting. She had always had police to protect her streets and the military to protect her country. She didn't *need* a gun. As far as Jennifer was concerned, everyone who *needed* a gun got one issued to them when they went to work.

When Roger dragged those guns out of the farmhouse, she had almost protested. But the encounter with the hunters had made her nervous. Being held at gunpoint in the fitness center had outright scared her. Then they were stopped by the military. The very people she had always been told were there to protect her and protect her rights were the ones taking those rights from her. They'd taken away their means of survival, taken their means of protection. Her mind still didn't fully accept it.

She gripped the rifle again. One thing was for sure, the next person who tried to take it would be getting the barrel first!

"Roger?" He startled at her voice. It was probably the first time she had spoken without being prompted since last night. "You're a gun-guy, huh?"

"If I say 'yes', can I change my answer after you define 'gun-guy'?" He almost cracked a smile as he looked at her across the bench seat.

"I mean you've always been around guns. You know about them, know how to use them. Right?"

"Sure. My granddad was in World War Two, great granddad was in World War One. Dad just missed Korea but went to 'Nam. I think, except for Korea, there was a Westover in every major battle Anglo-Saxons have fought all the way back to the battle of Stirling, between the Scots and the English. Heck I think we were on both sides of that one, Civil War too. Guns have been a part of my life…as much a tool as a hammer."

"But we don't have to hunt anymore. You know, to eat." Her mind switched over to the only other reason she could think of for using a gun, "And you don't strike me as the type to go around killing people. So they aren't really tools in the modern world, are they?"

Roger smiled for real this time, glanced at her quickly, then returned his attention to the road. "Having a hard time with what happened back there?"

Jennifer nodded and though he couldn't see it, he took her silence as confirmation. "I'm not a carpenter." He glanced over and saw her eyebrows knit together. "I'm not an auto mechanic. I'm not a painter. Hell, I'm not even a writer. But I have hammers, a set of wrenches and a word processor.

"If I waited until I needed to build something to buy a hammer I wouldn't know the best type for the job and wouldn't really understand how to use it. If I waited until I needed to fix a leaky pipe or change my thermostat on the truck to get some wrenches, I wouldn't have the skills I needed.

"Same with a gun. If you wait until you absolutely need it in order to get one or practice with it, it would be pretty useless to you. A tool needs to be used in order for you to become proficient. Properly maintained, it is going to be there and ready to perform at its maximum. It is up to the user to be ready."

"But what about, I don't know, I mean, ready for what?" She swept her arm, taking in the landscape outside and the entire truck. "Surely no one was ready for *this*. No one could have seen it coming."

Roger smiled again, reached across and patted her on the shoulder. This time she let him and didn't threaten to cut off his hand again. It was actually nice to have a little human contact. "Well," he said, "it seems no one *you know* saw this coming, but a bunch of people *I know* thought it was very likely. Remember the cabin in Arkansas I told you about? There are eight families. We each bought five to eight acres and formed up a pretty good sized piece of land. We've got a farm, off-grid power, wells, security, all that stuff. We call it a homestead but some people would call it more of a commune. That's where I'm trying to get to. If I can get the kids and get there, we should be set to ride this thing through."

"Really? Like back in the old west days, living on a farm, ranching, all that? People are really still doing that? People have been getting ready for all this?" *Surely he's kidding! Who'd give up modern life to be ready for something that just couldn't happen?*

"Maybe not this exactly, but for *something*." He glanced at her again, a questioning look in his eye for a moment, then continued, "Many people have said nothing like this could happen. We're the United States, we're the top dog. No one can take us down. But that was my job – to think of just how we could be taken down and what to do about it.

"The crazy thing is, most of us thought it was going to be a financial problem rather than an epidemic. The playbook was written for financial collapse. Sure, there were contingencies for epidemics but the main effort was concentrated on financial collapse. Turns out, that's two completely different responses."

Jennifer shook her head, he was getting off track. "Hang on. You're way down a road and I'm still in the driveway. You're a gun-guy because you thought the United States was going to have a financial collapse, and you have a bunch of friends who are setting up some armed compound?"

"Almost." He paused and she could tell he was obviously collecting his thoughts. "I'm a gun-guy, as you call it, because I'm a gun-guy. I like them. My family has had them all my life. I've taught Corey how to use them. It is a hobby, a sport, a form of recreation. Javelin throwing started as war practice. So did wrestling, fencing and many other ancient sports. When you think about it that way, historically speaking, it is more odd to have a pastime that does not include battle preparation than having a pastime that does."

He nodded and mentally shifted gears. "So that's why I'm a gun-guy. It just turns out that guns have become a good skill set to have. The homestead is a whole different thing. There's even a couple who are pretty much pacifists. Gene and Shirley. Good people. But most of us do have an interest in firearms. Not *because* we thought things were going south but *in addition to* thinking things were going south."

He wobbled his head as if that was only partially what he wanted to say. "OK, you ever been to a city where you didn't live?"

"Of course."

"Did you drive there?" He gave her another glance, like he was getting to his point.

"Sure." She drew it out to three syllables, almost a question, almost an answer.

"When you were a teenager you knew you were going to be in that other city and would need to get around?"

"No, not really. I mean, I guess I thought it was possible, but I wanted to drive. You know, it was fun and I could get around on my own. I didn't have to wait for someone else to take me places."

Roger nodded as if that was the answer. Almost a minute went by as Jennifer waited for a response and then her answer started playing itself over again in her head. Roger glanced over at her as a smile started to spread across her face.

"I get it." She nodded. *It kinda makes sense.* "I think I really get it."

Roger nodded again and paraphrased her words, "I guess I thought the country could go down the tubes. But shooting was fun and I could protect myself. I didn't have to wait for someone to come protect me." He paused, then looked at her again, "You know the old saying, right?"

Still smiling with her new understanding, Jennifer looked at him, "What's that?"

"When seconds count, the police are only minutes away." He smiled - as he had every time he told that one.

It took a second for her to think the statement through, "Oh! That's terrible! Police are hard working, just like anyone else!"

"True," Roger nodded, "but they have an impossible job. They have to be present in an area in order to be a deterrent and their very presence, most of the time, means that they are doing their job. But they can't be everywhere at once. We've come to rely on them to be our protectors, our infallible shield against evil in the world. They just can't. We must be able – now more than ever – to protect ourselves.

"In my mind, to turn your protection over, exclusively, to someone else is like abdicating a portion of your humanity. I chose not to do that. But we're coming up on the bridge so we need to keep an eye out. We've got hours and hours of discussion on the Second Amendment once we're safely across the river."

Back in Georgia crossing the Chattahoochee had turned out to be a non-issue. Not so with the Coosa. A red dirt road peeled off Route 22 to the right and, if Roger was reading the map correctly, it was the last road before the bridge. The problem was that the map did not show the house directly across the highway from the dirt road. When Roger saw it, it was too late. A man dressed in denim jeans, white shirt and black leather vest, his hair tied back with a bandana, was crossing the yard, a hand held up in the air. Behind him several other people were mounting motorcycles. Their engines filling the quiet rural lane.

23

Central Alabama

The benefit of motorcycles is fuel efficiency, the more direct connection with the road and the speed out of the gate. The particular motorcycles revving up for pursuit were large Harleys and similar. This gave them more stability and comfort over long distances but it also subtracted just a bit from their maneuverability. A major disadvantage was that most people are right handed and the throttles on most bikes are on the right hand side. This effectively eliminates the ability of the common driver to also be a shooter. Road bikes like these also don't handle well once off the road.

Roger knew he had to capitalize on his advantages and minimize his disadvantages. There were probably ten bikes revving up for pursuit. He glanced toward the bridge. Another group of men was waiting there. It appeared there was a barbed wire fence segment blocking the way. *Can't go forward. Just leaves going back.*

He stomped the brakes and skidded to a stop just as the first rider hit the roadway. The unexpected stop was enough to make the biker wobble and ram the rear of the truck bed. *One down.* He slammed the truck in reverse, using the soft shoulder of the road to complete a backward U-turn, then shifted back to drive. He knew they would catch up quickly, but he had to keep moving if he was going to buy time.

There had been no creeks or culverts or anything where Roger could try a blocking tactic. His map had shown that he was far away from any other route across the river. That was one of the reasons he had chosen this route. The only thing he could think to do was try and lose the motorcycles on rough terrain. The old pickup would surely handle off road conditions better than road bikes.

He remembered a utility clearance about half a mile back and made his way toward it. The next river crossing he could remember on the map was north. *Too far to go with people on my tail.* The way the roads curved out here, he was likely to dead end into the river if they tried to go south. As soon as the woods split, he snapped a left into the open space and plowed over the embankment.

The truck bucked and threw them both tight against their seat belts, then blasted up the loose dirt, showering the closest riders in a spray of red clay. About half the bikes split off as Roger made it to the top of the hill. The other four clawed away at the hill and slowly inched their way up. For the moment, the pickup was opening a distance.

He kept jerking the wheel side to side, attempting to make his next move random, hoping to ruin the aim of anyone attempting to shoot. So far, all was silent.

The truck sailed between the legs of a giant power line tower, ducking to the right of the cleared lane, drifting left, then right and a sharper right, only to pull away from the tree line at the last instant.

Scrub brush had over grown part of the lane and Roger powered over it, taking a moment to check his mirror. One bike had made it up the hill and was in full pursuit.

"You might have to learn to shoot real quick."

Jennifer looked at him them checked her side mirror. "What do I need to do?"

"Open that window." Roger used his head to indicate the sliding window in the back glass of the truck. Moving at more than 50 miles per hour over rough terrain wasn't a time to remove his hands from the wheel.

Jennifer flipped the latch and pushed the windows open.

Roger yelled, "Hang on!"

The truck bounced as he hit a patch of dirt rutted by heavy equipment and dried in place. Something shattered in the bed and Jennifer was thrown. Her head slammed into the roof on the way up and then into the dash on the way down. Her vision clouded, but she shook it off and returned to the window.

"You all right?" Roger glanced at her but immediately returned his attention to zigzagging through the lane.

"Hurt like hell! But I gotta job to do." She stuck the rifle out the back window and swayed as the truck continued to bounced under her. "What next?"

"Charge the weapon. That little stick just above the trigger. Pull it back and let it go." He heard the sliding sound confirming she had done as told. "Now, see that button down by the trigger?"

"Uh," she paused, "oh, yeah. I see it."

"Push it to the side so that the red ring appears. That means it is off safe. It is hot."

"Got it."

"It's a twenty-two. It won't kick. Just put it up to your shoulder and pull the trigger." There wasn't enough time for a full shooting lesson. If they made it out of the situation Roger would teach her more about it later.

The first shot rang out with an immediate *ping!* follow-up. "Shit! I got the tail gate."

"Aim higher!"

"No, kidding, right?" The second shot rang out. With the dirt cloud behind, him Roger didn't even attempt to see where the bullet went. Three more shots sounded in quick succession. The motorcycle jerked and slowed. Roger watched his side mirror as long as he could. Just as he looked away, another motorcycle was coming into view through the dirt spray.

Just ahead the road dipped away. "Hang on tight!" Roger hit the brakes to try and slow. It was too late. The truck went airborne as the lane dropped over the edge of a hill. Jennifer had nothing to hang on to. When she bounced up, the window frame knocked the rifle out of her hand. She hit the roof again. This time she fell forward, slamming her forehead against the back window.

The fog closed in again. This time when she shook her head she was assaulted with excruciating pain from her head and neck. Wetness splashed across her forehead and stung her eyes. She fumbled for the rifle and only once it was sticking back out the window did she realize her hand was splattered with blood.

Roger let out another yell and something impacted with the front of the truck. It grated its way up the hood, across the roof and rattle-slammed onto the bed before sliding off to the dirt. The corrugated metal gate burst apart. The truck slipped across a narrow road just as the biker made it through the now-cleared fence. Scrap metal twisted into the front wheel of the bike.

It wasn't like a movie. The guy didn't get thrown and fly through the air. One second he was riding, the next second the bike flipped over the front wheel, slamming the rider into the ground, head first. He never lost his seated position and the bike collapsed on top of him.

Jennifer didn't have much time to think about it. The truck dipped again as it went over another small hill. She wiped her face with her shirt sleeve and it immediately soaked through with blood.

Roger slammed his breaks at the bottom of the hill. He checked the mirror and the view behind was completely blocked by the hill. As the truck skidded to a stop, he turned it sideways so he wasn't locked into one direction to go.

"You OK?" He looked over at Jennifer and blood was cascading from a gash in her forehead. He grabbed a towel laying in the seat and dabbed at her head.

"You tell me? Kind of dizzy."

"You're doing great. Not a bad cut, just a good knock and head cuts bleed like crazy. You'll be fine."

Jennifer nodded, causing blood from her eyebrows to drip on the back of the seat. She hardened her eyes and nodded again, this time with more authority.

Roger smiled at her. "You're doing great." He leaned over and gave her a quick peck on the lips and shifted the truck into gear.

He looked down the lane, then back up the low hill, trying to determine where to go. There was a road right here he could try. Before he could make a decision, the rumble of motorcycle filled the truck cab. The two lead bikes flew down the hill. They slammed into the side of the truck, throwing their riders, mangling the bikes.

Roger jammed the accelerator, kicking up a cloud of dust. Another bike slid off the hill. The rider almost corrected enough but clipped his left leg on the truck bumper. He fell with his bike, clutching his shattered tibia.

The truck lumbered back up the hill. Roger snapped a right hand turn. He was just getting up to speed as the last of the bikers rounded the bend in the road and spotted him. The truck lurched forward. Roger wove through the woods on the narrow, winding road.

On the right side the red clay ground was higher. Some recent rain had washed the clay into the road. Roger drove through the dried clay, kicking up a screen of dirt. Jennifer was bent over on the passenger side of the bench seat, firmly holding the towel to her forehead, trying to get the bleeding to stop.

Roger had no idea where he was. All he knew was that none of the roads back here would take him across the river. That meant he was trapped. Just ahead, the clay-covered road took a sharp left turn. He did the only thing he could think of.

With the dirt obscuring the riders' vision, Roger slammed the brakes again, thrusting the truck into reverse before it had even come to a stop.

The wheels spun first one way, then another and the cloud completely enveloped the vehicle. Just as the truck began moving backward one of the bikes crumpled into the tailgate. The truck bumped to a stop.

The last bike flew by on the driver's side and cruised around the corner. Roger yelled at Jennifer, "Get in the floorboard!"

She slid down, still pressing the towel to her head. Roger flung open his door, grabbed the .22 and threw himself clear of the truck.

The massive vehicle, overcoming the inertia of the bike impact, continued to roll backward. Roger ran across the street and ducked into the edge of the woods. He could hear the bike slowly returning up the wooded road. Its engine was just above an idle, being cautious.

As Roger listened, the sound stopped. The *blat* from the tail pipe slowed. He checked the truck. The back tires had finished backing over the downed Harley, its rider pinned in place. The oversized truck tire had quieted any protest he may have made. The front tires were bumping against the bike, causing the truck to rock back and forth.

Roger returned his attention to where the last motorcycle was parked. There was a soft crunch of leaves as the rider took a shortcut around the peak of the turn, coming across through the woods. He was attempting to be quiet but the thick-soled biker boots simply weren't up to the task.

Roger faded back into the woods a few careful steps. The steps of the other guy didn't pause. Maybe he was making too much noise to hear Roger. Maybe he was somewhat deafened from riding his loud motorcycle at full speed.

Whatever it was, he stepped out of the woods just a few feet in front of Roger. Now that he was dismounted, his right hand was available to hold a weapon and he had taken advantage of that availability. The gun was impressive. Roger had read about them in magazines but he'd never shot one. It had an over-sized cylinder that was twice as long as normal revolver cylinders and it was chambered for a .45 long Colt or .410

shotgun shell. But, overall, it kind of appeared too short for the cylinder. Taurus came out with the design, called The Judge, and a few other manufacturers had copied it since. It was close enough that Roger could very clearly make out that it was a Taurus original.

The biker raised the weapon and yelled, "OK you assholes, stop the truck and get out." He thumbed the hammer back and closed one eye to sight down the under-sized sight rail.

The next bump against the bike dislodged the driver's side door. It swung open and the hand cannon blasted, punching a hole in the middle of the door. Had Roger been getting out, it would have torn out his stomach.

Unfortunately for this guy, Roger was already out. He quietly shouldered the rifle, just behind the biker's field of view. The revolver blasted again, punching another hole, this time at the edge of the door, next to the hinge.

Roger sighted down the length of the rifle and silhouetted the front sight post with the man's ear canal.

"Last chance!" The man yelled.

When the biker settled his head again to regain the sight picture, Roger pulled the trigger. After several minutes of the big truck's engine rumbles, the sound of motorcycles in pursuit, and two shots from the massive revolver shells, the .22 was virtually silent.

Roger felt the tap against his shoulder. The man's head twitched as the tree on the other side was sprayed with a delicate red mist and the man fell without even the slightest twitch. After retrieving the weapon and a pocket full of .410 shells, Roger crossed over to where the truck was bouncing off the crushed motorcycle.

He stepped up to the truck, just out of sight of the door. "It's me," he yelled just in case Jennifer had retrieved the old double-barrel. When he looked in, he saw she hadn't. Her eyes were the size of saucers and where her face wasn't streaked with blood it was devoid of all color.

It took an instant before recognition overcame the terror in her eyes. When it did, she crawled out of the floorboard and across the seat. Roger just barely caught her as she threw herself into his arms. The revolver and shells rattled to the ground as his arms closed around her. Their lips met. The kiss became harder and more desperate as they tightened their embrace.

Blood from her forehead slid down her face, mixing with their mutual sweat and smearing their cheeks. He didn't know how long they kissed but when they broke apart they were both gasping for air. Neither released their hold on the other. They simply stood together, arms locked, sharing their breath and thankful to be alive.

By the time the last of the bikers came across the scene, Roger and Jennifer were long gone, even the dust from their passing had settled.

☣ ☣ ☣

It took Roger over two hours to find a path out of the backwoods. The whole time Jennifer was tucked up under his right arm. Now that they had made contact, neither wanted to let go. He didn't even complain when his arm fell asleep. He let the 'sandbag' feeling just settle in and accepted it as small payment for having her so close.

By the time they crossed the Coosa over the northern route, they had burned hours. He stopped well short of the bridge, scouted ahead, stopped again, scouted, over and over again until they were across. No hassle this time. Shortly after, she laid down across the seat, her towel-wrapped head in his lap, and went to sleep. He was cautious as he continued across the state. He stayed on the back roads but gave any suspected choke point a wide berth.

It was interesting that the further west he went the more electricity was operating. As the sun fell, many of the street lights came on. This helped him stay clear of smaller towns. When they'd crossed over Interstate 20, it had been lit up in either direction as far as the eye could see.

When Roger saw a sign beside the road he decided to use a trait of human nature to his benefit. Most people in the US weren't comfortable around death or the dead. That might be changing. Familiarity increases comfort.

He had been driving slowly down the narrow County Road 2 with his lights off, looking for the Mississippi state line. There was enough light to drive by and enough to read the sign marking a cemetery. Pulling off the road at the black iron-railed, red brick-pedestal fence, Roger gently shook Jennifer. She lifted her head. He slipped out of the truck and lifted the gate latch, walking the gate open. Jennifer slid into the driver's seat and pulled into the graveyard.

Roger closed the gate and climbed onto the bed of the truck, sticking his head through the still open window. "Just drive around back and see if there is somewhere we can park out of the way."

She nodded and yawned, then proceeded to the back of the lot. It wasn't a large cemetery. The ornamental fence only extended about halfway down the side of the lot. In the back, it opened into a stand of trees. It wasn't the best place to stop as there were several houses around and there seemed to be a lot of light coming from the houses. Roger was tired and couldn't think about it at the moment. Between the Army stop and the biker chase, the day had taken its toll.

Jennifer pulled a tarp out of the back, along with a length of rope to begin tying up their shelter. The sky was clear but you never knew when it might rain. In the philosophy of *The World According to Roger*, it was better to have a shelter and not need it than to need a shelter and not have it. Right now she was just happy to be safe and to be with him.

That happiness lasted right up to the point that she heard a pump shotgun's ratchet and a blinding spear of light stabbed into her eyes.

24

Western Alabama

"Wa'ch'all doon ba'kair?" The light just could not be escaped. Jennifer tried to look at Roger but the halo of light was simply too bright. Her hands slid slowly up to shoulder level. It was becoming a natural position.

"Just trying to make camp." Roger was close but in the miniature sun shining in her eyes, she still couldn't make him out. Even when she closed her eyes the color spots were so bright there was no darkness.

It was the same voice. The accent was so thick Jennifer could barely understand what was being asked. She was certain the questioner was male but had no idea of age. "Ina sim'tairy? Wa'ch'all hyd'n frum you gotta hyd'n'a sim'tairy?"

"Figured we wouldn't be bothered in a cemetery. That's all." Roger stepped forward and blocked some of the light shining on Jennifer. In his shadow she could tell two large flashlights were being used because the beams converged on him but she still had no way of looking behind the light.

"You'da not been if it weren't a fam'ly sim'tairy." First one light and then the other shifted to Roger's feet. "Y'ain't armed?"

Roger sighed. "We have weapons. They're in the truck."

"Ya gunna go trespassin', y'otta least be strapped. Some folks ma'not take it kein'ly. Bu'cha stumbled on the right sim'tairy t'night. Looks like ya' hurt and need a bed. C'mon up ta th' house, we take care o'ya d'rectly."

As the evening progressed the rhythm of their speech, and depth of the accent, began to make more sense. Jennifer achieved some level of proficiency with listening to the family.

Mister and 'Miz'us' Wilson Cobb had the pleasure of accepting Roger and Jennifer as guests. So many people came in and out that Jennifer couldn't imagine they all lived in the one-story, ranch-style house. *It must be some kind of family commune or something.*

Sitting in the electrically lit dining area, 'Miz'us' Cobb, *Martha if you please*, was tending to Jennifer's head. Jenny's eyes kept drifting to the light bulb as if in disbelief. It's amazing how the human brain works. All her life she'd had electric lights and now just a week without and it seemed like some kind of magical thing.

Martha finished cleaning the wound and smeared it with an antibiotic laden cotton swab. She carefully applied a large adhesive bandage. "Tha' ya go, Sweetie. 'Til heel-lup nice. Be just as pretty after as b'fore."

"Thank you, that was very gracious of you."

"Think nuttin of it. What's people good fer if not hep'n anoth'rn out when needed?" Martha packed up her supplies and stored them back in the pantry. She took the blood-soaked rag and dropped it in a laundry basket just inside the wash room. "Now's food yur need'n. You're a guest in tha house, so you just sit pretty and I get sumthin heat'n."

As Martha puttered around the well stocked and still fully functional kitchen, Jennifer sat in her chair and carried on the conversation. Martha had seven children, twenty five grandchildren, with one on the way, and three great-grandchildren. They all lived within walking distance, most of them within sight, but you just couldn't beat the company of a guest from out of town.

☣ ☣ ☣

Roger was sitting with Wilson and Andy on the front porch. Andy, about the same age as Roger, was Wilson's youngest son. Both of the

Cobbs were seated on a couch that had obviously been outside for years. Various chairs and rockers were arranged around the couch. Wilson had a gleam in his eye from laughing. "Yez, I says to Andy here, 'Lookit that truck with no light on.'

"'Why ain't theys got lights on,' he said.

"'On't know. Try'n ta be crafty mebbee,' I said." Wilson shrugged his shoulders and looked at his son. Andy shrugged and Wilson continued.

"When ya stopped at the fence I said t'Andy, 'Cain't be ta no good, go'n to the sim'tairy in the dark like at.'

"Nope, no good t'all,' said Andy.

"That'll teach us! Gotta trust inna Lord. Here y'are, good people in needa help and we thought ya's up to no good. An' He blessed my fam'ly to be the ones t' do 't. He'll teach humil'ty if ya sit an's lissen. He will indeed." Wilson sat back and took a draw off his pipe.

"Well, we 'ppreciate you listening this time." Roger smiled at Wilson and Andy. "It has been several days since we saw a truly friendly face. There is no way we can repay you for your hospitality."

"Yu'on't owe me nuthin. Heaven's no. The good Lord blessed me with abundance an' this is how He wants me to use som'it. Who'm I ta say someone owes me sumthin for't? It's His to give an' I'm juss His hand ta'day. Juss you keep that ear out. When ya hear Him guiding you, you best lissen. When He does, you'll be alive t' hear Him. S'all I ask, 'cause Him and His Son is all paid up in my book."

"Again though, we certainly appreciate it. There are a lot of people out there not really caring what He says right now."

"He di'na tell me to preach to ya so I ain't gunna unless ya press me. But thay's people ou'tair who dinn't lissen when times was good. Now they ain't sa good, and they say He'd never allow it if He existed. So there's proof He don't. Hogwash.

"They's others 'at say we been runnin' from Him so long we's finally gotten so far He can't help us. Hogwash and blas'fme. He can do everything He can do no matter what we do to stop him. Yes, sir, He can."

"He can indeed. Yes He can," those might have been the first words Andy uttered since they sat down. He had his father's deep, rich voice with just about twenty years less smoke on the vocal cords.

"No, I tell ya, an' it's all I'll tell ya unless ya ask or He commands. I tell ya, sometimes ya gotta stick with the tough love. When the hugs and kisses ain't a-workin' ya might needa paddle."

"I took Andy here, and Mark too. Took 'em out inna woods."

"Yes he did! I 'member it. Did the same thing for m' boys too!"

"I took 'em out inna woods," Wilson repeated. "See I been tellin' 'em they needed ta get some d'rection in life. Took 'em out where they'd never been and left 'im there. Told 'im, 'He'll lead ya home or He'll lead ya where you're s'posed to be.'

"Made my heart proud to see 'em comin' out the woods two days later." He laughed at the memory, "They was scratched up, looked like they grabbed 'hold the wrong end of a bobcat and then got dragged by horses for a year, but they came back home. That'll open ya' ears to the Lord, but I ain't preachin'! I'm just sayin'!"

Wilson and Andy chuckled and sucked on their pipes. The thick smoke drifted into the cool night air. Some interesting smells were coming out of the house and just as Roger's stomach started to protest, Jennifer stepped out with a plate of food. Martha followed just behind with a folding TV tray.

"Such a nice night," Martha said, "be a shame to waste it sittin' at a stuffy table." She set the TV tray down in front of Roger. "But I'll not deny ya the table! Please don't think I would! I'll set it now if you'd prefer ta eat there."

"No, ma'am this is more than fine and more than generous." Jennifer smiled as she set his plate down. He smiled back as their eyes held one another for a moment or two longer than strictly necessary.

When Jennifer stepped away to follow Martha back into the house, Roger looked down at the plate and his eyes bulged. There had to be more food than he had ever tried to pile on a plate. The meat must have been a pound of pot roast, cooked like only a black iron pot with a heavy lid could do it. The pot roast was surrounded by small carrots, sliced onions and cubed potatoes. Next to that was at least a quarter head of cabbage. He could tell by the light sheen caught by the porch light that it was cooked with fat – probably pork drippings – like his mother had made, and like most cardiologist would tell you to stay away from. On top of it all was a slice of cornbread bigger than a man's fist.

Martha stepped out with another folding table and Jennifer placed her own food on it. Her plate was a scaled down version. It looked like it would only feed a family of four rather than a family of eight. The lady of the house sat back in her rocker and lit the end of a thin cigar that had been sitting in the ashtray, waiting for her respite. "Wish I'da known you was comin'. I'da fixed a proper meal for ya. But I do what I can with what I got, an' hope you don' think the less a' me for it."

"No! This is great!" Roger shot an imploring look at Wilson, "I was just telling Wilson how much I appreciate you all helping us out. I-"

"Friend Roger," Wilson cut him off, "you keep that up an' yer gunna make me start preachin'. I tol' ya it-"

"Hush, there, Wilson." Martha said it so quietly that Roger almost didn't hear her. "He's just bein' nice to say his thanks. Ya can let 'em do it and be thankful that we got some kind guests and not some of 'em we've seen crossin' by. Now let'um eat."

"Well, you right Mother. You know ya're." Wilson sat back on the couch as if that settled the issue. He and Andy took puffs on their pipes that would have appeared coordinated if they'd been anyone else. The same draw in, the same pause. The same exhale through the nose. For the next fifteen minutes the only sounds were tobacco crackling as air was drawn through it, wheezy exhales, and the clatter of forks and knives on plates as the couple attacked their meals.

☣ ☣ ☣

Roger finally admitted defeat with half his plate still covered in some of the best food he had eaten in years. When you threw out the modern rulebook about what you can have and what you can't have, and just went for flavor, even simple food could be quite exciting. "Martha, this is possibly the best meal I've had as an adult. I just don't think I could fit another bite in my mouth."

She pushed herself out of her rocker and cast an appraising eye over his plate. "A workin' man's gotta get all he can eat. N'Ah think that all men are gonna be workin' men again these days." She picked up the plate with a twinkle of pride in her eyes. In most interpretations of Southern hospitality, if a man has to go back for seconds it was always welcomed - but it was probably because there wasn't enough on the plate to begin with. Martha had passed the test she set for herself. She picked up Jennifer's plate with an equally appraising eye and nodded that there was some left there as well. "Ah'll be back wi'the cobbler d'rectly."

Roger and Jenny shot one another a glance that could have been interpreted as terror. Wilson, seeing the look, chuckled. "Don't worry 'bout it. Tha crusts so light, ya wone even know ya swaller'd it."

Jennifer reached over, squeezed Roger's hand and stood, "If you'll excuse me, I think I'll help Martha."

"It's fine, youn'lady. If ya wanna help Mother, that's fine. If it's something else I'm suspectin', the water's workin' as good as the 'lectric. No need to dig a hole in the back forty of the sim'tairy." Wilson chuckled as he leaned back on the couch. Jennifer just ducked back into the house, her face turning red. "She's a good woman ya got there, Roger. Good indeed. Ya don' find many of 'em that pretty and that quiet."

All three of the men shared a chuckle and Roger leaned forward, just coming to terms with how fortunate he was. Still, it wasn't right to let them go on with the wrong impression. "Really, it must be the bump on the head though. This is the quietest I've seen her."

"Don' look the gift horse inna mouth, there. Jus' sit back an' enjoy the quiet while ya got it."

"Yes, indeed." Andy took a long draw on his pipe though, he had finished it and already tapped out the spent tobacco. "Jus' sit back an' enjoy it."

"So you say the water is working?" Roger's head was spinning at the thought. At the nod from Wilson he continued. "As in a shower or a bath?"

Wilson smiled, leaning forward again. In a false conspiratorial whisper that could have been heard for yards he said, "I's hopin' you'd ask. See, Martha's a kind hearted woman but I'd not wanna hear her goin' on after ya'll lef' 'bout how ya stunk up 'er sheets." Father and son guffawed at the joke and after a moment Roger joined in.

I probably do stink compared to these guys. We had that bath last night but lake water and well water are two different things.

"Wouldn't want that, would we," Roger asked once the laughing died down. "I've got some toiletries in the truck, if you don't mind..."

"Notta'tall. Why don'cha bring the truck 'round? Park it ou'here where we kin keep a watch on it."

A few minutes later Roger pulled around in the truck and dragged both his and Jennifer's bags out. As he bounded up the steps to the front porch Jennifer darted out of the front door, grabbed her bag with a quick thanks and a peck on his cheek, then ducked back in the house.

Roger was still standing there watching where she had disappeared, a grin cocking his mouth to the side.

"Oh, ain't been so lucky for long, huh?" Wilson leaned forward again. "Love's still young 'nuff to keep the man standin' like sum'un clubbed in the back a' the head."

Andy shifted his weight, nodding. "Yes, sir! Yes indeed. Like a damned fool idiot."

"While I don' 'ppreciate the language, I cain't dispute the thought." Wilson leaned back.

Roger, still grinning, sat back in his chair. "I guess she's gone off for the showers so I have time.

"We met just as everything started happening." He judged the character of his hosts and felt the truth was the best course. "We were both stuck in the Atlanta airport. Just kinda fell in together and been together since."

Wilson leaned forward on the couch again, "Well the Lord, He work's those myst'r'uos ways people talk 'bout. Sure they's a reason for ya meetin' like 'at. Hope this whole mess ain't just so you two could meet though."

"Yes indeed," exclaimed Andy, "Those'ud be some true myst'r'ous ways! Indeed they would."

Roger chuckled with them again. It was a wonderful thing to share some camaraderie in a time such as this. He didn't think he'd share a laugh until he gathered the kids up in Denton or maybe even when he got to Arkansas if the kids had already left. *Hopefully they are still healthy and able to get to Arkansas.*

"Well, if you're at'a air-port, we heard 'bout that. Ya'll heard any news?"·

"Not much. Heard martial law had been implemented in places."

"In places. You kin say that. In places." Wilson leaned forward again. It seemed to be a habit. "Ain't nuff mil'tary lef's why I say they'n't done it ev'where. Mil'tary dyin' off with this flu jus like the res of us."

"I was wondering about that. You didn't worry about taking us in with the flu going around?"

"Weren't my choice was it? You drove up and tha Lord had me take ya in. I fig're He wouldn't lead ya here just to kill me off. But if that's His plan, who'm I ta say it ain't right? Just sayin'.

"Well, like all news, wha's hap'nin' depends on who ya talk ta. What I hear's this bug's bad. Real bad. They ain't got sure numbers yet 'cause they don't know where ev'ryone went. But from tha camps, they's saying this thing's killing over sixty p'cent those that got it. Seems to be gettin' a good number a' people too. Maybe over half by the time its done. Could be lookin' at one in three people dead.

"That's bad nuff. Next part, well, ain't no betta. All them dead people? Ain't nobody burin' 'em. We've taken care of ours who've passed, but we got our own sim'tairy, ain't we? Them dead, they do more'n stink, Lord take 'em and protect 'em. They's startin' to go back ta dust but they's taken a time to do it. In the meanwhile they's makin' people sick them-sefs."

Wilson leaned back and Roger thought he had finished, but the patri-arch of the house continued, "It's a bad way ta go, getting' sick off the dead. Ah'on't think the dyin' times done, sorry ta say."

"What has been the government response?" Roger knew the playbook. He knew financial collapse was the main focus of drills and planning for years. The pundits would say over and again that the United States was in no danger of collapse. That was already chapter three, so to speak, in the playbook. But the pandemic plan was well thought out. It had been vetted so well that it had taken a virtual back burner in favor of the plans which had not had as much attention.

"Just it, ain't it? They ain't been none." Wilson thumbed another load of tobacco into his pipe. Roger had watched several men prepare a pipe. Most cleaned it with a pipe cleaner, used a pick to dislodge burnt tobacco and then used a little metal plunger to tamp the new tobacco in place. Wilson tapped the old stuff out on the heel of his boot and used his thumb to press more in. He tilted a Bic lighter sideways and flicked it to flame. A couple of puffs later the thick smoke started drifting up.

"Ya already know 'bout martial law. Well, that's only where they can. Best I can tell, that's where the mil'tary's got 'nuff people ta make a stand. The flu's hittin' 'em jus as bad as the rest. They had what, a milyun and a half people when it all started, paper-pushers included. Fig're they got it half as hard as civilians, but I think they got it just as hard. So maybe one in six dead. Leaves about one point two milyun. Half them's overseas. Six hun'erd thousand stateside, half them wouldn't know what end of the gun to put to ta shoulder or what to point at the bad guy. Still, need 'em if ya gunna run such a thing. That leaves about thirty thousand ta each state. Some more. Some less. All a sudden, you jus' got nuff to cover your base. Ain't pretty. Defnit-ly don wanna get out with tha likes a' us and see if ya can get sicker.

"Politicians got it too. Both senators for Kansas? Dead. Gov'ner too so he can't appoint no one to take the place. No one can find the Lieutenant Gov'ner and can't really do nuthin til he's found or declared dead or unfit. At's a mess.

"President called a special session of Congress and they wouldn't come. They didn't wanna get gathered in a room with so many people, so they stayed home. Tried to do it virt'ally but too many city's without power to make it work. Even our innernet's real slow and lots of places ain't out there right now.

"President tried to declare martial law but the Supreme Court slapped 'im down. He can activate the mil'tary they said, but couldn't," he looked at Andy, "Wha'd they call it?"

"Abridge, suppress or set 'side civilian judicial function on US soil," Andy nodded and took another puff on his empty pipe.

"At's it! Accordin' to the Supreme Court the president ain't got the 'thority to set aside civilian law. Don't matter none though. Where they's still a mil'tary? They done it themselfs an' they ain't no one who can say dif'rent whose willin' to stand up."

"Well, I think-" Whatever it was that Roger thought went unsaid. He looked up and Jennifer was standing there in the living room, toweling off her hair. She was dressed in a long t-shirt he didn't recognize and there was just enough hint of shorts sticking out from under the shirt that you knew she was fully dressed but not so much that it stopped being enticing.

"Son, looks like you better get that shower." Wilson pushed himself up from the couch. He looked at Jennifer. "I expect Martha's shown you a room?"

"Yes, thank you." Jennifer smiled. In that light, with her wet hair laying in tangles on her shoulder, she'd shed ten years but lost none of her beauty.

"Well, you kids enjoy your night. Sleep well. We'll try to keep the gran'babies quiet so you can sleep in a bit, if ya can." He placed his pipe in a specifically designed stand beside the couch. "Wha'ch'all do's between you and the Lord but I don't wanna hear none of it."

As Wilson walked by Roger, the older man patted the younger's shoulder. "Doan worry none. I take my hearin' aids out at night." He chuckled as he made his way to the stairs leading to the bedroom level.

Roger turned to Jennifer, "Show me where the shower is?" She smiled and turned toward the stairs.

From outside Andy called, "Aye-ya. I ain't needed tha hearin' aids, but doan worry, I'on't embarrass easy! Indeed I don't!" He was still laughing as the new couple made their way up the stairs, both of their faces glowing bright red.

☣ ☣ ☣

After his shower Roger ducked into the room he was sharing with Jennifer. With the electricity on, he had tried his phone and got the little symbol that showed he had no signal. Even so, he knew that texting often got through even when there was no signal for a call. He sent a message to Ashley and Corey, letting them know he was delayed but safe, and that they should try to make it to the cabin. He would meet them there. Another text flew out to the homestead group letting them know he was alive and on his way. Of course Roger had no way of knowing whether the messages got through. The few messages he received were from before he left Atlanta.

He crept over to the bed and the springs squeaked as he sat on the opposite side of the bed from Jennifer. He peeled off his shirt but kept his sweat pants on and laid back on the old mattress. He had the full intention of hugging her close, maybe seeing what came of the situation.

Instead, he faded to sleep almost before the sheets had settled. All for the best; Jennifer had beat him to sleep by almost fifteen minutes.

25

The Cobb Household, Western Alabama

Jenny awoke. She was in a bed and there was the sound of slow, steady breathing coming from beside her. It took a moment for the events of the last few days to play themselves out and bring her to the present. When she was once again fully aware of where she was, she opened her eyes to the early morning light.

Roger was laying on his side, facing her. His mouth was gaped slightly open. He was breathing mostly in through it. By the state of his hair, it looked like he had come to bed with it still wet from the shower. It was twisted in tangles that would probably take another shower to correct.

What have I gotten myself in to? She stared at Roger. She was truly happy to be sharing a bed with him, and that their relationship had grown since their escape from the airport. But yesterday had been an emotional roller coaster. Not the up-and-down part of a roller coaster. No, the terrifying plunges, one right after the other. She knew roller coasters had safety crews that checked them out constantly. In this world, all the safety crews had taken vacation.

From what Martha had said, there was very little left of the old social order even where the electricity remained. Doctors and nurses did not report to work. Certainly some had died, maybe even a higher percentage since they were directly exposed to more victims. That didn't explain the almost complete absence of medical professionals that the rumor mill was talking about.

Police officers, sheriff deputies and even security guards failed to turn up at work. Most people theorized that these people had simply stayed home and taken care of their own families. Same with firefighters and paramedics. No one wanted to be away from home, taking care of others while their own families might be at risk. That left a lot of openings for crime. Martha said twelve people had died in a shootout just across the street.

The Cobb's had relatives who lived in the house across the way. When the family passed from the virus, they had been interred on the family plot. Later that night some Roamers, Jennifer heard the capitalization in Martha's voice when she talked about them, came through. All the other houses still had lights on.

Two groups of Roamers had come upon the house at about the same time. Wilson had said to let them have the house. The family didn't need anything that was still in the house as they'd already retrieved the few family heirlooms that were over. Besides, if these people could get what they needed and move on, everyone would be better for it.

After the first group went in Wilson almost changed his mind. They heard things breaking and crashing around in the house. That was something Martha said she couldn't get used to. People destroying things just to destroy them, especially at a time like this when anything could be needed in the future and there was no guaranteed way of getting replacements. The patriarch of the family stayed the course though and just waited for the Roamers to move on.

About that time, the second group came up. They must have been attracted to the sounds of destruction, and the mob mentality set in. They rushed into the house. There was even more noise and then gun shots. There had been screaming and yelling and shooting for over thirty minutes. Finally one young man stumbled out the front door and tried to get away down the street. A young woman climbed out a side window. Another young man ran out the back.

That last one shot the girl. The one that came out the front shot the one that came out the back and then continued to stumble off. The next morning buzzards were circling about a quarter mile away. When the

Cobb boys went to check it out, the stumbling kid was found next to the side of the road.

It had been a busy day Martha told her, getting all those plots dug, filled and marked. But good, God-fearing people couldn't let the dead just lie and rot. They needed to be returned to the Lord. It was up to Him to decide what to do with them at that point. They'd done their duty.

As Jenny thought back over the story, what she was having the hardest time accepting was not that people were going house to house and looting. She'd participated in that herself! It wasn't even that people were shooting at one another for what was probably just a couple of days of food. *No, the hardest part,* she thought to herself, *is that I can relate to that story!*

The United States wasn't some third world country where people *had* to shoot one another for food. There were *food banks* in the United States. Places where people had too much food and donated it to those who didn't have enough. There were social programs where food was given away.

A month ago some thought our biggest problem was that we were spending too much on social programs. We were too giving as a country and people wouldn't be self-sufficient if they didn't have to learn to support themselves. Now people are killing one another for a snack cake! And I can't say that in another week, I wouldn't do it myself.

So, she thought, *how did I get myself into this? I was in the airport. I was safe and people were going to feed me. No one was shooting at me. How did I let myself get drawn out of that security, into this bizarre world?*

Roger snorted, flung himself over, snorted again and shot upright in the bed. Jenny closed her eyes, then cracked them open just enough that she could see what he did next.

He swung his legs out of bed and stood up. Slowly he turned around and looked at the bed. His eyes traced her form out from foot to head and a casual smile tilted his lips. *It's a cute smile.*

Roger stretched both arms over his head and clasped hands then tilted to each side, stretching his obliques. Releasing his hands, he scratched his chest before reaching for the floor and coming up with a T-shirt that he slid over his head. Next he bent back to the floor, throwing both arms out in front in a traditional push-up position. She couldn't see anything for a moment but he let out forty quick grunts with forty quick inhales of air, then stood back up. His face was flushed from the exertion, but he wasn't the least bit out of breath. He sniffed the air and smiled again, saying, "Coffee," under his breath.

He crossed to the door and turned the knob. Before opening the door he turned to look at her again, the grin crossing his face again. "You don't have to pretend to be asleep. Ain't nothing happening in the bedroom you don't want to happen. If you ever want it to happen." He turned back to the door and then back to her, "Not that I'm trying to put it off one second more than necessary."

Roger slipped out of the room and closed the door quietly. Jennifer just relaxed in the bed for a few more minutes. The smell of coffee was quickly joined by the smell of eggs and frying meat.

She threw back the covers and looked down her body. She didn't have on a stitch of clothing. When she'd laid down last night, it was with the full intention of waiting for Roger and engaging in a little adult extracurricular activity. The cool morning air wrapped itself around her warm body, causing goose bumps to break out all over. She stood and stretched quickly. Slipping into her shorts and T-shirt she looked back at the bed.

Last night she had laid in wait for him. Night before that she had practically thrown herself at him. Her mind returned to the first question of the morning, *What have I gotten myself into?*

In the cold sober reality of morning her mind traced the path. She'd left the safety of the airport and had followed Roger around for the better part of a week because, as strange as it sounded, she'd rather be out here with him than back at the airport without him. The next time she had him in a bedroom, he wouldn't have to wonder about what she wanted to happen.

☣ ☣ ☣

Roger was at the breakfast table with a cup of black coffee and a half eaten plate of food. Two fried eggs, over hard, three pieces of toast and two strips of bacon with two patties of sausage. Another plate was covered with two biscuits split in half and ladled with cream gravy, heavy on the pepper. In other words, Roger had stumbled into his version of heaven.

Martha had gone out to collect another batch of eggs and the men of the house were out doing their morning chores. Jenny walked in dressed as she was last night. She looked at Roger with a mischievous gleam in her eyes, spoiled only a little by the jaunty tilt of the bandage across her forehead. He tracked her across the room as she poured herself a cup of coffee, then nearly choked as she opened the fridge and bent at the waist, looking for milk. Her T-shirt rode up and the satin jogging shorts fit her form uncomfortably well. She poured some milk into her coffee and repeated the process as she 'looked for' the right place to return the milk.

Roger's fork was poised halfway to his mouth as she stood on her tip-toes to look through the cabinet for sugar, then bent at the waist to 'examine' all the canisters on the counter. When she finally found it, she spooned in a helping then turned to look at him. The spoon slipped into her mouth and slowly slipped out from between her lips.

Jenny took a quick look around the room, then through the open doorway leading to the rest of the house. She could see Martha at the coop through the window. She rinsed the spoon in the sink and walked over to the table. Roger could smell the soap and shampoo of last night's shower, mixed with a smell that was undeniably just *Jenny*.

"OK, Mr. Genius Planner-man." She stepped back, set the cup on the table, placed her hands on both sides of the cup, then bent over. The slightly oversized shirt hung low in the front but just tantalizingly so. He couldn't see any more than if she was in a tank top, less even, but somehow this was more exciting. She slowly reached up to his hand and turned the fork full of egg to her own mouth.

He watched the egg disappear, the fork slide out and her jaws work as she chewed. "Last night," she said quietly, "I went to sleep in the same bed as you. The only thing I had on was perfume. Maybe you can smell it now." He could smell the perfume but his mouth wouldn't work so he couldn't tell her. "So as far as me wanting something to happen, you've got the green light. Nod if you understand me."

Roger nodded, he couldn't talk, could barely breathe, but he could nod. "Good. So you've got no excuse. Next time we have the opportunity and we continue on being frustrated, it's on you big man."

She leaned in and their lips met. He opened his mouth and she mimicked the action. His tongue darted out and she increased her pressure. When his tongue retreated hers followed. He dropped the fork and wrapped his hand behind her head. The fork clattered to the plate.

"Good ta' see ya healthy and happy," Martha said, "but careful tha plates. They's practic'ly brand new."

Jenny stood, her face beat red. Martha crossed to the kitchen counter. "Now we know ya ain't gotta a concussion girl, git upstairs and put on some real pants. Cain't have Father comin' an' gettin' a heart'tack seein' ya in his gran'dau'ter's runnin' shorts."

Jennifer bolted upstairs. Roger remained at the table, frozen in place by the sensory overload of the morning. "Not that she ain't got the body for it, mind ya," Martha said. "If I's her age with tha same shape I might do't m'self." She turned and pointed a spatula at Roger. "But I'd keep it in m' own house. And I'd keep it out the kitchen entir'ly! Ra'member that young man!"

"I will," he said.

"I know ya will. The kitchen ain't no place for those goin's on."

☣ ☣ ☣

Jennifer was just finishing her breakfast when Mr. Cobb stomped his feet on the wooden landing outside the back door. Roger could see his shadow bend over and a moment later, rise back up with an audible grunt. He opened the door and walked in, leaving his boots on the landing outside. Wilson smiled at his guests and crossed to the table. Jennifer shifted a chair closer to Roger, making room for the man of the house.

She had changed clothes. She had on the same T-shirt but had a button-down shirt over it, the bottom half buttoned. Over that was a windbreaker they had scavenged from Target. The boots Roger had found for her in the farm house actually fit. They poked out the bottom of a pair of blue jeans that were probably a little too form-fitting for Martha's kitchen but modest enough to not be outright protested.

"Well, you kids decide wha'cha' do'in'?" He placed his hands on the table and Martha set a plate down directly in front of him, as if it was a carefully timed maneuver.

"What we're doing?" Roger was confused. So much was running through his head this morning that he really did not understand the question.

"Well, we got 'nuff food here ta hep suppor'cha 'til ya earnin' ya keep. So if ya wanna stay, ya kin stay for a piece. But if ya need ta go, well, we unnerstand that as well."

"Now Wilson," Martha exclaimed, "it's not good manners to be runnin' off guests!" Even Roger could tell that her tone was right but the inflection and the set of her face didn't match the words. They needed to earn their own keep or keep moving. It just made sense in this world.

"We've got a destination in mind and need to get there." Roger pushed the last scrap of egg around his plate with his last piece of toast. He had finished eating once but had sat there so long Martha insisted on feeding him more. He'd eaten the second helping much slower in order to forestall yet another helping.

"But," Jennifer interjected, giving Roger a look, "we appreciate everything you've done for us. Is there anything we can do to repay even a part of your generosity?"

"Idle hands are the Devil's. Produ'tive hands are the Lord's. We'll not take payment for doin' His work." Wilson scooped a piece of egg onto a piece of sausage and into his mouth, then followed it with a bite from his toast. His jaw worked for over a minute and once he swallowed he looked around the table. No one offered a rebuttal, so he nodded and continued with his breakfast.

Roger dug his phone out of his pocket and turned it on. The screen lit up and he waited. "I sent a message to the group last night. Looks like either no one got it or they didn't respond. Either way, I have a responsibility to them so I really need to get out there."

Jenny's eyebrows squeezed together. "What about the kids?"

"Sent them a message too. Hopefully they're heading out as well. I'll keep checking."

26

Ashley's Apartment, Denton, TX

Ashley had left her iPhone on the solar charger's storage battery overnight to ensure it got a full charge. She turned it on and waited for it to boot up. When the Apple logo faded and her Home screen displayed, she waited for the little antenna symbol to light up, showing she had connectivity to the cellular network. It didn't happen.

It was weird when Professor Westover was talking about cellular communications in class. She'd really never thought about it, but since it went from one phone to another, she had just thought of a cell phone as a really advanced walkie-talkie. It wasn't.

Walkie-talkies were considered point-to-point devices. You pressed the button and the radio waves went out into the world and another walkie-talkie, or even some CB radios and most HAM radios, could pick up the signal if they were tuned to the right frequency. But the signal went straight from one point, your radio, to the other point, the receiving radio.

Cell phones were entirely different. A cell phone's signal went from your phone to a tower. The signal went from the tower to the same phone lines that landline calls travelled, then came out at another tower. It went from that tower to the recipient's phone. Along the way all kind of equipment was required to send the signal, route the signal, and get it from point A to point B. All that equipment required electricity.

All this flashed through her mind in the time it took the phone to go from the grayed-out antenna symbol to the antenna symbol with a circle and line through it.

Text messaging was very similar to cellular voice communications, but it was much faster and required less bandwidth for the towers and switches to process. It could also operate over greater distances. That's why text messages usually got through even when cell calls wouldn't.

Ashley opened the text feature on the phone. There were no new messages. *Even with all the bonuses, texts still needed power.*

She turned the phone off to conserve battery life, then tucked it into her back pocket. She'd keep checking, as she had for the last ten days. Either way, tomorrow was D-Day. Regardless of whether she heard from Roger. It would be nice to hear from her parents as well. But she was afraid what that news might be. Diverting her thoughts from that topic had become somewhat second nature.

Her GOOD Book was still open on her desk. She had laughed when Roger had used the term in class. Most people thought of the Good Book as the Bible. Roger used it as a play on words and said the GOOD Book was a *disaster survival bible*. GOOD stood for Get Out Of Dodge. It was a list of relevant information necessary to ensure you had everything you needed to increase your chances of survival in a disaster scenario. It was also a quick reference to make sure you didn't leave anything essential behind if and when you got ready to go. Roger had offered it as extra credit for those who weren't doing so well in the class and Ashley had decided to have a go at it even though she didn't need the extra points. Now she was glad she had.

Her lists had been extensive. The book was broken out into several sections and Section One was her list of lists. It outlined what was in every other section so that if she lost a list she would know what she needed to find or recreate. Each list was tucked into a waterproof protective sleeve, as were her essential documents - copies of her driver's license, Social Security card, birth certificate, passport and student ID. She also had an electronic copy of each document along with medical records, her high school diploma and college transcript. The thumb drive was encrypted and needed a password to access it. Really, the thumb drive and all the photocopies of the IDs were what worried her the most. Having the documents copied and in a book was bad enough as far as identity theft goes, but having it on a thumb drive that could be stolen or copied without her knowledge? It took a while to get accustomed to the idea and she wouldn't do it until she'd found the encryption program.

Luckily she'd had the forethought to make blank pages for each of the lists, and she kept a grease pencil in the notebook so she could write on the sheet protectors. She'd tried dry erase at first but one spilled Coke showed her the failure of that method. When she'd wiped the drink up, she'd wiped her notes off. Now she had her latest version printed off and some hand-written entries in the blank spaces.

The book was open to the medications section. Even with all the blank spaces she had left, she had still run out of room on the page after her trip to the hospital. She had just continued on to the spare page protector. They were handy to have.

Now was the time to really put the book to use. Section Two was titled 'Go Bag', Section Three was titled 'Vehicle Pack-Out'. Up until now Ashley had been using the bike to get around town. It was quiet and allowed her to go places that weren't necessarily accessible to cars. For getting out of town – or Getting Out Of Dodge – she was going to need something that would go faster and further. The main problem was that, being an apartment dweller, she couldn't store much fuel. She had a small storage area next to her parking slot, but the apartments expressly prohibited the storage of gasoline. It was a liability issue or something. She now wished she had used all the money she had paid into renter's insurance and applied it to a storage building. But insurance was the earliest form of disaster preparedness, so she got the peace of mind she had paid for.

Ashley looked out the window, across the now-ragged lawn between the apartment and the parking area and eyed her little truck. Technically, it was an SUV but it made her feel so *soccer mom* to say she drove an SUV that she referred to her Ford Escape as a truck. It was a couple of years old. That is, it had been a couple of years old when she'd bought it, and that was a few years ago. It had held up well in looks but she didn't focus on that too much.

Of course you had to keep your vehicle clean. In the brutal Texas sun you also had to keep it waxed with a good UV resistant wax if you wanted the paint to last and keep the body from rusting. But where she really concentrated was on what mattered. She was one of those obsessive people who kept up with routine maintenance religiously. A mechanic friend had told her, with the new oils, she could go 5,000 miles between oil changes. She changed it at 3,000 miles like her dad had raised her to do. Every other oil change, she had the tires rotated. She refilled the tank at about half full, and every five tanks worth, she filled with the high octane stuff just to flush the system out. Different people had given her differing stories on whether that worked and why. Like renter's insurance, it made her feel better so she did it. Lubes, battery changes and radiator flushes were all on her iPhone calendar, and she'd set a one-month advanced warning so she could save extra money if needed.

As it sat in her parking slot no one would know that. As soon as she realized looting had started, Ashley had taken precautionary measures. She had removed the fuses for the lights and ignition, then propped open the driver's door and the hatchback. She'd placed an old overnight bag in the back compartment and threw some old clothes in next to the bag. Like most college students, she had a few bags from fast food places already in the vehicle. She unwadded them and threw them in the vehicle haphazardly. Finally, she had rolled down the driver's side window and gathered some broken glass from a wreck a few blocks away. It was scattered next to the driver's door. She'd thrown old clothes and some items she'd dragged out of the Dumpster around the lawn to give the appearance of the apartment being looted. She tried the doors on other cars in the parking lot, and found two more unlocked. She'd staged them similarly, but wasn't going to *actually* break in to a perfectly good vehicle to make it *look* like someone had broken in. Somehow that just didn't make sense to her.

No one had come around for days but she didn't want to take chances. Just after sundown she would replace the fuses, back the Escape up to the base of the stairs, and load her equipment as quickly as she could. She ran her finger down the list again, ensuring she knew where each item was. After it was loaded, the Escape would return to its slot and Ashley would get as much sleep as possible. She'd then drive over to Traditions Hall, gather Corey and get the heck out of Dodge.

Ashley looked around her apartment. It really was a tiny space, just what she could afford as an office assistant at the mechanic's shop where she had her car maintained. Her extra work as a catering waitress, when there was a gig she could work, was her 'play' money. The tips were pretty good if she landed one of the corporate parties, and those jobs had funded most of her preparations. When Ashley and Corey had begun dating, Roger also helped along those lines. He'd given her some extra gear from his own preps. Even a caring father could recognize Corey's character, and Roger had given several items into Ashley safekeeping so that Corey wouldn't sell them. Each of those items were carefully inventoried and on the load list for the car.

For the time being, she set another cup of coffee on the Sterno stove, peeled the wrapper from a breakfast bar and sat back to reread a book she knew she was going to have to leave behind. Wistfully, she hoped there would be a day soon when she could start rebuilding her library, or even return here to claim the rest of her property. As gunshots sounded in the distance, that eventuality seemed to drift just a little further away.

☣ ☣ ☣

Corey sat back, surveying his hoard. *I totally am the King of the Hall!*

After Ashley left the other day he had no reason to keep his activities quiet or secret. She knew that he was getting out and she knew what he was doing. She'd said that she'd be back to get him when she was ready to leave, so she was obviously cool with the idea of collecting all the crap that these shitheads had left behind.

She's just too pretentious to actually give her blessing for taking stuff out of other people's rooms, Corey thought to himself. *Probably just pissed she didn't think of it herself!*

The haul was really amazing though. *Those little skinny jean wearing asswipes and BoHo bitches were loaded with stuff. Obviously their parents didn't have sticks up their asses Dad does. Most of the rooms had flat screen TVs, some of them as big as his.* Most of them had game consoles like his Xbox. Some were older than his but still, there were a lot of them in the building. Only a couple had a stereo as good as his, but he'd gotten that old piece of shit stereo years ago for his birthday, so it wasn't like he didn't deserve it or anything.

All that stuff was shit though. He didn't even bother picking it up. With the electricity out, there just wasn't a need for it. The stuff he got was *choice.* All totaled he had over fifteen cases of beer. It was totally against the rules of the building and most people who lived here weren't even drinking age, but here was his tower of proof that those little shits didn't give a damn about the rules.

He'd found about twenty one-ounce bags of pot and more wrapping papers than he took time to count. That was small potatoes. On the second floor one of the guys must have been a dealer. Corey dragged more than five *pounds* of pot from under the dude's bed. There was also over five grand in small bills. Now that Corey knew what they were worth, he literally wiped his ass with three 50s after taking a dump last night. *King of the Fucking Hall!*

The stash of prescription medicine had more than tripled. After some heart palpitations and hallucinations from taking a dip in his Punch Bowl of Fun the other night, he kept these meds in their bottles. Maybe he could sell them to someone later. He had been somewhat disappointed when he found one bottle of nitroglycerin tablets. That stuff was supposed to be explosive, but he wore his arm out throwing the little pills against the wall and the floor. But none of them went off. After getting totally frustrated with chunking them around, he pounded on a few with a hammer and they just crumbled. *Maybe they were old or something.*

Another big no-no he came across was weapons. The other day he had wandered all the way out to the freeway to look for guns and there were three right here in this building. He had found one in his earlier search, but he'd found two more as he went through the locked rooms. One was in the room with all the pot and cash, a nice little 9mm Keltec pocket gun, and the other was stuck under the pillow in another guy's room, a full sized Taurus 9mm. Best of all, they had ammo. The dealer had two boxes of full metal jacket and three boxes of jacketed hollow points with five full magazines. The other guy just had one box of hollow points with 17 bullets missing. They were loaded in the weapon. In all, it was a score of over 250 rounds of ammunition. *That* is what made him King of the Hall. He'd also gathered so many knives of different shapes and sizes that he didn't even count them.

His father had always gone on about this and that, doing his disaster ramblings. Every once in a while some of that shit stuck. What would happen if you were caught outside barefoot, he would ask. 'You need good footwear or you won't be getting very far.' 'If you freeze to death it doesn't matter how much food you have. Keep a jacket or coat nearby during fall and winter.' 'In freezing weather a blanket will be worth its weight in gold.' All this rambling crap about shit that could never happen. Now it had happened and Corey gathered all the quality footwear, coats, jackets, blankets and thermal underwear he'd found. Surprisingly, it was quite a mound in the hallway.

There were other backpacks and camp equipment mixed in as well. But if he knew Ashley, and he did *know* Ashley – he smiled at his own joke – she would probably already have all that stuff covered. *No telling what all she has, but if she is nice and* friendly *I might even share some of what I have.* It had been almost two weeks since he had done that little skank he'd met at Terrance's party, and he was looking forward to a little *friendliness* from Ashley.

Just the thought of having a return trip into Ashley's pants had him grinning. He picked up a pair of panties he'd collected from one of the dorm rooms and crossed over to his window. Staring across the street to where he'd offed Jerry and his buddy, Corey ran the silky cloth through his fingers while dreaming of how impressed Ashley was going to be with his haul. *Oh yeah, real friendly.*

27

Western Louisiana

The trip across Mississippi had been uneventful. They'd stopped a couple of times to stretch their legs. One utility corridor ran over twenty-five miles, past Meridian. After about an hour of crossing back and forth on country back roads, Roger had found another corridor that carried them through to Newton. Another helped them skirt around north of town and then run parallel to Interstate 20 to just north of Lake. At that point the corridor let out into open pastures so Roger had doubled back about a mile and taken a southwest-running branch. He was trying to stay as close to I-20 as he could, and that leg of the utility corridor was going too far out of the way. They had braved black-topped roads for over a hundred miles until past Jackson. Another power line clearing led them the rest of the way to the Louisiana state border.

These corridors were becoming the highways of the down trodden. They could hardly travel twenty miles without seeing someone or some group trudging through the humid backwoods. There was no telling how many others they'd passed or didn't see as they'd ducked into the forests.

Jennifer was heartbroken. The first group they came upon told a story with their eyes that was just as poignant as if they had acted out a full play. That group consisted of eight people from late teens to early seniors, probably three generations of what was left of a family. The only female in the group, probably the mother of the teen boys, looked up as she heard the truck. Her eyes were rimmed in red as if she had been crying for hours, maybe days.

The first look was fear. Those deep blue, red-streaked eyes spotted the truck and darted to the woods. She obviously wrote that off as too late. The whole group stopped and moved to the side though there was plenty of room for the truck to pass. Jennifer's eyes locked on the woman's. The fear faded, quickly replaced by hope. Maybe they'd get a ride. As the truck passed, the hope was dashed, and disappointment took hold. Jenny watched in the side view mirror until the group faded from sight. The woman never turned away. Tears rolled down Jenny's face.

After a brief discussion with Roger, much briefer than she had expected, it was decided that they would stop and offer rides to those going in the same direction. They didn't let anyone in the cab with them, but since the military had emptied most everything out of the bed, there was room enough for about fifteen tightly packed people. There were more than they could ever help, but at least they were doing something. *We can't make a difference to everyone,* Jenny thought, *but we can make a difference to these people.*

An elderly couple were their first set of passengers, destined for Vicksburg on the Mississippi-Louisiana border. They stayed in the bed of the truck as others got in, got out and shuffled around. For the entire sixteen hour bumpy trip, those two held on to the truck and held on to one another. It was a small payment to society carrying these two people across a state but it was some payment, and helped Jenny feel just a little more connected to humanity again.

Vicksburg was a bit disappointing. Not the city itself, it was quite charming in a large-town, small-city, Southern living kind of way. Its tree-lined streets and Victorian style houses portrayed a town steeped in history. Unfortunately, as Jennifer looked around, it looked like the clock had been turned back. Judging by the storefronts and restaurants they saw when driving through town, the electricity was out here. There were few people out on the streets and they seemed haunted. They drove past a park with tall, multicolored posts. It looked like there may have been fountains embedded in concrete. At another time it had probably been filled with kids being doused by spraying jets as they darted around under their parent's supervision. Those days were gone, and at times it was difficult for Jennifer to comprehend that those days were less than a month ago. *Geeze! Less than two weeks ago!*

Everyone else had exited the vehicle on the outskirts of town. Ted and Gloria, the elderly couple, had invited Roger and Jennifer to their home if they'd be kind enough to drive them in.

"You have any idea what the situation is like in town," Roger asked.

"Oh, it fine fo' du moes paut," Ted said. He had as much of the Louisiana side of the river in his voice as the Mississippi side. Roger had worked with several men from Louisiana during his career and there was more than a little Cajun drawl to Ted. "Nash'nal Gahd got da ri'vah bridge blocked but they stays close'nuff to it, they don't bother no one. Keep da town a bit quiet doe."

"If its quiet and settled, why did you leave?" Jennifer cast an appraising eye over their two-story blue-gray Victorian. "Sounds safer than anywhere we've seen lately."

"Safe'nuff," Ted responded with a nod of his head. He helped his wife step down from the lowered tailgate of the truck. Roger helped on the other side and Ted gave him a thankful nod. Gloria was frail. She had been when they helped her into the truck and her condition hadn't improved any from being bumped around over rough terrain. "But it go lonely ya see. We ra-tired ou'cheer ten years ago. Came to be with our boy, Davey, an' his fam'ly."

Gloria pulled a handkerchief from her sleeve and dabbed her eyes, taking slow, painful steps toward her front door. She pulled keys from the purse that had been wedged firmly under her arm for the entire trip, and turned the deadbolt.

"When da flu took Davey an' the gran'kids we figgered to head back east to Gloria's kin. Took us a week a walkin' and hitchin' rides. People, dae was cra-zy, an we didn't trus most no one. They didn't trus us neither, us two ol' people, too ol' a even think of doin' someone wrong." Ted wiped his feet on a welcome mat with the name Robeneaux, and stepped into his house. With a sweep of his arm, a smile and a nod, he invited in his guests.

"But when we got up ta Booneville, her people was taken by da flu too." Without a word, Gloria carefully made her way upstairs. "We started back tha nex' day. Gloria said she ain' got nutin' to go on fer now an' she wann'ed to be in'ner own home when she passed."

Ted took a forlorn look up the stairs where his wife had disappeared. "I be surprised, she make it a week. When a person's give up, they give up. Ya know watt'a mean?" Unshed tears pooled in the corners of his eyes.

Ted showed them to his pantry. It was practically barren. The house was still in great condition and did not appear to be looted. Most people simply did not keep food reserves. What little was kept, was generally refrigerated, and with the lack of electricity, that food was beyond saving.

Roger nodded at the state of the pantry. "Most people have less than three days food in their house. Here on the Gulf coast it is usually higher, maybe a week. If they'd stayed here rather than going to their relatives'? I bet there wouldn't be any left at all."

Jennifer gathered several cans that looked like they might make a balanced meal and turned to the stove top. It was gas so she started opening cans and pouring contents into pots and pans. When she turned on the burner nothing happened.

Jed responded to her question, "Oh, I forgot 'bout dat. That's gas-'lectric. Needs to be plugged in for the 'lectric sparker to catch. Somehow it know tha flame ain' caught an' stop da gas. Gloria take care moes da cookin', I forgot all 'bout dat."

He thought for a few moment. "Da Ericson boy ness door. He's got one dim gas grills wid a gas tank on it. One of the first to be taken on dis block so he wone be needin' it, rest 'im. Roger, if ya kin hep me, we kin roll it to the back yard and use it."

They made short work of the task and within an hour Jennifer was dishing out four plates of food. It wasn't quite the feast served at the Cobb household, but it was more than most people were getting these days. Ted carried a plate upstairs to Gloria and brought it down fifteen minutes later without a bite taken. He laid a towel over the plate and shared an embarrassed smile with Jennifer, "She ain' ready to eat juss yet. I'll take it back up t'er in a lil bit."

She patted his big hand and didn't say anything. They both knew it wouldn't be long if she had given up, and Jennifer didn't see a need in confirming what he already knew.

Into the evening Ted was telling them about Vicksburg. He had a town map and was instructing the younger couple on what they needed to do in order to cross the Mississippi.

"She's a big rivah, da M'ssippi. Ain' gone drive 'cross nowhere. Dim guards doe, day got da bridge blocked." He pointed to the river crossing on the map. "Y'ain getting' 'cross da rivah he'ah less dae le'cha an dae ain' let no one I know of. Dae call it controllin' viral spread."

He shook his head and wiped his hands over his face. "Dae ain controllin' no virus by standin' onna bridge an dae know't. Virus already on bote side da bridge. Can't stoppa leak by plugin' da hole once da water run out. But no matta. Dae got da bridge he'ah. Nex' one 'bout sevety-five mile sout' as a crow fly, in Natchez. Sixty-five north to Greenville. But you ain'a crow and I'ont know what between they an' hey dees days."

Ted sat back and wiped his face again. "Ya'll been good ta us so I truss ya mebbe more'n I should.

"Dae's a man I thin' kin hep. See, no ev'ry one 'round here truss the gu'ment, ev'n 'fore times turned. Some people wan'ned on the other side o' the rivah wit no one knowin' dae done it. I know a man can gitcha dis side ta dat wit no one knowin'. He do it 'cuz his daddy did it. But now, he might be one a duh few 'at kin. 'Course, you kin try Natchez or Greenville."

"About your guy," Roger started.

"He gotta ferry, if he still in da bidness. But if he still alive, he still in da bidness. Ya doen juss let yo daddy's way a life die out here like 'at. In dis day, dis time? I sho he be lookin' ta get paid doe."

Roger ran back through a mental inventory of what was in the truck and what they could spare. If they couldn't cross the river nothing else really mattered. The kids were in Denton or on the way to the cabin. Both Denton and the cabin were on the other side of the Mississippi. He was going to have to cross somewhere, might as well be right here where he could find help.

After making it obvious that he looked at both their hands for wedding rings, Ted showed them to separate rooms for the night. In the morning, the old Cajun went about arranging passage.

☣ ☣ ☣

The next night Roger pulled down a long dark road, lights off, windows down. Ted had told them that the water would sneak up on them quickly, so he was very cautious. He finally found the wide expanse of white sand Ted had told them about and he pulled off the road. The truck maneuvered around on the beach until the on-board compass said they were pointing northeast. Roger turned on the headlights for a two-count, turned them off for a five-count and flashed them quickly on and off once, all as he had been instructed. He turned the key off and the waiting began.

For a while nothing happened. He and Jennifer just sat there in the truck, quiet and still, just as instructed. After a few minutes, a vehicle passed slowly on the road, they could hear tires crunching on the gravel more than any engine noise. In the dark of night, and now down in the Mississippi River basin, they couldn't tell anything about it, so they just sat there. Eventually their breathing was the loudest sound they were making and it began to sound like a roar in their ears. Ted had told them that if this guy got spooked – and he never stated the guy's name – they wouldn't know anything about it until the sun came up and they were still on the Mississippi side of the river.

The waiting was like a weight pushing down on them. Each moment dragged out, feeling like an hour.

A light flashed to the northeast. It was a simple thing, on, off, on, off. Very fast. Just a light, no sound. It was such a surprise for anything to happen, and was such a break in the tension, that both Roger and Jenny gave an audible sigh of relief.

Jenny heard a large engine start on the Louisiana side of the river. Roger checked again to make sure everything was set as it should be. All their weapons were stowed in the cab but out of reach.

Ted had been adamant about it. He'd said, "Make a moo' fo' a gun an' no one'll ev'n know where ta start lookin' fo ya. Dees people, dae good people but dis serious work and dae don' play at work."

He got out of the truck and let down the tailgate, again, precisely as instructed. He laid out two 500 round bricks of .22 ammunition and retreated back to the cab. A few minutes later, the cab shook as the tailgate slammed closed. Both Roger and Jenny jumped at the sound. He wasn't sure who reached for who but they ended up with arms wrapped around one another in the middle of the seat.

Across the river the big engine was still idling. Two quick flashes of light illuminated the cab as someone behind the truck flashed a signal across the river. The boat's engine revved and began moving closer.

They tracked it by sound alone for the first few moments, then a huge shadow began slipping across the expanse of the calm river. Once they could make it out more clearly, this definitely wasn't like any ferry Roger had imagined.

To him, a ferry was a flat bottomed boat that pulled up to a landing. Over in Galveston, off the Bolivar Peninsula, they had a ferry that would fit probably a couple dozen cars. It was a huge vehicle dedicated to the cause of shuttling cars and trucks. In the old days, ferries were small boats that were dragged from one side of the river to the other by human or horse power. The thing moving toward them wasn't anything like either of those images.

The beast cutting across the water had a wide, flat bottom with very high sides. The front of the boat was very odd. Rather than coming up to a point, it looked like it was flat. Not only that, the front panel stuck up in the air at least three times the height of the side walls. The cabin of the craft was strange too. It was a box mounted on a thick scaffolding, giving it clearance to see over the projecting front.

There were no lights, but on the otherwise quiet and calm river, it wasn't difficult to monitor the craft's approach. It was over forty feet, maybe forty-five, in length. As it got closer, the hull appeared to be aluminum, and the only paint on it was an almost laughable attempt at camouflage on the cabin. Fifteen feet in the air, over a calm river, that paint job would attract more attention than a simple flat black. Roger had no idea why someone would do that. Then again, he didn't have any idea why people did a lot of things.

He started looking around for where the boat would dock and was getting nervous that it was just going to run aground. The thing just kept coming closer and closer, now just feet off the sandbar where the truck was parked. Jenny hugged him close and they both tensed as, just as feared, the boat beached itself.

Great! Now we're down a thousand rounds of ammunition to some crazy Cajuns. I know they won't give it back, not now that we've caused them to damage their boat.

The couple looked at one another. Jenny's eyes held the same questions that must have been in his. Roger just shrugged and looked back out the window, his mind already starting to think ahead to their next plan. The Mississippi was a huge river. They'd just have to keep going north until they found a bridge that wasn't guarded, or where you could bribe someone to cross.

Outside the truck window a whine rolled through the night air. At first Roger thought it was some mechanical device to try and push the boat off the sandbar. But as he watched, the weird flat nose of the boat started lowering. In less than a minute it was laid out on the sand, a ramp to drive up onto the flat deck.

A man walked down the ramp and across the sand. He was dressed in a long sleeved shirt and jeans. Work boots left imprints in the sand. His gloved hands came to rest on Roger's door. "You folks done whatcha should ta this point. Less juss keep it that away, aw-rite? Back 'er up and drive 'er on. We'll take care o' the rest. Once you get to tha othah side, we'll lower the gate again. You drive off. About fifty yards ahead of ya there'll be a road. Ya on ya own aftah that."

Roger and Jennifer nodded in unison and that seemed to be the appropriate response. The man's white teeth shined in the moonlight. "Aw -rite then. Let's git it movin'."

An hour later Roger was cruising the back roads of Louisiana. It was late and they had been up for more than twenty hours. Past time to get some sleep. The problem was that the land on this side of the river was entirely different than the Mississippi side. For miles in any direction, the land was worked farm fields and winding creeks and rivers. Despite his better judgment, Roger left the back roads and joined Highway 80 about ten miles east of Tallulah. As they passed over countless stretches of water, he knew there was no other way to make good time. He was beginning to think there might not be any other way to actually cross this state.

In the distance there was the slight glow of street lights. The road atlas indicated the glow was probably coming from the small town of Delhi, still several miles down the road. They passed a sign marking the community of Waverly. Just a little further up the road was a sign designating the Waverly Cemetery. *A cemetery worked out for us once, might as well try it again.* He turned down State Route 577 just past the large silos on the right.

When they pulled up next to the graveyard, it obviously wasn't going to do. It was only about fifty feet by fifty feet with one tree off to one corner. Everything to the east was open farmland. Just on the other side of the highway was a long line of trees. Roger investigated them and discovered they followed some creek or canal. There were only about twenty-five feet of trees between the roadway and the canal, but it was better than anything else he'd seen since reaching Louisiana, so they decided to risk it.

They pulled the truck as far into the trees as they could, set up a makeshift cold camp and curled up together against the chill night air.

28

Denton, TX

Ashley packed the last of her supplies into the Escape. Her vehicle load
-out sheet had all the boxes checked and she had purposefully left some of
the cargo area in the vehicle empty for whatever Corey might decide to
bring. To tell the truth, she had everything they were going to need to get
to Arkansas and probably enough for the two of them to survive through
the harshest part of winter as well. She hoped that Corey didn't try to take
everything he had scavenged over the last couple of days.

She cross-checked her lists. Her general inventory had items that
migrated into the vehicle so she made sure that she checked them off. That
was a bit weird, she knew. *I don't think I'll be coming back. Still, follow
the process through so you know you've done what you should.*

As she went down the list one item stood out. '.22 lr ammunition, 500
count box', listed as in her closet. She distinctly remembered carrying the
rifle to the truck along with some of her ammo. This box wasn't checked
off the list but she was almost certain she had packed it. A grease pencil
check mark removed the outstanding item from the list but didn't remove
the concern from her mind. After reading down the rest of the list, her eyes
drifted back to the ammunition entry. Finally she broke down, just to
confirm she had loaded the box in the truck.

The floor of the closet was empty. Everything that had been on the
floor, boots, her go-bag, a medical kit and a couple pairs of tennis shoes,
was now in the truck and faithfully checked off the list. There were still a
few items of clothing hanging. She had already packed the clothes she
considered rugged enough for farm living. There were also a few items
that she considered 'Sunday morning clothes' added to the vehicle load-

out. Never knew what could happen – that was the whole reason to prepare!

She backed up and stood on her tip-toes to peek over the edge of the shelf. Shoved in the back, against the wall, was the green and gray box. Grabbing the step stool from the kitchenette, Ashley reached the box and carried it back to the list. Just for good measure she erased the grease mark and then replaced it as she smiled to herself. *Once again; follow protocol. Maybe I should have put in an entry for where it was in that location. If I ever get a printer again I just might add that.*

Finally, she legitimately had every item checked off the list and loaded into the truck. It was returned to her parking slot, all the fuses replaced and all fluids checked. Ashley knew they wouldn't be able to make it to the cabin on one tank of gas. Under average driving conditions she had a theoretical range of three hundred miles. It was over three hundred fifty miles to their destination. Maybe four hundred if they had to leave the main roads. Ashley had mentally kicked herself when she strapped the spare fuel cans on the roof of the truck. She should have just stored fuel, regardless of the apartment policy!

Well, no. If nothing had ever happened but the apartments had burned down because of me storing fuel? That wouldn't have been worth it. You have to live where you are, when you are, and abide by the rules. If you're willing to chunk civilization out the window today, are you the type person we need tomorrow?

With that session of self-remonstration out of the way, she climbed the stairs for the final time and crawled into her bed for one last night of sleep in Denton.

☣ ☣ ☣

Corey had gathered all the salvage he could into his room. All day and all night he had heard noises, even saw shadows flitting around outside. He could have sworn there were people behind the convenience store earlier today. When he stopped looking out the window and went to drag more stuff into the room, whoever it was must have moved across the street and was standing on the ground floor, just around the corner where he couldn't see them.

He took another hit from his joint to calm his nerves. It had been the best night he could remember, and he couldn't even remember all of it. After gathering all the stuff, he'd sat back and taken time to simply enjoy the fruits of his labors. That bored the shit out of him, so he took a dip in the 'skittles' bowl.

All the multicolored pills had reminded some overly medicated kid of the fruit candy Skittles at some point. The term had spread like wildfire and now 'skittling' was a verb used on college campuses and high schools across the country for dipping into a big bowl of random meds. All things considered, it was Corey's fourth-favorite pastime. Right after video games, sex, and the new addition: blowing the shit out of someone who deserved it. He knew it was his fourth favorite because he'd spent a good portion of last night thinking about his favorite things and putting them in order.

He wasn't sure what he had taken, but he wished he knew because it had focused his attention like a laser. He sat there and thought about all his favorite things for more than five hours. The only catch was that he wasn't sure about the order. Sometimes sex was number one, sometimes video games were number one. If he could have sex while playing video games? He wasn't sure if that was all one or if it was really one and two but–

What the fuck was that?

He jumped up and went to his door. Whoever was out there wasn't *out there* any more. They were *in here*. They were whispering in the hall.

Corey opened his door. They must have heard him because they shut up. He knew this building better than anyone now though. He even knew what was in the walls. *That's right! I'm the fucking King of the Fucking Hall, fuckers!*

He grabbed a gun in each hand and burst out of his door. In less than five seconds he was at the cross hall, joining the two sides of the H. No one. *They couldn't have gotten away so fast. They must be in one of the rooms!*

He quickly shuffled down the hallway, using his left hand to hold up the seat of his sagging pants. At the end of the hall he kicked open the door to the first room on the north wall. No one was in there. It really stunk though. Since the water had gone out he had started using the toilets in the other rooms. Unfortunately, at night he couldn't be sure which one he had used and which he hadn't so he ended up revisiting some but not being able to flush. The water in the tank had been used the previous time. This was one of those rooms.

He closed the door, stifling back a retch. He crossed to the first room to the south and pushed open the door. *Nothing.*

This is going to take forever.

Back down the hall he heard whispering. It couldn't be far or he wouldn't be able to hear it. *Time to go* Black Ops *on their ass!*

Corey ran down the hall, both arms pumping. His pants sagged off, tangling his feet. He spilled into the floor searing a four-inch long carpet burn onto his right cheek.

He jumped back up and used both weapons to scan the hall. The whispering had stopped. Shaking first one foot, then the other, he dislodged his pants along with his right shoe. Now he could run without being tripped by the stupid fucking pants.

His momentum had only gotten back up to speed when he threw himself at the suspected door. Unlike in the video game, Corey simply bounced off, banging his head on the door frame and spilling back onto the floor. The revolver in his left hand caught at a weird angle as it pounded into the carpet. As his finger was on the trigger, ready to engage *the bad guys*, the weapon discharged. Pieces of carpet and wood blew upward as Corey's hand jammed backward.

Once again he pushed himself to his feet. He backed against the wall opposite the door, ran two steps, and kicked.

Unlatched as it was, the door slammed open. Inside, the door knob buried itself in the drywall, holding the door in place. He jumped in and swept the room. Nothing. He threw himself to the floor, peering under the bed. Nothing.

He ran back to the hallway, repeating the process. Bang, thunk, sweep, down, scan bed, up. Bang, thunk, sweep, down, scan bed, up. Bang, thunk, sweep, down, scan bed, up. Corey cleared half the entire northwest leg of the third floor and collapsed in a heaving, sweating mass.

At least the whispering had stopped. He was ready to-

Wassat?

The whispering was gone, but he heard footsteps running up the stairs. They were coming from the stairs directly across from his room. He pushed himself off the wall and took cover behind the corner at the cross-section of the H and his leg of the building. It made him have to use his left hand to aim, and that wrist was pretty sore from something, but he held the aim pretty steady.

The stairwell door burst open and a form darted out. It ran straight across the hall, into his room.

Corey charged, running halfway down the hall, taking refuge inside another room, now able to aim with his right hand, his strong hand.

The figure darted back out of his room, holding a gun. It turned down the hall, toward him. With the lights out he could not see who it was, but they were about to be dead!

He aimed at the round shape just above the shoulders. The front sight post lined up. His finger tightened.

The concussion from the shot was deafening within the confined corridor. Even with several doors open the sound reverberated, sending shock waves through him.

Corey shook his head, trying to make the ringing in his ears quiet down. The other person was laying on the floor. He walked over.

It was a small person. It had on a hoodie, like Ashley's. The jogging pants with 'Ain't an Angel' in stylized letters across the seat were just like Ashley's too. It even had a really cute ass, like Ashley. *Oh shit!*

He dropped his guns and knelt beside the still form. Corey grabbed one of her arms and with a heave, rolled her over.

He was greeted with a 9mm handgun pressed to his forehead. Ashley's eyes were ice cold. Corey had never even known she could be that cold.

She kept the barrel pressed to his head and slid backward, out of reach, then extended her arm, allowing her body to get even further back.

"What the hell Core? You almost shot me!" It wasn't the raving of a crazy person, it was just a simple statement and demanded a simple and very convincing response.

"I swear, I didn't know it was you." His hands drifted up in the 'I surrender' pose.

Ashley pushed back again, putting a bit more distance between them. "You shooting at everyone who comes up?"

"You're the only one that's come by," Corey shrugged, looking more than a little chagrined.

"So it's me? Just shooting at me?" She stood, still with the weapon pointing at Corey.

He dropped his hands but didn't make any indication he was moving for his weapons, "Look, sorry, OK? I didn't know it was you."

Finally Ashley got a good look at Corey. His hair was disheveled, appearing as if he hadn't washed it in days. There was still white powder in his hair, possibly left over from two days ago when she last saw him.

His eyes were sunken in and face gray-white as if he hadn't slept for some time. One cheek was sporting a carpet burn and his face was just healing from whatever bruising and lacerations he'd gone through earlier in the week. His T-shirt was too large for him, stained by sweat and food dribbles. His pants were laying in the hallway about fifty feet away, along with one of his shoes. The plaid boxer shorts looked to have seen better days.

"Core, what the hell happened to you?" She lowered her weapon, then reholstered it.

Corey bent down, retrieving his guns from the floor and ignored her question. "Why the hell you back?"

She shrugged. Whatever happened had to him, he probably wasn't infected with the virus, and it was time to get on the road. Beyond getting to Roger's cabin, any feelings Ashley had for Corey had died and been beaten until unrecognizable. Frankly, if she had a map to the cabin she would have been incredibly tempted to simply leave him. "Told ya I'd be back when I was ready to leave. I'm ready to leave."

"Just like that, huh?" Corey stalked back down the hallway and retrieved his pants and shoe. Carrying them past Ashley he said, "What if I'm not ready? What if I don't even wanna go to a stupid cabin out in the woods?"

Waving an arm in an attempt to indicate the city outside, "Haven't you noticed? Things are getting crazy out there. I've heard a lot of gunshots lately and there were two guys that attacked me the other day! I had to shoot one of them to get them to back off. I'm not staying here!"

"Oh, you're not staying here, huh? What if," he paused. "Two guys attacked you? You shot one of them?"

"Yeah. Two days ago. I stopped by to talk to you and you were out doing whatever you were doing."

"Oh, yeah." He got quiet again, "Yeah, it might be time to get outta here." He pulled his pants on, sitting on his bed to pull on his shoe.

"Look Corey, I know we're not together anymore, but you really might want to put on a belt, maybe tie the shoes. Something could happen. You might get tripped up and things...well, things have changed and getting tripped up these days might get you hurt."

"You know, you're right. We're not together anymore. You don't get any say in what I wear or how I wear it." He tied his shoes before standing up. His room was stuffed with salvaged items so it took a while to find a belt. Without further comment, he slid the belt through most of the belt loops and buckled it over his hips. Ashley refrained from telling him he'd missed a loop. At least he wasn't going to get himself killed if his pants fell off at an inopportune moment.

Corey threw some clothes into a backpack. Ashley couldn't figure out how he knew what was clean and what was dirty. Maybe he didn't.

"You know, Ash, we don't have to be 'not together' anymore." He paused for only a moment in his packing, not looking at her, but giving her a chance to respond.

Blek! Not a chance in-. She paused that thought. He was the one who knew how to get to the cabin. *I wouldn't put it past him to stall and then leave without me if I turn him down outright.* "Yeah," she said, holding out for a very short trip to Arkansas, "it's been a while and so much has happened."

"You don't know the half of it," he said.

"What?" She had been absently looking at the garbage he had gathered. Most of it was cheap, second-rate stuff. The backpacks were just a step up from some plastic 'Hello Kitty' crap a kindergartener would carry. They were made for students to carry books, and students want a new bag every year, if not more often. They just didn't have to last like the quality gear she'd purchased. "What do you mean? What half don't I know?"

"Aw, nothing." He shrugged and turned back to packing. "You got the Escape?"

"Yeah, downstairs. When I got here, I heard all the banging going on up here. What was that?" She sat in the only chair that wasn't covered in his collected crap.

"Aw, nothing," he said again.

She saw his 'skittle' bowl and an old Coke bottle with burned tabs of paper. Even before she saw the tabs, she knew that he'd been smoking pot. He always had whenever he could get some. When he smoked down to where he couldn't hold it any more, he'd tapped out the last of the marijuana and leave the scorched paper fragments wherever they landed.

Ashley had smoked her fair share, but with the deteriorating situation going on outside she felt she needed to be *more*, not *less,* aware of her environment. She had no desire to escape *reality* for a little while. She wanted to escape *the city*. Whatever his infatuation with 'skittling', she didn't share it. But thinking about it made her crave the real sweet, fruity goodness of the candy.

He finished cramming the backpack full of clothes and turned to her. "Alright, help me get this stuff into the truck, huh?"

"What stuff?" She looked around and frankly didn't see anything that she would consider worthy of the space left in the vehicle.

"What do you mean?" He extended his arms and turned in a circle, "This is my shit, man. I want to take my shit with me!"

"Core, there isn't much room. We can get some of it, but not all of it."

"What the fuck? You know how hard I worked for all this?" He picked up a Converse canvas shoe he'd scavenged, throwing it back on the floor, holding up a backpack for her to see, dropping it. "It was a lot of fucking work!"

"Come on. Come downstairs and take a look." She pushed herself out of the chair, her temper boiling up. "You tell me what food, what water, what medical supplies, what ammo, what *real gear* you want me to leave here so we can take piece of crap shoes that wouldn't hold up a week of real work in ankle or knee deep snow. Come on, come point it out." She stormed to the stairwell door and held it open for him.

"Fine, OK? Fine, fuck it." Corey swept his arm across the room. "What part of my shit will mommy let me take?"

"Look, Corey, I'm not trying to be a bitch-"

"Believe me, I know you don't have to *try*. Just comes natural for you."

Ashley slowly drew in a breath and let it out. *This is why you're not with him anymore. One, two days tops on the road and it's all over.* "Look, I left enough room for you to bring a lot of small personal items, a few medium sized items or one or two large items. I left some of my stuff at home too. We just don't have enough room to take everything. I wish I had a big ass U-Haul or something, so we could take everything we wanted and everything you dug out of where ever you've been. I don't. I just have the Escape."

"Whatever." Corey pulled the rifle from under the bed. He handed it and the backpack full of clothes to Ashley. "Mind taking these down, I'll get some more packed."

As Ashley took the first load to the truck, Corey packed another backpack with the weapons and ammunition she hadn't seen yet, along with the medications and dealer's pot. He stuffed more clothes on top and threw it on the bed where he could casually pick it up before they left. A final backpack got stuffed with the beef jerky, power bars, Pop Tarts and candy he had recovered from the rest of the rooms. By the time Ashley returned he was just cramming the last of his toiletries into a final backpack.

Corey threw both the backpacks over his shoulder and followed her back downstairs. He climbed into the truck without even looking at what Ashley had brought. It didn't matter. It would be fine. She was great at this stuff so he was sure she had the bases covered. The problem he had was that she was expecting him to remember how to get to the cabin. How the hell was he supposed to remember that? Sure, he'd driven a couple of times, but Dad was giving him directions so he wasn't really paying attention.

Besides, he never even liked that place. The Internet was slow, the cell signals were weak and they didn't have any premium channels on the TV. The place really *sucked*.

29

Outside Delhi, LA

Jennifer rolled over with a crinkle of the tarp. She opened her eyes just a slit and scanned the area in front of her, careful to not move her head. Both she and Roger had become more wary during their travels, more observant. The old rules no longer applied. Phones didn't work so you couldn't call 911. Even if you found a working phone there wasn't a police force to serve and protect anymore. So she looked around before giving any indication that she had awakened.

She could see under the truck. No strange feet. She glanced as far above her head as she could see and as far beyond her feet. Nothing. The next part was something she had never even thought of before, but she and Roger had practiced it several times now and it was eerie how accurate it was. She kind of cleared her thoughts and tried to *sense* if anyone was looking at her. She didn't feel anything unusual. Sometimes when she did that exercise it made her skin crawl. She knew someone was looking. During their practice sessions, of course, it had been Roger. This morning she didn't feel anything.

She rolled back over. This time the movement and sound of the tarp caused Roger to stir. He rolled over and went through the same process she just had. Watching his eyes slit open, roll up, roll down and then pause as he *felt* for someone watching was a dead giveaway that he was awake. Then he twitched and his head snapped around to look at her.

"Morning, sunshine," she said. "Looks like our morning ritual is as much a hindrance as a help."

He yawned and stretched out, his hands clasped over his head. "How's that?"

"I could tell you were awake a good thirty seconds before you could tell I was looking at you. That's a long time if someone really is watching."

He yawned again and nodded. "Yeah, we've gotta stop pushing it so hard. We need to bed down when we're still awake enough to keep a watch."

She nodded, "At least until we get to Arkansas."

He pushed himself to his feet and used the side of the truck as a support and stretched again. "At least. Once we get there, though, there'll be other routines and I'm sure we'll keep our fair share of watch then too."

"Think so?" The adhesive bandage on her forehead crinkled as her eyebrows knitted together. "How long do you think this will go on? You know, when will things get back to normal?"

He smiled a mirthless smile and leaned over to kiss her forehead. "One idea we may have to come to terms with is *this* might be the new normal. The way of life we got used to required automation and electricity. A lot will depend on what's been damaged and who has died. Maintenance had to be done on a daily basis to keep the cities and refineries running. If the infrastructure has been damaged and if the people who can repair it have died, it's going to be a while."

"Years? Decades?"

"Yup. Could be either. Could be a generation or more. All depends." He dug their toiletries from their packs and handed over her toothbrush. They dipped the toothbrushes into their water bottles to get them damp and smeared on the toothpaste.

Jennifer had never brushed her teeth in front of someone else. Even in all the time she had been married to Paul, it just didn't seem *right* to brush her teeth in front of him and she certainly wouldn't have spit while he was watching. Things had truly changed. She scrubbed her teeth, standing right there while Roger was scrubbing his own. She took a sip of water, swished it around, then spat it out, brushed her tongue, sipped and spat again. A final splash of water rinsed off the toothbrush and she flicked it a couple of time to dry it off. Roger followed his own version of the process and they packed the dental care products away.

In the old way of life she was a reasonably busy person and had only made time to brush twice a day, upon waking and before going to bed. Roger was some kind of dental avenger. He insisted that they brush at least three times a day, more if they ate more often, and had a couple of hundred of those dental flossers in his pack. They used them constantly. His reasoning was that they had no idea when they would come across a trained dentist again, and preventative action was certainly better than a dental procedure, especially with the potential of there being no anesthetic.

Many ancient people, he said, appeared to have been killed by dental problems. Either infection or starvation, likely due to it being too painful to eat. He wanted to become an ancient person himself, but one without tooth problems.

Once their mouths were clean, she smiled at him, and they exchanged a solid kiss. It was great to have companionship, especially in a world this uncertain. Speaking of uncertain, her mind went back to a question she'd had after he'd already gone to sleep last night.

"Hey, why do you think the smaller towns and places have electricity but the cities don't?"

"Just a guess, well, an educated guess, but I think it was a tactic to fight the virus."

"What?" She paused folding up the tarp. "How so?"

"I wasn't a part of the pandemic team. I was part of the economic disaster planning team. Some of us were on different committees, so some of the ideas were shared more broadly. I don't know, but I heard one theory that might explain it."

He helped with folding the tarp and continued while they dug through the few remaining food items, trying to find something that would start the day off as close to right as they could. She could tell that they had both lost some weight already and though she didn't mind shedding a couple of pounds, she had been pretty fit and didn't have too much to lose.

"See, there was this theory that was circulated. I thought that it was a horrible idea but I wasn't on that committee so I didn't say anything. Wasn't my place, you know? I was pretty sure everyone else thought it was horrible too so it wouldn't get traction.

"It went like this. At first you try controlled quarantine. Gather together those who are ill and separate them from the healthy. Treat them and try to get them healthy, but deny the virus another host and it will die out simply because it can't spread. The infected will get better or they'll die. Either way, the situation is contained."

"Brutal. People really think like that? The government sits around and figures out how many people they can let die, that kind of thing?" Jennifer was somewhat appalled that she might have been considered an acceptable loss back at the airport.

"Oh, sure. You've gotta. That wasn't the problem I had with the idea. That's simple battlefield triage carried to its next logical extent." Roger offered her a granola bar and though she had somewhat lost her appetite, she accepted it because she knew she needed it.

"No, the next part was what I had a problem with. See, most viruses need population density to really go haywire. They need to jump from host to host and continue breeding. So one thought was to spread the population out.

"We've seen in a number of scenarios that if the government gets involved, such as after Katrina on the Gulf Coast or Sandy in the Northeast, people tend to congregate again, but in camps. That's what looked like was going on in Atlanta. Well, moving people from a thousand people per square mile to a thousand people per acre is really just giving the virus more of what it wants."

He brushed his hands off and stowed the mylar wrapping from the granola bar in his pack. At times like these, one never knew what might become helpful and when.

"So they came up with a way that achieved several goals. It would spread people out in a chaotic fashion, helping to keep them from clumping. It would relieve the government of the expense of having to provide extensive medical care to thousands, maybe millions of people and feed millions more.

"See, after Katrina and Sandy lots of people in the government thought there wasn't a lot to be gained by providing shelters. No matter how well they performed, they were always punished for it. Incumbents tended to take a beating in the polls after a disaster with a major sheltering operation. Even if they won the next election, they had to spend more to retain their seat. In turn, that meant they owed more people more favors. It was becoming untenable."

"Hang on." Jennifer stood with her hands on her hips, really unsure that what she was hearing was what he meant to say. "Are you saying that they based disaster response strategies on *political gains* or *political strategies*?"

Roger smiled and gave her a one-armed hug. "Medical professionals treat medical problems. Teachers teach. Truck drivers drive trucks. Politicians act politically. That's why the forefathers wanted citizen legislators. They wanted people who had to live under the system they created and, more importantly, who brought the needs of the people to the government rather than imposing the needs of the government on the people."

"But," she paused, shaking her head, "but that's not right! That's not why we elected them!"

"I don't want to get too far into politics. Politics, religion and sex, three topics to avoid when possible." He smiled one of the few genuine, full-blown smiles she had witnessed from him. "But of the three, the last one is best discussed in a show-and-tell format."

Jennifer blushed a bit as they unfolded the map on the front seat of the truck. "All right. That was sex, we'll save religion. Get back to politics."

"OK, so we'll say disaster response was a no-win situation. Look at poor Christie. He got battered by conservatives because he commended the president for a good response during Sandy. Even acknowledging a good response is a bad move if it isn't the politically right thing to do.

"So anyway, to get people out of the cities and deny the virus a fertile field, so to speak, someone came up with the idea of shutting down the electricity in the cities. Turn off the lights, shut down the refrigerators, and people will leave. If it is during a chaotic time, they'll generally leave in a chaotic manner and stay fearful of one another. That way they keep their distance and the virus can die out."

"But doing that, they could kill thousands of people."

"Tens or hundreds of thousands, more likely." He paused and looked her in the eyes, knowing that if the rest were difficult to understand, this would really hit hard. "But, it will kill people more evenly. As long as the ratios stay relatively unchanged and people migrate back to their homes, Congressional districts won't have to be changed and the balance of power stays relatively intact. It also gives plausible deniability.

"If you let a virus like this run through a city, all of a sudden states like New York, California, Texas and Jersey lose a huge portion of the population and their representatives lose a lot of power. Under this scenario they might save lives and come back home once it's all over. That way the government can mourn with the people rather than getting blamed by the people."

Jenny just stared at him for a few moments, conflicting thoughts clashing with one another. "With thoughts like that bouncing around in your head, no wonder you don't smile much."

"Like I said, though, I thought that plan got scrapped. Either I was wrong about that or someone didn't get the memo."

"Makes me sick that anyone even thought about it, much less discussed it."

Roger shook his head, "Well, this might be the idea with the most far-reaching ramifications. But it wasn't the worst idea I've ever heard come out of a committee."

Jennifer shivered at that thought. What could be worse than letting thousands of people die for political gain? She really had no idea. She liked it that way. "So, Delhi," she asked.

"If my theory is right, we want to stay away from towns with lights. They'll draw people like moths to a flame. That means higher potential for exposure if the virus is still active and it also means higher potential for potential *human viruses*, those who feed on the weakness of others."

Jennifer traced the road LA-577 on the map. "So, north or south?"

"South is beautiful, but go too far and you're in the swamps. Staying north seems to be the best bet."

"North it is!" Many of the roads they took weren't even on the road atlas. Their next big decision came as evening fell, just after passing into Texas.

30

North Texas

Getting out of Denton was more of a challenge than anticipated. Of course Interstate 35 was out of the question. They'd both seen how it was stopped up by wrecks, and that stretch of freeway also seemed to be where most of the violence was happening. Houses were being looted all over the city, but Ashley had heard quite a bit of gun fire coming from the I-35 area, so she avoided it. That left two main routes out of town to the north, Elm and Locust.

All the other main roads were blocked off. It wasn't just that wrecks were blocking the roads. No, they were actively blocked off. Someone had pulled cars, trucks or buses across the road to deliberately prevent traffic from getting through. Whatever the reason, from unofficial tolls to outright assault, Ashley wasn't willing to participate. She drove around the entire city looking for a way out, watching as each mile and each fraction of a gallon clicked off her odometer, scanning potential exit points with her binoculars well out of what she considered rifle range. The good thing about this part of Texas was that it was pretty flat and the roads ran pretty straight. You had line of sight for over a mile in some instances.

She finally decided that she had to make a move. There was a reason she'd purchased a four-wheel drive truck. When you need four-wheel drive, two-wheel drive is not an adequate substitute.

On the east side of town, Paisley Street dead ended into a cul de sac. Well, it appeared to dead end if you were reading a map and hadn't spent a good portion of the last five years riding these roads when bored - needing some time to think away from everything. If driving in unfamiliar areas was your cure for insomnia, then you knew that Paisley Street was not a closed cul de sac. There was actually a north exit from the cul de sac that led into a field. Less than 750 feet of rutted field later, it crossed over Texas Loop 288.

Making that crossing caused Ashley to smile. Just less than a mile up the road was the Department of Public Transportation office where she had gotten her driver's license renewed last year. *They'd want it back if they could see me now!*

She took what was essentially the driveway through what was meant to be an industrial park that never quite made it. Her intent was to take Mayhill up to University. She was already outside 'the loop' and thought she was in the clear. Luckily, she was still being cautious and using the binoculars to scan major intersections before approaching.

At Mayhill and University, was a Racetrac gas station. It looked like it had been turned into a fortress. From her pre-Ankara nighttime roaming, Ashley knew there was a Georgia Pacific railroad building just a block or two further on, and there were always a bunch of trailers in the yard. It looked like someone had gathered them up and set them around the gas station. Somehow they had even managed to tip them over so that there wasn't a gap underneath. All the trailers were laying on their sides, their floors and supporting undercarriages providing just a little more security for those inside the perimeter.

Patrols were stationed on top of the trailers, walking the circuit. There was a stationary lookout atop the awning covering the gas pumps, one on each end. She could tell that only a few of these people had binoculars, but the stationary ones on the awning both had rifles with huge scopes. It simply wasn't worth the risk.

She changed her mind about the route and a couple of turns later, she was on Highway 377, heading out of town. They cut across, north of Lewisville Lake and were soon out of Denton.

☣ ☣ ☣

Corey just sat in the passenger seat, brooding or sleeping. *At this point, that's fine by me. The longer you're quiet the longer you're not pissing me off.*

Staying on back roads and avoiding large settlements was fairly easy to do in north Texas. The more difficult part was keeping from getting lost. With Corey being absolutely no use navigating, and Ashley having to stop often to regain her bearing and scan ahead for trouble when they, unavoidably, got close to a civilized area, what should have a ninety-minute trip to the Red River turned into a four-hour ordeal.

Durant to Hugo should have been another hour, but took another two. Ashley had gotten turned around but didn't realize it until she was well down the road. At one point Corey did speak up, but it was only to complain about being hungry. She reached behind his seat, grabbed an MRE and tossed it in his lap without comment.

The problem with reaching Hugo was two-fold. She was reaching the end of her fuel, especially considering the wrong turn, and she was about to embark upon the most dangerous part of the trip. Up to this point Ashley had stuck to the back roads. The next two hours were going to be on an established highway. There just weren't that many roads marked on her map in southern Oklahoma and southeast Arkansas, and she really wanted to stay away from main roads that crossed back into Texas. Going over the Red River just seemed to be a natural choke point. She thought bridges would be patrolled by people with less-than-honest intent. As the fuel light turned on, she made up her mind which of the issues was most pressing.

As she cruised down the road marked E 2021, Ashley kicked herself. She cleared a small thicket of trees and just to the south, right at the intersection of 2120 and highway 271, stood a huge building. More massive than anything they had passed yet, she just stared at it. They were on the backside so she couldn't see any sign but whatever it was needed a lot of room and a lot of parking.

"Casino."

Ashley didn't even realize that Corey was awake. His voice startled her. "What? I thought that was over in Durant, I made sure to go well south of it."

"Yeah, well, if you weren't such a little goody two-shoes, prissy pants you'd know they have more than one. I think this is the newest one. Came here with the guys last summer."

I'm certainly not a goody two-shoes! And who even says *prissy-pants?* She kept her comments to herself. At least he was being helpful even if he had to be a jerk at the same time.

"You need gas," he said, "and they've got a gas station. Only one for miles. Especially if you don't want to go into a town."

Ashley sat there and stared at the casino, then at the little building to the north that Corey said was the gas station. "I don't want them to know what all we have. I'm sure they won't take cash-"

"No shit. Cash ain't worth nothing." He said that like there was some underlying meaning but he didn't elaborate, so she didn't pursue it.

"The sun's going down so maybe they haven't seen the truck. I have two gas cans strapped to the top. That'll get us over half a tank. We should be able to make it the rest of the way on that. What do you say."

"Fine. Whatever. That's a lot for you to carry though." He leaned back his seat.

"Well, I could carry one and you could carry the other. It'll still be heavy but we can manage it. It's got to be less than two miles."

Corey looked over at her and she recognized the flat stare. It was precisely that stare that had caused her to break it off with him while he had been sitting there playing one of his stupid games.

☣ ☣ ☣

She had been dressed to kill in her little black dress and red heels. She had gotten her hair done that morning and had spent extra time applying her makeup. She usually didn't wear more than a little eyeliner, blush and lipstick, but it was their one year anniversary and she was trying to make an effort to see if she could ignite any spark that might still be there.

It was twenty minutes until their reservation at Keiichi. One of the few things they agreed on was that they both loved sushi, so Ashley had decided to splurge for their anniversary. It was expensive, for college students. She hoped it would be worth it.

But when she arrived to pick him up, he was on the Xbox, completely not ready to leave.

Ashley wasn't egotistical, but that night she knew she looked good. When she walked through the dorm she had drawn stares, and it wasn't because she had toilet paper stuck to her shoe. There are few times in most women's lives when she knew without a doubt that she was a complete knock out. This was one of those times.

By the time she'd gotten to the third floor someone must have called from the first floor because guys 'just happened' to be opening their doors when she walked by. Three doors down from Corey's room Ashley even heard one of the guys say to his friend, 'That dude is so lucky! Why do girls always-' His voice faded off so she didn't get to hear what else he had said. Whatever it was, she was feeling pretty damn good about herself. Right up until she opened the door.

Corey looked up, clothed in only boxers, tube socks and a headset. He looked her up and down with that look like he was hungry, and she was a steak, crossed his face. For a year she had tried to make that look generate an appropriate response but it disgusted her more than excited her.

Suddenly his head twitched. His eyes shot back to the television, and he threw his remote to the floor. "Now look what you made me do! I was *fucking* killing it!"

"Corey," she tried to be reasonable, "look, babe, it's just a game. You can-"

Obviously that had been the wrong thing to say. His face did that blankness-thing. He showed no emotion but it bubbled out in every other way. "Just a game? I was *thrashing* those assholes! I was about to completely *own* them! They were my *bitches* and you let them kill me!"

"Come on, Core. We have reservations. I just-"

"Fine, let's just make this about you, huh? Fine." He picked up a T-shirt from the floor, jamming an arm into one sleeve.

"Hey," she said softly. When he was in one of these moods, it was like a wild animal. No loud noises, no sudden moves. "Remember I asked you to get your suit cleaned? I wanted us to get dressed up to-"

"Oh, right." He slapped his hand to his forehead. "I forgot, this is all about you. I'll put on the stupid suit."

"Look, Corey," she was losing her patience, "I'd like this to be a nice night for us. You know, maybe we could get along. Maybe something romantic?"

"Fine, whatever." He buttoned his suit pants. "We'll play dinner your way, but we're playing after dinner my way. You're going to have to do something special to make up for *this*!"

"Ya know what ya little prick?" She jabbed a finger into his sternum. "I've already done something pretty damn special." Her finger started moving back and forth, jabbing with each emphasis. "I have," *poke*, "put up with," *poke*, "a year," *poke*, "of being," *poke*, "talked down to," poke, "made fun of, and," *poke*, "generally being," *poke*, "degraded. You should have considered yourself *lucky* to be going out with me tonight. You should have considered yourself," *poke*, "lucky that I went out with you at all."

He threw his shirt to the floor, "Think you can do better?"

"Know it," she yelled.

"Well tear your ass then," he yelled back, "Go for it!"

She turned and stormed out of the room. Three rooms down she pounded on the door. The guy who thought Corey was lucky answered. He looked young, probably a freshman. His mouth fell open. "Gotta suit," she asked.

"Uh, yeah, sure."

"Put it on. We've got a reservation at Keiichi in fifteen minutes."

"Uh, uh, Keiichi? Sushi? But I'm not-"

"Order whatever the hell you like. I'm paying and if you are in anyway not a disappointment," she turned to Corey's door to make sure he was watching, "you might even get grudge sex."

"Fifteen minutes?" The freshman asked.

"Fourteen now. I can do everything I plan to do tonight by myself." She glared at him. "I just prefer not to. Closing in on thirteen."

He was out the door, his pants on, shirt and coat in hand and carrying his shoes in three minutes.

The break up wasn't official until a week later when she had dropped off all the clothing and crap he had left at her apartment. He'd never let her keep any of her stuff at his place. She even had to take her toothbrush with her. Not that she necessarily wanted to leave her toothbrush in his filthy bathroom.

Tim, the freshman, had gone home full but otherwise unsatisfied. By halfway through the dinner she had calmed down and that calmness had hugely impacted Tim's chances of getting lucky. As a negotiated settlement, and he was going to be a great negotiator later in life if he made it through this pandemic, she had agreed to not deny that he had gotten lucky if she was ever asked. She didn't have to confirm it, just not deny it. For the scene she had caused outside his door, it seemed like a fair exchange.

☣ ☣ ☣

Ashley didn't say another word. At the moment, he had her over a barrel. He knew the way to the cabin. *Once we're there,* she reminded herself for the umpteenth time, *I can finally be done with him. We might live on the same slice of land but that doesn't mean I have to put up with his crap.*

She simply climbed out of the truck and unstrapped one of the cans. She reached in and pulled the keys from the ignition. Corey just smiled. It wasn't a denial. He'd obviously thought about it. Instead, he just laid back in his seat.

Ashley slung a gym bag over her shoulder and stuffed in several items that she had specifically chosen and stored for bartering. There were a handful of those tiny 'airplane' bottles of liquor and a few bars of hotel soap, even though she thought a casino with a hotel attached would probably have plenty. As a matter of fact, this place probably had most of what she considered direct barter items.

She dug through her personal use barter items and threw in five ten-count packs of tampons, a pack of feminine pads and a bottle of feminine cramp relief. There was the very real possibility that some women were in the hotel and they would appreciate these products if they didn't have them. If the women needed them, chances were the men would appreciate them too.

☣ ☣ ☣

Grabbing the gas can by the handle, she set out. As she walked by Corey yelled out the window, "Cute ass, Ash. I'll be sitting here thinking about it."

She turned and flipped him off with her free hand.

He just chuckled and called after her, "Get my gas first, then we'll talk about that!"

He is SO lucky I don't know where that cabin is. His ass would be left right here on the side of the road.

☣ ☣ ☣

When she walked out of sight, Corey dug the roadmap from her door panel. It took him over five minutes to find Dierks on the map. Most of that was spent finding Arkansas. *No one uses* maps *anymore! That's what GPS is for!*

He cursed his bad luck that his phone's battery had quit. It seemed stuff like that was always happening to him.

OK, so there's two roads leading out of Dierks, 70 and 278 to the north and 278 by itself out the south. It had to be 278/70 north. I know there is a river on the edge and a river crosses 278 but one also crosses 84 up here.

He spent the next hour trying to recall his dad's directions. While pondering his dad's words, he remembered that if an emergency happened and Corey needed to 'bug out', he was supposed to leave something behind to tell his dad he was safe and what direction he was heading. *Oh well, the old man will figure it out.*

31

126 miles away in East Texas

Roger turned his phone off again. This was the first time that his phone had actually said he had a signal. When he tried to make a call, however, it just went to dead air. He didn't even get the message that the recipient couldn't be found. The tower had power but somewhere between that tower and the switch something else was down.

They had stopped to stretch their legs, and that turned into an exercise of boiling some strained water just to top off their bottles. It was still too hot to pour into plastic bottles so they were letting it cool. Funny how 'stretching your legs' could so easily turn into 'sitting on your rear end again'.

He slipped the phone into his pocket and looked over at Jennifer. She was leaning against the door of the truck, staring off into the distance. She had a sweatshirt on over a button-up, over a T-shirt. It added some bulk to her frame but she still looked fit and trim. As a matter of fact, she looked a bit healthier with three layers of clothes on. She had gotten fairly thin.

If her thoughts were running anything like his, whatever she was staring at had a hamburger superimposed on it. The half pack of granola bars hadn't done much to satisfy his stomach this morning, and the last can of pork and beans they had wouldn't do much to satisfy him tonight. Unfortunately, none of the vehicles they had acquired gas from on their trip had been equipped with any food. Staying on the back roads had kept them fairly safe. It had also kept them away from potential scavenging sources for food.

A random thought occurred to him. "Don't you ever check your phone? No one you want to try and get in touch with?"

It took a moment for her to register his question. "Huh? What? Oh. No, not really. When you're married to the mob and then get separated from them...well, let's just say that your social circle really shrinks. I didn't even know who was in and who was out. Then when my friends who weren't in found out, they stopped talking to me. Got kind of lonely to be me. Had to change gyms, stopped going to the same stores, everything. Real uncomfortable. Now? Well, now there probably wouldn't be anyone who would even know I was missing."

Roger mumbled, "I would," under his breath.

"Aw," she leaned over and patted his leg, "I know *you would*, but I don't have to call you." Her hand squeezed his thigh and then she didn't remove it. He found that very acceptable.

"But what about the airport? You looked like you were dressed for business."

"Wow, huh? Two weeks. It took you two weeks to register that I was another real human being and had a life before you came into the picture." She smiled so he knew she was joking with him, and she said it so much like Melissa had that it was comfortable. *Oh, Melissa. How long since I've thought about you?*

"Yes," Jennifer said, "I was dressed for business. I was out for a job interview."

"Really? You flew to a job interview? I don't usually get on a plane until *after* someone hires me."

"Not all of us are nationally-renowned experts in our fields."

"Internationally."

"What?"

"Internationally-renowned. Some of my books have been translated into over twenty languages."

She patted his leg again, "I thought this was about me."

"Oh, sorry. You're right."

She smiled and kissed his cheek. "You'll get better at saying that. Comes with practice."

His eyebrows knitted together as she continued.

"I was in New York. Well, actually New Jersey, but I flew into and out of New York. So I was both. You know?" He started to respond and she held up a hand, "Rhetorical. No need to answer."

He nodded and she continued. "Paul's lawyer. We met while he was handling Paul's case. I was a paralegal, educated, certified all the way before I met Paul. Ironic, huh? A paralegal married to a mob assassin and didn't even know it." She held up a hand without even looking at Roger. "Rhetorical."

"So I actually helped handle part of Paul's case. His lawyer was impressed, so he called me up for an interview once the case was over."

"How'd it go?"

She turned to look at Roger, deadpan, "Fine, I think I start next week."

"When you get home, you'll have to give notice." He was deadpan as well, but she still didn't know him well enough to know if he was kidding or if he meant it. He clued her in by smiling and saying, "A joke. I can do it too."

She smiled, wrapping a hand around his arm, letting out a wistful sigh. "So that's the story, Little Jenny goes to the big city and the world friggin' falls apart."

"It happens." Roger paused. He liked hearing about her, but it sounded like she had reached the end of her story. "Never lived in the big city?"

"No. I lived in Avon." She glanced up at him and saw his quizzical look so she clarified. "Heard of Vail, Colorado? The resort? Avon is one of the places where the people who work at the resorts live. Vail is just too expensive.

"Paul had a place in Vail and I met him at work. My boss was setting up a trust for him and I was doing some of the background work, you know, figuring out the different rules between Colorado and New Jersey, where he was from.

"When we got married I moved into his house. It was huge. It was beautiful, but just needed a woman's touch. But Vail was the biggest place I ever lived and it had less than fifty-five hundred permanent residents."

Roger nodded. *Small town girl. I like that.*

☣ ☣ ☣

Unlike Louisiana, Texas had a lot of back roads to choose from. Looking at a map, Texas looked like they paved over everywhere that a cow might have wandered. And there were a lot of cows. Similar to Louisiana, what few utility corridors he found this far east tended to be short and run into fenced-off fields. He remembered reading somewhere that nearly seventy percent of car accidents happened within ten miles of your home. He drove cautiously because *other people didn't*! Jennifer didn't find that joke as funny as he did. Actually, she just looked at him as if wondering if he had even tried to tell a joke.

By the time they stopped, they were in the Little Sandy National Wildlife Refuge. The trees were dense, but he was able to meander his way through the trunks and underbrush until they were sufficiently concealed from the road.

He watched as Jennifer setup the tarp lean-to. He helped gather the pine needles together for a comfortable sleep. He had made such a habit of asking questions that once she had the tarp in place, covering the pine needles, she said, "We use the pine needles, or leaves, for two purposes. First it adds comfort and comfortable sleep cannot be over rated. Second, it provides a layer of dead air between us and the ground, making insulation and keeping our body heat from being drawn away by convection."

He nodded and smiled, "But I didn't ask this time."

"Nope. Beat ya to it," she smiled smugly.

He did his best *Kung Fu* imitation, "And now Grasshoppa', you must show me how to make a fire."

She had built several fires during their travels and he just monitored her while he cleaned the double barreled shotgun and The Judge revolver. Once the fire was going, he leaned over and kissed her forehead, and handed her the handgun. Loading shells into the breach of the shotgun, he stood and stretched his back. "I'll take first watch."

Jennifer opened the can of pork and beans, placing it near the fire to warm. After a few minutes she held the can with a towel she still had from the fitness center - a lifetime ago - and tried to savor the half a can she ate. It was almost impossible to stop eating it.

For Roger, it was equally difficult not to leave his duties and be attracted to the food. It was the last they had, *thank you Sergeant Schoop*, and they had a long way to go.

☣ ☣ ☣

The night progressed without incident. Jennifer relieved Roger after just a few hours sleep. He ate his dinner of pork and beans and laid down for his shift in the sack. Since Jennifer could sleep in the truck, she allowed him more actual time on the makeshift pallet. He rolled over, facing away from their small fire. It was about as comfortable as they could make it, really not that bad. What kept him up was the constant grumble from his stomach as it requested much more than half a can of what would ordinarily be a side item, not a main course.

Once he was up, they made breakfast of coffee. At least Sergent Schoop hadn't taken that from them. The strong flavor helped with the psychological condition of being hungry and the bitter drink served as an appetite suppressant. To kill their hunger though, they'd need gallons of the stuff and that would make for slow going when it wanted out of their system.

Jennifer returned to the truck with the little gardening shovel they had acquired at the old farmhouse. It had been their go-to tool for digging their 'cat holes' to take care of their personal business and then covering it back over. She tossed it in the bed of the truck and held up a half roll of toilet paper. "One roll after this and then the world really will come to an end."

"Shouldn't have to worry." He pointed at the map with his index finger and pinky, placing the fingers on two locations. "From what I can tell, it looks like we're about three hours from my house in normal times. I figure we should be able to make it in six if we're careful. We'll take this route," he traced the roads south of Dallas and wrapping around to western Fort Worth where he tapped his finger. "The house is about here,."

"What about the kids? I thought we were trying to get to Denton."

"Denton's north of Fort Worth. We'll get up there tomorrow if we get to the house today. They should already be gone by now, so I'll see what route Corey said they were going. He's supposed to leave a note. We'll follow behind to ensure they make it."

Jenny yawned and nodded. "Just wake me up before you drive us into any trouble."

"I'll try to plan ahead for any spontaneous attacks."

"That'd be sweet." She climbed into the truck and patted the seat. Roger climbed in and she laid her head in his lap. He wasn't sure, but he thought she was asleep even before they exited the woods - ruts, dips, stops, starts and all.

He followed Highway 80 all the way to Terrell, slowly, and kept a close watch. Driving sixty miles took an hour and a half. Terrell was thirty minutes from downtown Dallas under normal circumstance, as long as you weren't trying it during morning rush hour.

At this distance, he couldn't make out the downtown skyline. However, even at this distance he could see the dense haze drifting away from the city and could even smell a musky, chemical-laden burning smell. If the scent was drifting this far, even with a favorable winds, Dallas must have been devastated. He reconsidered his route. Lancaster and DeSoto may be too close. Anyone left around Dallas would likely be desperate.

When the truck stopped Jennifer raised her head, "Ambush?"

"Nope, change of route."

"OK. Wake me if you need me." She was asleep again before he could reply.

He doubled back a few miles and headed on a more southerly heading. It was probably going to add another two hours to the trip, but it was better to take an extra two hours and get there than not to get there at all. Since he was going that far south, might as well avoid Mansfield and Burleson as well. They'd go through Alvarado and Joshua, much smaller settlements. *Having a plan is important. The ability to be flexible with its implementation is essential.*

By the time they passed along the outskirts of Joshua and began the upward swing around Fort Worth, Jennifer was up and looking refreshed. They both avoided any talk of food. Their stomachs weren't as cooperative and after a while the rolling growls made it sound like their stomachs were talking to one another. As strange as it was, she began to laugh at the absurdity. It was infectious and he joined in. They laughed together for miles as their stomachs continued their conversations.

For Roger, who had lived in the Dallas / Fort Worth area for more than twenty years, traveling on these roads without seeing even one other person was surreal. Even on the furthest back road of the laziest Sunday morning, there was always traffic on the roads in and around the Metroplex. Even the looted shopping center in Atlanta didn't have as profound an impact on Roger as these empty streets. At long last he pulled onto the crushed rock road that led to his house.

He paused, looking ahead.

"What's wrong?" Jennifer looked down the road, trying to see anything that was obstructing their way.

Roger stared for a moment, still looking down the road. "This is it. This is the house I shared all those years with Melissa. I never thought I'd ever be bringing another woman here."

"Oh." She couldn't say anything else. There was nothing else to be said. This was something he was going to have to work through. She settled in for a wait.

It took less than a minute. "Never thought I'd steal a truck, shoot a biker or bury a family in their own backyard either. The agile mind must be ready to accept new situations."

With that, he shifted the truck back into gear and moved on. Jennifer shook her head. He was unlike anyone she had ever met. It had taken a while, but she had finally accepted that as a good thing.

☣ ☣ ☣

Jennifer had no idea what she was expecting. He was a quirky guy and his house could have been anything. If she was surprised, it was from the normalcy of the scene.

On this old crushed rock covered road, a huge entry gate arose on the swell of a hill. It was two towers of field stones, supporting a white painted pipe gate. The rest of the perimeter of the property was fenced by more of the four-rail, two-inch pipe. The spacing between the pipes was filled in by a two-inch wire grid. About every fifteen feet there was an upright post where the pipes were welded. Beyond the fence and gate was a black topped driveway leading to a ranch-style house that would have fit into practically any suburb from North Carolina to California. It was on the large side of modest but nowhere near as large as Paul's house in Vail.

There were a couple of out buildings she could just make out behind the house but otherwise it seemed oddly normal for Roger.

"Here it is," he said, "Home sweet home."

"It's nice!"

"You sound surprised." He looked over at her slyly.

"Well," she smiled, "I am kind of surprised."

He nodded at the house as he rolled down his window. "It had a woman's touch." She smiled at his reference to her story about moving to Vail with Paul. *There're worse things a man can do than listen when a woman talks.*

There was a keypad mounted on the driver's side tower. Beneath the keypad was an intercom. Roger typed in a code and the gate swung open.

"Wow, you still have electricity."

"What kind of emergency planner would I be if my own house couldn't survive the grid going down for a month or two?"

"A month?"

"Or two. Or sixty." He looked over at her. "That means hot showers too."

Jennifer leaned her head on his shoulder. "Mr. Westover, you really know how to sweet talk a girl." Her mind caught up with what he said. She sat up and looked at him. "Did you say 'sixty'? Sixty months? As in five years?"

"Well, not strictly speaking." He pulled through the gate and it swung closed automatically behind them. "I planned five years for three people, plus a twelve percent fudge factor and excess for charitable giving or barter. All told, with just two of us, we're probably looking at closer to, and I'm just averaging and using round numbers here, so don't hold me to it...," he paused waiting for her acknowledgment.

She held up her hand, the pinky and thumb curled so that they touched, the remaining fingers held straight up. Roger recognized the Girl Scout salute. "On my honor."

"For just the two of us, then we're looking at about nine years."

"Nine years of food?" She sat up to stare directly in his eyes. "Are you serious? What kind of, I mean, who would think, uh, I mean, really? Nine years?"

"Well," he started then paused himself, "yeah. Nine years. Um, here. More at the cabin." He sounded a little embarrassed by her reaction.

"More than nine years at the cabin?" This was just too much for her to wrap her head comfortably around. She had never met anyone who had more than two weeks of food. A year was insane! More than a year, she didn't even have a word for it.

"No." He felt some relief, she had misunderstood him, "No. There is *more* at the cabin. As in 'other', not a greater quantity. At the cabin there's probably only three years. There, I was counting on our colony becoming self-sustaining."

"Hang on. So, all told you have over *twelve years* of food for two people stored in two states?" Her face was incredulous.

"Well, yes. Food and necessities."

"Necessities? What necessities? What else do you have?"

"You know, batteries, toilet paper, clothing, water. Ammo."

"Oh my *god* Roger. What the hell?"

He pulled the big truck up to the garage and climbed out of the cab. She climbed out, looking around the yard.

"Seems weird to a lot of people, I know. I've heard it for years. Everyone who took emergency planning - what we call *prepping* - serious has heard it. We were the crazy ones." With a nod of his head he indicated the truck. Somehow that nod relayed the truck's recent history: the truck they had stolen, the food they had stolen, the family they'd buried. Siphoned gas, military commandeering. The biker and refugees, the ferry. He let her mind retrace their trek. "Looks like we might have been on to something."

The look of disbelief faded from her face, her entire disposition softening. Finally Jennifer nodded and shrugged. "Looks like you were."

He swept his arm toward a slightly overgrown sidewalk, and escorted her on the path to the front door. "Been a while since I used the front door. Car has a garage door opener. Its at the airport, in long term parking. Didn't realize it was going to be this long term." He paused and looked out at his yard, "Need to mow the lawn, looks like crap."

"There're probably more pressing things to do, don't ya think?"

He shrugged in acknowledgment, walking up to the door and digging keys out of his pocket. He swung the door open, "Welcome to Casa de Westover."

The master of the house stepped in behind her and typed a security code into another, larger, and more extensive keypad just inside the door. Jennifer cocked her head, looking at the panel. She had one similar at her home in Colorado. If someone tried to break in, it would signal the monitoring company. Out here she couldn't imagine that calling the police would do much good. The robbers could be in, have a party and pack a U-Haul before police could even find the place.

"Why bother? Like you said, when seconds count, the police are just minutes away."

He looked at her and then back to the panel, not understanding for a moment. "Out here they might be hours away. They do what they can. They just can't do everything that's expected." He paused to consider why she had made the comment.

"Oh! No, this isn't independently monitored. When it says 'armed', that isn't a euphemism for 'monitored'. This was custom designed for this house. When it detects a threat, it monitors the intruder's location, waits until they enter an exclusion zone, locks 'em down and knocks 'em out with enough gas to put a rhino to sleep. If they wake up before someone gets home to take care of them, or call the police, then it uses high frequency green strobes and ultra sonic sounds to keep them pacified.

"From what I understand, there is a pretty complex algorithm to help determine who gets pacified and who gets a pass. When I tested the system out, I could walk around the exclusion zone calmly and everything was fine. I could do pushups, no problem. If I started on some jumping jacks, it was all over but the crying."

"Wow. Sounds expensive." Jennifer looked at the control panel again, making sure it didn't say 'armed'.

"Prob'ly was. It was a prototype. The designer used my house as a proof of concept. Couldn't get the permits to do it like he wanted in a city limits until he did it somewhere else and was able to prove it's safety. Once that was done, he just left it for me."

Jennifer turned her attention to the rest of the house. "Any more Star Trek features I should know about.?"

"Just one. Wanna see it?"

She wasn't, sure but the gleam in his eye made her very curious.

32

Choctaw Casino

It was completely dark by the time Ashley made it to the casino. Luckily for Ashley, they had some lights on. They had a perimeter of razor wire that was virtually invisible in the darkness. She followed it around to where a driveway led into what she suspected was the employee parking area. A large spot light blinded her as her first foot stepped on to the driveway.

"What you want," called a voice close enough to the spotlight that she couldn't make out the speaker.

"I need gas," She called back, holding up the gas can as proof. "Ran out down the road and saw you guys. Thought I'd try to get some."

"Gas's 'pensive ma'am. You got something to trade?"

Well, that's encouraging, she thought. *Maybe I can negotiate with these guys after all.* "A little bit. I just need this can filled up twice. That's ten gallons." She held a hand up to shield her eyes from the light but it was no use. She still couldn't see who she was talking to in the glare of the light.

"Ten gallons is a lot these days."

"I know, but I brought stuff to trade. Guess you wouldn't take five dollars a gallon, huh?" She smiled her prettiest smile and got a laugh in response. *Wow, this is going good.*

"No," said a female voice very close. "He wouldn't."

Ok, well, not that good. "Didn't figure," she said out loud and backed up a couple of steps, the smile fading. Laying her bag on the ground, she unzipped it slowly, no sudden actions. "I just want to show what I have for barter."

She laid out a bottle of the alcohol. The woman didn't say anything. Ashley moved on to the bath soaps. Still nothing. She reached in and pulled out the bottle of Midol.

"What's that?"

Score! "You know," Ashley opened the bottle and poured a few out in her hand, "Midol, for cramps and stuff."

"No," came the response, "*that*." Ashley looked down. The edge of the tampon box was showing.

"Oh, tampons." She opened the plastic package and pulled one individually wrapped cylinder, as if the woman didn't know what it was.

"Ok. That'll get you your first five gallons."

"Oh! Sweet!" *That was easy!* Ashley picked up the gas and one the tampons.

After her first step the woman said, "Don't be stupid. All of them."

"The whole pack? That's ten. I don't know-"

"No, girl, *all* of them."

"That's fifty! I should get all ten gallons for fifty!"

"Or you could keep your tampons and we can keep our gas."

Ashley plucked all five packs out of her bag, but kept the bag pulled up so the woman wouldn't see what else was in it. She'd have to remember to break out her barter items into smaller units. Showing your hand obviously put you at a disadvantage. It wasn't like taking a $20 bill into a store and coming out with change. It looked like prices fluctuated to meet the 'currency' available, not the other way around.

"Alright." She walked up to the fence with the spotlight following her and sat the gas can down in front of the fence. She placed three of the packs on the gas can. "You get the other two when you bring the can back, full of gas."

One sun-darkened hand reached in to the circle of light, plucked the tampons off the can, then picked up the can itself. Footsteps walked off.

Ashley stood there in the circle of light, suddenly feeling a bit self-conscious to have so much attention focused on her while she stood there holding a couple packs of feminine hygiene products. It was a thankfully short time before the footsteps returned and the gas can was placed in the circle of light. Ashley walked back up and extended her hand, offering the final two plastic packs. The same hand came out and snatched them.

She knelt down, unscrewed the gas cap, and sniffed. It was certainly gas. She smiled and looked up. "You need anything else? For the other five gallons?"

"Got more of those?"

"No, not for trade. I don't know when I'll get more." Ashley thought about her other items. "Maxi pads? You know?"

"Yes, girl I know what they are!" The woman's voice had never been kind but it turned even more gruff. "Been using them probably before you ever troubled your mother!"

"Sorry." Ashley looked back at her bag. "I have some."

"How many you got?"

Ashley opened her mouth then snapped it shut. "How many for five gallons?"

"How many you got," the voice repeated.

"Thanks for the five gallons. That might get me where I'm going. At least it'll get me in to Hugo."

"Alright. Fine. What kind are they?"

"Allways? Ultra-thin regulars?"

"They come in like thirty-six or forty-eight to a pack, right?"

Again her mouth opened and snapped shut. "Maybe. But I might not have a full pack."

"Ok. Fine. I'll take thirty-six for your other five gallons."

Ashley lifted her bag and made a show of digging around in it. She tore open the 36 pack plastic bag and looked up. "How 'bout twenty?"

"You got thirty?"

"I can do twenty-five."

The other woman paused for a moment. "All right twenty-five for another five gallons."

Ashley dug them out of the bag and held them up for the woman to see. "Here they are. Now, they are the only things I'm bringing back with me. If the price changes, then I walk back to my car with an empty can and I'm just going to drive away."

"Don't worry, girl, we stand by our word."

Gasoline weighs just over six pounds per gallon. Multiply that by five gallons and suddenly Ashley had thirty pounds of dead weight to carry. It took over an hour to make the trek back, pausing every hundred feet or so to rest.

When she walked past his window, Corey looked out. Ashley was hot and sweating. The chill air was making her freeze despite the exertion. She was exhausted and her arms hung from her sides like wet sandbags.

Corey looked at her and said, "I'm bored." He sat his seat forward. "Think you can speed this process up?"

If she had the energy to spare she would have just slapped him. As it was, she used the remainder of her strength to tilt the gas can into the fill spout. She strapped the empty can to the roof and climbed into the driver's seat.

"What are you doing?" Corey sat up in his seat. "I thought you were getting ten gallons."

"I am." She started the car. "But that doesn't mean I'm going to lug another five gallon can back to the car. I'm going to drive around so I'm closer since I can't get any help."

Without another word she pulled the car forward. As she rolled up to the fence at the casino the spotlight engulfed the truck. She squinted through the light, reduced speed to a slow roll, and moved back to the driveway where the negotiations had taken place. Ashley slipped out of the truck, once again taking her keys with her.

"Who's that," the voice by the search light said as the beam swept over Corey.

"Just a passenger." Ashley pulled the pads out of her back pocket and retrieved the empty can from the roof.

"Don't let her fool you," Corey yelled. "I'm her boy toy, and she just can't wait to get me out behind the bushes somewhere!" He chuckled at his own joke as the exchange was made.

Ashley dumped the additional five gallons into the tank. Strapping the empty can once again to the roof, she shook her head, thinking about Corey. *He is just so* offensive *in everything he does. Surely he wasn't that bad when we were dating.*

She reached into the truck, inserted her key, and turned the ignition to the 'accessory' position. The fuel needle crept up past the three-quarter tank level. Maybe four gallons remaining, plus ten gallons. Twenty miles per gallon. Two hundred eight miles to go. Maybe one hundred miles to Dierks, hopefully less than fifty after that. *Should be plenty and then some!*

She stepped up on the side of the chassis and waved over the top of the truck. "Thanks! Good doing business with you!"

The only response was the spotlight turning off. She climbed into her seat and pulled back onto the roadway. Less than a mile along, a yawn stretched her jaws. She fought the sensation for a few more miles, but she was exhausted. Staying on constant alert, and even just having to keep her emotions in check being around the sulking Corey, had taken its toll. She shook her head, and focused on the road again. Maybe trying to talk would help, if he would cooperate. "Not too much further now. When we get to Dierks, just let me know where to turn."

Corey nodded then spoke up. "Hey, that gas looked heavy."

It was a lame way for him to reply, but at least he was talking and not just sulking. Then he continued, "And I can see you're tired. Why don't you get some sleep and I'll drive the rest of the way."

"Really?" Ashley looked over at him. He appeared sincere.

"Like you said, I have to tell you where to turn anyway so why don't I just drive it?" He offered a somewhat reserved smiled. *Maybe he is coming around. About damn time.*

"You're OK with that," she asked, still not quite trusting him. Maybe this was just a weird joke.

"More than. I was a jerk earlier. This will just be the first step to making it up to you."

Ashley smiled as she pulled off the road. He hopped out of the car and she just slid across the console to the passenger seat. There were times when you could tell that Corey really was his dad's son. It was those times that had made a whole year with him possible. Unfortunately, they weren't so frequent that it had made that year really worthwhile. Most of the time she'd felt like she had burned a year of social life, spent way too much money trying to make him happy. She'd also somewhat degraded herself trying to get him to be the person she wanted him to be rather than just accepting that he would never be that person.

He slid into the driver's seat, snapped his belt, and shifted the car into gear. "Just relax. I got it."

She intended to just rest as he drove, but was too tired. Less than five miles later, with the dim lights of the dashboard and white-noise sound of the road, the gentle rocking of the truck lulled her to sleep.

☣ ☣ ☣

Corey piloted the car, desperately trying to remember the street he needed to turn on when he got to Dierks. *At least with her asleep I won't have to hear her bitching if I make a wrong turn.* He was on Highway 70,

294 Brian S. Vinson

and that would take him straight into town. Dierks was a tiny town from what he remembered. Surely he'd remember where he needed to turn.

This trip was so different from the last time they had traveled this road. Last time they had come up, Corey was driving and his dad was in back. Ashley was still his oh-so-loving girlfriend. She had just crammed for two finals in the same week. She was working her secretary job and since it was end of the semester, there were a lot of parties in Denton. Her catering job had taken up most of her evenings. Really, the only similarity was that she was exhausted that time as well. By the time they had spent a couple of hours in the car, she was crashed out - just like she was tonight.

The big difference from last time was that she was in that really short skirt he liked. It was so short that it practically showed her ass while she was standing up. After she'd sat on a seat for a few hours, and moved around while she was sleeping, he pretty much had a bird's eye view of Nirvana. With her so busy with studying and working, they hadn't slept together in over three weeks. On top of that, he'd only been able to scrounge up one troll from the various parties he had hit. Sure, that one had been a *freak*, just the way he liked, but even that had been almost a whole week before they left.

The view of her bare legs and the little triangle of panties he could see had kept him pretty distracted for most of the trip.

His dad had no clue in the back seat. But that wasn't new. His dad usually didn't have a clue. He'd just kept yammering away, telling Corey what he needed to do. Corey needed to study harder. He needed to get a job. He needed to spend less time in bars. He needed to take life more seriously. He needed to treat Ashley better.

Corey's eyes had returned to that little patch of white in the seat next to him and thought of all the ways he would like to treat Ashley. He didn't know if they qualified as *better*, but they definitely qualified as *fun*. With that going through his head, it was no wonder that he couldn't remember a couple of stupid turns in some podunk, piss-ant town.

Today he hadn't seen a single cop the whole trip, so he just pushed the petal to the metal and let it cruise. He blasted down the freeway at eighty or ninety, slowing only enough to take corners at a speed that wouldn't wake Ashley. If he could make up enough time, maybe he could be through town before she woke up - even if he made some wrong turns. He made the seventy miles to the Arkansas border in under an hour and the next thirty into Dierks in less than half that.

Corey slowed as he entered the town. It was small and mostly residential. The largest business was the huge sawmill just visible in the darkness on the south side of town. Nothing was open tonight though. *Not that these yokels would have any clue how to get to his dad's ranch. Probably no one in town even knew who his dad was.*

Cruising up Main Street, he saw the sign for the highway 278 junction. He hung a right at 4th street, saw the sign saying he was now on 278 East and drove through. It didn't look completely right, but when he had looked at the map 278 went north and south through town. He came in to town from the south, so this had to be right. When he encountered the sharp left turn to the north he was certain he was going in the right direction.

A short while later the road took another turn, then began a slow, southern drift that was undetectable at night with no point of reference. When it dead ended into the village of Center Point he knew he had gone the wrong direction. *See, this is why I wanted her asleep. I'd never hear the end of it.*

He turned around and started going again, certain he'd just missed his turn. Maybe he'd recognize it from this direction. He looked over at his passenger. In the dim light he could just make out both of her legs and the V they formed, as well as the rise and fall of her chest. He checked the road quickly and looked back, his mind returning to the vision of the previous trip.

One thing's for sure, she is one serious lay. Can't wait to crawl back in there!

When they'd gotten to the cabin last time, Dad had stayed in his tiny little shit heap. Corey and Ashley had permission to stay at one of the other places. She must have gotten plenty of rest on the way up because by the time they had unpacked she was up for a bit of fun.

She was about all the fun he'd had there. It was so *fucking* boring! His phone didn't work in the cabin where they were staying. You had to go up to the freak-show house to get any television or Internet.

He'd started referring to Gene and Shirley as the freak-show because who would want to leave the city and go live in the middle of nowhere? It was just stupidly crazy. Not that they were weird looking like real freak-show people. Actually, Shirley was pretty hot, for an old lady. She was probably almost his Dad's age, forty or so. But Becky, her daughter, she was *fine*! She'd just turned twenty and from what Corey could tell, hadn't been anywhere near anything fun since she was eleven.

He tried to go *there* a couple of times, even catching her down on the bank of the river one day. He'd laid down all his best moves, but she was such a bitch! When he had taken her hand to lead her into the woods, she'd almost broken his wrist. He must of outweighed her by fifty pounds, but she twisted him up and flipped him around like a sack of horse feed. Next thing he knew, he was flat on his back with her heel resting on his nuts. She gave him the option of leaving or never being able to have kids. He'd decided to leave. Not that she was really *that* fine anyway. *Stuck up bitch.*

Becky actually kind of did him a favor. He was so pissed and upset that Ashley wanted to make him happy. She was always real generous when he was the most pissed, and he'd been totally pissed that night. *Those were some good times*. He adjusted his pants at the memories, even shifting the now ever-present .357 inside his waistband.

As he was staring at Ashley and recounting the good old days, Corey didn't realize the road took a slight leftward drift while he took the right fork. That road led off into the foothills of the Ouachita Mountains. A few curves later, a couple of attempts at backtracking and he was completely lost.

Ashley had been asleep for over two hours now. It was enough rest that if he stopped the car and turned on the light to read a map, she'd wake up and be pissed that he didn't remember how to get to the cabin. She'd be so much more *thankful* to him when he got her there, if she thought he had driven straight in, than if he woke her up. Besides, if she thought he didn't remember where the cabin was, she might get pissed about all kinds of crazy shit – she was prone to that kind of thing, the crazy bitch – and he'd have to find something else to do to make her thankful again. He wanted her in a *giving* mood as soon as they got there. No use wasting time.

But, if Ashley wasn't feeling it, maybe Becky had come to her senses. Best to try to keep the one on the hook while baiting another line though. There weren't that many roads out here, surely he could find his way back.

As the sun started to brighten the horizon, Corey was fuming. *These stupid hicks have no* fucking *idea how to put up road signs.* He was sure that he was taking different turns but he seemed to keep coming back by the same tree over and over again. He was going in circles *because these people had no idea how to* fucking *give directions.*

The little fuel light had come on over half an hour ago and now the needle was pointing to the line just under the 'E' for 'empty'. Starting up a hill the truck sputtered. They made it to the top and coasted down the other side. As they started up the next hill the truck sputtered and died. Corey slapped the steering wheel and unleashed the obscenities he'd been holding back for over an hour.

33

Roger's House

Once again Jennifer had no idea what she was expecting, but this wasn't it. Roger took her through the house. They entered through the formal living room. Two sofas, two chairs, a piano with bench, end tables and a coffee table with a large fireplace; it could have been a picture from a home design magazine.

Through the doorway was a short hall. Straight back, she saw cabinets and what she thought was the edge of a refrigerator. On the left there was a small closed door, probably a coat closet, and then another open door where a mirror and vanity indicated a bathroom. He led her through the other door in the hallway to the den, or informal living room.

This room had the big overstuffed leather chair with matching couch and loveseat, all arranged to point at the huge flat panel television screen. More end tables and another coffee table populated the room, but even with all that furniture, it still was almost barren due to its size. A back door led to a screened-in porch and then out to the back yard.

He held her hand and guided her outside. In the fading sunlight she saw a row of shiny panels, tilted up to catch the sun. Of course she knew what solar panels were, but she had never seen so many on personal property nor on the type of frames these were attached to.

Roger swept his hand across her field of view. "Melissa says most people don't care about the numbers so I'm not supposed to bore people. There is enough solar gathering potential there to power the essential functions of the house. See that little building to the right?"

She did. It was a squat cinder block building with a slanted roof. The roof led to a gutter and the gutter led down to a large barrel. She nodded and he continued. "That's the power relay station. You didn't see any electrical lines coming out here, did you? That's because there aren't any. Closest grid power is over ten miles as the crow flies - over thirty by road.

"But that relay station there, that collects from my three sources. That's the solar array there. You can't see the windmill system from here. It's up on top of the hill over there. I've got five Darrieus-style vertical axis wind turbines. Very efficient, very quiet. Very cool.

"Down at the creek I have a water screw and water wheel. They're a bit of a maintenance issue and I don't seem to have them dialed in for the best efficiency yet.

"But they all feed into the relay station. I've got my battery plant in there and it's the central location for power distribution with all the electronics necessary. You know, charge control regulators, inverters, monitors, surge protection. All that."

"Sure." She had no clue what he had just said, but this was one of the first times that Roger seemed to be just a regular guy. He was talking about something important to him and getting to show off his work to someone new. *Someone he cared about?* So Jennifer wasn't going to spoil it for him.

He looked at her, with a sparkle in his eye that was a rarity. "You know the best part of all that infrastructure?"

"What's that," she asked, giving him a smile to show him she was interested. She had no idea where this was leading.

"The best part about all that is the refrigerator is still working and we can light the stove." He returned her smile. He'd spent long enough living with Melissa that he knew even someone who shared his enthusiasm for preparedness could get overwhelmed by his added enthusiasm for the details that made it possible. He respected Jennifer for putting up with it.

"You mean, food?" Her eyes lit up and her smile turned from polite to excited.

"Food!" His eyes lit as well and they retreated into the house.

☣ ☣ ☣

They were cleaning their dishes after the meal. Roger was washing, Jennifer drying. He said that there was enough power to run the dishwasher, but that he hadn't run it in years because there were never enough dishes at one time to justify all the electricity and water. "Besides," he said, "that's a convenience we don't have at the cabin. No reason to get used to it now."

She agreed and it really wasn't that big of an issue. Two plates, a couple of pans, a couple of glasses and some flatware. They were done before they could have even loaded a dishwasher anyway. Standing there beside him doing something truly domestic was such a change from the previous two weeks that she actually welcomed it.

Once they were done, Roger flicked the scrub brush to start the drying process then leaned back against the sink as Jennifer finished the last pot and laid it on the drying rack. "Shelter, water, food. Top tier priorities are done. What's next?"

Jennifer thought back over their conversations. He dropped little conversational nuggets all the time. It had taken her a couple of days to realize that he actually expected her to remember what he was saying. Once she started really listening, she found the common threads. In his own, very *Roger* way, he was sharing his knowledge. That encouraged her to listen even more and it was amazing the information he was sharing.

"Shelter. Water. We don't need fire because we've got this awesome house. Medical and safety are taken care of. I'd say we've made it to hygiene."

"Gold star!" He smiled. "I have over twenty-three thousand gallons of water and on-demand hot water from over one thousand gallons of propane. If we're not prunes when we come out, we're not doing something right."

He showed her through the bedroom wing of the house with two guest rooms, Corey's old room, still decorated as if a high school student still lived there, and the master bedroom. There were three and a half baths. He showed her where the towels were as well as an assortment of shampoo, conditioner and soaps.

When Roger showed her to the first guest room her heart sank. *His house, his rules.*

She spent over an hour in the bathroom. The tub was deep and she soaked until the water turned cold. She washed her hair, brushed her teeth, and towel-dried her hair. It was wonderful. Roger had even placed a manicure set on the vanity. It was put to good use. When she emerged from the bathroom, she was entirely renewed, maybe better than ever. Even the gash on her forehead had healed enough that she no longer needed to bandage it.

She felt the smile slip from her face as she looked down the hall. Roger's bedroom door was already closed, light out. *His house, his rules,* she thought to herself again. She stepped into her room, still watching his door. Maybe he'd open it.

He didn't. Her door closed the last inch, blocking her view of the hall and his door. She leaned against the cool wood of the doorframe, wondering if she should go and knock. *Maybe he needed a reminder.* It took a moment, but she finally pushed herself off the doorframe and let her hand drop from the knob.

When she turned around, she startled. Roger was sitting in the chair beside her bed. He pushed himself up to a standing position. Long house pants, T-shirt and a subdued grin. That was it. No shoes, no socks. No pretensions.

"I was told that it would be my fault if we continued to be frustrated."

"Yup." She smiled and sucked her bottom lip between her teeth. "I think I remember that."

"I hate to be blamed for anything, especially if I can avoid it."

"Good policy."

"I heard I had a green light."

She nodded, the lip slipping back between her teeth again for a moment. "If it was any greener, they'd have to invent a new name for the color."

"You know, I hate wasting electricity. If a light's on, might as well do something with it."

"Might as well." Her lips just kept curling, her smile growing.

"I think I'm going to stop talking now." He took a step toward her. The room wasn't huge but there seemed to be a lot of space between them.

Jennifer just stood in place. *Let him work for it just a bit.*

He crossed the room slowly and raised a hand. When it touched her cheek it was as if she were jolted by electricity. That hand continued on and slipped behind her head, pulling her forward.

They skipped the pleasantries this time. Their first kiss was frantic, animalistic in its need. He pushed against her, she against him. Even with their bodies pressed together, there was still too much space between them.

Roger fumbled for the hem of her shirt. After two attempts he gave it up. He simply reached up, grabbed the elastic at the neck of the shirt and ripped it open. Her body responded to that mixed display of strength and desperation. She wrapped herself around him. It was the last conscious effort either of them took as their minds retreated and their bodies took over.

☣ ☣ ☣

Jennifer awoke confused. She was in bed and comfortable. The room was brightening from daylight filtering in a window. Her body was completely relaxed, even refusing to respond appropriately to some of her requests. It wasn't a disabled type of refusal, just a relaxed unwillingness.

The evening bubbled back into her mind, the bath, closing her bedroom door, Roger being in the room. A smile curled her lips. She looked over to the other pillow. He was still asleep, breathing slowly, rhythmically.

Jennifer slid closer and reached a hand over to him. A few moments later his breathing sped up, becoming more shallow. He rolled on his back, making his full body available to her. His eyes stayed closed, now it was from conscious effort rather than the relaxation of sleep. The breathing came in gasps and her smile widened.

She leaned over him, continuing her efforts. Finally his eyes opened. Her hair hung down into his face, her eyes shining with joy, her lower lip once again trapped by her teeth. Roger pulled that beautiful face toward him. Their lips engaged, encouraging their tongues, encouraging the rest of their bodies.

Over an hour later they lay back, relaxing into a tangled knot. Once their breathing slowed back to normal Roger stroked her sweat-laden hair off her cheek, slipping the strand behind her ear.

"You know what we should do next?" He continued to stroke her hair.

Jennifer moved her head so she could see his face. It was flushed from exertion but fading back to normal. His eyes were intense, focused on hers. Her lip trapped for a moment, she slid the tips of her fingers down his moist chest and back up to his chin. The lip slipped out as she smiled, "Breakfast?"

He smiled, "Exactly! Breakfast."

They followed the same routine for breakfast as they had for dinner the night before. He cooked, they ate. He washed, she dried. By the time the last dish was dried Jennifer's cheeks were cramping. She simply couldn't remove the smile from her face but she knew they had things they needed to get done.

Roger dried his hands on a dish towel, folded it, and laid it beside the sink. "We need to get up to Denton, make sure the kids made it out. Make sure they got to the cabin."

"So," she leaned against the cabinet, "you keep calling it a cabin, but there's a bunch of people there? Do they all live in the same cabin?"

He smiled. She had no concept of homesteading much less communal homesteading. "No. We have our own cabin."

"We?" Her smiled stretched as she teased him. Her cheeks were definitely going to cramp.

"If you want to stay." He was back in instructor mode and didn't realize she was being playful. "I would prefer if you stayed but we can talk about that if you want."

"I'm afraid you're stuck with me for a little while at least, Professor Westover."

He looked up, finally seeing the playfulness in her eyes. "Oh! Good." He grinned and continued, "So each family has its own home."

"Now we're a family?" She smiled again as he looked back at her.

"I -, I mean. Well, no. But-" He held up his hands, taking a step back. His face set in a mixture of confusion and fear.

"It's OK, Rog." She reached out and took his hands. She wrapped hers around his and stepped in, holding his hands against her stomach. "I was just kidding. I'll stop."

He rested his head on top of hers. She felt his nod. Jennifer closed her eyes and relaxed against his chest.

"So, each *group*," he said the word deliberately, "has its own home. Some of us have cabins. There are a couple of mobile homes and a couple were going to pull in travel trailers or RVs. I tried to talk them out of that but we'll see how that works out for them.

"All the houses are built pretty close together. Not like suburb close, but close enough that we can help protect one another if the situation arises.

"Each family, uh, group, has stored a minimum level of supplies in a communal area. That was kind of what we considered the communal buy-in. It ensured that we had enough to get through the first year until we could get established, if things fell apart before we got our individual places stocked."

He stepped back, looked her in the eyes, then nodded for her to follow as he turned away and continued the story. "So our idea was that we'd all bring areas of specialty and cross train the others. Additionally, we all increased our own stock levels to the point we figured we'd be comfortable.

"I haven't been up in over a year so I have more supplies to take." He opened the door to the garage.

There were three bays for cars. The first one was empty. The next one was occupied by a huge truck. It was a behemoth with a paint job that looked like those Army uniforms with the camouflage made of small multi-colored squares. It had an extended cab, extended bed, heavy-duty bumpers with a winch on the front and some bigger version of a winch mounted in the bed. Also in the bed, closest to the cab, was a metal toolbox painted matte black. Another metal box was mounted behind that. There was some kind of crank, but the most telling feature was a hose and nozzle like at a gas station. To Ashley, it looked like Roger had the vehicle and the fuel to get them there.

"On the other side," he said, "the trailer is ready to go."

She smiled and rubbed her hand across his back. "Well, good sir, looks like we have another road trip ahead of us."

34

Somewhere in Ouachita Foothills

The truck stopped and the inside of her eyelids were turning from black to red. It was morning and they weren't moving. Ashley's eyes flew open. They darted left then right, searching for the cabin or any other structure she remembered. Nothing. She remembered a dirt road leading to the homestead but they were still on a blacktop. As a matter of fact, absolutely nothing looked familiar. One quick glance at Corey and Ashley knew something was wrong.

He sat behind the wheel with *that look* plastered across his face, staring off in the distance. *Could it be a cop? That would be a blessing in disguise!*

Ashley checked the side view mirror and then turned to look behind them. Nothing. The road was empty as far back as she could see - to where the road faded off around a curve and up the hill behind them.

She looked around again. *Why did he stop? Why aren't we at the homestead? We should have gotten there well before sunrise.* Her eyes drifted to the fuel gauge. The light was on and the needle was resting on the little peg that stopped it from going lower. Ashley sat back in her seat, took in a huge breath and released it as a long sigh. She unlatched her seatbelt and stepped out of the car.

Without a word she grabbed the gas can from the roof again and dug a length of climbing rope out of the back. The rope could be used to fashion a carrier of sorts for the full can. The duffle bag with a few hands full of random barter items crammed in was slung over the other shoulder. She carefully closed the hatch, slinging the rope over her shoulder and across her chest. *Take it slow, take it easy. Don't do anything you'll regret. Anger makes you feel good at the time but can lead to long term consequences.*

The driver's side door opened. She heard a foot step out, followed by another. There wasn't even a reason to turn back. *All this time, all this frustration. Wasted. The ass never even knew how to get there, and he just led me along. Should have left his ass behind a week ago.*

There was no idea where he had taken them but looking around it was immediately obvious that he hadn't gotten into the Ouachita National Forest. That was a good thing. There was a lot of land up there with no settlements at all. No houses, no people, few roads. At least she could see that this road had worked fields on each side. *Why the hell didn't he stop and ask directions or something? Maybe even check the map?*

"Where you goin'?" He caught up with her. "We're in the middle of nowhere. You expect you're just going to shit out a gas station? Doncha think I would have stopped if I saw a gas station?"

"No," she said, sarcasm creeping into her voice with each word, "I don't think I'm going to shit a gas station. Why don't we just sit on the side of the road and wait for aliens to drop one down for us? That's so much better." She spun around to face him.

"Besides, no, I don't think you would have stopped if you'd seen a gas station. Based on what I've seen, getting out and asking directions would have been too much trouble for you. You obviously couldn't be even bothered to check a map!"

"I didn't want to stop and wake you up!" They had stopped in the middle of the road, voices inching up decibel by decibel until they were yelling at the tops of their lungs. "I knew you'd be pissed if I got lost!"

"Oh," she screamed, "you didn't want to piss me off? How's *that* working for you?" She spun on her heel, stomping away. *Wow, sometimes letting off some steam* does *help.*

"See? See? That's exactly what I was talking about!" He threw his hands in the air as she continued to walk away. "If you're going to just walk off don't expect me to follow like some puppy. If you're leavin', you're leavin'. Its on you."

☣ ☣ ☣

There were a lot of worked fields along the road but Ashley walked two hours before finding the first house. She was certain she had passed other houses but since she couldn't see them, she didn't want to risk crossing a field and potentially spraining an ankle wandering aimlessly over uneven and unfamiliar ground. Besides, she needed some time away from Corey even if that meant wandering through the rural roads of Arkansas alone.

The house she finally saw was tiny and set off the road at least a quarter mile. The long dirt drive leading up to it was well worn but didn't show any signs of recent traffic. The rocky red-brown dirt had been compacted by tires but it seemed to have been a while since the last rain. She would have expected recent use to have rendered the roadway powdery.

Well, doesn't look promising, but it looks better than another two hours walking. She turned up the driveway, idly swing the gas can as she walked. Her feet kicked up little puffs of dust on the gentle breeze. *Definitely been a while since someone drove through here.*

Ashley found herself distracted by the scenery. This was obviously a farmstead. The fields had been worked this season and the harvest had even been taken in. Now scraggly weeds were growing between the tilled rows and the uniformly clipped tops of whatever crop had been harvested. The trees to the south of the field were huge and dense, with their colors fading to winter brown. Even the air felt better here, less polluted than even a small city like Denton. It was a beautiful part of the country even with the chill air starting to settle in.

About a hundred yards from the house something snagged her foot. Before she could even look down there was an explosion to her left. Loud and violent. She threw the can and dropped to the dirt.

Looking around she saw what had snagged her foot. A thin piece of fishing line was tied to a stick on the left-hand side of the road. There was another stick on the right, probably where the fishing line had been supported. Over at the end of the fishing line was an old-style rat trap.

Someone had drilled a hole in the base board of rat trap and inserted a shotgun shell. The swing arm of the trap had a BB taped to it. The fishing line was tied to the trigger. The whole thing was painted brown with splashes of other earth tones.

When she had tripped on the line, the trigger had released the swing arm and slammed the BB into the primer of the shotgun shell. Either she was lucky that the device was pointed in the wrong direction or whoever had set it up had only intended it as a warning device. Whichever was the case, it indicated that someone was in the house.

It also indicated that they didn't really want visitors.

Ashley pushed herself to her knees and grabbed the gas can, realizing she had been lucky indeed. One corner of the can had been pelted. Small holes freckled the red plastic jug, rendering it useless.

Well, that's just great! She stood and threw the container to the ground calling out, "Why?" She turned in a circle, yelling, "Why would you do that?"

From the direction of the house someone yelled back. She couldn't make out what they said, but it was definitely a human voice. She started walking down the drive, this time glancing down with every other foot fall. *No reason to get surprised twice. Next time I might not be so lucky.*

She had travelled only twenty yards when the voice called out again. This time she was pretty sure what it said, "Stop! What'dya want?"

Ashley complied. She stopped, raising her hands to shoulder level. "I needed gas. Fuel! I don't want to hurt anyone."

The voice yelled something back. She wasn't sure what they said but it didn't sound angry so she slowly began walking forward again, hands still raised. When she was about thirty yards from the house the voice called out again. This time much clearer, "Stop!" She did.

"Hands over your head!" She pressed her hands higher into the air. The voice sounded young, probably a teenage boy.

"Now turn 'round. Real slow."

Once again Ashley complied, turning in place. "Alright," the voice said, "take off that holster and gun. Put it on the table."

She slipped the holster from her belt and left her weapon in it. She sat it on the table and backed away.

"You got anything else?"

"No," she called. *Damn it.*

"Alright. Turn 'round, back to the house."

She did as she was told. This angle revealed quite a bit about the residents of the house. They had actually done a good bit of preparation.

Directly at her feet was a rock about the size of a loaf of bread. The front of the rock, facing the highway, was left its natural color. The side facing the house, however, was painted white. As Ashley's vision drifted out across the acreage she saw other markers as well. About thirty yards out, posts were hammered into the ground, ostensibly to mark the edges of a path that ran between fields. Several of the poles had reflectors on them. If they had been intended to be used by someone on the trail, they would have been mounted on the south- or north-facing sides. These were only mounted in the eastward side so they could only be seen from the house. Twenty yards, fifty yards. At one hundred yards there was another loaf-sized rock painted white. One hundred and fifty yards was denoted by a pole that seemed to have no other purpose. Two hundred yards would have been right at the peak of a small rise in the ground that looked like the tiller had just missed a row, making an extra wide mound about halfway across the field. So it went out to four hundred yards, demarked in fifty-yard increments with various placed items or terrain features. The highway itself would mark approximately four hundred fifty yards. They had their own built-in range finder.

A door opened behind her, attracting all of her attention. Someone moved over to the picnic table, picked up her gun, then retreated back to the door. The voice spoke again, this time not yelling. It was definitely a teen boy. "Alright, ma'am. You kin turn 'round nah."

A kid, probably not even sixteen, stood in the doorway to the house, a younger girl in the shadows behind him. He was holding an AR-style weapon casually, slanted across the front of his body. The girl had a heavier barreled weapon, probably a 20 gauge shotgun. It was pointing forward and down. Both of them seemed very comfortable with the weapons.

"So," the boy said, "whacha need?"

"I was looking for gas. My truck ran out and I really need to get to Dierks."

"Dierks? Arkansas? Ma'am, that's a good way from here. Even if we had gas ta give, an' I ain't sayin' we do, I'ont know we'd have 'nough to get you to Dierks."

"How far is it?"

"From here? 'Bout a hundred mile. You got a truck? What, fifteen mile a gallon? That's six, seven gallon. Ain't got that'a spare ma'am." He relaxed a little, but was still vigilant.

"Look," she said, "are your parents home, maybe? I have friends outside Dierks. If I could find them, I'm sure I can get the fuel replaced or at least paid for."

"There'n back? Now ya talkin' twelve or more. That's a lotta gas these days."

"I know it is, believe me I know. Are your parents around?"

The girl reached up and wiped at her eyes, then returned her hand to the front stock of the shotgun, trying to hold back tears. The boy simply looked more stoic and tightened his grip on the rifle. "Ma'am we ain't got the gas you lookin' for. I'm sorry but we just ain got it to give."

"And your parents?" Ashley made it a question, hoping to press them just a little more. Maybe their parents would better understand her predicament. Maybe they would be willing to take something in payment.

"Mom and Dad, they gave all they got ma'am. Me 'n my sister here, we buried them more 'n a week ago. Had the fever like lots-a others."

"Oh," Ashley said. "I'm sorry to hear that." She meant it and it obviously showed because the teen relaxed a little again.

"We come in when the Lord wills it. We go in His choosin' too. That's what the preacher said when he come by."

"There's a preacher? He travels around?" Ashley's eyes lit up with hope.

"He did. Just a couple days after we buried 'em. A bunch of 'em came by, a whole church. The preacher heard we buried our folks and said a nice prayer over the grave. But they was movin' through, tryin' to get to Little Rock 'fore the snows start.

"They tried to make us come, what with our folks gone now. We didn't wanna go though, so we didn't. Had to shoot over their head a couple times before they believed we could take care of ourselves enough to stay." He shrugged, "I don't expect 'em back, least not til spring at the earliest."

Ashley was deflated. "Is there anyone else close? Anyone who might have some gas to spare?"

"Most people who was around here-," He took a moment to think, "Sorry to say, ma'am, most of 'em have passed on too. There was a big meetin' in Talihina just as ev'rythin' started. All the adults went. They all started goin' pretty quick after that. Preacher said they prob'ly all got infected there."

"Talihina?" Ashley was confused. "I don't recall seeing Talihina in Arkansas."

"'Cause it ain't, ma'am. You musta got turned 'round. You're in Oklahoma."

Ashley embarrassed herself with the string of expletives she unleashed. If Corey was still in the truck when she got back, the bitch-out he *thought* he was going to get if he woke her was going to pale in comparison to what he was actually going to get.

When she finally calmed, the boy was standing there, even more relaxed. It seems having an adult absolutely lose her mind had a calming effect on the boy. He waited for a moment to make sure she was completely done.

"Well, miss, Sissy's just had a good idea. We mi' know where ta get some gas. If ya help us bring some back f'us, we'll help you get some f'you."

Ashley's smile perfectly complimented her blush.

Billy - really William, but everyone called him Billy except Sissy who called him Bubba -pulled an old pickup around to the front of the house. The thing had obviously spent a good deal of time on the farm, probably after spending a good deal of time as the family's primary vehicle. Rust was showing through in more places than paint. What really mattered, though, were the mechanics, not the aesthetics. The mechanics were working fine. The motor growled without interruption and the brakes did not squeak when Billy pulled to a stop. Ashley climbed into the passenger side and Sissy, yes that was her real name – not like Billy being short for something, climbed into the bed of the truck. She had an Angry Birds backpack loaded down with shogun shells. Billy's AR was in the rifle rack mounted in the back window. Several spare magazines were laying in the center console which had lost its top.

Ashley had already helped them clean out several gray five gallon buckets. Back behind the barn was what the kids referred to as "Dad's Stuff". The way they used the words they thought of it more as a location than a collection of items. If it was in Denton, it would have been called a junk yard and may have violated several city ordinances. For the new world Ashley found herself in, it was a treasure trove. Of course there were the buckets, but lengths of pipe and tubing, remnant and new boards, and pieces of glass from the size of your hand to the front window of a convenience store. Nails, screws, wire and clamps were sorted into their respective sizes and types. Panels of corrugated plastic and tin along with stacks of brick and cinder blocks were arranged in separate areas. The buckets and their lids were loaded in the bed with Sissy.

Billy had never driven the truck off the farm property and he was nervous about it. He also knew that his young sister would not be of much assistance in lifting five gallon buckets of fuel into the back of the truck. He told Ashley, "If you ride with and help me learn to drive on tha road then help us lift the gas cans, we should be able to get enough for you to get where you goin'."

Billy drove down the dirt driveway and stopped in two places to disarm more of the booby traps. "You were lucky, Miss Ashley. I don't know why that shot didn't take off your ankle. Glad it didn't, for sure, but it shoulda. I'll have to make sure I set it right again when you leave."

Ashley thought about the explosion and the hole in her gas can. The can may have protected her leg from a couple of pellets, but it was more likely that the shell was simply pointed in the wrong direction by just a degree or so. She shivered at the thought of having her foot blown off. But she also shivered at the thought of what would happen to these kids if someone snuck into their farm. "Yup. Make sure it's perfect next time. You've got to protect Sissy and yourself. At least til things get better."

Billy turned right at the highway. He glanced in her direction, then back at the road. He took a deep breath and let it out. "You think things are gonna get better?"

Ashley opened her mouth and stopped. She closed her mouth, started to say something else, and stopped herself. This was a kid, but it was a kid who was going to have to grow up in a much different world than she had. Even if the virus simply disappeared, there were a lot of dead people. There might not be enough people left to restore the world she had knon. She thought about the last few years before the virus, struck she wasn't completely convinced that the old world was a better world.

"It'll get better," she said. "It might not go back to how it was, but we'll get used to the new way and some of the old things – like electricity – will come back. So it'll get better, but there is going to be a lot of work between now and then."

Billy stared out the window. For someone who hadn't driven on asphalt before, he was doing pretty good. He tended to over-correct and so ended up gliding from one side of the lane to the other. Since there were no other vehicles within sight, and since he seemed to be reluctant to get the truck above thirty miles an hour, it was a good first effort.

He nodded as if coming to a decision. "Thank you. That was an answer a adult would give a adult an' I 'ppreciate it." He nodded again, "I'm real glad that shell didn't shoot your foot off."

The sincerity in his voice made Ashley smile as she watched the countryside roll by. Oklahoma was a beautiful state, even with the farm land chopping it up in tracts. There were enough residual woods and rolling hills to bring to mind the images of how it would be in its completely natural state. Even the farm land itself was beautiful. Most of it had been harvested. There were miles of empty fields separated by vast stretches of other fields that looked like nothing had been planted, and the grass was growing tall. For the first time in quite a while Ashley found herself relaxing and swaying with the slow glide of the truck.

When Billy turned on his blinker Ashley smiled again. For an under-aged kid who had never driven off the farm, someone had instilled some good habits. It was unfortunate that those people were no longer among the living while people like Corey just continued on. Maybe that wasn't fair, but this world was starting to tilt toward *unfair* being the new normal.

She looked where Billy was turning in. There was a barbed wired fence surrounding the perimeter with a pipe fence blocking the entrance. The big truck simply inched up to the fence and Billy pressed firmly on the accelerator. The fence pushed inward and the chain holding it in place went tight. He didn't let up but didn't let off the gas either. He simply held the truck in place, stretching the chain. In one clattering pop the chain snapped and the truck rolled through.

His grin engulfed his entire face as he looked over at Ashley. She returned his smiled and nodded. "So, what is this place?"

"Frackers. They been out here a while, ya know, drilling for gas and stuff. Mom and Dad said they didn't used to be out here, but since they started fracking there's been a lot of people out here drilling." He pulled onto the property. "They got all these pumps out here and they got all these roads connecting them. Once you get behind the fence you can get to the whole field. That's what Timmy Alworth's dad said. He works in the fields, or he did."

He piloted the big truck slowly through the winding dirt roads. Just as Mr. Alworth had said, there were small clearings where pump jacks were stationed and other clearings where it seemed that pipes just fed directly into the ground. Unfortunately, the pump jacks all seemed to have propane cylinders, not gasoline. It was also strange to see them stationary. None of them were working. Maybe the pipelines were shut down; maybe they were set to timers. Ashley had no clue how these things worked, and since there wasn't any gasoline involved, she really didn't care at the moment.

They cruised around the field for over an hour before discovering the field station. It wasn't anything elaborate, just two aluminum-sided buildings. One was about eight feet across and maybe fifteen deep; a typical storage shed. The other was larger with a roll-up door that was currently rolled-up, revealing the interior. There were various tool boxes, tables and shelves, stocked with a variety of parts.

The trio climbed out of the truck. Ashley looked in the window of the small building. It was apparently being used as an office. There were two desks, five filing cabinets and a table with a map rolled out on it. Outside the door was a red bucket, half filled with sand and cigarette butts. Ashley tested the door, finding it unlocked. She pushed it open and stepped in. It took her a moment to locate this field station on the map. Once she saw the symbol they used to indicate the station, she found two more of the symbols on the map.

Outside the sound of yelling interrupted her search. *The kids!*

She drew her handgun and bolted out the door. She swept the handgun past the truck. It was clear. The yell sounded again. *Behind the garage.*

Ashley jogged to the edge of the garage. *What the hell? Who could have caught them?* A quick head duck around the side. Nothing.

She crouched. Another peek. Still nothing. Slowly she stepped around the corner, taking a slow, low step. *Steady, steady.*

"Ashley!" Billy yelled.

She calmed herself. Rushing in to an unknown situation wouldn't do anyone any good. Continuing in her low crouch, she took careful, quiet steps toward his voice.

"Ashley," Billy called again, "We found it!"

Ashley sighed. She stood, slipping the handgun back into her holster. When she cleared the back of the building, Billy and Sissy were standing there in traditional model poses. Between them were five fifty-five gallon barrels. Two of the barrels were marked as diesel, two of them were some sort of grease and the last one was plain old gasoline. The gasoline barrel and one of the diesel barrels had a hand crank attached to the top.

She smiled at the kids. "Great job!"

Billy used a knuckle to tap up the side of the gas barrel. At just under the halfway mark he stopped. "Less than half, but still, that's pretty good!"

Sissy smiled as well, but she still didn't say anything. Ashley hadn't heard the girl say a word since meeting them earlier. She had obviously talked to Billy on a couple of occasions but had never said anything within Ashley's hearing.

"Pretty good indeed!" Ashley strolled up to the barrel. "Think we can just walk this up to the truck?"

Billy grabbed the top of the barrel and tilted it. He rocked it back and forth, then set it back down, shaking his head. "Only about half full, but I don't want to drop it over. Ya know? Don't want any to spill."

"Good thinking," Ashley turned back toward the truck and used her head to show they should follow. "Let's get the buckets."

"Naw," Billy skipped ahead of her, "I'll just get the truck. Be right back."

Ashley smiled at his youthful vigor. She wasn't old by any means, but there was just something about a kid's enthusiasm. Maybe it was naivety, just rush in carelessly without fear of injury, but somehow by the time you got out of high school people were different.

Ashley watched as Sissy leaned her shotgun against the back of the garage and tested the pump. She jacked the handle to build up pressure and squeezed the nozzle. It appeared she had done this before. Gasoline shot out of the nozzle and Sissy smiled as her eyes found Ashley's.

"You guys have this all figured out, don't you?" Sissy smiled and nodded.

When Billy pulled the truck around, they busied themselves pumping the fuel into the buckets. Ashley told them about the two other locations she thought were similar to this one – where they might have gas. Billy nodded and Sissy smiled. They had a long day ahead of them.

Once the buckets were loaded and the lids were snapped in place Billy looked them over. "You know, I think we have enough buckets to get some diesel too. The tractor runs on diesel."

They had almost one hundred buckets and had only used four and a half. It took less than three hours to cover all three sites and return to the farm with their bounty.

35

UNT Campus - Denton, TX

Roger pulled to a stop. He was closing in on Denton and could see a number of smoke plumes ahead. Over on the left hand side of the interstate was an electronics supply warehouse. One of the smoke plumes started right there.

Probably not a lot of use for most of that stuff right now, but destroying it is shortsighted. What if the electricity comes on tomorrow? Unlikely, but not as unlikely as the lights going off in the first place.

He swept the road ahead with his binoculars. Jennifer had her own set and she scanned the area as well. When she lowered hers, he shook his head slowly. She did the same. Neither liked what they saw.

About half a mile ahead an overpass crossed over the interstate. Between their current location and the overpass, the road was clear. Just in front of the overpass and just on the other side, vehicles were jammed together, almost blocking the road. Roger assumed it was supposed to look like a major traffic jam caused by a wreck and it might have looked just like that if he wasn't overly cautious, or if he hadn't just seen what real, accidental traffic jams looked like across three states. This was a roadblock in disguise and he had no intention of getting trapped.

They both resumed their scans and he saw his first sign of activity just as Jenny said, "There! Did you see it?"

He had. On the overpass someone made a rookie mistake. Now that the mistake was made, Roger could make out the person with ease. It was a sniper, laying on the bridge underneath a truck. The big rifle had a scope mounted on it and it was obviously being used to sweep the road for targets. During one of the passes the scope caught the sun and sent a gleam down range. Roger estimated that range now and shifted the truck in reverse. *Too close.*

Something popped the window, punching a pencil-sized hole through the glass. The distant crack of the rifle followed a second after.

Roger spun the wheel. If he hadn't had the trailer he would have just floored it and backed down the freeway. With the trailer he had to take more time, be more careful.

The rifle cracked twice more. The truck was turned around on the open road. Roger stomped on the pedal. The engine lagged as if gathering itself, then roared to life.

They heard a ping followed by another snap of the rifle. The trailer must have gotten hit.

There was a quiet period. *Must be reloading.*

They lumbered around the bend in the freeway, shielding themselves behind houses and storefronts, putting anything they could between the truck from the overpass.

Jennifer turned in her seat, looking for movement. Her view was mostly blocked by the trailer so she kept adjusting herself, looking right and left, even hanging her head outside the window for a better look.

Her hair was a tangled mess a few miles later. "Looks like they aren't following."

Roger nodded. It was an ambush site, a location chosen for convenience. It was unlikely that someone who would set up a sniper ambush would follow. It had taken quite a bit of manpower to erect the gauntlet of broken down vehicles, so he had to be careful not to get too confident. That much manpower could easily translate into a roving crew.

Roger exited the wrong way, up an onramp. He followed the service road around until it wrapped under the freeway overpass and slowed to a stop.

Jennifer looked across the cab to where Roger was unlatching his seat belt, "What now?"

He pointed a thumb toward the rear of the truck. "Drop the trailer, find a surface road, and make our way in."

"What? You're still going in?" Jennifer slid out of her side of the truck, joining Roger at the tailgate.

"Got to." He unhooked the safety chains from the trailer hitch and lifted the latch. "The kids might still be in there. If they aren't, we need to know what route they took."

"But they're probably already out, right?"

Roger looked up as he started cranking the support stand down from the tongue of the trailer. "Yup. They might be out. But I don't know if we'll be able to find enough fuel to come back if they aren't at the cabin."

Jennifer looked back toward where the sniper was located, then at Roger bent over, cranking the support down. Her hands were stuffed in her back pockets as she pondered the situation. Nodding with decisiveness, she walked to the back of the trailer and opened the swinging doors. He had taken the chocks off the wheels when they left his house and placed them in the trailer. Jennifer reversed the process, taking them from the trailer and securing the wheels.

"You still want to argue, don't you?" Roger looked up from securing the chains.

"Yup." She kicked the chocks tight under the left wheel and crossed to the right side where she repeated the process.

"But you aren't going to?"

"Nope."

He stood and stretched. All this travel, not to mention last night and this morning, had caused a strange conglomeration of cramps in his lower back. "Why not?"

"It wouldn't change your mind, would it?"

"'Fraid not."

"So we'll do this one your way and I'll have one in the bank."

He quirked his head, "'In the bank'?"

She smiled, "Yup. It'll go something like, 'remember the last time you wanted to do something stupid and I didn't argue because it was important to you?' You'll say, 'I think so,' and I'll say, 'Remember how reasonable I was? This one's mine.'" She took his head in both hands and bent it toward her, kissing him on the forehead. "And then you will say, 'Oh, ok,' and we'll be done with it."

"One in the bank," he said.

She smiled, "One in the bank."

Roger nodded toward the front of the truck and made his way toward his still open door. With his quiet tone and the roar of the engine she didn't hear him say, "Let's hope you get to cash that check."

Less than two blocks from where they left the trailer, a fire station had burned to the ground, along with the neighborhood it had once served. Roger traced the neighborhood road on his map. He checked the landscape and tracked where he was going to have to go cross-country for about a quarter mile, then just spotted the road he intended to intersect by using his binoculars. Everything looked clear.

"Alright. The way looks good. I need you to drive. I'm going to handle security." Roger slid his AR-style rifle out of the backseat. He slipped into his dirt-brown tactical vest which was stacked with a variety of pouches. The front pouches at his waist were stacked two layers thick, eight pouches in total, each dedicated to a thirty round magazine of 5.56mm ammunition.

He slid a walkie talkie into one of the pouches and threaded the wire for a combination headset / microphone through his gear and clipped the device on his left ear. He gave Jennifer a matching setup and showed her the essentials of its use. They tested the sets and prepared to go.

Jennifer slid behind the wheel. Roger climbed into the bed. He chambered a round in the rifle and slammed the bolt release with his palm, loading the weapon. After ensuring the round seated properly and the bolt was closed, Roger patted the roof of the truck. Jenny gently applied the gas and moved out from the underpass, toward the burned out neighborhood.

They cruised between two neighborhood developments and up South Bonnie Brae. This was the part that worried Roger. They took the curve in the road where Bonnie Brae transitioned onto Roselawn. They would cross the field just ahead. At that point they would be in the open. He just hoped that the football stadium would block the view from the freeway. They were going to be kicking up a plume of dirt as they crossed the field and that could alert others of their passing.

This was a tricky crossing. I-35W, the freeway he had been on, approached Denton from the south. I-35E came in from Dallas from the southeast, merging with its sister route to press its way all the way to Duluth, Minnesota on the shores of Lake Superior. While they weren't going to have to travel that far, they were going to have to find a way to cross from the south side of the freeway to the north side.

Jennifer took the cross-field sprint expertly. A crushed rock road had drawn Roger's attention and, had he been driving, he would have used it to cross the field. Jennifer didn't. Her route was a bit rougher than his would have been but it kicked up far less dirt than his would have. She drove across the grass, about twenty feet from the crushed rock.

Perhaps it was her route or maybe it was the stadium blocking the view from the overpass. They crossed the field without incident. When they entered the neighborhood on Kendolph Drive, Jenny pulled to a stop. Roger scanned the area quickly then ducked down, looking in the sliding rear window.

Her hands were white-knuckled on the steering wheel, and she had herself pushed back in the seat, taking deep breathes. He could see her mouth moving but she wasn't pressing the push-to-talk button on the radio so he couldn't hear her. Based on the mantra-like rhythm of her words, he probably wasn't meant to hear. He stood up again, keeping watch, letting her collect herself. After a moment she released the brake and started picking her way across roads, over the freeway and through the campus.

When they arrived at the dorm Roger could see where another vehicle had pulled up on the grass next to the stairwell leading up to Corey's room. He had only been to the room once, on the day Corey moved in. Roger had tried giving Corey some independence, *some space* as Corey referred to it, so he wasn't very familiar with the building. He had passed by on several occasions and looked up at Corey's window but he had waited to be invited back. That invitation never came.

He hoped that the vehicle that had been at this door was friendly. So far not much else in Denton had been. A burned out gas station with three dead bodies was now the first impression of the campus. Cars were clogging the streets and more than a few dead bodies were laying next to the cars or on the sidewalks. The cool weather may have helped a bit with the smell, but after a week or two even relatively cool bodies were pretty ripe. Roger tried to focus past the sights and smells.

The next major sign of how events had changed the town was directly across the street from the dorm. The little run down convenience store had never been a place that inspired comfort. Roger even remembered Corey saying that he preferred to walk several blocks to another store rather than go to the one practically outside his door. Even with that reputation, the car with two dead bodies which had obviously been shot cast the place in a whole new light.

Roger radioed instructions to Jennifer and she pulled up on the sidewalk next to the Hall. A black metal fence supported by tan brick columns separated the grounds of Traditions Hall from the outside sidewalk and street. Jennifer pulled up next to the building, just outside the door, hoping the small shrubs between the columns would give a little concealment. They both climbed out and scanned the area.

It was amazing how much you could hear in a dead city. Denton had a remarkable amount of open space, especially for urban living. That was mostly centered here around the athletics portion of the campus. Even so, revving motors and infrequent gun shots sounded in all directions. Yelling even drifted through the air. Roger had the unnerving feeling that if they could easily hear others, they could just as easily be overheard. He nodded toward the door.

Jennifer reached back into the truck and pulled out the handgun she had adopted from Roger's collection. It was a 9mm off brand that one of the guys at the homestead had worked on for him. It had started off as a nice enough weapon, but if Roger had had to pay for all the work, the gunsmithing would have cost more than the weapon itself. Now it was a finely tuned machine like pretty much every other weapon Roger owned. *When your life depends on your equipment, take care of your equipment like your life depends on it.*

He crossed to the door. There was a broken piece of brick propping it open. Roger wasn't a trained tactical operator, but he did his best to sweep the bottom landing of the stairway. Jennifer opened the door for him and he swept right, then left, up the stairs. Nothing. He moved into the room and checked under the stairs. Still nothing.

He waved Jennifer in. She kicked the brick out of the way, tested to make sure the push bar worked, and pulled the door closed.

Roger methodically cleared the stairs. He crept up one floor at a time, sweeping the stairs with his rifle, then the next section, then the stairs above. At each landing he waved Jennifer up. When they reached the top, both were drenched in sweat from tension more than from exertion.

The top door was closed.

"Ok," Roger quiet talked, "his room is directly across from us. There is a long hall leading off to the left. You push the bar, count us down, then push the door open. I'll do a quick scan of his doorway then cover the hall. You cover his room and keep the door propped open unless we start taking fire. If we start taking fire, get back in here as fast as possible."

She made a face as if he had just told her the sky was blue and grass was green but didn't say anything. She just slid the bar in, freeing the latch from the doorframe.

"One," Jennifer nodded with emphasis. Another sharp nod. The third nod.

Her shoulder rammed against the door, throwing it open. The 9mm pointed directly across the corridor into an open doorway then down the corridor. The rifle slid around the doorframe, sweeping the corridor and came to rest pointed across the hall.

Nothing.

Jennifer raised from the crouched position she didn't even remember assuming, careful not to point her gun at Roger. He turned his attention back down the hall and they crossed to his son's room.

The place was a sty. It was littered with virtually everything Roger could imagine being in a college dorm. Backpacks, pens, paper, clothing, boots, shoes, sheets and blankets, even soaps and shampoos. It looked like someone had used Corey's room as a dumping ground.

"Wow," Jennifer looked around, "was he always this messy?"

Roger shook his head. "No. He was usually quite fastidious. Very clean. But I haven't been up here in a couple of years." He used the toe of a boot to push some of the items around. "This stuff doesn't look like it has been here very long. It isn't compacted or anything."

"Ok." Jennifer lowered her weapon, letting it hang loose by her side. She remembered Roger's caution about leaving a finger on the trigger and deliberately moved her finger so it rested on the frame of the gun. "If that is the case, it looks like your boy has been very busy the last week or so."

Roger nodded, still trying to comprehend what could have happened, "Very busy." He tore his eyes from the junk, glancing at the magnetic whiteboard on Corey's closet.

There were four mushroom-shaped magnets on the whiteboard. Two red, two blue. When Roger had hung the whiteboard he had placed the magnets in each corner, red ones in opposite corners and blue ones in the remaining corners. The symmetry had appealed to Roger. He had also attached a dry erase pen to a little Velcro strip at the top of the whiteboard. An eraser was attached by another piece of Velcro at the bottom of the board. Roger had envisioned this would be where Corey would place pictures and write notes for himself – reminders for class and that kind of thing.

He had left only three instructions for his son. Do your best. Have fun. If you ever need to leave - leave a note on this board. Tell me where you're going and how you're getting there.

The board was still hanging right where he had left it. If the magnets had been moved, they had been replaced exactly as he had left them. Both the marker and eraser were still attached to their Velcro strips, just as he had left them, a fine layer of dust hinting they had not been moved in more than two years. Nothing was written on the board. From what Roger could tell, nothing had ever been.

He sighed and shook his head. "Let's go. He didn't leave a note."

"What?" Jennifer looked around the room as if she could find anything in the jumbled mess. "How do you know?"

"It would have been right here," Roger pointed at the board.

Jennifer looked at his face. Disappointment had completely washed out all other characteristics. She started to say something but the squeal of brakes outside the window cut her off.

Roger darted across the room, leaning out. "Not good."

Five people had pulled up behind his truck in a new-looking BMW. By the time he saw them, they were already surrounding his truck. It was boxed in now. The fence hemmed the truck in to the front and right side. The building was on the left. With the BMW behind, there was no way to get the truck out. *If we get a chance, we'll have to plan that better next time.*

The gang made a cursory check of the truck. Seeing no one inside three of them began scanning the area, weapons in hand. The others tried the doors and pried at the pickup's locked bed cover.

Roger watched for a moment, staying just out of sight at Corey's window. Just two weeks ago he would have called the police. Now there weren't any police. He raised the rifle, taking aim.

"What are you doing?" Jennifer's whisper was quiet but harsh enough to get his attention.

"Those guys. I can't let them just take our stuff."

"But you'll kill them!" Jennifer tried to angle herself to see out the window as well.

"If we let them get our stuff, they're killing us." Roger lowered the rifle. He nodded out the window. Jennifer looked out. Not just at the courtyard but at the whole city. Smoke was billowing out of buildings across the horizon. Random pops sounded, indicating small explosions or gun fire. "I don't want to do this," he said, "but we have to get out of here and that truck is our means of doing it. Friendlies would be calling out to us, not trying to break into the truck. If we give them a warning shot or try to talk, it's two versus five."

It took a moment. If Roger had not been intently looking for it, he would have missed it. Jennifer's eyes slid from appalled confusion to equally appalled acceptance.

330 Brian S. Vinson

He raised the rifle to his shoulder and had to lean his entire body out the window to point at his first target. The shot reverberated through the room. Over the ringing in her ears Jennifer heard a cry from outside. Roger ducked back in just as popping sounds ripped through the early afternoon quiet.

Dust and brick fragments exploded around the window, showering the window frame with tiny clay projectiles. Roger pulled himself all the way into the room, throwing his back against the wall. The pops and fragment shower continued for a moment and all went quiet.

He thrust himself back out the window, cracking off three shots in quick succession. His first target was crawling toward the back of the BMW. The second fell to the ground. Roger had shot through the passenger's side door. He wasn't sure if his bullets had survived penetrating the thin steel so he placed all three shots close together. Consciously avoiding the driver's side, Roger was hoping these people would just leave.

Instead, they finished reloading. He pulled back in as the bricks around the window exploded again. "We have to get out of here."

Jennifer nodded, turning back toward the hall. She swept the area with her handgun to make sure no one had snuck up on her. As she reached for the handle, Roger tapped her shoulder, shaking his head. "That'll take us right down in the middle of them. We have to go around."

Jennifer nodded and they sprinted down the hallway. Roger stopped. "Here's what we do. Your gun isn't going to be much good at range. They're all using handguns as well. If they are in range, so are you. Got it?"

She nodded.

"'kay. Good. So I want you as a distraction. You go to the opposite end of the building and get down the stairs. I'll stay up here to make sure they don't come up.

"When you're at the bottom of the stairs, press the talk button on the radio twice. I'll come down these stairs. When I get downstairs I'll click twice. Two clicks, OK?"

"Two, got it."

"When I'm in place, you open your door and shoot. Draw their attention. Hopefully that will draw them into the open courtyard and I can take them out. You come back through the building and meet back up with me. If I haven't taken them out by then, we're all going to be in range of one another."

Jenny nodded again, her face deadly serious. She didn't say anything else, just turned and jogged down the hall. Roger returned to his position, opened the door to the stairs, and waited. Outside the gang must have been trying to break down the door because the heavy banging boomed up the stairs.

It seemed an eternity, but he finally received the double click of static indicating Jennifer was in place. He sprinted back to the crossbar and down the stairs. It had to be fast - if the gang penetrated the door, he would lose his advantage of knowing their location. It was a small advantage but it was all he had.

He knelt at the front door. The banging was still going on. It sounded like someone was trying to knock the metal door down with a sledgehammer. For all he knew, that could be precisely what was happening.

Roger gently pushed the front door open, shuffling into the opening. He wanted to give himself room to retreat if he needed and didn't know if the door would lock him out. At the end of the courtyard he could see the truck and rear bumper of the BMW. Two of the assailants were propped against the fence behind the car, one of them rocking and moaning. The other lay completely still.

Roger clicked his talk button twice and drew the rifle to his shoulder. He didn't sight down the barrel, opting to keep both eyes open until a target presented itself.

A shot rang out. A red plume jetted out of the chest of the rocking moaner and he went quiet. In the back of his mind Roger reminded himself not to tick off Jennifer if she had a gun in her hand. That was a fantastic shot for a new shooter.

The second, third and fourth shots pinged off the back of the Beamer, taking out a tail light and spider webbing the rear window.

Return fire came from the gang. Roger pressed the rifle tighter to his shoulder. It was about to be show time and he couldn't afford to get sloppy now.

The first assailant showed himself again. He jogged over behind one of the brick posts, peeking around the side, looking for Jennifer's position. Roger wasn't too surprised to see that the guy was carrying a sledgehammer in his left hand, a large caliber handgun in his right. Given their relative positions, Sledgehammer guy was behind cover in relation to Jennifer - fully exposed to Roger.

The professor once again snugged the rifle to his shoulder, lined up the sights, and laid the front site image over his target. His finger slowly drew back on the trigger.

36

Ouachita Foothills

Corey had been sitting at the side of the road for *hours*. He had napped, gotten out and walked around the car, eaten a couple of meals, tried every station on the radio, and kicked the truck until he thought he may have broken a toe. A couple of times he thought he heard engines, motorcycles if he wasn't mistaken, in the distance. They could have been around the next bend but in these hills, they could have been a mile or more away.

The sun was already starting to dip toward the horizon. *Just like that bitch, leaving me out here to suffer while she is off doing fuck-knows-what! I don't know why I've carried her this far!* He had dragged a tent out of the back of the truck and into a harvested field when he heard an engine.

He settled into the field, his trusty revolver gripped in his hand. *Ain't no one getting my shit. They better just keep driving.*

The truck coming down the road was beat up. It looked like it had seen better days, then had new tires slapped on it and even they were past their better days. It was old, maybe even older than Corey.

The college student turned rural explorer leveled his gun at the driver's side half of the windshield. It was still too far away for a good shot and he didn't want to waste bullets so he held his fire.

The old beater seemed to take forever to cruise up. As it did he was able to make out that there was a passenger and someone in the truck bed as well. The sun was behind the truck, placing the windshield in shadow but casting a good silhouette of the rider in the back. That one was small but was holding a long gun. Corey swallowed and flexed his fingers around the grip of his pistol. *This is going to be a challenge.*

The truck slowed and the engine calmed as if the driver had simply let up pressure on the gas pedal. It slowly rolled down the slight hill and stopped behind his truck. His fingers flexed again, sweat beading on his brow. He had to take them before they knew where he was. Fortunately the truck stopped just on the other side of some trees, concealing him for the moment.

He crept up to the edge of the road, carefully moving aside dried twigs and branches, desperately trying to avoid snapping any and giving his position away. The person in the bed was a young girl. She couldn't be more than ten or twelve. Still, she had a shotgun. That made her a threat. *Play big-people games, pay big people prices.*

He carefully lined up the shot. The blade of the front sight seated itself in the notch of the rear sight. She was standing in the bed of the truck, so he needed to aim high. She was at the far range of his weapon so he inched it higher for bullet drop, then a smidge higher for aiming up. People tended to aim low when shooting on an uphill or downhill slope.

The other two had gotten out of the truck, but Corey could only see them through his peripheral vision.

"This it?" It sounded like a kid, a teen boy probably.

There wasn't an immediate response. The question made Corey wonder what *it* was. Had someone seen him while he was sleeping? Could someone have been following them? No. If they were following, they would have come by sooner. Maybe they'd heard something.

The boy spoke again. Corey couldn't make out all the words over the sound of the engine. He was pretty sure he heard the words 'he', 'gas'. 'far from anywhere' and 'idiot'. That last word really spun him up. Some punk kid was calling Corey an idiot?

Maybe he should take out the kid first. He shifted his aim just over the hood of the truck where the top of the boy's head just showed. It was quick work to line up the shot. Front sight focus, overlay the target. Squeeze the trigger. Don't jerk. Squeeze. Let it break cleanly.

"I don't know!" Corey recognized that voice. Ashley. "He could be anywhere. Let's fill it up." Corey lowered the gun.

The boy got back in the beater and pulled forward until the bed was lined up with the back of Corey's truck. Ashley reached over the side and retrieved a nozzle. Just as Ashley was turning back to insert the nozzle, the girl yelled.

"Watch out!" Her shrill voice pierced the air and the shotgun leapt up to her shoulder.

Before he understood what was happening, Corey had all the attention in this part of the world. Three barrels were pointed at him. The shotgun presented the biggest problem but the AR the boy carried wasn't far behind. Ashley's handgun was probably the least effective at this range but Corey had seen her shoot. He wouldn't put it past her to score a clean shot and then two more while he was falling.

"It's me Ash," he yelled. "Fucking-A. Who the fuck were you expecting?"

Ashley stood up so she could see over the bed of the truck. "Corey! Language! These are kids."

"Kids that have me in their fucking crosshairs! You want me to stop fucking cussing, get 'em to lower their fucking guns!" *I can't even fucking believe we're having this discussion. What the fuck does she expect?*

He looked over; the kids had lowered their weapons. The boy had a sweet chest rig for the AR. It allowed him to have it held high on a sling but still let go of it if he needed to use his hands. *If I'd popped that asshole, that'd be mine now.* He sighed, *Well, the night's young.*

Lookie at that! There was a barrel in the bed of the truck, attached to the nozzle Ashley was going to use. Must be over fifty gallons of fuel. *The bitch scored! Wonder what kind of favors she had to give the little shit for that much gas. Hope the kid enjoyed it.* From Corey's vast experience though, he estimated a roll in the sack with Ashley to be worth only ten gallons, not fifty.

The object of his thoughts returned to inserting the nozzle. The girl pumped a handle in the barrel and a few minutes later the nozzle clicked. Corey busied himself with collecting the tent. It looked like they were going to be on the road tonight after all.

Ashley made a big fucking deal over the brats, giving them hugs and telling them thank you, even expressing thanks on behalf of Corey, *as if,* who just stood there waiting for them to be on their way.

"All right," Ashley said, looking at the boy, "remember what I said, right? Don't let anyone know you have fuel and go straight home." Her eyes shifted for an instant and if Corey didn't know better he would have thought she was giving the kid some kind of signal about him. "Hide the truck, don't let anyone see where it is."

The boy gave her another hug, tears pooling in the corners of his eyes. *What a fucking wuss. Go find another piece of ass somewhere, kid. This one is mine.*

Ashley stooped down and hugged the girl. "Nice to know you can still speak." *Whatever that means.* "You take care of your brother, ok? I'll try to come back in the spring and check on you. All right?"

The girl had tears in her eyes as well. She just nodded and that sloshed the tears out of her right eye. It streamed down her dirty face and made a little mud spot on Ashley's shoulder.

The two climbed into the truck and the boy fired it up. Corey yelled, "Hey! What about the rest of our gas?"

"What?" Ashley looked at him, her face contorted in confusion.

"That gas. Ain't it ours?" Corey pointed at the barrel. "We could fill up my gas cans at least. What do they need it for?"

"No." Ashley kissed her hand and waved at the kids. The boy popped the truck back in gear, executed a sloppy five point turn and headed back in the direction he'd come. "We split the gas," Ashley continued. "I told them I would help them if they would let me fill up."

"Well, that's fucking stupid!" Corey walked to the far side of the truck and unzipped his pants, taking a leak on the side of the road. He talked over his shoulder while she turned away. "You could have bargained for more. You know, shake that ass a bit, bat those eyes at him. At that age he'd have shit himself to impress you."

"You know, you're one disgusting S-O-B at times."

He zipped up and turned around, shaking moisture off his hand. He ended up just wiping it dry on his shirt. "Hey, if you don't want to face reality, that's on you. Now what if we can't find the cabin again? You going to dig a couple more magical kids out of the woods? How the fuck did you even find them?"

"Don't worry about that. I found them. I got gas. Now we can go." She looked in the car, then back at him. "Where are the keys?"

"I figured I'd drive." He held the keys up by the fob, then whipped them around so they slapped in his palm.

"Give me my keys, Corey. My truck, my gas, my rules." She walked over and snatched for the keys. He easily avoided the grab.

"See," he said, "I think possession is nine-tenths of the law. I got the keys. The keys start the truck. The truck has the gas. I think I'm making the rules now."

"Corey. Give. Me. My. Keys." She was trying to look serious or something but he could tell that she was getting a little scared. *About damn time she took me seriously!*

He just ignored her and walked around to the driver's door. She tried to step between him and the door. He just stepped back. *Just like training a real dog, this one's just got to learn who is alpha.*

"Look, Ash, you can get out of my way and sit your happy ass in the passenger seat or you can fucking walk." He stepped back to give her room to move.

"Look, Corey," she paused for some reason, as if to add effect of something, "it's my truck. The only reason you're here is because I brought you. The only reason I brought you is because you were supposed to know the directions to the damned cabin! You have officially become useless. Now give me my keys and consider yourself lucky that you aren't walking!"

Her face was red. He hadn't seen it this red since that night she stormed out of his room. *Man, if she only knew the shit storm she had called down on that kid Timmy. Corey chuckled to himself. The little prick had been on a scholarship. Missing two weeks of class from his hospital stay dropped his GPA and, boom, that was the end of that. Scholarship revoked. Asswipe had to go home to Mommy. That's the price of messing around with one of my bitches.*

"What the hell are you smiling about? Give me my keys."

Corey dangled them in front of her and snatched them back as she made a swipe for them. "Just get in. I didn't come this far with you to have some kind of pissing fit on the side of the road."

"Why the hell did you come?" Ashley was fuming now. The red face was purple, her hands were flitting around like he'd never seen. *She's fucking wound up!*

He smiled. It was good to see he could draw out this kind of emotion. It would make it all that much better when they finally had some time to themselves for her to properly express her gratitude. "Look, I just came along to help with the repopulation strategy. We might be the last breeding couple left."

He chuckled. When her slap snapped his head around it was completely unexpected.

"What*ever* you are, whatever *I* am, *we* are not a couple. We definitely *won't* be breeding." She had to pause to regain some composure. It didn't help much. "And we won't be *practicing* either. We're done! Nothing left! All gone! You had your chance. You blew it. There is nothing here for you. How much more clearer do I need to be? No part of you is ever, ever again touching any part of me without me cutting it the hell off!"

Corey's mind was absolutely clear. That slap had brought his entire world into focus with a clarity he had never felt before. *She's led me on for over a year. All I ever was to her was some kind of fucking map. That's too bad. She's hot but surely there's gotta be someone else out there just as hot.*

Ashley noticed his blank stare too late. Her slap had turned his head. When he turned back his face was completely devoid of emotion.

It was a fluid motion that guided his arm forward, the revolver firmly gripped in his hand.

Ashley backpedaled, her hands coming up.

She did not hear the shots. Her chest was punched twice. Somehow it wasn't as painful as she thought it would be. As she fell, she saw that one of the bullets had torn through her left hand before landing the hammer blow that was toppling her over.

His face never changed. His eyes tracked the arch of her chest as she spilled over but nothing else changed. He didn't flinch at the sound of the discharges. There was no fear. There was no shame. There simply was nothing behind those eyes.

As she watched, Corey simply turned from where she lay on the road, slipped into the car and closed the door.

There was a strange thrumming sound in her ears and the edges of her vision began to blur. It was surprising how comfortable the road was. Why had she packed a sleeping pad if asphalt was this comfortable? She wished she could tell people how comfortable this was. They could save so much money if they just slept on the road. She'd have to tell someone when she woke up. Amazing. Gunshots don't hurt and asphalt was so comfortable.

Darkness closed in on Ashley and she didn't resist. The logic of her mind was still cataloging all the things she needed to let people know when she woke up. For now though, the darkness was inviting, welcoming, beckoning. She let it slip over her.

☣ ☣ ☣

Corey whistled as he cruised down the highway. Everything had become so clear. All his life people had taken advantage of him, used him for their own plans, manipulated him. It was amazing he had never noticed it before.

Jeremy and Mitch had only come over because he had the best game system and weed. Sure they brought their own sometimes, but it was crap - nowhere as good as the shit he had. They'd basically used him to trade up their shit for free.

Ashley just used him to get to his dad or to get laid. Corey knew he was good in bed so she just got her jollies while waiting for the old man to notice her. If she's thought about it she'd be thankful he'd ended it for her.

Of course, all that lead back to the old man. His dad had to do something to keep his mom around. She was way too good for the old man and his dad knew it. Corey had to be the only reason that she stuck around. Corey was her world, they all knew that. All these years he hadn't been able to understand how his dad had kept his mom around. Now it was clear. He had threatened to take Corey from her. It all made sense now.

☣ ☣ ☣

Corey didn't know how long he drove, or precisely where. The compass had mostly pointed east and there was some vague memory of crossing over into Arkansas. The clock in the dashboard read well after midnight, and he realized that sleep had slipped up on him. Pulling off the road, Corey pulled out the tent from earlier.

The tent, a sleeping pad and a few minutes was all he needed. In less than thirty minutes he fell into a deep and blissful sleep.

37

Traditions Hall - Denton, TX

It felt like hours since Jennifer had pressed her talk button. She was seriously considering calling Roger to make sure he was getting in place, that he hadn't been hurt. Then his clicks came.

It was just two bursts of static. How could she be sure it was from him? Could someone else be using the same frequency? Could she be receiving some false signal? Any two bursts of static were indistinguishable from any other two bursts of static. Maybe they should have made it two clicks then one click. Maybe two then three. That would be more definitive. She-

Jennifer forced herself to pause. She sucked in a deep breath and slowly let it out through her nose, just like her yoga instructor had told her to do. The next breath was deeper and more stable. The next exhale even more cleansing.

That was the signal. He had given her the signal. An appropriate amount of time had passed and she'd received the signal. It was Roger, and he was depending on her.

Jenny had checked her gun several times while waiting. She resisted the urge to check it again. *Time to just do it.*

Her hip slapped the push bar on the door. It was heavier than expected. The latch retracted but the door didn't move. She bumped it again. It was stuck. She threw herself against the door.

It popped open, throwing her off balance. She pointed her gun toward the Beamer blocking in their truck. There were two men leaning against the fence. One big guy was pounding on the other stairwell door with a sledgehammer. Two more were standing there, urging him on, covering the window three stories above.

Before she could pull the trigger the door bounced back, slamming into her wrist. The weapon discharged, bucking in her hand. One of the guys against the fence slumped over. Jenny instinctively shook her hand. The gun bucked again. This time she had no idea where the round ended up. Getting the weapon, and herself, back under control she fired off several more rounds.

When the guys collected themselves and started moving in her direction, Jenny slipped back into her door, pulling it closed. She pulled her magazine and dug some bullets out of her pocket, taking a moment to refill and reseat the magazine.

Outside she heard more shots. They were muffled but she was sure it involved Roger. There wasn't a reason for anyone to fire if he hadn't seen them or they hadn't spotted him.

She grabbed the push lever. It wouldn't budge. She tried again. Still nothing. It was jammed.

Now there were multiple weapons firing. The shots were too close together for it to be just one gun. Roger was under fire and she was stuck in the stairwell!

Jennifer made a quick decision. A quick yet solid bump with her butt popped the door open. Expecting the spring back this time, she braced herself and drew down on one of the looters.

The guys had obviously forgotten about her when Roger opened fire. The one with the sledge had moved behind the Beamer. He was now lying there in a pile with his friends. One had made his way all the way across the courtyard and stood at the corner, his back to her, almost within reach. He began to turn as the door popped open.

Jenny's gun barked twice before she even knew she had pulled the trigger. The man crumpled to the ground.

Bricks exploded near the head of the last man standing. He was at the corner of the building, facing into the courtyard, trapped between the dorm and the BMW. Roger's weapon shattered the bricks again, kicking up another dust cloud. Jennifer took careful aim, trying to adjust for the distance.

The guy looked up as more bricks turned to powder in front of his face. His eyes locked on Jennifer's. He backed away from the corner, holding his hands up, spilling the gun to the ground.

Jennifer kept her gun leveled but nodded over the top, signaling him to leave. He backed his way to the driver's side door, hands still in the air, then sat awkwardly on the seat and swiveled into the car.

She walked to the edge of the building and kicked the gun away from the hand of the man she had just shot. Her gun stayed focused on the man in the car. Out of the corner of her eye she saw Roger approaching across the courtyard.

Under attention from both weapons, the driver was very cautious. He backed out just far enough to maneuver around the fence, turned his wheels and slowly inched off the curb. When he turned the corner, the engine revved and tires squealed.

Roger relaxed his stance, dropping the rifle to a more comfortable position. "We've got to get out of here. That might not have been all of them."

Jenny nodded and sprinted for the truck. "Let's get to Ashley's. Maybe she left a note."

"Wish I could." They climbed into the truck, Roger looking across the seat at his girlfriend. "I was her instructor. It wouldn't have been appropriate for me to go to her apartment."

"So, a master planner and his star student and neither know how to contact the other?"

Roger nodded. "That about sums it up. You can't think of everything all the time. We anticipated that cells would keep working or Corey would leave a note. Hopefully we get a chance to correct that error."

"Hopefully," Jennifer said, "sounds like a nice kid. I'd like to meet her."

☣ ☣ ☣

It had been a risky move, but Roger followed the same trail out that Jennifer had taken into the city. His mind was racing through the possibilities. Was Corey injured and couldn't leave a note? Had he needed to flee before he could leave a note? Was he caught outside and couldn't get back in? Of course those lines of thought were directly followed by the what-ifs. If he was injured, could he find help? If he was caught out, was Ashley caught out as well? He stared blankly out the window, driving by habit rather than intent.

Both he and Jennifer got out of the truck under the freeway. He was reattaching the trailer. Thinking about the plight of the kids, Roger forgot what he was doing and tried to lift the tongue of the trailer by hand rather than cranking up the stand. Pain shot across his back. He grunted and backed away, bending over and flexing backward, trying to work out the cramp.

"Ok," Jennifer stepped over the tongue of the trailer to his side. Her fingers went to work on his back and he sighed with the mixture of pain and relief they brought. "You've zoned out enough. You aren't safe like this. I know it's hard and I know you're worried, but you can't do anything to take care of them, or find them, if we're in a ditch somewhere. So I hate to sound like a bitch, or even worse, like Cher, but *snap out of it.*

"We're still not in a safe enough place that we can fall apart. Once we get where we're going we can see what's up and then we can take time to have whatever breakdown we need. Got it?"

Roger nodded. She was right, of course. He needed to get to the cabin and evaluate the situation based on what he found. They wouldn't do anyone any good if they didn't make it away from Denton. He stooped back to his work with the trailer but the twinge came back. He backed away and Jennifer completed the job. She seemed to have done this kind of thing before. When he mentioned it she just said that Paul had a boat on a trailer. *Guess you never know what experience you can draw on in an emergency.*

He had no idea what route the kids would have taken. To further complicate matters, he couldn't drive through town and take a logical route out. With the type of activity they had been through, he simply wanted to avoid Denton all together. Highway 377 looked like the most likely route out of town but, it also meant going one hundred-eighty degrees around Denton. It was to the northeast and he was on the southwest side of town. Swinging out far enough to stay away from town would cost precious time. *So will sitting here trying to read their minds. Just get moving.*

He suited actions to words and started driving, following the route he felt was safest and most likely for the kids to have driven. Once across the Red River, he stopped and topped off his tanks from the spare fuel he had in the bed. He had no intention of stopping for anything other than the kids once he hit Highway 70, and it was just a few miles ahead.

The couple stretched their legs by walking laps around the truck and trailer, scanned the horizon with their binoculars, and had a quick meal from some randomly selected MREs. Honestly, neither of them paid much attention to the food. It was for simple sustenance at this point, not for flavor. A quick trip to take care of necessary functions at an abandoned gas station that was still relatively clean even if completely looted, and they were back on the road.

Roger bypassed even small towns using the back roads. Cutting south of Durant and swinging east, they caught Highway 70 about ten miles out of town. He turned to his passenger, "This is it. Seventy will take us within five miles of the homestead. Hopefully we'll find them between here and there."

Jennifer just reached over and patted his leg. She wanted to reassure him but didn't want to lie. The first thing that came to mind was to say, 'I'm sure they'll be fine.' But she wasn't sure. In the last two weeks they had seen more dead people than living, and it seemed half the living were trying to kill the other half. She was anything but *sure* that they'd be fine. Her best option was to just not say anything and let the quiet speak for itself.

Roger seemed to understand the sentiment and remained quiet himself. With the open road in good condition, he ran the speedometer up to 85 and set the cruise control. Maybe they would be able to blow past any potential problems if they just didn't slow down.

38

Southwest Arkansas

Engines. He could hear them. Lots of engines. Corey peeked under the car. There was a funeral procession. A black car was driving with its headlights on, followed closely by several long, black hearses. As the first hearse passed, Corey could see in the side window.

They were turning at the corner where a sign had an arrow pointing to New Bethel Cemetery. Corey remembered a sign like that from not long ago, maybe even last night while he was driving around. It seemed very familiar. *Where the hell was* old *Bethel Cemetery?*

The hearse recaptured his attention. It was one of those old-time hearses, more like a buggy. It was pulled by black horses that were draped in black cloth. The buggy had those big swags of black fabric that hung in drapey kind of swoops. A guy sat on the seat at the front of the buggy, holding the black reins in his hands, guiding the horses along.

His mother was sitting in the back where the coffin should have been. She waved out both sides, smiling as if she were a queen waving to her people. It was so good to see her awake and happy. It had been forever since he had seen her. The last time was when the babysitter had arrived and his mom had bent down to kiss him on the forehead. She had said, "Now you behave for Willow and you can have dessert. I'll be back as soon as I can."

Even at his young age he had thought 'Willow' was a strange name for a girl. He remembered a movie named *Willow* and it was full of strange looking people dressed up in weird armor. *Why would anyone want to be called that? Who is the stupid idiot that would name their kid that?*

It really didn't matter now. He had grown up and he'd never seen Willow again. When they'd learned that his mom had died, his dad had pretty much cut him off from everyone. He'd just hung around the house and wouldn't let Corey go anywhere or do anything without him. It had taken him years to shake the old man.

Now his mother was happy and waving at him. He waved back.

The next hearse was new. Like maybe made yesterday kind of new. It was big and sleek and polished to the point that he could see his reflection in the paint. The driver's compartment was tinted dark so he couldn't see in, but he could see in the back.

Ashley was sitting there. She wasn't anywhere near as happy as his mother. It looked like she had been crying. As she looked out the window and saw him, she pressed herself to the window, tears streaming from her eyes. He could see her mouth working and could just make out the words through the glass, "I'm sorry, Corey. I always loved you. So sorry."

The car passed, and he nodded. At least she understood the situation now. If she had just understood it a little earlier she could have skipped that car ride. She could be lying here beside him watching the poor fuckers parade by. "It's okay," he said, "I forgive you."

Ashley smiled a sad smile and mouthed, "Thank you."

He just smiled and nodded.

The next hearse was surprising. It wasn't old-fashioned like Mom's and wasn't brand new like Ashley's. It was just a regular hearse like you'd see every day. Ol' Stuttering Mitch was sitting there in the back. He had that same pouting look on his face that he usually had. When Mitch looked over and saw Corey, he just raised his middle finger. Corey returned the favor. That ass would never learn anything. He was a waste of skin and air.

Jeremy came through next in a hearse just like Mitch's. He was alert and looking around, but he just kind of shrugged when he saw Corey. It was almost like Jeremy didn't recognize him. "Well screw you too, Jer!" Corey flipped off the hearse. Jeremy laughed and looked out the window.

"You always were an ass Corey! Thanks for the weed, ya prick!" Corey used both hands to flip him off until the hearse turned the corner and the last one came into view.

This hearse looked like it was from the 1970's or something. It was a huge land yacht with the bubble back. At one point it had been black, he was sure, but now it was faded and closer to charcoal gray. The paint was peeling and the tires were flat. The faux leather top was ripped with the dingy almost-white padding showing through. Corey saw his dad sitting in the back.

His dad was sitting there. His eyes locked on Corey's. Those eyes were filled with the disappointment Corey had seen every day since Mom died. He shook his head as he looked out at his son. His lips curled as if revolted by what he saw. Roger leaned forward and called through the glass. "Wake up Corey! Wake up."

The voice shifted. Dad's mouth kept moving in the shape of 'wake up' but the words fell out of sync.

"Well, lookie what I see." His dad's hearse limped its way to the curve, and all the hearses were gone. "I think we just might have us some fun."

It definitely wasn't his dad's voice and it didn't make sense.

Another voice spoke up, "Holy shit, man! Look at all this stuff!"

Corey came awake. He was in the tent about ten yards from the truck. Through the mesh window of the tent he could see headlights focusing on the truck. About ten people milled around and poked through the vehicle's contents.

Corey watched for a moment. The dream was fading but he was having a difficult time trying to determine which scene was more real. He knew everyone in the dream, and he didn't know anyone that he could see now. In the dream everyone was acting like they should. Mom was happy, Ashley was sorry, Mitch was sad, Jeremy was a prick and Dad was disappointed.

Looking out the window, these people were going through his shit. That doesn't make sense. People don't just go through a man's shit like that.

He shoved his Taurus into his waistband. The Keltec got stuffed in his back pocket. He had taken to sleeping with the guns. It made him feel comfortable and safe. The rifle was still in the truck, but the handguns were more appropriate to this use anyway.

Pushing the tent flap open, he stood up and stretched silently. It was dark out and with the interior lights from the truck and the headlights from their cars and motorcycles Corey knew they would be light-blinded. *Poor strategy, asswipes!*

He had seen it so many times in movies, he had always wanted to try it. Taking the Keltec from his pocket he held the .357 in one hand and the 9mm in the other. He leveled the barrels at the crowd and just opened up.

The revolver barked five times. The little Keltec barked seven. It was pretty amazing. Those bullets tore into the crowd. It seemed a couple of the bullets may have hit more than one person. He'd have to ask, or count the holes later.

Since both of those guns were empty, he just dropped them. He drew the Taurus and it coughed up several slugs, knocking down a few more in the now-thinning crowd. When it ran dry, he dropped it as well.

Corey walked up to the truck. People were on the ground moaning, a couple of them were perfectly still. He reached in the back. He knew where one of Ashley's handguns was and he slipped it into his belt.

The guns were fun and all, but it was time to take it up a level. He retrieved a baseball bat and turned around. A smile split his face as he saw his next target. It was a woman standing beside her car. Both hands were over her mouth, her eyes just about popping out of her head.

Batter up! Corey strolled over to her, cocking the bat over his shoulder, setting up for a homerun swing.

His arms tightened. The bat wouldn't move. He tried again. It still wouldn't move.

Corey turned to see what the problem was. It turned out the problem was a small guy. Like five-six, five-seven, less than one hundred thirty pounds kind of small. But with the bat over his shoulder, Corey hadn't had leverage and the guy had just reached up and grabbed the bat.

That led to a bigger problem. The people who had been hiding started coming out. Now that Corey wasn't using a gun they got a bit of their nerve back. The little guy kept a hold on the bat and the scared lady jumped on Corey's back. Her trashy fingernails dug into his face and neck.

Corey started laughing. This is so crazy. These people think they can fight me in my dream? I could fart and blow these people straight out of my head.

Someone caught him with a lucky punch to the side of the head and he staggered. It was *fucking* hilarious!

More kicks and blows rained down until Corey was driven to the ground. He laughed the entire time. None of these people knew he was the master of this world. For so long people had taken advantage of his generosity and now he wasn't giving anymore. These people were just little fleas on the ass of a big dog and he was the big dog's master.

He couldn't control his laughter as his shoulder dislocated, his ribs cracked and his jaw shattered.

Just as the darkness was closing in, just the tiniest sliver of doubt intruded on the hilarity: *Is this what death feels like?*

39

West of Dierks, AR

Roger dropped out of cruise control. The road was going to take a hard left ahead where 59 and 70 split.

"About twelve miles to Dierks at this turn. Another twenty or so to the homestead."

Jennifer smiled at him. It was going to be nice to get out of the truck. It felt like forever since they had stopped at the Red River. She was hungry, tired and in dire need of a potty break.

Roger made his left-hand turn. They passed the Highway 70 road sign. Dierks was, in fact, eleven miles away. On her side of the road there was a low scrub brush field that gave way to a stand of trees. Less than a half mile further on, the trees gave out and a red dirt road ran off into what looked more like pasture land than crop fields. At the intersection of 70 and that red dirt road was a small sign pointing to New Bethel Cemetery.

Since that night with the Cobb family, pulling into the little cemetery and having the family be so gracious, Jennifer found herself noticing these small cemeteries all over the place. It was hard to drive fifty miles without seeing a little family or community plot.

She stared off the side of the road. A smattering of trees somewhat obstructed her view. There were long barns close to the road, and a few more in the back of the pasture. Off in the very distance, just before another stand of trees completely obscured her view, she could see a gathering of vehicles. It looked like another funeral might be taking place. *Sad*, she thought, *so many people have died. At least this one is being buried properly.*

The trees once again swallowed the view on the side of the road. Roger looked over and gave her a strained smile. She gave him another reassuring squeeze on his arm. He was such a caring guy. He was hard to figure out sometimes because he was so different from everyone else she knew.

Not every man would have taken her on at the airport. If they had, most would have expected some kind of payment for their efforts – up front, so to speak. Roger had simply accepted her and helped her as he helped himself. Even when they finally had made love he wasn't extracting a payment. He was simply a partner, engaged in an act of pleasure. She could have done much worse with her choice of rescuers.

The apprehension of drawing closer to the homestead, as he called it, was becoming tangible. They knew they were getting closer to an answer about Corey and Ashley. It was strange that she lumped them together in her head, like they were both Roger's kids. She hoped they would accept her.

That was a strange thought. Jennifer had not given conscious thought to what would happen when they arrived at the cabin. But it seemed the wheels in her brain had been cranking away on some hidden thoughts. If she hoped the kids accepted her, did that mean that she was now a permanent part of Roger's life? That he was now a permanent part of hers? Was this a matter of convenience or had it become something more?

Some time before Highway 70 made its lazy S-shaped route through the hills and woods leading up to Dierks, her mind had settled. She slid over and wrapped her arms around her rescuer, her lover, her *partner*. The kiss on his cheek was tender but also relayed a bit of what she had just discovered in herself. It was loving. Her head rested on his shoulder as the miles ticked off toward their destination.

She was looking forward to meeting Corey. If he was anything like his father, they would get on fabulously. Ashley sounded like a really smart, wonderful girl as well. Jennifer had never had children, but she was sure some motherly instincts would kick in and they could try to make a family of it. *Don't push too hard though*, she admonished herself, *just be yourself and let them be who they are, not what you want them to be. That path will lead to success.*

☣ ☣ ☣

Roger had driven this road over a dozen times. The emotions and thoughts surging through his mind made this trip more challenging than any before.

Part of him was utterly content. Another was utterly torn. Jennifer was a wonderful woman. He was feeling more for her than he had for anyone since Melissa had passed. That was the source of the distress. Could you love another without diminishing the love for the first? He knew that what he felt for Jennifer was more than friendship, but would allowing it to be more be a betrayal of his wife?

Even more, was it a betrayal of Corey that Roger had found happiness even while he was unsure of his son's safety?

The highway became the main artery through town. It entered on the southwest, ran along the railroad track that was primarily for serving the saw mill, then became Main Street and shot north, back into the country.

Roger looked over at Jennifer, "Take in the view. I suspect we're going to be seeing a lot of this place. It's the closest town of any size to the homestead. If we have buying, selling or trading to do, it'll be here." He looked out the window with renewed interest himself. The Dierks of his memory was a healthy, robust, electrified rural community. With the pandemic, things took on a new meaning.

The town was virtually unchanged since he first saw it. Sure, there was new paint here and there, even a couple of new houses. But if you went to sleep on Main Street the first day Roger drove through with Melissa and woke up today, you could walk straight home and probably not see much difference other than the clothes and the cars. There had been a little expansion to the southwest a little while back, and they had even put in the new elementary school. Before that, the storage and sorting yard for the mill had retracted, but for the most part it was the same town.

On the way out of town the Dierks Drive-in, which began life as a Dairy Queen, was closed and looted - directly across from the NAPA auto parts store that had shared the same fate. The last businesses on the way out of town that could still be considered part of the town were the Dollar General store and Dierks Supermarket, which would hardly be considered *super* by big city standards, but was certainly *super* for the residents of Dierks. Looters had not only made off with all the merchandise, but burned the buildings to the ground.

Looks like some things have *changed,* Roger thought to himself.

"What's with all the trees?" It was the first thing Jennifer had said for miles.

"What do you mean? They're trees."

"No. Well, yes, they are trees. But so many of them are just growing in rows." She pointed over to her side of the landscape. Off in the distance a stand of trees was growing and, as she said, they were growing in well ordered rows. Even closer were smaller trees, all about the same height and lined up with military precision.

"The mill." Roger hooked a thumb back over his shoulder. "That saw mill back there. They own a lot of the land. When they cut something down they replant so they have a crop in the future. Very little of this, maybe none of it, is virgin land."

She nodded as the tall green soldiers marched by. "What about your property? Many trees out there?"

He smiled the first real smile in miles. "Yup. We got trees. Our property is right on the river. Right in the kink of the river. Nice fertile ground. That's where the homestead is. Where we have the houses and fields. Between all the families, I don't even know how many acres we have now, over a hundred I believe. But the beauty of that property is out the back door, so to speak.

"See we're in a little notch in the Ouachita National Forest. It is to the east and west of us and all the way across our north. You could say we have almost two million acres of tree-covered, mountainous backyard."

Jennifer smiled at his smile. It did sound wonderful. She knew they were in the Ouachita mountain range, but being from Colorado, she was having a hard time seeing these hills as mountains. Avon was over 7,400 feet in elevation. Denver is famed for being the 'mile high' city but Avon was another half mile higher. If she remembered her geography right, the Ouachitas didn't even make it to 3,000 feet. *Hardly a mountain to an alpine skier!*

Roger hung a left at an unmarked two-lane road without a shoulder. They zipped down the road between more of the orderly rows of trees encircling open horse pastures. The hills had gotten more pronounced but it was still practically flat land to her. He made a right onto another two lane. This one with a soft shoulder. It seemed easy enough to find, if you knew where you were going, but she was already lost.

As they came up on a bridge he hooked a thumb to his left. "Right there." When Jennifer looked over, he was smiling again and nodded his head toward the driver's side window. "About a quarter mile over is the creek and everything beyond that to the hill you can see rising up. That's where we're going."

He took a left at a country road that was surprising well maintained. It snaked back into the woods. These trees were not in the orderly rows. It was just natural growth and beautiful.

The next turn led down a dirt road that appeared to have been recently graded. A little berm of dirt was still mounded. Loose dirt blew off the top with the passing of the truck and trailer.

Two turns and Roger stopped. The road dead ended into a black pipe gate. Two support poles raised a sign of flat metal with the words "Day After Ranch" cut into it.

He opened the ashtray and removed a key. It wasn't on a key ring and didn't appear to be marked in any way. If you didn't know where it went, it would be practically useless to you.

Roger popped the door open and climbed out while the truck chimed its protest. Kicking up little puffs of dirt, he crossed over to the fence and unlocked the gate, then walked the gate open. He waved Jennifer over to the driver's seat and motioned her to pull through.

She watched the mirrors to make sure the trailer cleared the gate and came to a stop. Roger walked the gate closed. Jennifer slid back over as he climbed back in.

As soon as the truck started rolling again Roger's walkie talkie began mumbling. He picked up the radio and uplugged the earpiece. "Say again," he said into the device, "I didn't copy."

"Welcome home, Roger!" It was a good voice, a nice voice, but something was off. There was a strain in Willie's voice that hadn't been there before. The smile on Jennifer's face faded for a moment with the next sentence. "Please pull up to your house, get out and go directly in. You are in quarantine for the next seven days."

Roger spoke back into the radio. "Willie. I appreciate the caution but we're clean. We are asymptomatic. No signs at all."

Willie's voice came back, this time completely removing her smile, "Great to hear Rog. Now drive to your cabin and go in. We'll see ya in a week. I have to inform you, if you deviate from this course of action, we will be forced to take direct and irrevocable action."

Roger nodded and somehow his voice didn't shake when he replied, "Understood."

"Direct and irrevocable?" Jennifer's voice shook a bit just asking the question.

"There's a lot of guns out here. You can't call back a bullet."

She nodded. Jennifer wasn't stupid and she had a good feeling that was what Willie had meant. Now it was confirmed. She tried to lighten the mood. "So, what on earth could two completely uninfected people do with a whole week to themselves and no one to bother them?"

Roger's smile returned. They leaned across the seat and shared a kiss. He drove forward. When the trees spilled back Jennifer saw a little slice of paradise. Farm lands opened up down a gentle slope, leading to the river Roger had shown her. Several small houses and other buildings were scattered around the property, each with its own yard. The only thing out of place was the remnant of a large bonfire that was smoking itself out on the bank of the river.

There was a central building that was at least twice as long as it was wide, maybe forty by twenty feet, possibly sixty by thirty. It had a chimney, as did all of the houses, on one end. The sides seemed to be made of cloth rather than field stones.

The truck pulled up next to a respectable cabin that would have likely fit into the living room and dining room of Roger's main house. Probably with room to spare. Despite its size, it looked sturdy and well tended. Obviously someone had spent a good bit of time on upkeep.

He shut off the engine and they both popped their doors open, climbing out and stretching. He crossed over to the door and slid the latch. There wasn't a lock or door knob. *Rustic, very rustic.*

Inside was a main living area with a couch and a wall stuffed with books and reading material. A couch, a loveseat and two chairs made up the furniture along with end tables and a coffee table. The fireplace was the main focal point of the living area. Behind the couch was a kitchen and dining area combined. The stove appeared to be an old wood burner. *Good thing I never thought I could cook! I'd never learn to use that thing,* Jenny thought.

A set of steps led up to a closed in loft space. Under the steps, next to the dining table, was a bench seat against the wall and two chairs opposite. "That bench folds out to a bed. For guests, or the kids. Speaking of-"

He walked back out to the truck.

Jennifer looked up the stairs. A conspiratorial smile crossed her face and she glided up the steps. Opening the door she peeked in to the small bedroom with one tiny window about six inches across and two feet high. It was inset with glass but the glass could be swiveled back.

She heard movement downstairs and ducked back out. Roger closed the door and looked up. Jennifer's sneaky smile returned as she started unbuttoning her blouse. "Ready to break quarantine?"

Her lover smiled up at her, obviously more than ready. He nodded, "Just one sec though." Lifting the radio, Roger said, "Willie, Roger. Where'd you put the kids?"

There was a pause. The voice that came back was tinged in sorrow. "Uh, the kids?" Willie's voice cracked. After a pause it came back, "Corey and Ashley you mean? Sorry, man. We haven't seen them."